"I don't care who started it!"

By

Jez Taylor

TALES OF A LIFETIME
IN TEACHING

Jack Turner has seen it all in his life as a secondary school teacher. Starting as a humble RE teacher in a large Sussex school, he rose to become an assistant head and school leader. This book is a series of snapshots that recall significant moments, heart-warming times, steep learning curves, frustrations, mistakes and much more. Anyone who has been a teacher or has worked in a school will resonate with Jack's story, will laugh and cry, and share in his rollercoaster life at the chalk face.

Jack Turner, the central character has lived through it all, and this book tells his story. Whilst Jack and all the other characters are fictional, sometimes they are amalgams of teachers or students I have encountered. The school too is fictional, however, the incidents Jack recounts are based on real events that took place in schools across Sussex.

Each chapter can be read in isolation as a unique story, but together they represent the best and worst of a life in education.

Dedication

This book is dedicated to my late brother Peter Taylor, my hero and inspiration as a child and the best brother a man could have. Gone but never forgotten.

Acknowledgements

Thank you to my wife Sandra for her unwavering support and help with editing. To Hugh Betterton my brother-in-law, a former teacher and Ofsted inspector, for his help with editing and providing insight and advice on all matters educational. Finally, thanks to John and Ingelore Demetriou, for reading it as non-specialists and suggesting some adaptations to help the reader.

Other books by Jez Taylor

On This Rock. (Peter the Rock book 1)

I will Build My Church. (Peter the Rock book 2)

INTRODUCTION

Education is one of those industries where everyone thinks they know what goes on and what it is like because we all went to school. Most people have clear memories of their time at school and this creates either a positive or negative view of education. Often this is passed down to children and even grandchildren. However, the truth is very different. It is the same in every industry. Could I claim I know how to plumb in a central heating system, just because I have one in my home or I saw a plumber hang a radiator? Could I claim to be able to fly a jet plane just because I've been to Mallorca on my holiday or I saw a pilot in the cockpit? Not really. Our experience of education as consumers just scratches the surface. There is so much more than children, parents and the public ever see. It is this element that brings so much joy, frustration, tears and laughter to teachers, administrators, teaching assistants and all those who work in a school. This book tries to capture just a tiny portion of those experiences. The book is divided into three sections:

Part one: The early years.

1984-1989

This was an age where health and safety barely existed, let alone safeguarding. A time pre-computer where chalk and talk were your main weapons and creating a worksheet took time and neat handwriting. It was a time of great educational change. A time when the teachers controlled the curriculum and could shape a young mind. However, it brought with it complacency and a lack of accountability in recognising diversity and challenging bigotry.

Part two: A seasoned professional

1990- 2009

The era of Ofsted, the introduction of computers, the internet, and emails. A time when the focus shifted from learning to exam success. A time when CPD really took off and educational "experts" came to tell teachers how to do it right. There was a growing awareness of the need to recognise the range of cultures and ethnicities that were prominent in schools. Personal Social & Health Education became serious along with the desire for children to have a life education as well as an academic one.

Part three: The leadership years

2009-2021

This was the time when education struggled to maintain its soul. Where progress and achievement became more important than welfare and enjoyment. Successive governments have altered the nature of schools in an effort to drive up standards. This is an age where academies were deemed to be better than schools and competition for places drove the leadership decisions. The art of learning for learning's sake has been lost. Despite this loss, teachers are amazing, finding ways to be creative amidst a tight curriculum that focuses much more on exams than broader values. In this age, accountability and excellent practice are high on the agenda. School improvement and league tables are the driving force. This is not necessarily bad, but it certainly changed the focus from the child to the school.

CONTENTS PAGE:

PART ONE- THE EARLY YEARS.
1984-1989

CHAPTER ONE

The first day

South Coast Comprehensive School sits in the suburbs of a beautiful Sussex seaside town. Its buildings are a mix of a drab and dark 1930s brick-built sanatorium and the functional and glass-filled constructions of the sixties. Further extensions had added a sports hall and a dreadful, quick-build ROSLA block. ROSLA stands for "raising of school leaving age". Some fifty years ago someone had the great idea of ensuring children stayed in school until they were sixteen. This meant that most schools had no space to house these often unwilling participants and money was found to erect poorly constructed classroom blocks in which to contain students who were expecting to work but had to remain in school. Also evident are large playing fields and playgrounds, with dark corners a long way from the prying eyes of teachers. It is here that students smoke, frolic, and generally misbehave at every break time.

My name is Jack Turner, I am just twenty-two years old, newly married and this is my first teaching job. The year is 1984. It's 3rd September and I am nervous as hell. I trained as a Religious Education teacher in London and am now sitting in the assembly hall of South Coast Comprehensive School. I didn't always want to be a teacher, my first dream was of course to play in goal for Fulham and England, but I stopped growing at five foot eleven inches and if I'm honest, I probably wasn't good enough. I loved RE at school, my teacher was a good laugh and inspired me to want to know more. That's what I want to do. I want to inspire children, challenge their thinking, give them a love of learning and make a difference. *Yes! I want to make a difference.*

The floor of the hall is parquet and highly polished, just right for sliding great distances in your socks. I have a plan to do just that at the end of the day. *Brain, don't let me forget!* The room is full of teachers and office staff all waiting patiently for the Head to arrive. The man behind me blows smoke from his cigarette and it wafts over my head and into my face making me cough.

"Sorry mate," said the man leaning forward and speaking into my ear. His breath was even worse than the smoke he had just exhaled. "My name is Tony, I'm the NUT rep." He was tall, gaunt and looked like he lived alone. I later discovered he was divorced. He took another drag and blew the smoke out all over my face as if that were a normal thing to do. Apparently, he thought it was, as he made no apology this time. I blew the smoke away and replied: "Hi I'm Jack Turner the new RE teacher." I offered my hand to shake but Tony was busy offering a cigarette to the tall, skinny PE teacher who had sat next to him. He lit up and blew smoke in my face as if it were normal. He didn't offer a name, so I turned away, not wanting to look stupid or needy.

"Jack, can I sit here?" I looked up to see Janet Smith, the new girls PE teacher. We had interviewed on the same day and both were appointed. To be fair we were the only ones that had turned up for the interviews for our jobs. So it was either employ us or start over again. I think they took the easy option.

Janet was about my age, maybe a year or two older, and looked like a PE teacher, if you know what I mean. She had long, wavy blonde hair, tied in a ponytail and a big, beaming smile. We became instant friends.

"Hi Janet, yeah, please, sit down. Good to see a friendly face." She plonked herself in the seat next to mine. We passed the time waiting for the meeting to begin. The room filled up quickly and Matt Rogers came to sit next to me on the other side. Matt was my head of department. To be honest it was just me and him. My predecessor had left with a stress-related illness. That filled me with hope! Matt was about ten years older than me but looked twenty years older. He was tubby, balding and dressed as if he had slept on a bench. He was unshaven and a bit sweaty. We exchanged pleasantries and I introduced him to Janet.

There was a rumpus at the back and I turned to see four, what I can only describe as, old teachers. They looked old enough to retire. When I say old, I mean in comparison to my youthful charm and good looks they were old. They were talking excessively loudly. One was very tall, muscular, and balding with a comb-over. Another was shorter and had a bushy, unkempt beard. He was wearing a corduroy jacket with patches on the elbow. I thought that was only seen on the telly with teachers or lecturers from the OU programmes. The third had hair that clearly was a wig: black as coal, not a hint of grey. He wore jeans a collarless shirt and a big, baggy cardigan. He hadn't shaved for a couple of days and had a cigarette behind his ear. He had to be an art teacher. The final one was short, with neatly cut, grey, thinning hair, a trimmed beard and wore a faded green, shiny suit. His tie was military in style and neatly knotted. He looked grumpy. They sat together in the back row, loudly sharing stories of their holidays, their ailments and how dreadful the children at the school were.

Janet nudged me and pointed with her eyes. I turned to see the head walk in, followed by a detail of subordinates, whom I assumed were the deputies. The Head was a tall, thin man, with wiry, silver hair, not quite a Brillo Pad but close. He wore a brown pinstriped suit and a brown tie to match. He looked grey in the face. His cohort of subordinates were two men in grey suits and two women. One wore a long flowing dress, with a long cardigan that went down to her knees. Around her neck was a chunky necklace of costume jewellery. Her hair was supposed to be up in a bun but it seemed to be coming loose. There were hints of pink in her blonde hair. The other woman looked severe in a turquoise skirt and matching jacket with a white blouse. She wore large glasses and her brown hair was cut short to the collar.

They all sat in a row at the front of the hall, facing the rest of the staff. Behind them was a portable screen and an overhead projector. The Head carried a series of slides in a brown folder, to match his suit. In my head I wanted him to be called "Mr Brown." The others carried similar folders.

The hall gradually fell silent and a dull haze filled the room from the smoke of several cigarettes. "Mr Brown," his real name Mr Robinson, stood.

"Welcome back everyone, I hope you have had a pleasant holiday and are ready for the rigours of a new year!" There were sniggers and moans from the back of the hall. Some chatter began as well.

"Hush, hush!" said Robinson, "I do wish you wouldn't smoke in here, it creates a nasty atmosphere. The children will notice. We have a staffroom for smoking. Please would you use that instead." The art teacher with the black wig called from the back. "There's no law against it, I'll smoke where I please." There were murmurs of agreement from amongst the smokers on the staff.

"Let's talk about that later, Mr Grant. For now, we have new staff to introduce." The Head moved swiftly on, avoiding any further discussion about the smoky atmosphere. Mr Robinson proceeded to introduce several new staff including Janet and me. I stood meekly, at the appointed time and turned to face all those in the room, who stared blankly back at me. Janet and Matt smiled at me. This was going to be tough, I thought to myself. As the meeting progressed, I tried making notes, so that I could remember everything that was said, but the slides went up and down too fast. Last summer's results were displayed. There were percentages and names of top performers. There were "oohs" and "aahs" at the mention of students' names who had achieved highly.

"Ruddy heck, how did Tom Jennings get those grades, he was never here, lazy toe rag!" The voice was from the tall, muscular, comb-over man whose name I later discovered was Leslie Baker. He taught woodwork to the boys. There was an eruption of laughter from the older teachers at the back. I desperately wanted to laugh, but felt I ought not to.

"Come on gentlemen, please, Tom was a gifted student, but troubled…" Mr Robinson was floundering. There were stern looks on the faces of the underlings who sat beside him. The fearsome lady in the turquoise twin set stood up.

"Perhaps we should move on, Headmaster, we have spent enough time on the past. We must let our colleagues know what is in store for them this term."

"Quite right, Miss Higgins, we can celebrate further when we have our certificate evening." Robinson was relieved to be off the hook. Miss Higgins took up the slack. She began to talk about routines, timetables, collecting stock, detention rotas, and duties. It was a whirlwind of information. My notepad was a mess. Janet nudged me and leaned in and whispered in my ear. "What is a CAT test? And why are we testing cats?"

I shrugged, I had no idea, I hadn't even seen any cats in the school. I said as much in a whisper back to her and she sniggered. Miss Higgins stopped speaking abruptly and stared at us.

"Miss Smith, is everything all right?" She smiled, but there was menace in it. As if she were really saying: *"How dare you interrupt me."*

Janet spluttered a response. "I'm fine, just a cough." She cleared her throat to emphasise the fact. Miss Higgins peered over her glasses, smiled the menacing smile again, and then continued. She introduced the underlings and their new roles. Apparently, there had been some movement in job titles over the summer. I wasn't really sure what that meant, so I let it go. Miss Higgins was now in full stride.

"As Deputy Head, I will be taking on the role of discipline..." I shuddered, she was a scary woman. Bizarrely I conjured up a mental image of Miss Higgins, whom I'd never met before, in a corset, stockings, and a military captain's hat, holding a whip and handcuffs. I quickly shook my head to clear the image. *Please, no. Don't let that thought come back!*

"Mr Jackson will take on the administration of the timetable, internal and external exams and oversee the Year Heads. Mr Jackson appeared to be about sixty years old. His hair was thinning, he looked tired and his grey suit seemed threadbare. He appeared unhappy about his new role. Janet leaned into me again and whispered. "Internal exams? I don't fancy an internal exam from him." I nearly choked on the pen that I was casually sucking. Again Miss Higgins stopped and looked at both Janet and me. She smiled the menacing smile and waited for an explanation. I had none, so I remained quiet, hoping she would not take it further. Thankfully she did not. She turned and pointed to the second man in a grey suit. He was about six feet tall, ten years older than me, and looked smart. His suit was sharp, his shirt pressed and his tie done up properly. He was Indian by ethnicity. "Mr Choudri will take charge of the curriculum and oversee curriculum development and planning. All heads of department will report to him every month." There were some moans, but also some positive sounds from the remaining staff. It seemed that Mr Choudri divided opinions.

"And finally..." Miss Higgins turned and held out a hand towards the lady in the flowing dress and baggy cardigan with the pink hair. "Ms Lovejoy will be responsible for student welfare, our pastoral leader." Miss Higgins emphasised the "Ms" as if she thought it were distasteful and then followed it up by almost sneering when she said "our pastoral leader."

Even as a naïve twenty-two-year-old with little or no life experience, I could see Miss Higgins had no time for "Ms" Lovejoy and her pastoral care.

The doodles in the margins of my notebook expanded rapidly as the meeting ploughed on. In the end, I had to turn the page, or I would have been forced to concentrate on all the details about how to complete the registers correctly. With hindsight, I wish I had concentrated, as I got it completely wrong for about a month. Finally, the Head once again stood and dismissed us from the hall and into our departments to collect resources and organise our classrooms.

I sat for a moment bemused and slightly overwhelmed by what I had just experienced. I realised I had no understanding of what really went on in schools. All the background work, all the details that no one sees, the discussions and decisions that take place. *Why didn't they teach me this at college?* I wondered whether one day I would be sitting at the front and new teachers would look at me with some kind of awe and wonder. *I can't imagine myself in one of those roles. How do you even begin to aspire to become a school leader?* I was wet behind the ears. Could I become a school leader? Would I be good enough? *If I want to make a difference, then I'm going to have to try and become the best I can possibly be! There is so much more than just turning up, teaching the kids and having fun.* I was beginning to realise the enormity of the role I had taken on.

"Follow me, Jack, I'll show you your room and where all the resources are." Matt Rogers strode off quickly and I gathered up my belongings and scurried after him like a puppy.

"We are a small department, just you and me, but we have a lot of resources and the kids love RE. One thing to remember, book the TV room early if you want to watch a programme. We now have a VCR so you can use video, if you can record a programme yourself at home. Do you have a VCR?" I shook my head, I only had a small portable black and white TV. Matt continued the one-way conversation. "The school now has three TVs. One in the TV room, one in the English corridor and one in the Geography rooms. You can book any of them, but you have to swap rooms if you use the English or Geography ones. The staff get a bit cranky if you leave it too late." My mind was spinning. Why would you want to watch TV? What was worth showing? Nobody really mentioned TV in my training. It was all about discussion, reading, and textbooks and getting the children writing as quickly as possible so it was calm in the room. Before I could speak and ask a question, Matt was off again.

"Aah! Here we are, room 101, I'm in room 102, there is a connecting door with the stock room in between." He opened the door. It was a half-glazed affair with the metal wire embedded in the glass to stop it from cracking and breaking if damaged. It looked as though someone had head-butted it, as right in the centre, the glass was shattered and was being held together by the wire mesh. I stepped into the room. Room 101, that somehow seemed like an omen. It smelled musty and dusty at the same time. There were old-fashioned desks with lids that opened and inkwells on the top. They were covered in graffiti. I glanced down and saw a giant penis scratched into the surface of the desk, with the words, "Rogers is a knob" scribbled underneath. I smiled at the raw emotion and dislike of Mr Rogers, that some poor kid must have had. I promised myself that no one would write that about me.

I scanned the room further, noticing how shabby and uninteresting it was. There was nothing to stimulate any child with a desire to learn new things.

"All your books are in the cupboard. One book per child per year is free, but if they lose it, they pay 50p for a new one. I suggest you get them to cover books as your first homework.

Make sure the boys don't cover them with pages from Playboy. It upsets the Head." Matt turned and disappeared into the stock cupboard. "In here boy!" he called. I didn't like the sound of it but felt I had little option. I stepped into the cupboard. It was a room about six by eight, lined with shelves. It was filthy and untidy; chalk dust, regular dust, an apple core, and biscuit crumbs lined the floor. Waste paper, student work, and piles of textbooks on the shelves, in no particular order. Matt stepped up close to reach past me for a pack of biscuits. I stepped back quickly, the smell of stale sweat caught my throat. I coughed and moved back into the classroom desperate for some fresh air. After a couple of deep breaths, I braced myself and stepped back into the cupboard.

"Fancy a biscuit?" Matt held out an open packet of Custard Creams. "They've been in here since last July, but they should be OK." He took one and wolfed it down. I took one and took a bite. It wasn't OK, but I still ate it. I made a mental note to bring in my own biscuits. Matt began to show me all the resources that there were. He was right, they had a lot, including interesting artefacts like Seder plates, a replica Torah scroll, prayer mats, and even a Buddhist prayer wheel. Not that I knew that at the time.

Matt was on a roll and keen to give the whole tour of the school.

"Come on, Jack, let me show you the Banda room and teach you how to use the machines. We have a paper sorter and staple machine too!" The excitement was overwhelming.

The Banda room was really a walk-in wardrobe with a long

table and a series of shelves filled with packets of paper and other stationery. It hadn't been cleaned in a while and felt dusty. On the table were two machines. A Banda machine and a paper sorter. Attached to the edge of the table was an electric staple machine.

"It's not quite Star Trek, is it?" Matt looked at me funny. Clearly he didn't watch it. The comment was lost on him. The room smelt of strong alcohol spirit, and by the time I had learned how to use the Banda, I was covered in purple ink and felt a bit tipsy. My head was throbbing.

The Banda machine is a thing of technological beauty. A drum, into which alcohol spirit is poured. A handle to turn it. A clip to fix the inked Banda sheets to the drum- (having spent hours writing out a worksheet on it without making any mistakes. The times I got to the final sentence and then spelt a word wrong and had to start again. Oh, the frustration!). Once you have slotted the sheet onto the drum (the right way round!), placed the right number of sheets of paper into the feeding tray, you could start to turn the handle. What joy at seeing sheet after sheet of purple-inked worksheets fly out into the receiving tray. If you were not covered in purple ink by the time you finished it was a miracle.

I was keen to get back to my classroom and begin to transform it into a beautiful, sensory learning space, where children would flourish, be inquisitive, learn to think, and leave better human beings than when they entered. We were heading back to our rooms when we were met by several of the staff heading out of the main door. Janet was with them.

"Jack, we're off to the pub up the road, apparently it's where we all go every Friday lunchtime during term time. Wanna come?" I shrugged; I am never one to refuse a pint. I did have a nagging concern, that I really should be cleaning up my classroom ready for the children to arrive tomorrow morning. *There is always this afternoon*, I thought.

The pub, The Royal Oak, was decorated in an imperial style, like a Gentleman's club in India during the Empire. There were large, comfy leather sofas, rugs on the floor, portraits of elephants and Indian gods, potted palms in the corners, and large ceiling fans. The food was fine: Beef sandwiches with a garnish of crisps. The local ale was tasty and full of hoppy flavour. I began to get to know my new colleagues, it was a good decision to join in.

By the time the afternoon was over and the caretaker came round jingling his keys, my new classroom was nearing perfection. Noticeboards were backed and covered in appropriate spiritual posters that I had found lurking in the stock cupboard. They looked a bit 1970s but who was I to complain? I had created a display of world religions. A map of the world, that I had rescued from the back of the stock cupboard, was pinned in the middle of the board at the back of the room. Around it were posters linked to several of the world's religions. Red ribbon linked the posters to locations in the world. On another wall, I had some "Big Questions" such as "Is there a God?", "Where do we come from?" and "Who made this earth?" The aim was to stimulate thinking and discussion. I had cleaned the roller blackboard with a damp cloth and found new boxes of white and coloured chalk. The room now looked fresh, clean and ready for learning. Books were neatly piled on the shelves and labelled by class, ready for distribution, and the desks were arranged in what I thought was a modern, friendly way, to encourage learning. It is actually quite hard to make it friendly and inclusive when each child has their own desk, with a lid they can lift to hide themselves behind. I had discovered some disgusting things inside some of the desks, which explained the musty smell. Old, once damp, now mouldy, PE kit. Rotten and putrefied apple cores and banana skins. It took a while to remove it all and wipe down all the desks. I had moved my desk to one side and turned it so there was no barrier between me and my learners. Apparently, children learned better this way.

I was sat at my desk, completing my class registers, writing out names, desperately trying not to miss any out as it would ruin my new, blue, hardback register/ mark book. I had also been given a diary, that started in September and ended in August. I marvelled at the fact that these even existed. It made sort of sense, but I had never thought about it before. I wasn't sure what I was going to put into it. No one had really shown me what to do. The jingling of keys stopped at my door. I looked up and saw a thin man of average height, wearing a brown overall coat, the type Morecombe and Wise wore when they did stage set removal while Shirley Bassey was singing. He had spectacles and he was bald on top but had quite thick hair at the sides. I noticed he wore a shirt and tie under the coat.

"Hurry up lad, it's getting late." I looked at my watch, it said five o'clock. I didn't think it was that late, but I was not going to challenge the man in the brown coat.

"Oh ok! I didn't realise." I began to pack up as quickly as I could. It was a Monday night and the last night before term started. I expect the caretaker still had many jobs to do.

"My name is Jack Turner, I'm new. But then you know that I expect." I was floundering, feeling under pressure. The man just stood and waited for me.

"I'm Derek, the caretaker. I actually run the school, but please don't tell Robinson. It would upset him so!" Derek grinned. "Pleased to meet you, let me know what I can do for you." I wanted to say, clean the room properly, especially the cupboard, but I thought better of it. Why make an enemy, when you can make a friend?

I was sitting on the small two-seater sofa in my flat, bag at my feet, coat draped over the chair by the dining table. I was knackered. This was before I had even begun the real job. This was just the preparation day. I still had lessons to plan. I heard keys in the lock and the door opened and in walked my wife, Sandy. She looked exhausted too. A fellow teacher on her first day at the local infant school. I stood up, crossed the small room, took her bags, and dumped them by mine. She stood, her eyes glazed; she had a purple smudge on her nose. I stared at it. She noticed. "Banda?" she said. I nodded and grinned.

"Wine?" I asked. She smiled and nodded.

CHAPTER TWO

The first lesson

I had not slept well on Monday night. It had been a late one. Sandy, my new wife and I had been up late planning lessons. We were both starting in new schools as probationary teachers. I recalled the angst I had felt as I reviewed the documentation that Matt Rogers had given me yesterday. I had four one-hour lessons to plan. Three of them I felt comfortable about. Introducing Islam to Second Years (Year Eight in modern parlance), Jewish festivals with the Third Years (Year Nine), and the life of Jesus with Year One (Year Seven). The fourth lesson, which was actually the first of the day at ten o'clock filled me with dread. Sandy had laughed out loud when I had shown her the curriculum plan. How could a simple typed piece of paper cause such dread?

As I walked to school I recalled the moment I had read the plan. I remembered the blood draining from my face, the light-headedness and beads of sweat.

"What the…? What's this? I don't understand." I had struggled to get my mind around the content of the first topic of the year for the Fourth Year. (Year Ten, aged 14-15 years old).

"What is PSE anyway? I thought I was an RE teacher. What has this got to do with RE?"

Sandy took the piece of paper and skimmed through it. Her face lit up and then she began to laugh. Her sparkling blue eyes were filled with mirth as she tossed her head back to laugh and her wavy blonde hair flicked across her face.

"What do you know about all that? We've only been married a month. You're still discovering what the outside of a woman looks like naked, let alone the inside of one!" She fell back onto the sofa and continued to find the whole situation wildly funny. I was not impressed. PSE apparently stood for Personal and Social Education and involved topics such as sex education, smoking (not teaching them to, they already know that!), drug abuse and careers. I knew very little about any of these topics. I was in the dark. I couldn't contact Matt, my head of department as he had not given me his home number. Anyway, as yet we had no phone installed in the flat, so I'd have had to go and find a phone box.

"I don't know what the inside of a vagina looks like. It was all holy books and festivals with my training! The closest we got to body parts was a picture of a Rabbi doing a circumcision!" The anxiety in my voice was palpable.

"Look," said Sandy, "here is a worksheet attached to the plan." She held it up. It was a purple, Banda sheet with a drawn diagram of a cervix, ovaries, and fallopian tubes. There were labels to fill in on the diagram. Sandy showed me a second sheet with a giant penis, scrotum, bladder, and prostate; also with labels to complete.

I took the sheets and examined them carefully. The purple ink was smudged and the handwriting was even worse than my own. *These would not do,* I thought.

"Is there a lesson plan or suggestions of what to do with this? What's the point?" my voice was filled with trepidation. Sandy flicked through the sheets of typed paper and shook her head.

"All it says is: 'Aim of the lesson; to understand the reproductive organs.'"

"That's more like a science lesson! What are they doing in science? Evidence for God's existence?" I was getting annoyed. Sandy had to work hard to control a smirk and not giggle. I slumped down onto a dining chair and sat at the table.

"I'm going to have to re-draw these sheets and think of some way to present it, so it looks like I know what I'm talking about." I rummaged in my bag and retrieved a handful of Banda sheets and my pencil case. "This is not what I signed up for!" I muttered to no one in particular. I turned, hoping for some sympathy from Sandy, but she was now busy cutting out letters on coloured card.

It was after midnight by the time I had created new Banda sheets, planned four lessons and packed my bag again. Sandy was already asleep in the small bedroom of our tiny flat. I undressed down to my underwear and slipped into bed under the duvet. Sandy mumbled in her sleep. *There's no chance of a last-minute refresher course on the intricacies of the female form,* I thought to myself. I rolled over and tried to put the lesson out of my mind.

Arriving at school at just about 7.45 am I went straight to the Banda room to print off the day's worksheets. To my dismay, there was a queue, several people all with piles of sheets ready to print off. They were chatting happily about summer and holidays. I could not cope with the light atmosphere; I was feeling stressed. I went up to my room. The room of doom, 101. This could be where my whole career disappeared on the first day. As I approached my room, I spoke out loud in the empty corridor.

"Pull yourself together Jack, it's just a vagina and a penis." As I spoke a young and rather pretty teacher emerged from the room opposite. She stopped and stared. I blushed. Inside my head, I cringed and silently said. *You idiot, you idiot.*

"You must be doing PSE today, I had to do that last year! It's not that bad once you've done it once. Hi, I'm Sally Le Croix, I teach French and German." She held out a hand, I took it and we became friends and allies.

"You don't sound French; I mean Sally isn't a French name."

The moment I spoke I realised that I sounded like an idiot again.

"My husband is French, I studied languages at University and met him on an exchange stay in Lyon."

"How come you had to teach PSE last year if you are a French teacher?"

"My timetable was light and they needed a PSE teacher. I expect you're nervous and wondering how it is going to go. Well don't worry, I survived."

We chatted some more and then Sally left to join the Banda queue. I suddenly felt more confident. *If Sally survived it, I am pretty sure I can.* I said to myself confidently. I entered my room and sat at the desk. I took a couple of deep breaths, closed my eyes, and prayed. Sandy and I were not overly religious. We both had been baptised as teenagers, and we openly identified as Christian, but at present, it was not a life-changing thing. My prayer was more out of desperation than certainty.

I looked down the line of Second-Year students standing in the playground. I was their new form tutor. They stared intently at me, studying me; *looking for weakness,* I thought. I returned their stares, attempting to exude an air of authority, in the hope that they would respond to me. I was going to spend the next hour with them, sorting out timetables, giving out homework diaries, and generally getting to know them. A short, blonde girl with hair in bunches smiled at me. She had train track braces. *An ally* I thought. Further down the line, I noticed a slightly tubby boy with what could only be described as a naughty boy haircut. It was longer on top but cropped at the sides with a swirly pattern shaved into it. He was chewing. I opened the large beige register and scrolled down the neatly written list of names. My eyes caught a name. Clinton. *That's got to be Clinton, the name and the hair match.* I recalled one of my education lecturers at Roehampton, describing how it was possible to make a summary of an individual within fifteen seconds, just by their clothing, mannerisms, and hair. *Have I just done that?* I had never, until then, believed it to be true.

Tutor time had passed without much incident. The class had behaved as well as I had hoped. Clinton was indeed the boy with the naughty boy haircut. The smiley blonde girl with the train tracks was called Sara. She did become an ally and was keen to hand out every bit of paper she could.

"Sir," said a tall, smartly dressed lad called Joseph, "are you related to the Chuckle Brothers?"

The class erupted into laughter. I inwardly smiled but needed to maintain control. I knew why he had said it. I had neatly cut spiky brown hair, and a full moustache carefully trimmed to fit my upper lip.

"Joseph, explain yourself, what do you mean? The rest of you, settle down. Let him explain himself." Gradually the class settled in expectation of Joseph's reply.

"Well sir," he said growing in confidence, knowing that I was playing along and not going to get cross. "It's just that you look so much like the Chuckle Brothers, the hair and the moustache. I thought you might be the missing brother, a long-lost relative." The class were enjoying the banter.

"Well Joseph, you'll have to wait and see. It may just be true if you spot them in town or hanging around the school."

"They're starring in the Panto in town this Christmas!" shouted one lad from the back. "Are they staying with you? Can I have an autograph?" Several in the class joined in, seeking an audience with Barry and Paul Chuckle.

From the back of the room, I heard a song beginning... "Chuckle, Chuckle Vision, Chuckle, Chuckle Vision..." Several joined in and the class was soon singing the refrain. I had to make a split-second decision that would define my teaching career.

"ENOUGH!" I bellowed, using my best goalkeeper's voice. I knew the years of football would somehow come in handy. My voice rang in the ears of my class and even echoed down the corridor. The door opposite opened, and Sally stood there looking at me through my open classroom door.

The tutor group sat in stunned silence. No one moved a muscle. They were all shocked that I could shout so loudly. One, small, mousey brown-haired girl almost began to cry. Joseph's boldness had disappeared and he was looking nervous. Even Clinton looked worried.

I spoke slowly, and in a measured way to show I was not angry. "If you're going to sing, let's at least do it properly! On the count of three, this side start," I pointed to the left-hand side of the room. "Once they have sung it through once, you lot start." I pointed to the right.

"One, two, three..." The singing began. "Chuckle, Chuckle Vision, Chuckle, Chuckle Vision..." Sally just stood at the door, smiling. The stock room door opened and Matt poked his head through. He grinned as he saw me conducting the tutor group in singing. That was it. From that day onward, for many years, my nickname was "Chuckle."

The tutor group filed out at ten o'clock, just after the bell blasted out three short rings.

"Thanks, sir, Nice to meet you," said Sara.

"Thanks Chuckle!" said Clinton cheekily.

"It's 'Sir' to my face. Chuckle behind my back!"

"Gotcha!" said Clinton turning back and smiling. The rest of the class filed out chatting. Some others thanked me, others just smiled nervously. I looked up and saw a queue forming in the corridor. Bigger students, more menacing, less smiling. My nervousness returned.

As the class of Fourth Years filed in, I spoke. "For today, sit where you like. I will sort out a seating plan for the next lesson. Today we just need to get in, get going and get to know each other."

"I'm not sitting next to a boy!" said a rather rotund girl with short brown hair and a very pointed nose. Her eyes were beady and she looked angry.

"No boy wants to sit next to you," responded a tall, greasy-haired, spotty boy. He emphasised the word "wants."

"Now, now, ladies and gents. Be nice to each other." It was the best I could think of in the heat of the moment. "No one has asked you to sit next to a boy, have they?" I spoke gently and directly to the rotund girl and smiled. She scowled and turned away to sit at the back of the room.

By the time the rest of the class were in their seats and settling down the incident was forgotten. I called the register and discovered that the rotund girl was called Rose Steele and the spotty boy was Finlay Gilbertson. There were also two Sams, three Claires, each with a different spelling, a Mercedes, and a Ravi, the lone non-white face in the class. He was tall, and thin and was already developing a fine growth of hair on his upper lip. He sat alone.

"Good morning, my name is Mr Turner and I am your new RE teacher. I will be taking you for both RE and PSE. This is a non-exam class but just as important as your O-Levels as it will help you develop a positive approach to life and living with other people." I spoke with confidence and casually walked around the room as I did so. There were a few grumbles and mutters but generally, my first sentence had gone well. I got a couple of willing volunteers to give out A4 blue, exercise books; I wrote my name on the board and the class code and room number.

"I haven't got a pen," said one scruffy-looking boy at the front set of desks.

"How can you not have a pen? It's the first day!" I turned to my desk, picked out a black biro, and handed it to the lad.

There was a low hubbub as the class settled into organising their exercise books. Instructions were given about how to set out work, and the school expectations.

"Remember, the date goes on the top right-hand side. Always write the title and underline it using a ruler." With a deep breath and a silent prayer, I launched into my very first lesson.

"Calm down everyone, it is just normal human biology. We've all got either a penis or vagina."

The class had erupted into chatter and giggles the moment I had announced the topic. There were jeers from several boys and moans from some of the more reserved girls.

"Do we have to do this? It's embarrassing?"

"This is science, why are you doing it?" I could not help but agree, but I didn't voice it.

"Oh my god! He's drawn a dick on a worksheet" The voice was Rose Steele's. It was loud. She continued; "My fanny doesn't look like that either!" There was raucous laughter from around the room. Things were getting out of hand; I needed to gain control quickly. I decided to use my booming voice once again.

"Enough!" And once again, it stunned the class into silence. Rose stared at me, mouth open, not sure if she should speak. I held up my hand to indicate she should not. She closed her mouth. The class waited, expectantly. Taking the moment of silence to think, I decided to take a big risk.

"Listen," I said with as much confidence as I could muster, "we all have to get used to talking about human bodies, private parts, sex organs and think of it as normal. If we can't, we will never fully appreciate how amazing our bodies are and how amazing sex can be!" Once again there were some jeers from the boys.

"I can't wait!" called Finlay from the far side of the room. He began signing the act of intercourse with his hands; his index finger thrusting into an imaginary vagina made from his other hand.

"Gross!" shouted Rose. "It'll be a long time before that happens." Several of the girls laughed at him and he quickly settled down.

"Pack it in you two! Let's get on. What I want all of you to do is to come up to the board and write on it a word that describes a penis or a vagina. I'll start, Rose has already shouted out two, so I will use those." I walked up to the blackboard and in big letters in white chalk wrote 'dick' and 'fanny'.

"We need to know all the words, so we can decide which are appropriate and which are not." I stood holding chalk in my hand, waiting. Slowly one or two stood and walked towards the board. "Don't worry if someone else has already written it, I want everyone to write something."

After a couple of minutes, the board was filled with an array of synonyms for penis and vagina. Some written big and bold, others scrawled in a corner. There was even a picture of a penis. *No surprise* I thought when I saw it.

As the lesson progressed, the class settled into copying the diagrams of the male and female sex organs. The fun started when I had to explain what each part was for. I had never learned this in school in the 70s or at least I couldn't remember learning it.

"Sir, why have they named the girl parts after a Swedish car?" said one lad whose name was Tom. He was a quiet, apparently shy boy who was not one of "the lads" in the class.

"What?" I said momentarily confused, but before I could correct the boy, there was a response from elsewhere in the room.

"It's the vulva, you muppet, not Volvo!" Finlay was laughing as he said it. Several others joined in, including some of the girls. Finlay turned to a pretty blonde girl who was sitting across from him, she was one of the Claires. "I'd like to have a go in Claire's Volvo!" he shouted. She momentarily blushed, then responded with a quick wit. "I'd have to be dead first!" Once again laughter erupted. "How about you Mercedes, fancy a drive?" Finlay was on a roll. She turned and called out, "Up yours!" she flipped her middle finger at him.

"Hey! That's enough Finlay!" I was beginning to get cross. "And the rest of you. You speak with respect to each other." My voice was loud and firm. The message was clear. Finlay was about to complain but a stern look and a hand held up dissuaded him.

"Pens down and listen, now!" my voice was authoritative. This was an important moment. I recalled my lecturers talking about respect and the teaching of positive values to students. Now was the time to begin this.

"I know you are full of hormones and going through puberty, but that doesn't mean you can behave like animals to each other. We are all human beings and deserve respect. We speak kindly to each other. Try to think of how others may be feeling." I scanned the room, there were a few faces that looked remorseful. Most looked blank. Rose and Finlay just looked angry, as if I were telling them off personally.

Rose spoke; "Finlay's a dick, he always says stuff like that."

"Not to you, you fat cow," said Finlay with some vitriol. The class was now quiet as the two protagonists faced off. I needed to resolve this quickly. I was about to speak when the classroom door opened and in walked Miss Higgins. She stood watching, a sternness in her gaze.

"Is everything all right, Mr Turner? I was passing the room and heard raised voices. It sounded like Rose and Finlay." She stared at the two teenagers. They stared at me, their eyes pleading for me not to say anything. "They sometimes struggle to be civil to each other. This would not be the first time," Higgins continued. She appeared determined to catch them out. She stepped further into the room and began to wander about looking at the work in the books. She glanced at the blackboard, the penis and the synonyms still evident. She said nothing.

"They were expressing their views about sex and got carried away. I think they will be fine." I turned to them and stared, in the hope that they would receive my unsaid message. *Don't let me down, I'm on your side. Work with me.* Higgins eventually left the room and there was an audible sigh of relief from almost everyone.

"You two are lucky, you'd have been in trouble if Turner had grassed you up," said Mercedes,

turning round to them. "Why didn't you?" Mercedes asked.

I paused before speaking, I wanted to say the right thing, to let them know I wasn't a pushover, but to also let them know, I was here to support them and help them.

"Because," I began, "we haven't finished the lesson, and I didn't want them to miss out. Next time, I will grass them up. Next time, you will discover that my bite is as bad as my bark, but for the moment, you need to know that I want us to learn together. I want us to learn to respect each other. I want to teach you to think about new things, develop opinions and learn to disagree without slagging each other off. Finlay, Rose, you and I will have a very brief chat at the end of the lesson to work out how we are going to get along next lesson." They immediately began to grumble and protest. Others in the class began muttering too.

"Hang on!" I said. "You didn't expect there to be no consequences, did you? Every action has a consequence. One minute of your break is all I am asking. Either that or ten minutes after school. Your choice! Now, where were we?" With that, I closed the discussion and moved on.

The lesson progressed without any further major incidents. Diagrams were drawn and labelled. I escaped being found out that my knowledge of the inside of a woman was just as limited as most of my class. For that matter, my knowledge of the inside of my own body was pretty limited too. I managed to explain the intricacies of intercourse without too much embarrassment, but it was a close call. There were beads of sweat on my brow and I could feel myself getting hot and bothered. My heart was racing.

"Sir," said one of the Claires, "when did you first have sex? What was it like?" I wasn't expecting that. I wasn't sure what to say.

"Look, he's got a wedding ring on. I bet it was on his honeymoon." An eagle-eyed girl at the front spoke out.

"Nah! Everyone does it before they get married. I bet he's had loads of girlfriends." Finlay had recovered his front.

"Shut up Fin, you know nothing. Sex is a private thing, very intimate. It's not something you shout about or do with anyone. I think it's sweet that you get married first. It makes it special. I think I would like to wait until I found the perfect person that I want to spend the rest of my life with." Mercedes spoke with real maturity and I noticed it.

"That's lovely, Mercedes. A very mature and adult response." She turned and stuck her tongue out at Finlay in a very immature way, then smiled smugly to herself.

Just then the bell sounded its three short blasts signalling the end of the lesson. I was rescued from a decision.

"Right, pack away please, and stand behind your chairs. No one goes until the room is tidy and you are quiet. Rose and Finlay, stay behind for one minute for a quick chat."

I had survived. Just!

CHAPTER THREE

The Video

"Please can I remind you that block booking the television and video is not permitted, as it creates an unhealthy reliance on technology and often prevents others from using, what is potentially, a positive educational tool." Mr Robinson, the wiry-haired Head Teacher was reading a notice from a list on a clipboard.

South Coast Comprehensive was at the cutting edge of educational technology and had purchased three brand new televisions with video players. The televisions were fixed to tall, mobile trolleys with a metal box in which was locked a video player. One was located in the Video/Careers room and the others were in the English corridor and the Humanities corridor. To book them, you needed to plan way ahead. A logbook in the staffroom was effectively a weekly timetable of the three rooms where the televisions were housed. You added your initials against a time/lesson and the television was yours for that hour. The next job was to inform the teacher in that room at the time, that you needed to swap rooms or collect the television at the start of the lesson. This usually meant sending two of the naughtiest children in your class to do this tricky job. In general, they would be desperate to watch anything on TV rather than do any real work, so you could rely on them to do the job correctly.

"Can I also remind you to speak to the English or Humanities teachers before you arrive at their door wanting to use the rooms? It can be most disruptive." Robinson sounded quite pompous as he read out the list of weekly notices and instructions to staff on this cold October Monday morning. The staffroom was filled, every seat taken and several staff standing around. A fog of smoke rose to the stained ceiling; three or four staff were smoking during the meeting.

I stood near the door, I had arrived too late for a seat. I needed to get to the video booking logbook before old Fred Winter from the History department block-booked it. It hadn't taken me long to learn that the History and Geography departments had a monopoly on the TV. Fred Winter had a large collection of World War Two documentaries that he had recorded on TV and he used to show them any chance he could. It only took one child to mention the war and he was off into his cupboard to find a video. Even if the topic he was covering was "The Romans!" He had a habit of booking the TV, just in case he needed it.

Fred Winter was part of the Silent Generation; he grew up during WW2. He had lived it. His cupboard was full of memorabilia, including his childhood gas mask that the kids adored and always wanted to try on. He had done national service and stayed on for another three years before becoming a teacher. He was always dressed smartly, although his suit was now old and had a sheen to it so it looked like it was shiny when the sun hit it. He wore his regimental tie every Friday, and each Friday the kids in his class would ask about it, knowing it would distract him from the lesson and they would get to watch another documentary on the war.

The meeting ended and the staffroom began to empty, the fog of smoke was released into the school corridor. I squeezed past staff, as I was moving against the flow of traffic. I kept my eyes on the logbook hanging on the noticeboard by the far door. Next to it were three keys each with large wooden key fobs made by the Woodwork Department; one in the shape of the letter C, the others H and E. With a sense of relief, I reached the logbook and opened it. I flicked the pages until I found the current week. To my dismay, the initials FW were scrawled in several of the slots he needed.

"Bloody Winter," I muttered. Fortunately, the Video/Careers room was free on at least three of the occasions he wanted. I quickly scribbled my initials in the slots in the logbook and dashed off to greet my tutor group.

The Video/Careers room was a small classroom with shelves on three sides, it had a window that overlooked an outdoor quadrangle space where classes would line up. There were benches and a bin in the middle of the open space. Inside the room sat a desk by the window and two tables put together with four chairs around. The rest of the room was empty except for three stacks of chairs and the television trolley with the locked video cabinet attached to it. Teachers would march their classes down to the room and there would be a scramble, once the door was unlocked, to grab chairs and sit as close to the 32" screen TV as possible. Generally, the boys would muscle their way to the front, leaving the girls to either sit on the floor or fight for the remaining few seats. When I was in there what usually followed was a discussion about fairness, equity, sexism and justice, leading to several boys, not so graciously, giving up their chairs.

"Walking in silence please, so that we don't disturb other classes, make your way to the Careers room and line up outside. Wait for me." The class stood up and began to make their way out.

"Do we take our bags?" said one small lad, whose uniform seemed a little large.

"No, I 'm locking the door and we will be back before the end to do a summary in our books."

"Oh! Do we have to? Can't we watch more of the video?" The same lad replied.

"You'll get to see all you need to see," I said encouragingly. Since September, I had learned that video could be a great way of providing visual stimulus and posing ethical questions, something my university lecturers never really mentioned. I was beginning to enjoy showing clips and sections of films. The problem I had was I only had a small portable black and white TV. Sandy and I couldn't afford to buy a new TV or even rent one from Radio Rentals, let alone have a video recorder as well. I had found copies of "Jesus of Nazareth" in the stock cupboard, the TV mini-series directed by Franco Zefirelli and starring Robert Powell as Jesus. I was now using it regularly to teach the First Years the stories of Jesus.

"Right! Settle down. Make sure you have a pen and your exercise book. Turn to the back and be ready to make notes, and write down anything you don't understand, so you can ask afterwards." Immediately a hand shot up.

"Yes, Clinton?" It was said with a little weariness, as Clinton always had some issue that would prevent him from working or would slow down the lesson.

"Jason wasn't here last lesson, so he missed the video from last week. Can we go back and see it again?" There was an expectancy in his voice. A few in the class nodded, including Jason himself. Jason also smiled hopefully.

"In a word, no! We'd never get to the end if we went back and watched it all again, just because someone was away. Now, why don't we let Jason know what we watched and talked about in the last lesson, then he won't miss out. Also, we can all remember and be ready to move on!" I was pleased with myself, I had avoided any major disruption and led it neatly into where I needed to be in the lesson.

"So," I paused momentarily using the silence to get everyone's attention, "where did we get to last lesson?" Several hands shot up into the air, keen to give a summary, including Jason!

"Jason, you weren't even here, put your hand down."

"But sir," he protested, "can I turn the lights out?"

"I'll pull the blinds down!" shouted a girl from the back who was sitting on the teacher's desk as there were no chairs left. Three children got up and raced towards the windows in a race of Olympic proportions in order to close the blinds. The lights went out and the calm of seconds before was lost.

"Stop!" My voice was booming. The chatter stopped immediately but the battle for the blinds continued. "Leave the blinds alone." I continued to boom. My voice almost echoed around the sparse room. "Lights on, blinds open. We're not ready to watch yet. Jason doesn't know what we did last lesson." I pointed at Jason for emphasis. "Everyone sitting down, let's try again. Remember, the more time you waste, the less of the video you get to watch. Where did we get to last lesson?" Two girls stood by the blinds holding on to the pulleys, waiting patiently for their moment to shine and be the girl who shut the blinds.

"Sara, Emily, sit down!" I said it firmly but not angrily.

"But sir, what difference does it make? I'm still listening!" Emily pleaded.

"It is not what I asked you to do. I asked everyone to sit. I know you can listen from there, but I asked everyone to sit. Please sit and follow instructions as asked." I was using a technique I had learned at my placement school in Tolworth, South London. My mentor there told me how to respond without becoming emotionally involved. Not to respond with a counterargument, like a child might do, or demand obedience, like a parent; but just to reiterate the instruction, calmly and explain the need to follow instructions. I was to discover, many years later that this was called Transactional Analysis.

Emily and Sara reluctantly returned to their seats looking like they had lost a pound and found a penny.

"Where were we?" I said confidently, having restored calm to the class.

Clinton chipped in, "About to turn the lights out?" Several children laughed and once again calm was lost.

"Clinton, one more comment like that and you won't see any of the film." Transactional Analysis went out of the window. "Jane, please help me out, tell us all where we got to last week!" Jane was a popular girl in the class, humorous and clever without setting herself apart as a result of her academic ability. She proceeded to explain the story so far in enough detail to show she had been listening but quickly enough to ensure the rest of the class kept listening. "... So, Jesus is about to be crucified. He was found guilty by the Jewish leaders and then sent to Pilate, is that right sir?" I nodded my approval. Jane was doing well I thought. "Pilate asked him loads of stuff about truth but Jesus didn't say much. So then Pilate lets the crowd choose who to kill or save. It was something to do with the festival, I can't remember the name..."

"Passover!" a shout from the back of the room.

"Well done Tommy, but don't call out." I nodded and smiled at Tommy. "Thank you, Jane, that was excellent. So today is a bit gruesome. In this section, we will see how the Romans used to execute criminals..." I went on to explain how Jesus was scourged and then led out to a place of execution. I described crucifixion in some detail, talking about the nails, the bones, the difficulty breathing and then having legs broken or your side pierced.

"Sir, I feel sick"

I looked in the direction of the voice. It was a small blonde girl, very thin and quiet in nature. She rarely spoke. She looked a bit green.

"Shelly, are you ok? "I went over to her. The rest of the class began to stare and make assumptions about Shelly.

"Yuk! She's going to puke!" Clinton pretended to be sick on the floor. The boys around him laughed and joined in.

"She's such a wuss! It wasn't as if sir was going to actually crucify anyone."

"I think she's going to faint."

"Leave her alone, she's not well." The class were taking sides. The girls were protective, and the boys displayed alpha behaviour to show their manliness.

I was at her side. The last thing I wanted was vomit all over the floor. Then things would really kick off. I led her outside and sat her on a bench in the quadrangle. Slowly her colour returned and the green faded.

"Sit here for a moment. When you feel better you can come back in." I left her in the quadrangle and returned to the class. I could see her from the window. The class were now getting impatient.

Finally, I was ready to press play on the video. The class were settled and expectant.

"Right! Here we go." I said hopefully. I pressed play. Nothing happened. The TV screen remained blank, there was no hum and click from the video. Silence.

"Have you plugged it in?" said one helpful child.

"Of course he's plugged it in, he's not a complete idiot!" said Sara from the back, where she was perched on the teacher's desk.

"Thank you, Sara, I'm not sure whether that was a compliment or not. Your use of the word 'complete' casts some doubt!" She looked at me and smiled, not really understanding what I meant.

I bent down to check the plug and casually flicked the switch on. Sadly, it did not go unnoticed.

"I told you it wasn't plugged in," said the helpful child revelling in his glory.

"It was plugged in; it just wasn't switched on." Sara leapt to my defence. "I told you he wasn't a complete idiot!"

"Thank you. My mental capabilities are not up for discussion. Right here we go. Let's hope it works this time." I was slowly losing the will to live! I pressed play again. This time the video player sparked into life and a picture appeared on the screen.

"We've seen this bit, last week!" Clinton shouted.

"Wind it forward!" The helpful child spoke again.

"No, I missed it last lesson," said another. Quickly the room dissolved into chaos. Children debating what they had seen, where it should start, and how to get to the correct starting point.

I quickly pressed fast forward on the player and tried to settle the class. More time had been wasted on preparing to watch than there was left to watch the film. Frustration flooded through me. I kept my cool and as calmly as I could, spoke to the class.

"Ok! OK! Settle down. We've got there." I waited until the class had calmed down again.

"Right, in this section we will see Jesus being whipped and crucified. Try to note down any questions you have and any observations about what was happening. I will be looking for evidence of note-taking before we leave. So no excuses Clinton!" I looked at Clinton, who was about to protest when I winked mischievously at him. Clinton grinned.

The video came on. Robert Powell winced as he was scourged, his hands gripping the iron rings that held him to the whipping post. There were groans and mutterings from the class. The boys enjoyed the violence being played out, not realising that Bible stories were so gruesome. I noticed Shelly, looking through the window from the quadrangle. She looked green, and just at that moment, she puked. Fortunately, the window was closed and the class were facing away from her, otherwise, there would have been a riot. I sighed inwardly and quietly moved towards the door. I looked back at the class. All were silent, engrossed in the drama of the crucifixion being played out on screen. For some, this would be the first time they would have seen the story, for others a reminder of personal beliefs or previous learning.

Clinton broke the silence. "Sir, did they really do that to people? Hang them on crosses with nails? It's gross. No wonder Shelly felt ill." Others followed suit in responding to what they were witnessing.

"Why would he do that? He could have escaped!" said one girl, puzzled by the self-sacrifice of Jesus.

"His disciples were chicken; they just ran off. I'd have fought the Romans off with my sword!" Jason made swishing noises like a sword whizzing through the air.

"Come on, quieten down. Watch the rest and then we'll talk." I hushed them up.

I suddenly remembered Shelly vomiting outside the window. I was about to leave to see to her when the final straw broke my proverbial camel's back.

Bring, bring bring bring… the continual ringing of the fire alarm.

"Bugger!" I whispered. The class erupted. Noise and movement, chairs scraping, falling over.

"Do we take our books?"

"Is it a drill?"

"Sir, I'm scared, is it real?" The questions kept coming.

I put on a firm and loud voice. "Just leave everything, walk quietly out of the door, turn into the quadrangle and out the other doors into the playground. Remember to line up in your assigned places."

"I can't remember mine!"

"Why can't we go through the hall?"

"Sir, I'm not leaving my make-up!" Emily picked up a small handbag and marched out.

"If she's taking hers, I am too!" Several other girls turned back to retrieve bags.

"Just go now! Everything will be safe!" I shook my head and sighed.

The last of the class filed out. I looked at the TV screen. Robert Powell was hanging on a cross, talking to the sky and looking rather lonely. I pressed pause.

"Gross! Shelly's puked!" Clinton's voice could be heard echoing around the quadrangle.

"Clinton! Walk quietly!" I bellowed. I closed the TV room door behind me.

CHAPTER FOUR

The Banda Room Incident

People outside of teaching have no concept of the stress caused by trying to produce handwritten worksheets, spelt correctly, with perfectly drawn diagrams onto a Banda sheet, ready to print using a spirit duplicator or "Banda machine." I have already referred to this marvellous piece of machinery in a previous chapter, but there is so much more to be said.

I sat at the dining room table surrounded by Banda sheets, textbooks and my pencil case. It was 11.30 pm and I still had two more sheets to produce before I could go to bed. Sandy had finished her preparation and gone off to bed, leaving me alone with the Banda sheets and a cup of tea. I silently cursed as I misspelt 'Mediterranean' on the worksheet. Vainly I tried to correct it neatly but the handwritten sheet looked a mess. As a left-hander, my handwriting was inconsistent anyway, as I could never find the right angle to place the paper. I sighed and screwed up the sheet and took a fresh one from my rapidly diminishing pile. I threw the crumpled mess into the waste bin and noticed that there were already four or five in there. The problem with creating worksheets is that if you make an error, there is no real way of correcting it without it looking like a mess. I was not a perfectionist, but I did want the work to look clear and neat. I expected that from children, so I had to set a good example. So I started a new Banda sheet and began to carefully write the title, underline it with a ruler and then set out my worksheet. The map of Israel was carefully redrawn and labelled, this time with 'Mediterranean' spelt correctly. Slowly and methodically I wrote out the tasks and questions, that I required the class to complete. It was agonisingly slow. It had to be neat and it had to be correct. By the time I had completed the A4 sheet, my hand ached and my brain was fuzzy. I sighed with relief as the pen in my hand dotted the last full stop. I sat back and looked at the sheet. It would pass. I carefully lifted the top sheet on which I had written to see how well the purple waxy ink had transferred from the sheet below to the shiny side of the top copy. *Not bad* I thought, no smudges or faint lines that need going over on the top page. With a slight nod of approval, I placed the completed sheet carefully onto the pile of others that I had worked on earlier in the evening. I took a sip of tea, it was cold. Glancing up at the clock, I noticed it was after midnight. It had taken me forty minutes to redo the sheet. I made a snap decision that I would not use a sheet for my second-year class (year eight), I would do it as I went along, by drawing and writing on the rolling blackboard. I packed up my papers and headed off to bed.

It was spitting when I left the house to begin the fifteen-minute walk from our flat to school. Sandy had left earlier and taken our little Fiat. She worked in the neighbouring town, a ten-minute drive, but too far to walk. I hated walking in the rain. Even with a coat, I felt damp and uncomfortable by the time I reached work. I headed straight to the men's toilets where there were lockers and hooks to hang coats. Mine was beginning to drip. I hung it up, checked that my hair had not gone flat under the hood of my coat and left for my classroom. It was 7.45 am.

At my desk, I checked my handwritten lesson notes for the day. My teacher's planner was open on the right day; the books were ready. All I needed to do was get all my worksheets copied in the Banda room. Despite the dismal start to the day because of the rain, I felt quite optimistic that today was going to be good.

"Morning Jack, everything ok?" Sally stood at my door smiling.

She had been assigned as my "buddy" to help me settle in and guide me through the first few months. She had given me lots of reassurance and several tips on how to manage classes. Ones that she had got from her buddy last year.

"Morning Sally. Yes, all good. I have a good feeling about today. Great classes, a bit of free time this afternoon and everything ready to go. I have just got to copy my worksheets and I will be set for the day."

"That's great, if you need anything, give me a shout!" She turned and headed back to her room opposite. *Sally is becoming a good friend to have.* I reflected on our developing friendship. *She is a good teacher, kind and supportive and there is no awkwardness between us. We were both happily married and have no interest in each other.* With that, I stood, grabbed my pile of Banda sheets and headed off to the Banda room to copy my sheets for the day.

Yes! The room was empty. This was rare indeed. I set to work. I placed a couple of hundred sheets of plain A4 paper onto the input tray, and then selected the first of my Banda sheets. I carefully peeled back the top copy and separated it from the carbon copy. Opening the grip on the main drum of the duplicator I inserted the top of my worksheet. I was careful to ensure it was straight and in line with the drum edges. Clipping it safely in, I rolled the drum handle to help the sheet stick to the drum. All set. I pumped a button on the side that released the alcohol spirit that helped remove the waxy ink from my sheet to the plain paper as it rolled through the machine. I began to turn the handle on the side of the drum, that fed the paper into the machine and out the other side, hopefully with my worksheet now printed on it. The plain paper began to spit out of the machine as I turned the handle. Nothing! The paper was still plain; my sheet had not been copied. I stopped turning the handle and examined the machine.

"Shit!" I shouted to the empty room. I had placed my master sheet the wrong way. The shiny inked side was facing the drum and not facing outward. No wonder, it had not been copied. I bent in close to unclip it and turn it over, hoping that the writing had not been smudged too much. To my great relief, it had not, but the smell of the alcohol spirit went straight up my nose. I nearly fainted it was so strong. Shaking my head to clear it, I turned the sheet around and tried again. To my great delight, copies of my sheet began appearing in the out tray as I turned the handle. I counted in my head... 7,8,9, 10... until I had counted 30 sheets. Success. I looked around, no one else had entered the room, so I continued. If I could get all the sheets done now, I could do marking in my free lesson. That would be a bonus. That would mean I could plan for tomorrow in my free time and after school, which in turn led to less time tonight at the dining table. A win, win situation.

I quickly unclipped the sheet and placed it carefully on the carbon copy, to protect it. I grabbed another Banda sheet with diagrams and tasks all about the life of Jesus. Without rushing, I clipped it into the machine as quickly as I could and began to turn the handle. Purple printed sheets spat out the other end. 18, 19,20, 21... I tried to turn the handle faster to speed up the copying, but disaster struck. In my haste several sheets of plain A4 had entered the machine cockeyed, some had creased. Partially printed sheets emerged, some folded with bits of the printing now on both sides.

"Shit and double shit!" I was beginning to panic. Time was ticking, the clock on the wall said 8.15. I made a major decision to save the day. This class would just have to share. I still had three more sets to do. I unclipped the master sheet and began all over again. I pumped the button to release more spirit and the smell hit once again. It made my eyes water. As fast as I could I printed the remaining sheets.

"Are you going to be long?" I jumped. I hadn't noticed Andrew Chisholm walk in. He was carrying a pile of sheets to copy.

Andrew was one of the older teachers, nearing retirement. He taught Geography. He was short in stature and had bushy hair and an unkempt beard. He always wore a cord jacket with patches on the elbows. I had learned that he had served in the military as a teenager at the very end of World War Two. He liked to let everyone know that fact and the fact that he had travelled extensively, which enhanced his ability to teach Geography. However, the rumour was his classes thought he was boring.

"No, nearly done." I smiled at him to show I understood the frustration of waiting in line. "Just one more set to do." As I fiddled with the Banda machine, Andrew Chisholm picked up my sheet with the map of Israel and examined it.

"Bloody Arabs," he said with a little anger in his voice.

"I beg your pardon?" I was a bit confused. I thought I might have missed something.

"I served in Palestine when it became Israel. Bloody Arabs. Dirty people, liars and cheats all of them. They made the transition to Israel very difficult. I almost got killed by one. A sniper's bullet just missed me. Bloody savages!" It was clear he had a personal hatred of Arabs as a result of an incident in his youth. I wondered whether to tell him that I was of Arab descent. My grandfather married a local Palestinian girl during his service in Palestine after World War One. My dad was born in Haifa and grew up during the war and the troubles afterwards. He had his own stories to tell.

"How do you know it was an Arab sniper? Did you see him? The Jewish insurgents were killing soldiers too." He hadn't expected that response and it threw him.

"I'm not racist, but the Jews were clean and nice people, very friendly. It was an Arab; it must have been. They were the ones causing the problems, they are liars and cheats. The Jews were just fighting for what was theirs." I looked at him; *not racist? You bloody are!* I took my sheet back from him, unclipped my

Banda sheet and removed all the copies from the machine. I collected all my bits of paper. I was seething inside. My dad had experienced the terrorism of the Jewish insurgents led by the former Israeli premier Menachem Begin.

As I went to leave the room, I turned to Andrew and spoke gently to him. "I am sorry that you feel that way, but the war there is two-sided. Many Palestinians and Jews have suffered. Please don't lump all Arabs as evil and nasty. They are definitely not." I walked away breathing heavily, my heart racing. I hated that kind of conflict. I could not believe how racist he was. *I can't believe it, the man is a racist, how dare he speak about Arabs like that? I know, I'm part Palestinian, and I have Jewish friends. I went to school with Jews and trained with some to be RE teachers, I love the Jewish culture and religion.* Angry and frustrating thoughts rampaged through my head. *If I'd spoken about Jews the way he spoke about Arabs, he'd have called me anti-Semitic.*

I got back to my room, just as the bell went. I placed my sheets on the desk and went to stand by the classroom door to await the arrival of my tutor group. Sally stood opposite.

"You look stressed and angry, what's happened? Banda problems?" She pointed to my hands which were smeared in purple ink.

"You could say that." My teeth were clenched and I could feel my muscles tightening.

"Take some deep breaths and slow down. Your class need you to be Mr Lovely, not Mr Grumpy!" I inhaled a few big breaths and my heart rate began to slow just as the class appeared in the corridor. I turned to Sally and said: "Thanks, I'll tell you all about it at break time."

The class began to line up, Sara, Clinton, Joseph and the rest, single file down the corridor.

"Good morning!" I said firmly but politely. I forced a smile. I needed to make sure my day was not going to continue to be a disaster.

"Who is going to believe me?" I was sitting in the staffroom drinking coffee, Sally and Janet sat opposite, leaning forward listening to the tale I had to tell.

"I do. He gives me the creeps. I think he's a bit of a letch as well. I've noticed him staring." Janet was clear in her dislike of Chisholm. She sat back and sipped her coffee.

"Am I a racist? I call my husband dirty and smelly?" Sally was trying to find a compromise.

"That doesn't count," I said, smiling. "All husbands get called dirty and smelly at some point in their married life. You're not lumping all French men together when you say that, are you?"

"If all married French men get called dirty and smelly by their wives, as you suggest, then yes I am lumping them all together!" We all laughed at the absurd way the conversation went.

"This isn't helping me decide what to do about Chisholm." I was in a quandary. As a probationary teacher, I was new to the school and education. Andrew Chisholm was a teacher at the end of a long career. Who would believe me? Was Andrew Chisholm really a racist, or was he a man with a bad experience that has scarred him? Was I to be the one who destroyed his career? We continued to discuss it through break time, using hushed tones, huddled together in a corner of the smoky staffroom.

"That's not racism, it is just expressing a dislike based on experience, you can't damn a man for that." Tony, the NUT rep blew smoke in my general direction, as if it were a normal thing to do. I had decided to seek out union advice and popped along to see Tony at lunchtime. We sat in the equally smoky staff workroom. We were the only ones in there.

"But doesn't racism stem from the simple stereotyping that Andrew was using? The moment we lump all people of a race as being the same, we negate their individuality and assign common traits." I was recalling what my lecturer in Education had taught me. He was a great teacher and had experienced racism first-hand. There were not many black teachers when he had begun his career and coming from the Caribbean he had struggled at first, facing prejudice and discrimination. I had learned a lot from him.

"The man fought for our country at the end of the war, he fought racism." Tony was keen to defend his colleague. "How can he be a racist now?"

"I'm not sure it is as easy as that. Look I have no desire to make trouble or to see him punished. But he can't go around making comments as he did. What if he is saying things like that in his lessons?" My main concern was that he was not passing on these messages to children. It would be very easy in his Geography lessons to talk about his travels and the people he has met, and do so in a disparaging way. I expressed this to Tony.

"What do you want me to do, monitor his lessons?" He was being sarcastic. I began to see that this was a hopeless situation.

"Thanks, Tony, thanks for your help." I got up and left, waving the smoke out of my face as Tony just sat there smoking.

The rest of the day passed without much incident, the classes were unaware of my frustration and the Banda issues I had faced in the morning. They were happy enough to share sheets or, allow me to write work on the board. To them, it was just another day, although I had learned a different and difficult lesson.

CHAPTER FIVE

The mysterious disappearance of the HOD

I was at work early, I had plenty of Banda sheets to organise and get printed. Over the half-term break, Sandy and I had spent days working on planning and preparation for the next term. We had managed some early Christmas shopping and a trip to both sets of in-laws, but most of the holiday was spent working.

I greeted other staff members as I walked down the central corridor from the Banda room to my classroom.

"Is Matt in yet?", I called to Sally as she strode towards me. Her classroom was opposite Matt's and mine, she would know. She smiled warmly, and we stopped in the corridor to chat.

"He's not in yet, his room is in darkness and the door is shut."

I shrugged, "Oh well, I will see him at registration. Anyway, how was your week off? Did you get to France with Philippe?"

"Yes, we did. We stayed with his parents. They have a house near Nantes. It was surprisingly warm. We got back last night. I'm a bit behind, so I've got to dash. Catch up at break?"

"Of course! See you then." We went our separate ways and I arrived at my room, unlocked the door and plonked myself down at my desk.

Having organised my worksheets, opened the register and entered the date at the top, I began sorting out the books I would need for the day and then sat down to quickly mark a set of First Year (modern year 7) books.

Why is it, that a simple instruction like, 'underline using a ruler', can be so hard to do? I thought as my red biro scribbled two simple words on the page. *Underline, please!*

Just then the door opened and Mr Jackson, the senior teacher, walked in. I noticed that he still looked tired, even after a week off. His suit was still the same old threadbare one he always wore and he looked a little defeated.

"Jack, I have some bad news for you, Matt Rogers won't be in this week I am afraid. You will need to step up and organise cover work for all his classes. We will have a supply teacher coming in to cover but they will need work to deliver. Can you organise that, please?" There was even tiredness and resignation in his voice. I felt sad for him. It seemed like he was just disinterested in his job and waiting to retire. I made a mental note never to get into the same mindset.

"Of course. I'll get on to it right away. Is Matt ill, is he OK? He normally calls me if he won't be in."

"I'm afraid I don't know the details." Jackson's mouth said the words but his eyes indicated he knew a lot more than he was letting on. He turned and left the room.

"Curious," I said out loud to myself. I stood up, pushed my chair back and walked round to the cupboard that connected the rooms. I almost tripped over a pile of books on the cupboard floor. I flipped the light switch. The cupboard was a mess. Several piles of books were scattered everywhere. The tin that had biscuits in was on the floor and the biscuits in crumbs mingled with the scattered books. It looked like a scuffle had taken place. I stepped over the mess and opened the door to Matt's classroom.

Just then, Matt's classroom door opened and Sally entered. She flicked the light switch. She held her keys in one hand.

"I just heard, Matt is off all week, I thought you might need a hand sorting his cover. Is he okay?"

"No idea, but something is going on. Jackson was very cagey when I asked, and our cupboard is a complete mess. It was tidy when I left on Friday before half term. I'd appreciate the help sorting it out. I can't do the cover until I know that all the books are here."

"I'll sort the books you work out what lessons he has got today." Sally headed straight for the cupboard and looked in.

"Bloody hell!"

"I know; it looks like someone had a fight in there!" I was searching Matt's desk for his planner and timetable.

"It looks like someone has thrown everything off this desk then just picked it up and dumped it on again." I was a little frustrated and puzzled. Clearly, something bizarre had gone on after I left for half term. I recalled tidying my room, putting things away neatly in the cupboard and popping my head around the door to say goodbye to Matt. He was at his desk, marking, with two Fifth-Year (yr. 11) students in detention; a boy and a girl.

I found the planner and timetable and proceeded to plan simple lessons using textbooks. It mainly involved reading and copying with the occasional diagram or map. I provided resources and found the appropriate textbooks. I placed them carefully on the, now tidy, desk and Sellotaped the lesson plans to the desk. The school bell blasted out its five rings, telling everyone it was 8.40 am and school was beginning. I instantly heard children's voices in the corridor, shouting, laughing and preparing to line up outside rooms.

Sally emerged from the cupboard. She blew the misplaced hair from her eyes and then tucked the loose hair behind her ear. "It's just about sorted, I found this on the floor." She held up a condom, still in its wrapper. There is a whole box on the top shelf."

I looked quizzically at her. "That's odd. They only arrived last

Friday before we broke up for half term. They are for our Sex Ed lessons. Matt put them on the top shelf, out of sight of prying eyes."

"Well, the box is open and this one was on the floor." She tossed it to me and I caught the packet. I smirked and said; "Perhaps he was borrowing a few for the holiday." I laughed at my own joke.

"Eeww! That's gross, I don't want to imagine Matt having sex!" she laughed as she spoke.

The noise from the corridor was growing more intense as more children arrived, ready for the day. Sally turned and left the room and crossed the corridor to her own. I hurriedly replaced the condom, shut the cupboard door and emerged into my own classroom.

I ushered my tutor group into the room.

"Settle down, settle down. Morning Sara, did you have a good holiday?" Before she could answer, Clinton, burst into the room. He was wearing a sombrero.

"Olay! Olay!" he danced across the front of the room showing off his new hat. "Guess where I went in half term, sir? Go on, guess!"

"Bognor!" shouted one smart lad from the back. Several people laughed. Others joined in, all of them deliberately avoiding the word 'Spain'.

"London!" "France!" "Eastbourne!" "Russia!"

Clinton was slightly crestfallen. He had wanted his friends to be impressed. I settled the class down.

"I suspect you went to Spain, Clinton, am I right?" He beamed at me.

"Yes sir. It was brilliant. I've never been on a plane before, never even been out of England. It was so hot. There was a pool, we went out to restaurants, and all the girls wore bikinis!" There was a cheer from some boys at the back.

"Not in the restaurants, I hope! Once we've done the register, you can tell us all the best bits okay?" I was keen to make Clinton's story feel valued and important. I knew that his friends wouldn't be so kind about his Spanish adventure. Clinton nodded eagerly and trotted off to his seat and sat down. Sombrero firmly on his head.

"Sara, do me a favour, please. Can you go to the office and collect a supply teacher? The one who is covering for Mr Rogers. There was a snigger in the room from one of the girls, and a boy named George called out "Wahey". I looked at them sharply. They stopped.

"What does he look like, sir?" asked Sara.

"I don't know; I haven't met him. Just ask at the office and they will show you the right person! Bring him or her up here." I sent her off on the mission and then turned back to the class. There was a lot of chatter and laughter. The boys at the back were taking turns in trying on Clinton's sombrero.

"Clinton, you had better leave that with me today, otherwise, it will get confiscated and you'll end up in detention. Come and tell us all about Spain. Did you learn any Spanish?"

"Olay!" came the reply.

Peter Malcolmson was tall, thin, balding and had a moustache similar to mine. He wore a grey pinstripe suit with a waistcoat and was about five years older than me. He was the supply teacher called in to cover for Matt.

"Thanks, Jack for making the day so easy for me. The lesson notes were clear and easy. The classes were generally good and had a go at the work."

He was sitting at Matt's desk, sorting out books and

worksheets. I sat on a student desk in front of him.

"No problem, thanks for stepping in at the last minute. It can't be easy waking up in the morning thinking you are doing one thing, then getting a call to ask you to come and work." I liked Peter, we seemed to hit it off almost immediately when we met that morning.

"Oh no, I knew about this last Tuesday, during the holiday. I got a call from the agency saying that South Coast Comprehensive needed an RE teacher for at least three weeks."

"What?" My voice showed my surprise.

"I thought you knew. I'll be here for at least three weeks." Peter was almost apologetic.

"No, I was told Matt was off for a week. Is he ill? Did they tell you why? Oh God, I hope it's nothing serious. He is a bit overweight; I hope he's not had a heart attack or something." I was genuinely concerned for my Head of Department.

"I've no idea, I just got told it would be a minimum of three weeks with the possibility of it continuing further. Look, seeing as I am here for a while, I am happy to plan lessons and do the marking. If you point me in the right direction and show me the schemes of work, I can work out where each class is and plan from there. It will save you a lot of work and make me look good in front of your boss!" He grinned as he said the last part.

I laughed. "A deal, I knew I liked you!" We sat down together and spent the next hour planning work.

By the end of the week, the rumours were rife. Sally, Peter, Janet and I were sitting in my classroom after school.

"You know that the rumour is that Matt was caught shagging a Fifth-Year (yr. 11) girl in the cupboard." It was Sally who was speaking. "Personally I can't see anyone wanting to shag him, let alone a sixteen-year-old!"

"I can't believe Matt would do that. Anyway, who was the girl and where did you hear that?" I was mortified at the news.

Sally continued. "Sharon Williams, apparently."

"Ha! She's had more boyfriends than there are days in the month. She's the school tart! If it's true, she probably seduced him!" Janet was laughing as she spoke. But there was an element of truth to what was being said. Sharon was a troubled young woman, who, it was later discovered, had been the victim of child sexual abuse by an "uncle" and was exhibiting overly sexualised behaviour at a young age. She had been caught allowing boys to touch her, intimately, whilst on the playground at break times. She craved male attention, wore excessive makeup and the more sexually aware boys were keen to be with her.

"Even so," I said, "surely Matt would realise that it was wrong. He's not a fool."

"Sharon's not been back to school yet this term. Has anyone heard anything? Matt's not here, she's not here. It all adds up!" Janet was beginning to play detective.

I interrupted. "Anyway, Clinton in my class, told me today, that his mum knows someone whose child was assaulted by Matt on the last day of last term." I had just recalled this nugget. I had dismissed it as childish storytelling.

"What? Why didn't you say so? This adds a whole new dimension to the tale" Janet was intrigued.

"Alright, Sherlock! I forgot, I didn't think Clinton was serious. I thought he was fooling around. It's Clinton, when do we ever take his stories seriously." I was a little defensive, but at the same time, a little guilty for not trusting Clinton.

"We don't know if this is true, any of it. It could all be lies and Matt could be in hospital having major surgery." I was trying to end the conversation before we all became embroiled in excessive speculation, and rumour and gossip became the truth.

Peter, as the newcomer, had remained silent until now. "Surely, if he was just ill, or in hospital, we would have been told. This seems like something more. I never met Matt, I don't know him or any of the children you mention, but there is often no smoke without fire."

"Exactly!" said Sally, "something is going on."

"I'll tell you exactly what's going on!" said a gruff and grumpy old voice. We collectively turned our heads to see David Grant, the crusty old art teacher standing behind us. David took a long drag from his cigarette and blew smoke out as if he were Liza Minelli on stage in Cabaret, having a guilty pleasure. We were all transfixed waiting expectantly for a revelation that would explain everything.

"He was caught shagging a student." He paused and then continued. "It wouldn't be the first time a teacher has done that. He just got caught!" He winked as he said it. Took another drag of his cigarette, turned and walked away as if he were making a dramatic exit, stage left.

"What!" I said bemused "Do you think...?" I was cut off before I could say any more.

"Don't take any notice of him. He is just winding you youngsters up! He doesn't know any more than you do." Lesley Baker, the tall and broad woodwork teacher stood where Mr Grant had previously been. "He likes the drama, he's a frustrated actor. My advice to you is to wait and see and not speculate. It is easy to condemn someone without knowing the truth." I smiled and nodded. Lesley was becoming an ally and friend. He was speaking sense.

The next two weeks passed without any further news of Matt. The senior staff were tight-lipped, and I had no access to a phone number to call him. Peter had settled in well and the kids really liked him. The rumours continued. All teachers were asked to quash any rumours relating to Matt and to report any they heard.

"I don't get it, why aren't they telling us what is going on?" Janet was still keen to get to the truth. I had resigned myself to the fact I would never know. Janet was driving me home as it was raining and I had a set of books to mark. Walking home would have been a disaster.

"I expect Matt will be back soon, he can tell us if he wants to. Anyway, I've been asked to a meeting with the Head, tomorrow after school. Perhaps he will tell me then!" I was a little nervous about it, I had only spoken to the Head Teacher once, and that was at my interview.

"You never said anything," said Janet disappointedly. She stopped the car outside my flat.

"I only found out at the end of the day." I pulled out a note written in the Head Teacher's trademark purple ink. "It was in my pigeonhole. A good job I checked. I've no idea what he wants. I can't recall doing anything wrong, so I can't be in trouble!" I laughed nervously.

I waited for the rain to ease a little then opened the car door, got out, took my carrier bag of books from the back seat and my work bag and shouted goodbye as I pushed the car door shut with my leg.

"Come in Jack, thank you for coming. I know this is all a bit of a rush and a bit unexpected. Would you like a cup of tea? Or coffee?" Mr Robinson spoke calmly and gently.

"Please. A coffee would be great." Robinson used his intercom to ask for two coffees and some biscuits. I relaxed. If I was being told off, I wouldn't be offered coffee and biscuits.

When the drinks arrived the real conversation began.

"Jack, I have a proposition for you." I shifted in my seat. I was intrigued.

"Matt Rodgers will not be returning to South Coast Comprehensive. Therefore, we have a vacancy for a Head of Department. I would like you to fill that role, at least for the rest of the year. If it goes well, we will make it permanent. How does that sound?"

I was nonplussed. "It sounds great, but why? Where is Matt?"

"Before I answer, I need to know two things from you. Will you accept the role? And secondly, do you think Peter Malcolmson is good enough to stay on to take over Matt's classes for the rest of the year." Robinson sat back and waited. He picked up his coffee and sipped it.

My brain was suddenly full of questions, all buzzing around. I needed to make sense of them. I did not want to be disloyal to Matt, nor did I want to let the school down. I also wanted to further my career. I liked Peter, he was becoming a friend. He was a good teacher, should he be the Head of Department?

"Can I ask a question?" I tried to sound casual. I leaned forward and picked up my coffee and took a sip.

"Of course." Robinson smiled.

"It is definite that Matt will not be coming back, isn't it? Has he resigned? Is he ill? Has something happened?"

"That's four questions." Again he smiled, but this time there was a subtle difference in his eyes that I could not quite measure. "I will answer the first two and then you need to tell me if you want the job. Agreed?"

I nodded: "Agreed."

Robinson put down his coffee and sat back in his chair. "Matt has resigned with immediate effect. He will not be coming back, ever." Robinson paused. "With that in mind, will you take the role of temporary Head of Department, until July 1985?"

"Will I get a pay rise?"

"Not yet, if you do well we will move you up to scale two for September 1985." Robinson waited for me to speak, anticipating the next question.

"So you want me to do extra work for free for nine months?"

Robinson sat forward, there was a sternness in his eyes and his body language changed from relaxed and benevolent to tense and business-like. "Look at it as a training opportunity. Not many probationers find themselves with this opportunity. I hear that you are a good teacher, the children like you, the staff like you."

How does he know that? No one has been near my room to see me teach, I thought. I knew I was being used, but it was an opportunity for career progression that otherwise would take much longer.

Robinson continued his pitch. "You fit in here. This is an excellent opportunity to show your commitment to the school." I sat for a moment as if weighing it up. I was always going to take the role, as soon as I knew Matt was not returning. I had so many ideas to develop the department.

"I'll take it. With regard to Peter Malcolmson, he is excellent. I think he should stay."

"Excellent news. Thank you, Jack. Work hard in the role and I am sure the rewards will come to you." Robinson picked up his cup and took a sip.

"Sir? Why did Matt resign? What went on?"

"You have a right to know, but I agreed with Matt that it would not become public. I have also agreed to something similar with the parents of two students, on the condition that Matt resigned."

I spoke quietly. "I promise I won't say a word to anyone."

Robinson sat forward in his chair. "On the Friday we broke up for half term, Matt had two final year students in detention. Sharon Williams and Martin Benson."

"Yes, I saw them sitting in his room. He was marking books and they were at desks sitting quietly." I interjected.

"They were in detention for poor behaviour in a lesson. Towards the end of their detention, Matt had told them he was going off to print some worksheets ready for next term. He told them to sit and wait until he came back."

I nodded in understanding. Not wanting to give away the fact I knew that Sharon was likely to be involved. I was becoming a little uncomfortable. Perhaps the rumours were true after all.

"He returned to the classroom after about fifteen minutes. The room appeared empty. He thought they must have run off. However, he heard a noise, a yelp, from the cupboard, opened the door and caught Sharon and Martin in a compromising position. Apparently, they were boyfriend and girlfriend. She had her skirt up around her waist, her underwear in her hand, and his trousers were down. You can guess the rest."

"What? You mean…"

"Yes, that is exactly what I mean." Robinson was still clearly angered by the incident. "They had even broken into the box of condoms that the department use for sex education."

"So why did Matt resign? Surely leaving students unattended in detention is not that bad, is it?" I had done it on numerous occasions.

"The story doesn't stop there. Matt was furious with them. As you'd expect. However, he acted on instinct. He grabbed them both to separate them. They struggled, both embarrassed at being caught. One of them lashed out and struck Matt in the face. He reacted and slapped them both. He began shouting at them, ranting and raving about how disgusting they were."

"Bloody hell!" I didn't know what else to say.

"Quite! Sadly, it didn't stop there. He failed to let them dress properly for at least five minutes while he ranted at them. He then tried to manhandle them both down to my office, but they pushed him off and ran away."

"No wonder the cupboard looked like a bomb site and his desk was a mess." Robinson nodded in agreement.

"So what happened next? Why did Matt resign? I know he struck a student but look at what he caught them doing. He just lost it, a natural reaction." I was wanting to find the positives in Matt's actions.

"Matt came straight to see me and told me what happened. He was upfront and honest. By five o'clock that night I had the parents and the two students in my office. They both admitted their actions and confirmed the story. Martin Benson seemed a bit sheepish, but Sharon was more intent on blaming it all on Matt. The parents were more outraged that Matt had caught them and reacted in the way he did, than the fact their children were having sex in a school cupboard!"

"That's crazy. I know Matt overreacted, and what he did was a mistake, but it was out of shock, surely?"

Robinson shook his head. "Apparently, according to Sharon's mother, Matt is a pervert who needs to be locked up, and Mr Benson thinks Matt is a violent man who likes to hit children. The more the meeting went on the more they were out to see Matt punished severely. The outcome is that I had a call from County Hall on the Monday of half term suggesting a meeting with Matt and the parents that day. Benson's father had contacted them. It took place and the County representative chaired it. In order to protect the school, Matt offered his resignation rather than be suspended and have a local authority investigation. The parents of the students agreed to transfer to different schools. They are now at the local boys' and girls' schools respectively. The aim was to keep it out of the public arena to protect the reputation of the school. The parents have agreed to keep quiet and so have we."

I was bemused and upset. I was just getting to know Matt and liked him. Now his career was effectively over. No school would hire him with that on his record.

"So Matt loses a career, Sharon and Martin get shipped out with no support or even a hint of a reprimand. Doesn't that suggest we are not interested in why two underage teenagers are having sex in a school cupboard? Surely they need some support?"

Robinson shrugged in a resigned way. "Kids." He was not going to get drawn into an explanation of the decisions that were made.

"You also, need to promise to keep this to yourself. We have an agreement."

"Of course. You have my word." I sighed.

****

"So? Why did Matt leave?" Janet was keen to get the lowdown on my meeting with Robinson.

"I've no idea. Apparently, he just handed in his resignation and walked out." I was uncomfortable about lying but I was under oath. "Robinson just told me I could be Head of Department on a trial basis until July, and that if I wanted Peter to stay on he could!" I turned to Peter and said: "It's a good job I like you!"

"So what about all the rumours? Sharon's gone to the girls' school on the other side of town." Janet kept pressing for more information. I just shrugged.

"Anyway, Peter and I have a department to run. Come on Peter, you can be my apprentice." I slapped Peter on the shoulder, stood up and left the staffroom.

CHAPTER SIX

A trip to Devon

"Of course I'll come. Why wouldn't I? It sounds fantastic." I was excited that Simon Pedersen the Head of Geography had asked me to be part of the residential field trip to North Devon.

"It is a week off school and a week living in a caravan with me and Sergey." Sergey Belinsky was the relatively new Geography teacher who had replaced Andrew Chisholm when he had retired a couple of years earlier.

"I think I can put up with that!" I had become good friends with Simon and Sergey who were like a Geography double act. Simon the comic and Sergey his foil. Simon was tall, with thinning ginger hair. He was about thirty-five years old, had a lumbering gait and looked clumsy. However, he was an excellent teacher with an unrivalled passion for his subject plus kindness and generosity that impressed me. He was also the head of Year Three (nine). Sergey was shorter, stockier with a thick mop of black hair. He also sported a beard, neatly manicured around his jaw. He was very efficient and his lessons ran like clockwork.

I suddenly had a panic. "Are you sure I am ready for this? This is only my third year here."

"Jack," said Simon, kindly, "You are head of a thriving RE department. You're organised, the kids love you and you deserve a chance to be on the best trip of the school year!" Simon was never shy in promoting how good his Fifth-Year (eleven) Geography trips were.

"You must be mad!" said Sandy, my wife. "A week on a caravan site with fifty teenagers." She shook her head in despair. "Rather you than me. I couldn't think of anything worse." She smiled as she spoke. "At least I'll have the house to myself for a week. A week of pampering and self-indulgence!"

"I think it will be fun, all I have to do is drive the minibus and shepherd a few kids about various locations." I was wanting to let Sandy know that this was going to be easy. A week off from the slog of lessons. I wanted her to be jealous, but she wasn't falling for it.

Sandy came up to me, hugged me and then said: "If you'd rather spend a week with two men in a cramped caravan surrounded by kids, rather than be with me..."She let the sentence trail off. She turned away but not before she winked seductively at me.

"Humph! You know that's not the same... right? It IS work!" I'd lost and I knew it. It is not that she minded at all about the trip, it is just what we did, teased each other.

****

It transpired that the preparation involved in going on a trip for a week was immense. I had to plan every lesson in detail, leave all the books out, marked up to date, textbooks in piles and labelled for each class. Simon, as well as the scary deputy, Miss Higgins, wanted a manila folder of all lesson plans plus copies sellotaped to my desk. There needed to be no excuse for cover teachers not to deliver the lessons planned. We were due to leave on Monday morning. It was the Friday before; school had finished and I was putting the final touches to all my lessons. Twenty-one lessons planned, all books marked and sorted. The room was tidy and ready for the supply teacher. I slipped the handwritten lesson plans into the manila folder and headed off to the Banda room to copy them. Thank goodness for photocopiers. The school had invested in upgrading from Banda machines to a photocopier. Simply place the sheet of paper on the glass beneath the lid, close the lid and press the big red button. The copier hummed into life, the light flashed under the lid and a copy of my work popped out into the paper receiving tray. It was more complex if your work was double-sided. I tried to keep mine simple.

"Here we are," I said, handing the manila folder to Simon. "All my lessons in date order. All the books are sorted and the room is set up for the supply teacher. I've also left a set in Peter Malcolmson's pigeonhole."

"Well done! Are you all set? All packed and ready for Monday. You have got everything on the kit list, haven't you?" Simon was a stickler for ensuring everything was perfect for his trips.

"All except the wellies. I don't have any. The forecast is good weather, so I don't think I'll need them." I was hopeful that this would be a reasonable response.

"It's not about the weather Jack, we will be wading in a river and walking through the watershed. It will be boggy. Trainers won't do, nor will walking boots."

I sighed. "Really?"

"Really! Get yourself a pair this weekend. Millets in town have got loads."

Monday arrived. I kissed Sandy goodbye and she dropped me off at school. I am sure she smirked as she drove off. She was looking forward to a week of peace and solitude; early nights and soaking in the bath without me bothering her.

It was beginning to drizzle, the clouds were thick and it looked like it was set in for the day. Simon and Sergey were already there as were Sally Le Croix and the frightening Miss Higgins, the Deputy Head. She looked very different out of her twin set, almost human. She wore jeans, trainers and a sweatshirt. Tied around her waist was a cagoule; clearly, the drizzle was not enough to make her put a coat on. I had learned early on that Higgin's first name was Linda and that she was a geographer by subject. I had never called her Linda, only Miss Higgins.

"Jack, glad you could make it!" Simon tossed a set of keys in my direction. I caught them. "Load your stuff in your bus and then collect your registers from Sergey. Tick the kids off as they arrive. Load their stuff onto your bus and get them sat down. No wandering off! We need to be away by eight!" There had been a series of meetings leading up to this day; in each meeting Simon and Sergey, the Morecombe and Wise of our school, talked us through every aspect of the five-day trip. I had a folder with the itinerary, maps, locations, lists, phone numbers etc. Everything was accounted for, even the menu for each day. Simon had somehow managed to arrange with a local supermarket in Devon to have daily deliveries of food, enough for each student and staff caravan to cook their own meals.

I opened the minibus and packed my holdall, walking boots and shiny new wellies under the seats. The seats were side-facing, there were no seatbelts and there were boxes of equipment piled up behind the driver's seat. My ten children would pack their belongings under the seats, as I had done, and then sit facing each other. If you were tall enough, you could just about comfortably put your feet up on the opposite seat. I stood by the open rear doors and ticked the students as they arrived. I watched them struggle to pack their gear under the seats; some of them had no idea. I would imagine this would be the first time away from home.

"Oi, Tina, take over ticking students off as they arrive. I'll sort out the packing of kit in the bus." I couldn't watch them struggle anymore. We'd never get away on time. Tina was a sweet, hardworking Fifth-Year student, who was always keen to help. She had big, round wire-rimmed glasses and blonde hair tied in a ponytail. She was wearing camouflage combat trousers and a grey sweatshirt bearing a Fruit of the Loom logo.

"Ok sir, I'll do it." She jumped out of the back of the van and almost snatched the tick list from me. I hopped into the back and began to reorganise the attempts at luggage packing. The three other Fifth Years in there tried to help. It was a learning opportunity for them.

By 8 am we were set to go. All my charges were on board, luggage stowed. I had five lads and five girls on my bus. We had negotiated in the student meeting the previous week, that all ten would take it in turns to ride up front and navigate. Simon had provided detailed instructions and an AA map book of the UK. Our first destination was a service station on the far side of Salisbury. All buses had to rendezvous there for a toilet stop and to check everyone was ok and knew where to go next. Tina was first up riding shotgun. I hoped that I could just follow the other buses. I was third in the convoy with Simon leading and Sergey as rear-guard. Sally and Linda (I was still struggling to think of her as Linda and not Miss Higgins) were second in line.

Simon and Sergey arrived at my window. I wound it down. "All set Jack? Everyone in and accounted for?" I nodded and spoke at the same time. "All set. We're all raring to go aren't we?" I turned round to my charges, my team looking for support. Three of them were plugged into Sony Walkmans, and two of the girls were reading books, two lads were already asleep and the other two were eating crisps. "See, look at them all, keen as mustard. They're just very good at hiding their excitement."

They both grinned. "The same in our buses too. Right, see you in Salisbury. If there are any issues, find a phone box and call the school. We will check with the school at every stop, so if you don't show at least we know what has happened." I was beginning to get a little nervous. I had driven the bus several times, but that wasn't the issue. This was a long distance; we were on our own. Me and ten teenagers, on an adventure in a bus, all the way to Salisbury and beyond. I turned the radio on. Southern Sound Radio blared out. The Breakfast Show, the DJ was playing classics from the 70s. I was in heaven!

"Sir! Do we have to? This is so old." Trevor spat crisps out as he spoke.

"That's gross Trevor, pack it in" A rather demure girl called Fiona pulled a face as she spoke.

"Ha! Ha!" said Trevor, "Packet in, get it?" waving his packet of Golden Wonder around.

"Just stop spitting crisps! I'm already feeling sick and we haven't even gone anywhere yet!" Fiona said in a rather prim voice. I panicked. I didn't recall anyone in my group telling me they got travel sick. "Are you ok Fiona? Do you get travel sick? Have you taken anything?" I began to scrabble around in my manila folder looking for Fiona's medical form.

"No sir, I'm fine. It's just Trevor, he makes me feel sick!" The bus erupted into laughter. Even Trevor laughed, crisps spewing as he did. I smiled to myself, *I think this is going to be ok* I thought, *even if it is just me and them alone in a bus for 200 miles or so.*

As we pulled out of the school gates, I started singing, well sort of singing, along to the tune on the radio. "That's neat, that's neat, I really love your tiger feet, I really love your tiger feet!" I tapped my fingers on the steering wheel.

"Sir! Please stop, or at least put a cassette in that we all like." Tina was pleading with me.

I glanced at her, grinned and said, "Tina, I'm just getting started! That's neat, that's neat, I really love your tiger feet, I really love your tiger feet!" She shook her head and focussed on the AA map.

The rest stops at Salisbury and Taunton came and went without issue, Tina was replaced by Trevor, who turned out to be an excellent navigator and map reader. I relented and put a cassette in the player. Trevor's mix tape. Everyone sang along.

We pulled into the campsite near Barnstable at about 2.30 pm, right on schedule. No one had got lost, no one had broken down and even better, no one had been sick.

Once all the luggage had been offloaded and caravans allocated to students and staff, Simon gathered them all around. He introduced the campsite warden who explained the rules and how not to blow up your van by leaving the gas on and having a sneaky fag in it. Smoking was obviously banned!

"Right, we meet back here in 45 minutes. Be appropriately dressed for walking. No flip-flops, high heels or expensive trainers that you don't want to get muddy. It's not going to rain so don't bother with a cagoule or jacket. Just bring a jumper. Remember we are starting five days of work, so no moaning about it! Right, off you go." Simon dismissed them and soon the teachers were left alone in the centre of the site.

"Jack, Sally, Linda, make sure you know where your kids' vans are, round them up in about 35 minutes. In the meantime, unpack and let's have a quick cuppa and I'll tell you what we're doing." Simon turned and strode off towards our van. Sally and Linda headed off next door to theirs.

The afternoon was spent orienteering, practising OS skills and generally getting lost in the vicinity of the campsite. I was on point duty with Linda at the crest of a hill with a trig point on it. Our job was to mark the kids off as they arrived and give them some more coordinates to take them to where Sally was about a mile away by a church.

"So Jack, I don't really know you that well. I hear you are a good teacher." *There's that phrase again* I thought. *I've been teaching for two and a bit years and still no one has come in to see if I am a good teacher. Everyone just seems to hear it!* Linda and I had been chatting on our stroll to our hilltop location. She seemed human out of the school setting, approachable and even cracked a few jokes.

"Thank you. I've heard it too!" I panicked for a second, thinking

I had overstepped the mark. But she laughed. I discovered she was a Liverpool fan and liked amateur dramatics. She was part of an AMDRAM society in the Sussex village where she lived. She had a sense of humour and we got along.

"Give us a tune then, Linda," I used her first name. It made me nervous.

"What, now?"

"Well, if you're that bad there's no one to hear it but me, and I won't tell!" I swept my hands around indicating that we were the only two around for miles!

"Cheeky sod!" She grinned and then burst into song. The first verse of Beauty School Drop Out, from Grease. I was taken aback. She had a great voice. I clapped her and whistled.

"That was great!" I was genuine. It was, considering there was no music, no words, no preparation.

"I played 'Frenchy', last year in our AMDRAM production of Grease. I love it. I am really a frustrated actor and singer." She laughed; I discovered that I had misjudged Miss Higgins. She wasn't a scary monster, but just a normal human, with hobbies and interests, who just happened to be great at her job and very efficient. Over the next few years, until she left to become a Head Teacher, Linda and I would cross swords over many issues to do with school but we always remained friendly. Disagreement does not mean dislike.

Two figures approached, climbing the hill to the trig point. Linda got her tick sheet ready to mark them off and give them new instructions. As they came closer, I realised it was Trevor and Fiona. I had paired them up deliberately at the start of the exercise to try and get them to communicate and learn to get on. Fiona strode purposefully up to me and stood directly in front of me with an angry look on her face. It was quite out of character for such a polite and well-restrained young woman. "Sir, I really hate you! Why did you have to put Trevor with me? He is such an arse!" Linda looked around sharply ready to reprimand Fiona but saw my face. I was trying not to smirk. She could see it in my eyes.

"Because, Fiona, we all have to learn to get along, even with people we think we don't like, isn't that right, Miss Higgins?" I turned to Linda and smiled.

"Absolutely correct, Mr Turner, sometimes we think we don't like someone because we haven't spent time getting to know them. We can have a false image." Linda knew how I had felt about her before our walk and long conversation during the afternoon.

"But sir, he farts a lot and then tries to waft it in my direction! It's gross!"

"Perhaps he is trying to impress you, it's the sort of thing boys do when they like someone." I was trying not to laugh, as was Linda.

"Eww! Please don't tell me that he fancies me! That makes it worse!" Fiona screwed up her face as she spoke. At that moment Trevor finally arrived at the trig point.

"Slow down Fi, it's as if you don't want to work with me. What have I done to upset you? I've shared my crisps and I've even let you do all the work!" he grinned at that last bit.

"Teamwork Trevor, teamwork. Fiona is upset because you can't control your wind! She's not a fan of your ability to fart the alphabet. She would rather you helped her with the work and talked to her about things you both are interested in. Isn't that right, Fiona?"

"Sir? I can't fart the alphabet" Trevor hadn't seen the sarcasm. Fiona had and was laughing.

"Thank you, sir! By the way, I don't really hate you. It's just Trevor can be such an…" She was cut off by Linda.

"We don't need reminding of what an arse Trevor can be. I

think he knows it as well!" Miss Higgins smiled at Trevor, then winked at him conspiratorially. "I have a feeling you won't be for much longer, will you Trevor?" Trevor and Fiona were staring at Miss Higgins, trying to take in that she had used the word 'arse' when referring to Trevor.

"Miss, are you allowed to say that?" said Fiona, strangely defending Trevor.

"To be fair Fi, I was being an arse, you said so yourself" Trevor was defending Miss Higgins.

I decided to intervene. "Why don't you two head off to the next destination and continue to discuss if Trevor is an arse or not."

"Sir! Don't you start?" Everyone began to laugh, realising the absurdity of the situation.

"Go on, clear off to the next point and try to get on. Trevor, no more farting. Fiona, make sure Trevor does some of the work!" Linda gave them the next coordinates and before they headed off across the top of the hillside, Fiona turned to Linda.

"Miss, are all boys like Trevor?"

"What do you mean Fiona?" said Linda genuinely puzzled. She smiled at her encouragingly.

"Well, it's just that all the boys seem to be preoccupied with food, football and farting. They don't seem to want to talk about anything else. Is that normal?" Fiona seemed genuinely frustrated by the immaturity of teenage boys.

"I'm pretty sure they think about other things too." Linda winked and smiled at Fiona.

"Miss!" Fiona squealed and blushed a bit.

"It's normal Fiona, they get over it, don't they, Mr Turner?" Linda turned to me for support.

I grinned. "Yes, they do, by the time they reach about the age of forty. And sometimes not even then!" I couldn't help it. I was a bloke, and still a big kid at heart. I winked at Trevor who had been standing quietly listening and waiting to leave.

"Sir, that's no use!" Linda and I laughed a bit and Fiona turned to Trevor. "Do as sir says. No more farting. If you do, I'm going to smack you round the head with my clipboard!" She threatened to do it and Trevor dodged out of the way. "Cheers sir, miss, see you later!" he chirped. In the distance, two more students strode up the hill.

It was midnight, the air was cold but at least it was dry. I was tired and feeling drowsy. Sally and I were patrolling the caravan site, or more accurately checking the static vans where the students were staying. We both had torches and we stood quietly outside one of the boy's vans. There was chatter and laughter from inside. We listened in, standing close to an open window.

There was a loud fart and the van erupted with giggling.

"Trevor! You're such an arse!" More laughter.

"Turner was right; you do nothing but fart! I bet you could fart the alphabet" It was difficult to tell who was speaking but clearly everyone knew about Trevor and Fiona's experience on the hillside.

"I'll give it a go if you want to?" Trevor's voice was distinct.

"No thanks, Trev! If you do, stick your bum out the window!" More laughter erupted.

Sally and I were trying not to laugh as we listened in, either side of the open window.

"Is it true what Turner said, that you fancy Fiona?" The voice was toying with Trevor.

"He never said that!" Trevor was getting a little defensive.

"I bet you do though, she is fit!" several of the boys in the van began to jeer.

"Get in, there Trev!" "Ask her out!" "Wahey! Trevor!"

"F... off you lot. I don't fancy her!"

"I bet you do! I do she's hot! If you won't ask her out. I will!" said a lad named Sam. There was more jeering

"You wouldn't ask your mother out!" This was from Trevor who was beginning to regain some status in the conversation.

"I'd ask Sam's mother out, she is fit!" Again followed by jeering and laughter.

The noise was building up. Sally and I looked at each other and nodded. Time to intervene.

I banged on the side of the van. "Time to quieten down lads. Enough of the banter!"

"Shit!" said a voice. The van went quiet very quickly.

"Shiiiit... do you think he heard us?" There was a whisper from one of the lads.

"You will never know what we heard. You will have to face us in the morning and wonder what we heard. How embarrassing!" Sally spoke clearly through the open window.

"Shit, that's Le Croix, she's there too. Shut up, everyone." Trevor was clearly embarrassed.

"She's hot too, though!" Sally laughed out loud and we turned away to check the next van.

Torchlight flickered from the door of the van opposite. As Sally and I approached we saw Fiona and Tina, my helpful map reader on the journey down here. sitting on the caravan step. Tina seemed to be consoling Fiona. Sally stepped forward. "What's wrong, girls? Why are you out here? You know there is a curfew of 11 pm."

Tina looked up. "Yes miss, but Fiona is upset and we didn't want to wake the other girls."

Sally knelt down beside the girls, I took a step back. This was not my area of expertise.

"What's up Fiona?" Sally's voice was calming and kind. Fiona looked up, she had been crying.

"Nothing miss, it's just boy trouble. I like this boy but he's such an arse! Why can't he just be nice to me?"

"Sometimes boys don't know what to do or say to girls. They come across as strong and tough, but inside they are scared of showing how they feel. I expect this boy likes you too. Why wouldn't he?"   I stepped further back into the darkness leaving Sally to counsel the girls on how to understand teenage boys.

In the days that followed, we visited a dockyard, the Dartington Glass factory, and a farm that was diversifying into a tourist attraction as farming alone was not financially viable. We did beach profiles, walked a dry river valley, discovered the source of a river and followed it down to the coast. My wellies were essential. We drove the convoy of minibuses around the Devon countryside. I learned a lot about Geography during that week.

I was standing in the small river, the water about two inches below the top of my wellies. My team of ten from my minibus were gathered around me. They had nets and jars. I stood with a clipboard and a pencil ready to log down their findings. We had a stretch of the river to profile. How many fish, eels, snails etc... pollution, in terms of rubbish or litter. The plant and animal life that lived along the banks. We had been there about an hour and I was now getting bored.

"Sir, how much longer, my hands are freezing and my feet are wet?" Fiona was looking a bit bedraggled. Her usual smart appearance had been somewhat lost during the day as we had followed the river from the watershed at its source down to where we were now.

"Trevor will keep you warm!" Sam called out from the back of the group. Several of the girls giggled. Fiona stuck her tongue out at him and gave him a vicious stare. Trevor nudged him in the ribs.

"Ow! What? Well, you do fancy her, we all know it. Give her a cuddle!"

"Shut up Sam!" Trevor was going red.

"Enough you two, let's wrap this up and get out of the water!" I said quickly to break up the fuss.

"Thank God!" said Fiona and she scrambled out of the river onto the bank. Other teams were finishing too, further down the small river. After everyone was out and I had collected all the data and equipment from the team, I sent them off to sit and have a snack and drink. They sat together under a tree. I noticed Trevor and Fiona, sitting close to each other but not yet acknowledging each other's presence.

I stood by the river bank, watching the water, giving myself a moment to reflect and be still. All of a sudden there was a scramble behind me and I turned to see my team, all ten of them descending on me. "Get him! Quick!" I turned and tried to run as fast as I could but wellies are not made for running. It was no good! Trevor jumped on my back. Sam grabbed my legs in a rugby tackle and before long I was on the ground!

"Quick! Lift him, get him in the river!" I began to struggle.

"Wait, hang on, you'll get in trouble! You can't..." I tried to reason with them but ten against one was overwhelming. At last, I saw help coming, Simon and Sergey, Sally and Linda all running my way. Behind them were the rest of the students on the trip. There was shouting and cheering.

"Simon, Sergey, get them off me!" I was struggling to escape. Trevor and Sam were exceedingly strong and had my hands and feet securely pinned down. Most of the others, including Fiona, had various parts of my clothing gripped in their hands in an effort to keep me still. To my horror, I saw Simon holding the video camera, a massive grin on his face. Sergey, Sally and Linda just stood and laughed. It was then I realised, I had been set up. Now I realised why Simon had insisted that everyone, including staff, brought a change of clothes on the trip today. This was planned! I relaxed a little. "You bastard Simon! Sally, I thought you were my friend." They just stood there. I stopped struggling and allowed the ten students to lift me and carry me down to the river bank. There was a gentle slope with a tiny sandy beach. They walked me down and out into the middle of the river and dropped me unceremoniously into it! Simon stood videoing the whole incident. There were cheers from all the kids around. I stood up, dripping from head to toe. Then suddenly I grabbed Trevor, who had foolishly stayed too close. Before he could resist, I took his legs from under him and he fell right in. There were cheers and screams all around. The rest of my team began to make a run for it. I managed to grab Sam and trip him up. He too went under. I saw Fiona scrambling up the beach. "Oh no you don't!" I grabbed her around the waist, carefully avoiding any sensitive areas, turned and carried her back to the river. "Sir no, I didn't mean it!"

"Too late for apologies!" I dunked her under and let her go! She came up spluttering.

By now several others had begun to jump in the river and dunk each other. Sally and Linda were in, trying to trip up other students. A mass water fight broke out in the middle of the normally quiet section of the river. For the next ten minutes, every child and every adult got wet. They even managed to get Simon in… once he had stopped filming.

"I forgot to mention," said Simon, "it's a bit of a tradition that I get one group to dump their team leader in the water. We have a water fight every year!"

I stood there emptying my wellies onto the ground.

"I have to say they did it rather well. They were quite keen!" I towelled my hair and tried to take off my cagoule. It was clammy and sticky.

We had sent the girls off first, back to the busses to dry off and get changed. Simon, Sergey and I remained with the boys, who stood around, dripping.

****

I sat in a fold-up garden chair outside the men's staff van. I was clean, dry and relaxed. I had been let off cooking duties as a reward for being thrown in the river. I was enjoying a cup of hot tea and a piece of cake, made by Linda. Simon was cooking and Sally and Linda would join us for dinner once they were showered and changed.

Sam, whose mum is apparently hot, came running up to me.

"Sir," he said, "how do you make omelettes?"

"What? Omelettes?" I said slightly bemused.

"Yes, We've got the oven chips in the oven but none of us knows how to make omelettes?"

"Really? None of you?" Sam shook his head.

"No, sir. Please, can you help, I'm starving!" Sam looked pleadingly at me.

I stuffed the last piece of cake into my mouth and washed it down with a slurp of tea. Put my cup down and got up out of my chair.

"Come on then, time for a cookery lesson!" I walked with Sam back across the campsite to his caravan.

As I stepped into the caravan, the smell hit me. Not oven chips, but sweaty socks and stale farts. A bacteria-laden caravan, full of teenage hormones, sweaty clothes and damp shoes. I nearly gagged.

"Crikey, it's steamy in here, like a football changing room, but worse! Open some windows." A couple of the boys got up and reluctantly opened the windows.

"That's better. Keep these open for a while, and let some clean air in. Right, omelettes!" I went over to the small cooker. It was a mess. It hadn't been wiped over or cleaned for several days. There was an open tub of margarine, half a loaf of bread in a bag, a pot of jam with the lid off and half a packet of digestives all scattered around the cooking area.

"Fellas, you need to learn to keep things tidy. Look at this mess! Come on let's clear up. There is a fridge and cupboards to put things away. Once you've done that I'll show you how to cook omelettes. Come on all of you help out. No helping, no omelettes. I'm watching." The small team of boys got to work, getting in each other's way in the small static caravan. Eventually, the kitchen area looked a little tidier.

I proceeded to teach them the art of the perfect omelette. Each boy took their turn in making their own, cracking and mixing the eggs, a little milk, and some salt and pepper. I showed them how to stop it from sticking, and how to use the grill to make it fluff up and cook fully.

By the time I had left them, they were all replete and enjoying lemonade and cake for pudding.

"Thanks, sir, you're a diamond!" said Sam with a mouthful of cake.

"Diamond? Where are you from, the East End of London?" I smiled. "My pleasure lads. At least I know you have learned something on this trip!" I turned back when I was at the van door. "Don't forget to wash up using hot water and washing up liquid. Grease won't come off in cold water! Tidy everything up and don't let anyone get away with doing nothing." I stepped out of the van just in time to see Sally and Linda heading off to our van to enjoy our omelettes and oven chips.

We sat around the table planning the following day's activities and going through the itinerary. A bottle of wine was in the middle of the table. I picked it up and filled everyone's glass.

"I still can't believe none of those lads could cook an omelette. This is 1986, not the 1950s." I took a sip of my red wine and sat back.

"It may be 1986 but sexism and gender stereotyping are still rife," Sally commented. "In all of the girls' vans, they not only made the omelettes but made a salad too with their sandwich provisions. Tomato, cucumber and lettuce. It was even in bowls and put on the table!"

"I bet their vans don't smell of sweat and damp shoes either!" I continued the dialogue.

"Nope! It's all sweetly scented and immaculate!" Sally was laughing now.

"Unbelievable" I shook my head in despair for the future of the male species of the human race. "I know I'm not a totally modern man, but I can do a bit of cooking and make a salad!"

We continued drinking and planning, playing cards and chatting until 11 pm when we all went out on patrol again. This time on day four of our trip, all was quiet in every van.

The drive home was uneventful. We waved goodbye to the campsite, then to North Devon and steadily made our way back eastwards towards Sussex. We sang songs in the van until I noticed I was the only one singing. Glancing in the mirror, I saw that everyone was asleep. When we got to Salisbury and stopped for lunch, something had changed. We were parked up at a petrol station that had a 'Little Chef' attached to it. I stood by the van stretching my legs. Fiona and Trevor walked hand in hand into the restaurant.

"Oi Sam," I called. "Are they going out?" I nodded my head in Trevor's direction. Sam shook his head. "Of course they are! It was on the cards. They have liked each other for ages, it only needed someone to give them a nudge."

"Oh, I see," I said non-committedly. I watched them disappear into the restaurant.

"Sir, you know that was you, don't you? You put them together on the first day. You gave them the nudge!"

I smiled. *So I did,* I thought.

Sam turned to me and smiled. "You're OK, for a teacher. Thanks for this week, it's been brilliant. Thanks for looking after us all.

"You're not so bad yourself, for a kid! Now go off and get your lunch."

I glowed inside, moments like that made it all worthwhile.

CHAPTER SEVEN

The magic trick

T he hustle and bustle of students leaving school at the end of the day was always a good time for me. It meant another day done, lessons taught, children educated, and a day closer to the weekend. Not that I was wishing my life away or hated my job; in fact, the opposite was true, I loved my job. It just meant I could move on and get ready for the next challenge. As the sound of children exiting the buildings began to fade, it was as if the buildings themselves heaved a sigh of relief. Peace began to descend, staff members slowed their pace a fraction, stopping to pass the time of day, checking up on each other, and ensuring everyone was well after the teaching day had ended. It was a time to share your successes; a lightbulb moment when one of your class suddenly understands. Also your frustrations; the class that will not respond, that misbehaves despite your meticulous planning.

It was Monday afternoon in the Spring of 1987. It was, as in many schools, meeting day. Today I was in a Humanities meeting led by Simon Pedersen. In most schools, there is a hiatus between the end of the day and the start of a meeting. A time to use the facilities, make coffee, do some photocopying or play with the Banda machine until, out of sheer frustration, you swear in an attempt to make it work. I was making coffee in the staffroom, people were milling about preparing for their own meetings or generally taking a breather.

"Make us all a coffee, Jack, and I'll crack open the biscuit tin."

Simon's booming voice filled the room.

"Deal! Make sure there are chocolate Digestives!" I set about gathering several more mugs and a tray to carry the precious load up to the Geography rooms. Simon disappeared carrying a large sheaf of papers.

"He's playing you for a fool, Jack!" Fred Winter, the crusty old History teacher was sitting in a comfy chair reading the Daily Mirror. "He should make his own coffee, not get you to skivvy for him."

"What's up with you? Have you had a bad day? You're not normally THIS grumpy!" I deliberately emphasised the 'this'. I smiled at Fred letting him know I was teasing him.

"I just don't like more senior staff taking advantage of the young ones." Fred seemed more morose than usual.

"It's all part of my grand plan, Fred. To take over the school. If I am nice to everyone, then they can't refuse me anything!" I smiled and winked conspiratorially at him.

"Humph! You're just being put upon and you can't see it. You're too naïve."

"So you don't want a coffee, then?" I was teasing him again.

"Yes, please. White, one sugar." Fred was blissfully unaware of the irony.

I placed the tray of coffee down on the table. Several desks had been rearranged to create a large conference-style seating arrangement. The coffee and also the biscuit tin sat in the centre.

"Help yourself, there are three with sugar in the white mugs, the rest of us are sweet enough, eh Fred?" I said.

"Humph!" Fred took a white mug, helped himself to a handful of chocolate digestives and sat down.

Fred and I were the last to arrive. Around the table sat Simon, Sergey, Linda Higgins from the Geography Department, Peter Malcolmson, my partner in RE, Fred Winter and Amy Watson a new History teacher this academic year. Amy was quite short, with brown hair cut in a bob and as left-wing as they come.

"Stop grumbling Fred, he's only taking the piss. And besides, you've been really grumpy today, what's wrong?" Amy had quickly got the measure of her Head of Department and treated him like a miserable grandfather figure. She never pulled her punches.

"I'm not grumpy!" he said in a very grumpy fashion. "This is me being happy." He stuffed a digestive in his mouth and began to munch it.

"I'd hate to see you when you're miserable, Fred," said Amy with a grin on her face. "Anyone would think you'd been asked to join the Tory party." Fortunately, Fred had a mouthful of biscuit otherwise he would have filled the room with expletives. Instead, he stuck two fingers up at Amy. The team began to laugh at the exchange going on, it was entertaining.

"Time to get on, otherwise we'll be here all evening," Simon spoke gently but with authority.

"Agendas are on the table, help yourself. Item one, year 1-4 exams and year 5 exam preparation. Please can you fill in the exam form letting me know what you are planning for internal exams? Also, can you let me know what you are planning in terms of revision in class for your Fifth-Year classes?" A discussion broke out about exams and revision. Comments going back and forth. I tried to stay out of it and spent the time completing my exam form. I showed it to Peter, who nodded in agreement. I slipped the form across to Simon who nodded his thanks.

"When are we going to get sample papers for this new GCSE exam then? Why couldn't they leave things alone? If it ain't broke... don't fix it. That's what I say. There was nothing wrong with O levels. Bloody Tories messing everything up. If it's not Thatcher bleeding us dry, then it's that ponce, Baker. Have you heard about his plans for a national curriculum? Bloody ridiculous, everyone doing the same thing, that's just nonsense." Fred was quickly getting fired up.

"Fred, I gave you sample papers weeks ago." Linda Higgins, the Deputy Head, spoke sternly. "What have you done with them?"

"He gave them to me," said Amy quickly, before Fred put his foot in it again. "I've been reviewing them. I've got a plan for preparing the first exam class, don't worry." Amy looked at Fred, concern in her eyes.

"Sorry, I must have forgotten. I've got a lot on my mind." Fred sunk back into his seat.

"Anyway, moving on..." said Simon, trying to get the meeting back on track.

The meeting had been going about ten minutes when the door opened and a nervous face appeared. Everyone in the room stopped and turned to see who was there.

"Hello? Sorry to interrupt, but I've been out here." Duncan was a Fourth-Year student. He was short and had wavy brown hair that needed a cut as it hung over his eyes. His jumper was frayed at the cuffs and his laces were undone. Let's just say he was in the bottom sets for most things.

"Hello Duncan, what can we do for you? Shouldn't you have gone home by now?" Sergey was the first to speak. "We are in a meeting so make it quick."

Duncan nervously entered the room. It was easy to see he was uncomfortable around so many teachers in one space.

"Um... it's just that you put me in detention, and I couldn't find you, so I've been wandering around searching the school. Now I've found you." Duncan was doing his best not to be scared and as such had not identified the teacher he was speaking to.

Linda Higgins spoke up, "What did your detention slip say? It must have had a room number on it. Who put you in detention?" She turned to the assembled staff accusingly. This was a mistake by someone and it was made in front of the Deputy Head. She turned back to Duncan and spoke. "Well, Duncan, who put you in detention, and why?"

"You did miss! I was climbing the fire escape to get my ball off the roof at lunch yesterday." He almost smiled but thought better of it. However, there were clear grins from several of the assembled staff.

Embarrassed by her faux pas, Linda Higgins turned to Simon. "I'm sorry everyone, I seem to have made an error. Would it be OK if Duncan sat in the room in the corner for a while? I don't think we are discussing anything sensitive, are we?" There were mutterings of approval from around the room.

"At least I'm not the only forgetful one!" Fred was suddenly grinning. His mood had brightened somewhat.

"All right Fred, none of us is perfect!" Linda ushered Duncan into the room and sat him in the corner.

"He can sharpen some pencils to keep him busy. Might as well make use of his skills." Simon got up and placed a box of coloured pencils in front of Duncan and a pencil sharpener. It was one of those educational ones with grips that pull out and a plastic see-through container to collect the sharpenings.

"Right... let's get on. Item two, feedback on Baker's new education bill. The head sent round the key points for us to mull over. Of course, it is only in the preliminary stages but it's planned to be law by September 1988. Let's go round the table to hear what we think. You all know my thoughts. Learning is lifelong and should be enjoyable. Schools are not exam factories, nor should they be." Simon gave a wry smile as he said the final sentence.

"Jack, why don't you go first?" Simon smiled at me encouragingly. *Shit,* I thought, desperately trying to organise my thoughts.

"I'm not clear on why we need Grant Maintained schools. Or even what it actually means. Also, why do we need key stages and exams at every step of the way? Also, I think league tables will take away the joy in learning and force schools to be exam centred."

Phew, I got away with that. I sighed. My comments sparked conversation, that at times got quite lively. Amy with her socialist background did nothing but rip apart anything Tory, even if it may have had merit. Linda was all for improving schools and creating competition that would push up standards. The debate raged, people expressed often extreme views and Simon interjected regularly, trying to focus on children's enjoyment of learning and how a national curriculum may stifle this. He tried to maintain a calm and friendly atmosphere as the discussion progressed. Duncan sat sharpening pencils.

"Miss, can I go now? Look at the time." Duncan pointed at the clock. It was half-past four.

"Oh goodness, I forgot you were there, Duncan, you've been so quiet." Linda Higgins pushed her chair back and got up.

"Another memory lapse for our deputy, that's a free pass for us, I do believe." Fred piped up.

"In your dreams Fred." Linda smiled as she spoke. She went over to Duncan who was arranging all the sharpened pencils into colours.

"Well done Duncan, an excellent Job."

"Thanks, miss, my Maths teacher lets me do this in lessons when I can't do the work. It stops me from getting cross." Duncan was unaware he was giving away information that could be used against his teacher.

"Does he, indeed?" said Linda. "Interesting!"

Simon broke into the conversation to stop Linda from questioning him further.

"Oh, Duncan, can I show you a magic trick before you go? I've been practising it in order to show my children at home."

Duncan shrugged. "I suppose so. Will it take long?"

"No, it's very quick." Simon dug around in his pocket and pulled out a ten-pence piece. "Look," he said and held the coin at arm's length in his left hand between his thumb and first finger.

"Watch carefully, you'll like this… not a lot but you'll like it." There were smiles from the staff sitting around, even from old Fred.

"That's what Paul Daniels says, isn't it sir?" said Duncan, now staring at the coin in Simon's hand.

"Watch carefully!" Simon swept his right hand over his left as if to grab the coin. The coin dropped silently into his left palm. With his right hand, he made a big show of flinging the coin away.

"Ta-da!" said Simon, "it's vanished." There were cheers from the staff at this simple trick.

"Sir, that's brilliant!" Duncan was clearly impressed and had not seen this done before.

"Wait!" said Simon dramatically. "What's that behind your ear?" Before Duncan could raise his hand to check Simon leant forward and with his left hand ruffled Duncan's hair and ear. He stood back and held up the ten-pence piece in his hand. The crowd around the table went wild in mock shock. Cheering and even whistling. Even Linda Higgins clapped politely.

"Wow, sir, that was amazing. How did you do that? Can you teach me?" Duncan was excited that a magic trick had been performed on him. "I want to do this to my mum."

"Ok! But no telling anyone else. Deal?" Simon winked at him.

"Deal!" Duncan was beaming.

Simon showed him the trick, slowly placing the coin in one hand, pretending to take it in the other. He showed Duncan the coin safely in his left palm while pretending to throw it away with his right. It took several goes before Duncan truly got the trick.

"Wow, sir you're great. My mum will love this!" Duncan headed for the classroom door. Simon went to sit down. The meeting was in disarray; it was almost time to end it.

"Sir?" said Duncan, appearing at the door again.

"Yes? What is it?" said Simon.

"Just one question. I get how you made the coin disappear, that's easy. But how did you get it to come out of my ear?"

There was a stunned silence. Duncan was serious. Simon looked at us all in turn, not really knowing what to say. We all just shrugged. Then, as if inspired, he said:

"Now that's magic!"

Fred trudged down the corridor, and Amy and I followed.

"Wait up Fred. What's up? You're not right, are you?" Amy's voice carried concern.

Fred shook his head. He stopped in the corridor.

"Don't say a word, you two. I trust you both. But I think I have cancer." Amy dropped her bag, stepped in and hugged him tightly.

"Shit," I said. What else could you say?

CHAPTER EIGHT

A special visitor

I sat in the back of the staffroom, with Amy, Janet, Peter and Sally. It was early September 1987. The Headteacher, Mr Robinson had called a special staff meeting before our usual Monday one.

"Anyone got a clue what this is about?" Peter asked as he leaned into the group of us huddled around a low coffee table.

"I bet he's retiring," said Sally.

"Let's hope we get a woman replacement!" said Amy enthusiastically. She took every opportunity to promote gender equality. David Grant, the slightly camp art teacher with the thick black wig 'humphed' at Amy's comment. She stared sternly at him.

"We're all getting a pay rise?" I said hopefully. At that, everyone laughed.

"No chance!" "In your dreams Jack!" "Not with the Tories in charge!" Everyone around the table responded.

Robinson entered the room followed by Linda Higgins, Tom Jackson and Francesca Lovejoy, the whole senior team. They stood by the coffee station and waited for the room to settle.

"This must be important," said Sally. "The whole team is here."

The room quickly settled, people realising that something significant was about to be said. There was an air of expectancy. Robinson stepped forward.

"Thank you all for giving up your free time before meetings

tonight. I know how precious this time can be. However, I have some significant news that I need to share with you." He paused. There were a few murmurs from around the room. "Today I received a communication from Her Majesty's government. I will read it to you." There were further mutters from around the room. People were intrigued. I leaned forward in anticipation. Robinson continued.

"Dear Mr Robinson,

I am delighted to announce that your school has been chosen to receive a visit as part of a unique tour of the United Kingdom. Your visitor, who, for security purposes, will remain top secret until the day before the visit, will arrive for a tour of the school, watch selected lessons and meet staff in a reception afterwards. The school will be assessed before the day of the visit to identify the security needs of the site and organise the route of the tour and finalise the reception details. Due to the current unrest in Northern Ireland and the threat of terrorist incidents on the mainland, the final identity of the visitor and the exact date will only be announced twenty-four hours in advance. Her Majesty's Government expects the school leadership to use discretion in sharing this information within the school and not to share it with the general public."

He paused and looked up at the staff. There was a stunned silence.

"I'm going to hand over to Linda who will explain further." Robinson stepped back. He was beaming with pride.

"Thank you. At this time, we genuinely don't know the exact date of the visit but further documents were received that stated it would be in mid-October, a month from now. We have no idea who will be coming or the purpose of their visit. However, we have been given strict instructions about not sharing information outside of the people in this room. Security is of paramount importance; we do not want to make our school a target for a terrorist attack. Please don't discuss this with family or friends." Linda stepped back. Immediately there was a chorus of questions and chatter.

"If it's Thatcher, then I'm not going to be in the same room as that witch!" Amy was loud. There was a ripple of laughter and a few calls of "here, here".

"I do hope it's the Queen! She's so lovely" said one lady staff member who taught in the cookery department. Robinson let the chatter continue for a moment or two and then stepped forward again.

"This is an important and prestigious day for us. I would ask you all to respect the details of the letter and only discuss it when you are out of earshot from children or parents. It is vital that we maintain the security that is asked of us. Thank you." With that, the meeting was over.

The planned Humanities meeting was now in disarray, everyone just wanted to discuss the secret visitor. We all had our theories as to who it was going to be.

"It's got to be the Queen; I mean who else demands such security?" Fred Winter was quite upbeat; he was a bit of a royalist at heart. His recent cancer scare turned out to be a benign tumour in his stomach, which he was due to have removed in a few weeks.

"If it is our Lizzy then you'll miss her. Won't you be having your operation in October?" Amy Watson, Fred's apprentice in the History Department, said. She was not a particular royalist, more of a republican. It often led to interesting discussions. Two generations viewing life very differently.

"My money is on Thatcher," said Simon. There was a hint of malevolence in his voice. "After the IRA missed her in Brighton in '84 her security has been increased ten-fold. If it is top secret, then it has to be her." I knew Simon was a staunch Liberal and was totally frustrated by the Tory government and their repeated lack of investment in the public sector.

"If it is her and I get the chance, I'll tell her what we need in schools! How are we supposed to compete with the private sector and have an equal education system if they refuse to invest in it?" Simon was beginning to show his true liberal colours.

"They don't want everyone to be equally educated, that would mean they would probably lose power. They definitely don't want that! If state schools produced the same results as private schools, then the populous would soon see through the Tory lies! There is no way a Tory government will invest in education. It is not in their interests." Amy spoke with authority and passion. "A Labour government would soon reverse all the funding cuts."

I chipped in, "Whilst I am definitely no fan of Thatcher, I'm not sure the country is ready for Neil Kinnock." Amy looked at me sternly. "What?" I said defensively.

"Who else is there?" she said.

"Well… David Steele?" said Simon hopefully. We all stopped and looked at him.

"Seriously?" said Fred. Everybody laughed, even Simon.

"Ok…. Ok… let's start the meeting before I get ridiculed anymore." Simon called the meeting to order. Secretly I felt sorry for him, I quite liked David Steele.

September rolled into October, and the excitement faded as we got on with the business of teaching. The usual successes and failures took place in my lessons. The regular questions that got asked by disgruntled teenagers. "Why do we have to do RE? I don't even believe in God." Or even worse, "My dad says RE is a waste of time, we should be doing more Maths and English. If we hadn't let all those immigrants in, then we wouldn't need to know about Muslims." This one was the most challenging to answer because whatever you said would appear to challenge the authority of a parent and undermine their opinions, even if those opinions were based on lies, misunderstanding and poor education. I usually managed to produce an answer that gave positive reasons such as: "We live in a world of many different beliefs, it is important we know and understand them all. That is how we combat racism and prejudice. You want to be properly educated, don't you?" The mention of race and prejudice often quietened them down. Not many would want to see themselves as racist or prejudiced, even if they knew they were.

In the second week of October, a note arrived in my pigeonhole. The school rule was that pigeonholes were checked twice daily, in the morning and evening before you went home. Pigeonholes were very exciting. Every day you never knew what would turn up in it. A note from a colleague asking a favour or an important question, such as "Can you look after my class for five minutes at the end of the day so I can nip off to the doctor?" Strictly this was not allowed, but everyone did it. Why wouldn't you? You are helping a friend. You were supposed to go to the Deputy Head and ask permission. This note, however, was different. I unfolded it. It was written in purple ink. It was from Mr Robinson, the Head Teacher. It read:

Dear Jack,

Your classroom and one of your lessons, a second-year class (Wednesday lesson 3), have been selected to be part of the tour by our special visitor. Over the next 24 hours, please ensure all displays are updated and graffiti free. Ensure the classroom is tidy. You are invited to a private reception after the tour. You will need to provide a detailed lesson plan to me by Tuesday morning. There will be a brief meeting for all those selected for the tour on

Wednesday morning.

It was signed by the Head. I stood there and read it again. I looked at my watch to remind me what day it was. Stupid really because I knew it was Monday. A mass of thoughts flooded into my head. *Bloody hell! They are coming to watch me teach! What is that class? Who is in it? Are they well-behaved? What are we learning about? Who will be coming? Can I tell anyone? What will Sandy think?*

It was Monday afternoon. The school was quiet and meetings had been cancelled in order to allow staff to ensure all rooms were at least presentable in case the visitor wanted to go off the tour route. I showed Sally and Peter the note.

"Blimey, Jack. You had better get that lesson sorted. You might be teaching in front of the Queen." Peter smirked as he spoke. Sally whipped out her note. It was identical to mine.

"You too eh? We must be special!" I turned to Peter. "Obviously they only want to let the visitor see the crème de la crème" I patted him on the back. "Never mind mate. Maybe next time."

"Less stress for me!" he retorted. He grinned. "Just you wait, you'll be sweating like mad. Damp armpits in front of the Queen. Not a good look!"

"No pressure, Pete. I've got it covered. Definitely no sweat." My brain was working overtime thinking of ways to make my lesson more interactive and more stimulating.

"Well, I'm off to plan some singing in French. We are learning irregular verbs and we are going to sing them." Sally waved her note as she spoke, turned and left the room.

"Well then, I had better leave you to tidy your room, sort your displays and plan the best ever RE lesson. I've got next door to sort out." Peter slipped into the cupboard that connected our rooms and disappeared. I stood there alone in my classroom. "I'll tidy up first, sort my displays and think of the lesson as I'm doing so," I said to no one.

At 8.00 am on Wednesday morning, ten of us were huddled in the head's office. I stood next to Sally and a tall, slim, slightly balding English teacher called Marcus Taverner. He was the Head of the English and Arts faculty. I leaned into Sally and whispered in her ear.

"I feel like we're all about to get told off for smoking in the toilets or something like that." She sniggered and the Head looked at us. Marcus turned to us and whispered. "Yes, I know what you mean. It's all a bit tense."

"Thank you for coming," said Robinson. "Late last evening I received notice that our special visitor is arriving today at 11 am. They will already have been to the FE college in town. Here is a schedule of the tour and when you can expect a visit from the tour party." He passed round copies of a typed sheet with times, rooms and staff names on it. I glanced down the list. My name was clearly there. There was no mistake. I saw Sally's, Lesley Baker's, Marcus' and of course everyone else in the room. This was really happening. Some important VIP was going to watch us teach. This, as yet, unnamed VIP was coming halfway through my lesson. *OK, that's fine, we will be in a good discussion by then.* I was getting a little nervous.

"Can we ask, who the VIP is?" Lesley Baker's booming voice seemed extra loud in the confines of the office.

"Of course, it is now in the public domain. The schedule has been made public. We are going to be visited by…" There was an air of excitement and expectation. Would it be Thatcher or the Queen? "The Secretary of State." There was an audible sigh of disappointment from some in the room. "I know many of you were hoping for the Queen or the Prime Minister, but nevertheless, this is our opportunity to influence education policy and even the proposed new Education Act." There were mutterings and nods of assent. Robinson continued, "Once your lesson is over and the tour is finished, please come straight down to the staffroom for a private reception, where you will have the opportunity to chat with the Secretary of State. He will leave here at 2 pm. If you have a class during that time, cover has been arranged. Thank you. Have a good day." With that, we were dismissed.

The morning passed slowly, the tension growing as I ploughed through the first two lessons. The students were now aware that there was a special visitor and were asking questions.

"Sir, who is this bloke? Why is he so important? And why is he coming here?" By the time morning break arrived, I was exhausted from answering these questions, let alone the tension of being watched by a man with such influence in government. It suddenly dawned on me. *"Someone is actually going to watch me teach! Even if it is someone who has no clue whether I'm doing it right or not!*

Morning break was spent in a mild panic. I used the toilet at least twice, checked my classroom (again), reviewed my lesson plan (again) and ensured that all worksheets were ready in piles on my desk. My heart was racing and I was beginning to sweat. I eventually made it to the staffroom, grabbed a swift coffee and a biscuit and sat down to gather my thoughts. Sally sat opposite me, also looking a little nervous.

"Worried?" I asked knowing the answer. She nodded and smiled weakly at me.

"Me too, but I am sure it will be fine. We have to remember he is not a teacher; all the experience he has of education is his own public schooling. He won't know if our lesson is good or not unless the kids are running riot. They won't be, they know how to behave with visitors!"

Just then the warning bell rang, indicating that there were five minutes to the start of lesson time. We stood together, left our coffee mugs on the table and exited the staff room.

"Jason, can you tell me what you think a miracle is?" I was in full flow. The lesson about the miracles of Jesus was going well. We read some examples of miracles and shared what we thought about them. The students were giving their opinions on Jesus' miracles and reasons for their views. Before Jason could answer the door opened. The room fell silent; they were expecting the visit. I had prepped them. In walked, Mr Robinson, the Head, followed by the Secretary of State and a small posse of security and dignitaries from County Hall. They lined up against the side of the classroom looking out across the room. I continued as if they were not there. He looked just like he did on the TV: quite tall, grey suit, dark hair parted to the left and the large trademark thick-rimmed glasses.

"Jason, what is your view?" *Please say something sensible, please?* I silently prayed just to back up my wishful thought. There was a pause for what seemed to be an age whilst Jason prepared his answer.

"Well, sir," he began. *Good start, nice and respectful. Keep it up, Jason.* "I'm not sure I believe in miracles; I mean it isn't scientifically possible to walk on water or to feed five thousand people, is it? There has to be a different explanation... or it's all just made up."

Phew! I can cope with that, well done. "Excellent response Jason. Can anyone give an alternative explanation?" Several hands in the room shot up! I made a big show of thinking about who to choose, but in reality, I was always going to choose Emma. She was bright as a button and had a Christian background. I had seen her at the church Sandy and I had started to go to. She would be a safe bet.

"Emma," I said, pointing at her, "how would you respond to Jason's view?"

"Well, sir, if the story is just a story then we should dismiss it and assume miracles don't happen." A few in the class began to chatter in agreement.

"Hush now, let Emma continue." I glanced up at the dignitaries watching, beads of sweat on my brow. Robinson smiled encouragingly. The secretary of state just stood there watching. The rest looked disinterested.

"However," said Emma feeling confident of being centre stage, "If Jesus was or even is the Son of God, then wouldn't he be able to do those things? He would have God's power. I think the miracle stories show that Jesus was God, just like he said." At this several hands shot up in the air, there were even groans as if to say Pick me, pick me."

"Emma, that is brilliant, some excellent thinking by both you and Jason, well done!" I tried to emphasise that so that the Secretary of State would be aware. I'm not sure he noticed. He just stood and smiled.

The discussion continued, further contributions were made, and arguments and counter-arguments were put forward. I orchestrated the discussion, prompting students to think more deeply about why they had opinions and how they might justify them. The Head escorted the dignitaries around the room and they looked at student work. They spoke quietly to a few students, who, thank the Lord, responded with polite and positive answers. Eventually, after what seemed like an age, Robinson interrupted the lesson. "Mr Turner, thank you for allowing us to disturb your lesson." He turned to go and began to lead the party out of the room. The Secretary of State turned to me and spoke. "Thank you, Mr Thompson and excellent lesson."

"It's Turner, Jack Turner." *If it was excellent, then at least get my name right in your report.* The door closed behind him. I didn't know if he had heard me.

The whole class sighed a sigh of utter relief and chatter broke out. "Sir, I never knew your name was Jack!" said one small lad sitting at the front. "You do now." *And I hope that Tory politician knows it too.*

The private reception was in full swing. All the dignitaries were standing around in one group and all the staff, hovering around the buffet table as if they had just been set free from a prison camp. There was even alcohol. There was a calmness about the room, occasionally broken by the bark of someone laughing too loudly. I had noticed that the Secretary of State had downed two gin and tonics and the Head was drinking wine. I stood with a plate of sandwiches, sausage rolls and a scotch egg in one hand and a bottle of lager in the other. Sally stood nearby nursing a single sandwich and glass of wine.

"How did it go?" I asked. I looked at my food and my bottle of beer, a difficult dilemma, which to put down. In the end, I plumped for the food. I swigged my beer greedily.

"Great, I think. The kids joined in the singing, even he had a go." She nodded in the Secretary's direction.

"Crikey! In my lesson, he just stood and smiled. You must have done all right then." She shrugged. Sally was a great teacher but very humble and never thought she was good enough. "I suppose so," she said in a resigned sort of way.

At that moment the Secretary of State broke away from the dignitaries and headed straight for us. He had a fresh gin and tonic in his hand. As he approached us, he held out his hand. I took it and shook his hand. He looked me in the eyes and spoke:

"Mr Thompson…"

"Turner," I said quickly before he could continue. "Jack Turner."

"Sorry… Mr Turner. I meet so many people, names can get so muddled." He leaned in close to me and spoke a little more quietly.

"Thank you again for your excellent lesson. I want you to know that it is good to see the Christian faith being taught so well in school and also to let you know that your subject is safe with me." He was so close that I could smell the alcohol on his breath. He almost wobbled but steadied himself.

"Yes, your subject is definitely safe with me." He repeated. He took a swig of the gin and turned to Sally. He offered his hand. She took it and he covered it with his other hand and patted her hand. "And you my dear are…Miss Le Croix. What a beautiful name. What part of France are you from?"

"Actually it's Mrs. And I am English, I have a French husband." I could see Sally was cross. His sexism was subtle but it was there. He was flummoxed for a moment and then tried to recover.

"You speak French very well," he said, trying to get back on track. Sally was not going to let him off the hook so easily.

"Yes, I have a degree. In fact, I speak three other languages. What does the future hold for my subject, sir?" There was a little tension in the word 'sir'.

"Ah! Your lesson was so lovely, what a good idea getting children to sing. You must have practised a great deal with them." *A politician's answer if ever there was one. Avoid the question and change the subject.*

"Thank you…but…" Sally was cut off by a County Hall dignitary butting in.

"Sir, Mr Secretary, it is time to move on." The County Hall representative ushered him away from us and back to the main body of dignitaries. Sally was about to say something when I took her by the arm and led her away to the buffet.

"I can't believe that smarmy…" She was furious.

"Not now, Sally." I didn't want her to make a scene and get herself into trouble. She was a friend and I was protecting her.

"Did you see how he spoke to you and then to me, the

difference? How sexist can you get?" she was bubbling up and finding it hard to calm down.

"I know, he's an old-fashioned, sexist bloke. He was also drunk; I could smell the gin on his breath. But at least he liked your singing!" I was taking a risk. This would either work or explode in my face. Sally turned to me, rage on her face.

"Jack! How dare you…" She turned to face me ready to lay into me as well and then saw the look on my face and knew I was winding her up. She suddenly guffawed and began to laugh loudly. People turned to see who was making a spectacle of themselves.

"You bastard," she muttered under her breath to me. I smirked. "I had to do something to break the spell. Otherwise, you might have punched him. I can see the headlines now. 'Secretary of State decked by sweet, singing French teacher!'"

"Alright, alright, you win. He's still a sexist sod though!"

"Agreed," I said, "but at least my subject is safe in his hands." We turned back to the buffet to find some more drinks but decided to go soft. We still had afternoon lessons to cope with.

PART TWO: A SEASONED PROFESSIONAL
1990- 2009

CHAPTER NINE

A new era.

It is September 1991 and I am sitting in my new office. Yes, I have an office. I am now, not only the Head of the RE Department, but also a Head of House. To be precise Columbus House. Our colour is green and I intend to make us the best house at South Coast Comprehensive School. The house system is a funny thing, it originated in private schools and has filtered down into the state system. Our house system uses explorers from history; the aim is to see exploration and learning as improving us and the world. It kind of ignores the imperialistic nature of conquest and empire that caused a significant amount of war, pain and suffering. The four houses are Columbus, Polo, Cook, and Scott. They are designed to be for pastoral care, developing a community spirit and teamwork amongst students. I am now responsible for the welfare and academic progress of two hundred students. I share the office with Mary Johnson, a formidable but kind-hearted maths teacher. She is my deputy. Mary is in her mid-forties and has long black hair and large round spectacles. I have to admit I am a little nervous about working with her. *She scares me,* I thought.

Everything seems to be changing as if a new era is beginning. Janet Smith my first friend, whom I met on my first day, had left for a role in a girls' school in Chichester. I will miss her friendship and wisdom. Mr Robinson, the Head Teacher, has moved to the Isle of Wight to lead a failing school. Tony the unhelpful NUT rep has moved on to higher things in the union. I expect he is being unhelpful there as well. *Stop being so judgemental, Jack.* It is a habit I am struggling to break. Tom Jackson, the weary Deputy Head, had retired and been replaced by a dynamic young, PE teacher called Martin Simpson. He had already been at South Coast for several years. Fred Winter had also retired after his cancer scare, deciding to make the most of life. I got a postcard from him yesterday on holiday in Mallorca. *Lucky sod.* Finally, my partner in the RE department, Peter Malcolmson left to become a Head of Department in a school in Crawley. My new partner in crime is a woman called Jackie Jones. She is older than me by a few years and she also runs the Careers Department. Jackie is tall and blond. She is extremely organised; we get on well. Our new Head Teacher is a woman called Melanie Franks, she appears to be a career woman, who has risen through the ranks in education very quickly. She dresses similarly to Linda Higgins, in smart two-piece outfits, with scarves and brooches. She has a very precise way of speaking and rarely wastes words. As I reflect on this now, I suddenly realise I am surrounded by powerful and assertive women. *I am going to have to work hard, just to keep up.* On a personal note, Sandy and I had moved into a house on the outskirts of town and had even acquired two children. Two amazing boys, Joe and Sam. Life was certainly changing.

****

"Please can you have your assembly rotas into me by next week and your three ideas for house charity events? I know this is quick but I would like to get the calendar sorted as quickly as possible. Please also ensure that you use your logbook to record phone conversations and dealings with parents and students. Please take one for you and one for your deputy." Samantha Lovejoy was my line manager, I was in a meeting with the other house heads and Martin Simpson the new deputy who had oversight of PSHE.

"Can I hand you over to Martin who will explain how we will deliver some of the PSHE work this year?" I liked Martin, we had already struck up a good working relationship. He was personable and we had a shared interest in religion. I was a believer; he was a Humanist. He was always keen to engage me in a debate about faith, God and morality. He began to speak and outline how key elements of PSHE such as careers and money education would be delivered by tutors and the rest incorporated into the RE curriculum.

"If you give me more time and one extra full-time team member we could deliver the whole lot properly." I was ready to fight for this. PSHE is unique as a subject yet is treated like an add-on. *I wish people would take it seriously.* To be fair, Martin did but was constrained by current staffing budgets.

"Properly, Jack?" said Samantha. "Are you suggesting we're not doing it properly?"

"If I am honest, then yes. Tutors with no training, skill or interest, teaching vital life skills and trying to develop our students into positive young adults. You wouldn't get any school letting untrained tutors teach Maths, English or Science, would you?" I was getting on my hobby horse. In the last six years, I had learned the value of excellent PSHE. I'd come a long way since that first lesson.

"Well of course not..." said Samantha, "Those are important..." She stopped before she said it all, but it was too late. Samantha slumped in her chair and sighed. "It's not as easy as that Jack, we are restricted by budgets and staffing costs. We simply don't have the money for another department member in RE."

"But you have for English or Maths." I looked her in the eyes, I knew I was right, they had just employed two new teachers, one in each subject. None had left, but now they had extra staff.

After the meeting, I walked down the corridor with Martin

Simpson. "You didn't help me out much. Why not? Thought PSHE was your thing." He looked a little sheepish and a little resigned.

"I am on your side, in principle. It is just she is right about the budgets. English and Maths will always take priority. It's the law of the jungle." I stopped him in the corridor.

"Wait. OK, I get it. Will you back me if I can create a case for an extra RE teacher in two years to help deliver lesson time PSHE in the curriculum?"

Martin smiled at me. "Of course, I bloody will. You know I believe it is important. I have faith in you, Jack. You can build the case for PSHE You have the passion."

"So you do have faith then? You do believe?" I teased him.

"Shut up, you muppet!" Martin turned and walked away. I grinned!

****

Snow was falling heavily and settling quickly. The playground was covered in a thick layer of snow. The road outside the school was also white. Cars moved slowly for fear of skidding; the sky was laden with snow and there was a luminescence in the atmosphere that you only get on days like these. It had begun snowing at around 6 am and it was now nearly 9.30 am. I looked out of my classroom window. The lesson had gone to pot, the year eight students (Old year two. This year everything changed to a new system. Reception to year 13) just wanted to look out of the window. I was desperately trying to interest them in the Five Pillars of Islam, but the snow was infinitely more interesting. I live in Sussex; the South Downs protects it from most of the severe weather from the North. Snow is a rarity unless it comes from the East. This was from the East and it was heavy.

"Sir, are they going to shut the school?" said one girl, who looked slightly worried. "I've heard the buses are cancelled! How am I going to get home?"

"Sir, please let us out at break time." Mohammad, a tall and handsome boy originally from Nigeria, pleaded. "It's perfect for snowballs!" Several others, both boys and girls began to plead.

"Sir, please" "Sir, let us!" "Go on sir, please!" "Everyone else will. Go on sir!" The pleas came thick and fast.

I held my hand up and asked for silence. They eventually responded. Snow is a big distraction.

"I don't make those decisions. Ms Franks will decide. She will get instructions from the local authority. They will advise us. Now can we get back to the lesson please!"

Just then the door opened and a young Year Seven child walked in and handed me a message. He stood and waited. I stood and read the message to myself. The class were expectant. Outside the snow was still falling, and cars in the carpark were covered in a thick layer.

"Sir, are we going home?" "Have they shut the school?" "I bet we have to stay indoors." The class were desperate to hear the news. They were bubbling up again and getting excited.

I cleared my throat. And began to read the note out loud to them.

"To all classes. Due to the extreme weather conditions, and the cancellation of all bus services, the local authority has advised all schools in the town to close." There was an instant cheer. There were fist pumps, clapping and a few whistles. Again I held my hand up and "shushed" the class. "There is more." I waited. They settled a little. "All students are to return to their tutor bases and be dismissed from there. Tutors will receive a list of students whose parents have previously consented to their children leaving the school in the event of an emergency closure. Those students may leave. The rest must stay on in their tutor bases until the end of the school day when they will be dismissed as normal." There was a moment of silence whilst the class processed this information. Then all hell broke loose!

"I hope my mum signed that form, I ain't stayin' 'ere!"

"Me neither. I don't care if I can go or not. I'm going!" There were nods and murmurs of assent.

"Sir, what if I get the bus, how do I get home? I live on the other side of town." The worried girl looked even more anxious. "Can I stay even if I am allowed to go?"

"I'm going straight up the Downs when I get home." Several of them were making arrangements. Others were cheering and packing up as quickly as they could.

"Wait!" I said in a very firm tone of voice. "There is still more." The class stopped and listened. "Any parents who did not give consent are being called right now in order to receive verbal permission."

I handed the note to the boy who was still waiting and he departed to the next room. There was noise in the corridor, classes emptying and children talking loudly, shouting in excitement about snowball fights and sledging. The classroom emptied and I stood there for a moment. I shook my head in disbelief. *This is Sussex, we don't do snow.*

Just then Samantha Lovejoy walked in and handed me a list of names.

"Jack, these are the names of the children whose parents have not consented to emergency closure release. Home and work numbers are listed here. Please start to phone, we need to get rid of as many as possible. This weather looks set to stay. We don't want students hanging around all day. The staff of course will be expected to stay if they live locally. Those who live in other towns can leave once their class has gone. Please can you tell your tutors?"

"Sam, is this the right decision? Is this really such an emergency?"

"The buses have been cancelled. People are being advised to stay off the roads. All the local radio stations are advising people not to travel. So yes. It probably is." We both stared out of the window. My car was covered in about two inches of snow.

"Ok, I'm on it. I'll tell the tutors first and then get on the phone." We both turned and left my room. I spent the next ninety minutes phoning parents, finding their contact details in their files, calling, explaining, justifying and apologising.

"Yes, I do understand Mrs Bates... Yes, I know it is inconvenient... yes I am sure it is, but... I know, but the weather is the weather. I've just been asked to get your permission... No, I understand that we are supposed to look after them... The local authority... Please, Mrs Bates, can I send Katy home or shall we keep her here? Thank you, that is all I needed to know. Goodbye, and thank you again." I put the phone down before she started again.

Mary Johnson looked over her glasses at me and grinned. "I'm glad she was on your list and not mine. She infuriates me, that woman. Nothing is ever right, the school is always at fault. Her poor Katy is always a victim of the school's incompetence. The fact that her darling Katy is a pain in the backside and can be rude and arrogant is often overlooked by her mum."

"Correct!" I said wearily. "Apparently the school is to blame for the weather and it is inconvenient as she now has to cancel her hair appointment. I tried to explain that the weather is not in our control but she wasn't listening. Anyway, why can't Katy go to the hairdressers with her?" Mary just shrugged.

"Are we all done? How many are left in school from our house?" I asked, hoping that it wasn't too many. I wasn't looking forward to supervising disgruntled children for the rest of the day. Mary totted up the names left on the list.

"Fifteen, mainly in Year Seven. That's not too bad. We can take turns supervising. It won't need two of us."

"Mary if you round them up and bring them to my room, let the tutors go home and I'll meet you there. I'll just go and report to Sam what we are doing. Ok?"

It was well after midday, the snow had stopped falling, the fifteen children sat in my room glued to the TV screen. I had borrowed the mobile TV and video and they were watching Raiders of the Lost Ark on video. It was a department video, usually shown at the end of the term under the premise of it having religious themes. As I looked out of the window, the clouds began to break up and the sun poked through. There were coats and gloves draped over the big iron radiators under the window, wisps of steam still rose and evaporated from these damp items of clothing. Students had been let outside at break time under strict supervision. No throwing snowballs or running in the snow. Pointless instructions that no child was ever going to obey. They all came back soaking wet and happy. No one got seriously hurt, a few bruises and hurt pride but nothing more.

I had marked three sets of books and was on the fourth and Indiana Jones was searching for clues in the sewers of Venice when the door opened and Mary came in to relieve me. She went straight over to the window and looked out. To the right, you could see the Downs and there were masses of black specks moving up and down on the snow. Children sledging, snowballing and enjoying the strange January day.

"Poor buggers," she whispered to me indicating the children watching the video. "They should be out there enjoying themselves. Not stuck in here with us." I nodded in agreement.

"So should we! I love a good snowball fight."

"You big kid!" said Mary. I didn't disagree as I walked out to go and eat lunch in the peace of my office.

At 3.15 pm when the bell rang to indicate the end of the school day, the sun was shining as strongly as it could in January. It was warm outside, the ground was wet, and there was absolutely no snow to be seen anywhere. I looked out the classroom window, my car had returned to its original dark blue, the sky was clear and the sun bounced off the glass to make me squint. The Downs were now quiet, the white blanket that had covered it was almost fully green again, a few white patches remained in inaccessible places. A bus stopped at the bus stop outside the school, and half a dozen children got on. Normally they would be scrambling for places, but today they had the pick of the seats.

I wonder if Mrs Bates got to the hairdressers. If not, I expect it's probably my fault.

There were a few bemused staff left in school. We sat and chatted in the staffroom, not really understanding what had just happened. We debated the rights and wrongs of the decision to close and all eventually agreed that hindsight was a wonderful thing.

****

Spring was in the air, the sun was shining and the daffodils were everywhere. This was the time of year when some children eventually came out of their shells. Their behaviour grew more confident and they felt comfortable in their year group. Katy Bates, the same Katy Bates whose mum had had to cancel her hair appointment due to a snow emergency sat in my office. I sat behind my desk and Mary Johnson sat at hers. Katy looked sheepish. I looked at Mary and she tried to repress a grin. I was struggling too, but this did have a serious side.

"So Katy, tell me what you've been up to?" I spoke kindly and smiled at her. Katy was in Year Nine; she was just fourteen.

"What do you mean, sir?" her head was bowed slightly; she knew exactly what I meant.

"Well, tell me why you are here, sitting in my office?" Again, I spoke gently not wanting to upset her. She shrugged in the way only a sulky teenager can do.

"Dunno," she said. Mary chipped in to move the interview along. She was going to play bad cop to my good cop. Her voice was sterner and carried a gentle threat. "Katy, stop wasting time. Tell us why Miss Smith brought you to us here in the office. What were you doing?"

"She told you, you already know. So why are you asking?"

"Because we want to hear your side of the story." I was trying not to smile.

"Why were you doing what you were doing in Miss Smith's lesson?" Mary again playing it tough. Again Katy shrugged. "Dunno, I was bored?"

"Ok," I said, "let's try another approach shall we?" I picked up a pair of pink, fluffy handcuffs from my desk. The sort you can buy from an adult shop. I held them up, desperately trying not to smile. "Katy, please can you explain why you have these handcuffs and why you handcuffed Simon Thomas to his chair in your English lesson?" The handcuffs dangled from my hand. The key was on my desk, it too had a pink fluffy fob attached.

"Katy, this is very serious." Mary sounded stern. "Not only have you caused major disruption to a lesson, but you are in possession of items that a child of your age should not have." As Mary was speaking I was biting my lip, trying not to laugh. Yes, it was serious, the disruption to the lesson was major. Simon Thomas had tried to escape, he had stood up, raised his arm and his chair came with it. Chaos ensued and he fell over. The class was shouting, thinking there was a fight. Ms Smith had trouble restoring order and had called for Mary or me to sort it out.

"Katy, where did you get them? These are not children's toys. You could have hurt Simon; he could have broken his arm in the struggle." I was still trying to play good cop, keeping my voice calm.

"I would have let him go, he didn't need to panic. It was only a wind-up. He wanted me to do it. We were just messing about." Katy slumped a bit in her seat, a sense of defeat emerging.

"Ok, thank you for being so honest. Now Katy, please tell us where you got these. Did you find them? Did you buy them? If you did, the shopkeeper will be in serious trouble." I was pretty sure I knew where they came from but I needed to hear it from Katy.

"You are in trouble for the disruption, don't make it worse." Mary was still playing her part.

Katy sighed, "They're my mum's. I found them in her bedroom drawer. I don't know why she's got them, or where they came from. I just took them because they looked funny. I thought it would be a laugh to bring them to school."

I looked at Mary and we both smiled, trying not to laugh.

"Thank you, Katy. I will keep these here for safekeeping and call your mum and let her know that we have them. She can come and collect them in person. I am afraid you can't have them back. It's not safe." Inside I was laughing and at the same time trying not to imagine Katy's mum, her bedroom or her using the handcuffs.

"Please sir, she'll kill me."

"I'm sorry Katy. I am afraid they are your mum's and she will need to collect them. Mrs Johnson, can you issue a detention slip for Katy for the disruption to the lesson." I smiled at Katy.

"Sir, that's not fair. It wasn't just me. Simon wanted to do it too." Katy was getting agitated now.

"We'll talk to Simon Thomas and see what he says" Mary handed Katy the slip. "I expect he'll get a detention as well." Just then the bell went for break time, and children emerged from rooms, talking, shouting and running out to be the first in the queue in the canteen.

"OK, Katy off you go," I said and sighed. She stood, glared at us both and left. She slammed the door behind her. For a second, there was silence then we both burst out laughing.

"Denise Bates is not available, please leave a message after the tone." The recorded voice of Denise Bates rang out of the speaker from my office phone. Mary and I sat and waited for the beep of the machine.

'Beep' went the answering machine. "Good morning Mrs Bates, it is Mr Turner here, from South Coast Comprehensive. I am afraid Katy has got herself into a bit of trouble today. She borrowed your pink fluffy handcuffs from your bedroom drawer and brought them into school. She handcuffed a boy to a chair which caused major disruption to the lesson. Katy will be punished for her actions, but we cannot return the item to her as they are of an adult nature." I winked mischievously at Mary. "So if you give me a call you can arrange to come and collect them from me." I reeled off the office phone number and extension. "I look forward to hearing from you. Thank you. Goodbye." I put the phone down and sat back. We both grinned like school kids pulling a phone prank.

Strangely we never heard from Mrs Bates again for the entire time Katy was at school.

CHAPTER TEN

There's only one F in Ofsted

The first time anyone with any expertise in education ever saw me teach was in 1991, six years after I started. An HMI visited the school as part of a low-key County inspection; the inspector swept into the room, swanned about, smiled and left. I received no feedback nor was I ever aware of the outcome of the inspection. Then, in 1992, Ofsted was born as part of the Education Act of the same year. For many teachers in schools, it became a fearful word, a team of nosy inspectors snooping around in your classrooms, inspecting your filing cabinets, wanting to check your mark books and generally causing extra stress. It was not welcomed by many at the "chalk face." In truth, though, Ofsted was to be key in transforming the quality of education provision in the UK and raising standards. Despite its many failings and mutations since 1993 when the first inspections began, Ofsted has ultimately been a good thing for schools and education as a whole. All areas of public service and private industry need to be held accountable and measured against agreed standards, otherwise the lazy, the greedy and the downright criminal can get away with anything.

The sun shone through the hall window and I squinted and then blocked it with my hand, held over my eyes. It was the summer of 1994. "Why are we here?" whispered Amy Watson, the newly promoted head of History. Amy was in her early thirties and had been at the school since the late eighties. She was a competent and dedicated History teacher with a passion for left-wing politics as well.

"The rumour is that Ofsted is coming." I returned the whisper. At that moment the head walked into the hall followed by the senior team. Their faces looked stern. The hall, full of staff, from cleaners to teachers, fell silent.

Melanie Franks stood, waiting, assessing the receptiveness of her audience. Once satisfied, she began.

"This morning we received notification that we are to be inspected by Ofsted as part of their first wave of inspections under the 1992 Education Act. The statutory six weeks preparation time began today. There is much for us to do in preparation for the visit and as such, each Head of Department will receive a booklet of actions which they will share with their team, after this meeting. By the end of your department meetings, the senior team need your action plan. You will find a template at the back of your information booklet. Members of the senior team will visit department meetings today and respond to any questions you may have."

She paused and the staff began to chatter and respond. Several hands went up, staff wanted to ask questions. Melanie settled the room again and continued. "This is, of course, new to us all. There will be many questions, some we can answer and others we cannot. Please bear with us. We are all in this together. We need to show the inspectors what a good school we are." She smiled, hoping this would allay some of the anxiety that was growing amongst some staff.

"Melanie, Melanie!" The voice from the back was that of Leslie Baker, the Head of Technology. An old school teacher, tall, muscular, balding. He was loud, and frightening but had a heart of gold and was brilliant in supporting any boys who found school a challenge.

"You do realise," he said with a grin, "that six weeks from now it will be the summer holidays."

"Yes Leslie, I do," she grinned back. "We are extremely fortunate that our six weeks is actually twelve weeks.

The inspectors arrive on Monday 13th September. The lead inspector is a Mr Beaver..." There were sniggers from several staff around the room. "There is a team of twelve inspectors, with specialists for each area of the curriculum. The list of names is in your pack."

She fielded several more questions including; "Will they check our filing cabinets are tidy?"

"Will they come in the staffroom?" "How will we know they are coming?" "Will we have to plan every lesson in detail?"

"Shit!" said Jackie Jones my counterpart in the RE department. She ran her hand through her wavy blond hair. I had copied the information booklet for her and we scanned through it together.

"They will grade lessons from outstanding to poor, with good and satisfactory in the middle." I could see Jackie was getting anxious. She was a good teacher and incredibly organized but sometimes lacked self-belief.

"Look here," I said and pointed to a section in the booklet. I read it out loud. "Each department must produce a department handbook outlining their philosophy and approach to teaching, a plan of their curriculum for all five years, broken down into terms. This should include an explanation of the thinking behind each topic and how it will develop skills and understanding. It must include a catalogue of resources, a list of staff, with their experience..." I trailed off, my finger still scrolling down the list of about twenty sections the booklet had to contain.

"Bloody hell, that's a piece of work." I puffed out my cheeks. "Just as I thought we could wind down a bit after Year Eleven left. I have to organise all our curriculum plans into a booklet, just for Ofsted!"

"At least we've got some. I pity the PE department who seem

to make it up according to the weather!" I laughed and she continued. "Look at this bit," Jackie pointed to a paragraph on the next page. She proceeded to read it.

"Displays in classrooms should be fresh and stimulating and include examples of student work. Classrooms must be orderly and arranged in a way as to promote learning." She pulled a puzzled face. "What does that mean? 'Arranged in a way as to promote learning.'"

"I think it means, don't have all the desks facing the back of the room!" I smirked as I spoke. She swore under her breath at me and I grinned.

We spent the remainder of the meeting filling out our action plan. Martin Simpson came in and we shared a joke or two and he managed to answer a few questions for us.

"Jack, your department is good, you know it, Melanie knows it. It is on the up… despite you teaching a load of twaddle about God and spirituality." He had a mischievous twinkle in his eye when he spoke. I picked up a pencil from the table and flicked it at him. He ducked and it rattled the whiteboard behind him. "And you're a crap shot!" He turned and left the room. In truth, Martin Simpson was fully supportive of RE and PSHE in school. He was a Humanist who had grown up in a Christian environment and rejected faith but respected those who had it. He believed in educating the whole child and that included spirituality. He was a good friend and ally.

The final six weeks of term passed by in a flash, and the usual excess amount of free time being used to catch up with marking or planning for next year, was not available. Every moment was Ofsted-focused. In every meeting, lists were checked and re-checked. Every department was pre-inspected by the senior team to ensure we were ready. I even sorted my filing cabinet out, just in case an inspector happened to look inside. The notice board in the staffroom was now an Ofsted countdown board with daily notices and cleaning and decorating schedules being pinned up. The school slowly went through a transformation. Cupboards that no one wanted to tidy, miraculously got sorted, and things got thrown away that had been laying around for decades.

Sam White, the Head of Science walked down the corridor, holding a skeleton. It was tricky as he was not the tallest man and it was a life-size skeleton.

"How many times have you been told, Sam? You can't lock kids up if they're naughty. Look what happens if you forget them!" I grinned as I spoke.

"O ha ha," he said sarcastically, "I'm on my way to show him to Melanie. We don't use him anymore. We have an artificial one now."

"What? Artificial? You mean…?" I was flummoxed.

"Yep! Bob, here is a real one." He patted Bob on the skull. "We used to use him. He's been around for about forty years, apparently. But now we have a plastic one. Bob's been living in the technician's cupboard for years. It creeped the kids out knowing there was a real one lurking around!" I laughed at the idea that we had a real skeleton in school.

"What are you going to do with him? You can't just chuck him on the skip… we'll have the police round in a flash thinking there's been a murder." I was grinning at the thought.

"Exactly Jack, we don't know what to do. That's why I'm dumping him with Melanie. There has to be some sort of protocol. She can sort it."

"He could be the newest member of the senior team!"

"Na, he'd get too much done and the others would be jealous!" Sam's retort struck a chord that was common among middle managers. Often senior leaders were thought to be a little lazy and reluctant to get their hands dirty in department work. Sam wandered off towards Melanie's office with Bob's arm around his shoulder as if he were a long-lost ex-colleague.

By the time the summer holiday arrived, the RE department at South Coast Comprehensive School was ready for anything. The department handbook was printed with a snazzy cover full of religious symbols and the school logo in the corner, the filing cabinets were spick and span, and the displays were fresh and ready for September. Both classrooms had been painted and the cupboard that linked them was as tidy as it had ever been. Jackie and I were knackered, as were all the staff. The end-of-term party was a little quiet.

Once again, I sat in the hall shielding my eyes from the sun.

This time it was Friday the 10th of September. A whole staff meeting had been called after school for one last push to ensure no stone was left unturned in the quest for a good outcome from our first inspection. We held in our hands a timetable of expected events, meetings and observations. Melanie was talking through the schedule, but so many of us were not listening but instead reading the sheet of paper we had been given. Fatal mistake, never give out a worksheet too early! I was going to be observed at least four times in the week the inspectors were in school. I also had two meetings. One as Head of RE and one as a pastoral leader. I was Head of Columbus House. It was going to be a busy week. I thought ahead to the lessons in which I was going to be observed. I mentally ticked off the planning. Some were sorted and just needed sheets printing, but my new Year Ten GCSE class was as yet unplanned. This needed to be a good one. As the meeting progressed, I mused over how I was going to deliver a lesson on images of Jesus and the use of symbolism in worship.

"Any questions?" said Melanie, and I realised I had not concentrated on the meeting at all. I nudged Jackie, who sat beside me. "I wasn't listening, too busy planning in my head. Did I miss anything?"

She shook her head. "No, it's all on the sheet here anyway."

"If there are no more questions, have a good and restful weekend," Melanie said with a smile. There were groans and laughter at the comment. Many staff would spend the weekend in final preparations.

I headed back to my classroom, I wanted to plan the Year Ten lesson so that my weekend was restful. I looked at my watch, it was four o'clock. By six I was confident it was done. There were still several cars in the carpark as I slipped into my Datsun Cherry and drove home for a quiet and restful weekend. *Yeah, right!*

Kevin was a bit of a rogue. He was a likeable fourteen-year-old, who had come from a challenging background; his father was in prison and his mother was on the dole and smoked and drank too much. Kevin, found it hard to engage in education when his elder brother was earning good money digging foundations on a building site and making up shuttering. He had left school with no GCSEs, why should Kevin worry? He had chosen GCSE RE as an option to avoid doing History and Geography as he thought they were 'too much like hard work.'

"Sir, what's all this? Our room is all different? What's all that stuff?" Kevin was at least observant. The room had been reorganised into 'stations'; on each station was an object or picture and a sheet with some questions to stimulate thinking. The class filed in quietly, following the strict instructions they had been receiving since returning to school the previous week.

"Just file in and stand around the edge of the room," I said encouragingly. "What I want you to do is just look at what you can see. Think of questions that might help you understand what is going on in the room today. I will do the register and then we can get on." The last person to enter the room was a middle-aged woman with black hair tied in a bun. She had sharp features and large black-rimmed spectacles. She wore a long skirt, a white blouse with a silk scarf and a grey lightweight jacket. She had flat shoes. This was my inspector, Mrs Roberta Finchley, a former head of RE and now a consultant and adviser for the Birmingham City Education Authority. She smiled and stood by the door. I handed her a couple of sheets of planning and continued the lesson.

With the register complete I dived straight in. "So, initial thoughts?" I said to the fifteen GCSE students standing around the edges of my classroom. Kevin put his hand straight up. My heart sank.

"Yes, Kevin." *Please. Please don't let me down.*

"We don't normally have the desks like this, why have you done it today? Is it because she's here?" He pointed at Mrs Finchley. The rest of the class fidgeted, uncomfortable at Kevin. Several of them looked at me sympathetically, apologising to me on Kevin's behalf.

I sighed inside, but outwardly I maintained an air of joviality. "No, of course not Kevin, yes the desks aren't normally like this, but that is because today you are in for a treat, an experiential extravaganza that will help you understand so many new things about Christian worship." *I turned that around, take that Kevin!* "Remind me, what we learned about worship in the last lesson…" Several hands shot up.

"Yes Katy" Katy proceeded to recap quite clearly a good definition of worship and the idea of liturgy and liturgical objects. She was helped by a couple of others, a mix of girls and boys. *Phew!* After a couple of minutes of recap, I led them on to the main purpose of the lesson and explained that at each 'station' was a different object or image relating to Jesus or the worship of Jesus. There were questions to stimulate thinking and some tasks to ensure a depth of understanding was achieved. The class could start at any station but had twenty-five minutes to complete all four stations. There was a hubbub as students collected their books and headed off to different stations. I began to patrol the room ensuring students could access the materials and knew what to do. I was aware of Mrs Finchley wandering as well. She was gravitating towards Kevin! *I knew she would. Why do they always do that?* I was about to intercept her when a girl called Courtney asked me a question. She was standing at a table that had a variety of crosses and crucifixes on it.

"Sir, isn't that a bit gross, I mean an image of Jesus being murdered. Look it's even got all the blood painted on. That's just sick." Courtney pulled a face. There were a couple of others around her looking equally perplexed.

"Why do you think Christians might find this helpful? How might they use it in worship?" I tried to ask open questions to make them think. "Have you read the information sheet that goes with it?" None of them had. "Read the sheet and then see if you can answer my question, Courtney. I'll be back in a minute." I weaved my way around the room and came up behind Kevin who was focusing hard on a large print of Holman Hunt's 'Light of the World.' Mrs Finchley stood to the side watching closely.

"So Kevin, what do you see?" I asked hopefully.

"Some old painting. Looks boring." He said without any enthusiasm. Katy and another girl took intakes of breath, letting me know their disapproval of Kevin's words. I turned to Katy and winked at her conspiratorially then turned back to Kevin.

"Boring! Far from it Kevin. This is one of the most famous paintings of Jesus. There is so much to learn. Katy, could you read the information sheet out, to help us?" She quickly picked it up and began to read.

"Thanks, Katy. So anyone, what is the picture called?"

"Light of the World," said one boy, again without much enthusiasm.

"If it is about light, why is it so dark in the picture?" Kevin was getting interested. "Is that Jesus holding the light at the door?"

"Yes Kevin, well done… Katy, what did it say on the sheet about the door?" She scanned the sheet again. "It represents our heart and is all overgrown because we haven't opened it up to God."

"But there's no handle!" said Kevin pointing at the picture "How is Jesus supposed to open it if there is no handle? That's stupid!"

"It's not stupid, Kevin, we try not to be rude about things we don't understand. There must be a reason. Why don't you read the Bible verse that goes with this picture? Holman Hunt painted this picture based on this Bible verse." I could see Mrs Finchley standing behind Kevin, smiling. Kevin took the information sheet from Katy and cautiously began to read. His reading was not fluent but he got through it. "*Here I am! I stand at the door and knock. If anyone hears my voice and opens the door, I will come in and eat with that person, and they with me.*' I don't get it." For a couple more minutes I guided the small group of students through the intricacies of the image and how it may be used by Christians to understand deeper theology of our lives being overgrown with sin and Jesus waiting to share life with us, shed light on it and clean it all up, but we have to ask (although I didn't use the word theology, that would have been too much for Kevin).

"So, we have to open the door, is that what the picture means?" Kevin was pleased with his own progress. So was I. Mrs Finchley moved on around the room.

"Right Courtney, how are you doing with that crucifix? Michael, have you worked out why Christians might use icons?" I began to circulate again ensuring students were on track and had gleaned the most pertinent bits of understanding needed. I had learned early on in my career that if you give children the opportunity to question and learn independently, then they will often have a go. *Teaching,* I thought *requires a wide range of styles and techniques all used in harmony.* I was pleased with how that went.

"Thank you, Mr Turner, for a very interesting lesson. I thoroughly enjoyed the way you presented the different aspects of iconography, art and symbolism. The movement around the room and the questioning helped to engage the students. The planning was meticulous although you tended to hover around Kevin too long." She smiled knowingly.

"I will let you into a secret, Holman Hunt's 'Light of the

World' is my favourite painting. I loved the way you drew out the meaning and helped Kevin and Katy understand it. Well done." We continued to chat for several minutes more. Roberta Finchley gave me detailed feedback on my planning and delivery, the behaviour of students and the attainment and learning. At the end, she handed me a template sheet of paper with notes written on it. "Thank you again, I think I am observing you again tomorrow. I look forward to it." She stood and left my classroom. I heaved a sigh of relief. Jackie stuck her head around the door.

"Well? How did it go?" I looked at the piece of paper in my hand. I stared down at it, there in black and white was the word 'outstanding' against the planning and delivery section, another 'outstanding' against behaviour and another against attainment and learning. There at the bottom was her signature next to one final mention of the word 'outstanding'. I smiled and handed it over to Jackie to look at.

****

"They're all over the bloody place!" said Amy Watson as she slumped into a chair in the staffroom at the end of the day. It was Wednesday evening and the inspectors had been in school for three days.

"I even saw one in the gents' toilets? What was he doing there?" grumbled David Grant the ageing art teacher, his scruffy brown cardigan catching on the arm of a comfy chair as he sat down. "Shit," he mumbled.

"David, even inspectors need to go to the loo! They are human after all!" I tried to sound encouraging.

"Are they? Are they really?" David was clearly disgruntled, more than usual.

"What's up? What's happened?" I asked.

"I'll tell you what's up." He pointed a finger at me. "Bloody art inspector was more concerned about my attire and the image I gave to the students than he was about my ability to teach art." He was stabbing his finger in my direction quite aggressively to back up his point and visualise his anger. "What the hell is wrong with my clothes? I'm not going to wear a bloody suit and get it messed up by Year Sevens who don't know one end of a paintbrush from the other!" I looked at him, carefully assessing his clothes. His shoes were brown leather brogues with paint splatters on them, they had seen better days. He wore baggy, dark green corduroys that were threadbare at the knees, a collarless white shirt with paint stains on and his scruffy brown cardigan with a packet of Silk Cut protruding from the right-hand pocket.

"It's not for me to say David, but I'm pretty sure you won't win any awards at the Paris fashion show this year!" Amy sniggered at my comment. I grinned my cheekiest grin.

"F**k off!" He stuck two fingers up for good measure. "You're not exactly James Bond, Darling!" There was bitchiness in his voice, but he was grinning too. I looked down at my own attire, my black shoes were scuffed, my shirt was hanging out and my tie was low with my top button undone. "Touché! Fancy a coffee David, to cheer you up a bit?" He nodded his assent.

"Got any whisky to go in it?" He was smiling now.

"If only...don't let them get to you. David. They will be gone soon. Thursday tomorrow, the last day they can come into lessons." I made the coffee and also my excuses, I had a department head meeting with my favourite inspector, Roberta Finchley.

"So tell me, Mr Turner, what do you consider the main purpose of RE in schools?" Roberta smiled and sat back in her chair. We were in my house office, from where I lead Columbus House.

Is this a trick question? Is there an official answer? I decided it wasn't and there was no set response that she was looking for. "Well," I said, slightly nervously, "I have always believed that if I can get children thinking about things they would not normally consider, to ask questions and to reflect on their own beliefs and values, then perhaps I am on the right lines." She nodded sagely and jotted some notes down on a pad.

"And if a child is not religious, what then?" She tilted her head and again smiled. *I know this one!* "It makes no difference; we live in a multicultural world. The world is shrinking and knowledge of other cultures and belief systems is vital if we are to maintain and develop a more peaceful and united world. We learn French at school, we are not all from France. We learn about Japan in Geography, but we might never go there. RE is about appreciating beliefs and values so that we become better people." I stopped before I started getting in a muddle.

"Thank you." She nodded encouragingly. "Moving on, how do you know that a child has understood what you have been teaching? How do you know they have made progress?"

The questions kept coming and I kept on answering, using all the things I had planned and prepared. There were questions on how the department planned, how we assessed work and how we grouped children. Roberta kept plugging away, digging into the department. "So Mr Turner, what about your vision for the department, how do you intend to increase numbers at GCSE and improve your outcomes?"

"Ideally, I would like whole cohort RE at GCSE and increase provision for lesson-led PSHE rather than tutor-led, which in my opinion never works effectively. RE needs experts, just as Maths, English and languages need experts. I have asked for a further member of staff and have set out a two-year plan to achieve this vision." I continued explaining my dream of expanding the department and providing RE for all up to Year Eleven. I had shared this first with Martin Simpson the deputy and then at a senior meeting with the whole leadership team, with mixed responses. Roberta occasionally interrupted and asked a secondary question. The conversation lasted a full hour, by which time I was mentally exhausted.

It was my turn to slump into a chair in the staffroom. This time Jackie made me a coffee and quizzed me on how the meeting went.

"You really think, we can get an extra staff member and do whole cohort RE?" Jackie was excited by the vision.

"Why not? After all, we are the Mary Poppins department!" I grinned mischievously at her.

"Eh?" Jackie was bemused.

"Well, we are practically perfect in every way!" She shook her head and rolled her eyes.

The party in the function room of the Royal Oak on Friday evening was a raucous affair. I sat in a booth, pint in hand, and some of the less adventurous members of the Humanities Faculty sat with me. The Head, Melanie Franks was dancing as if there was no tomorrow and several of the other members of the senior team were also letting whatever hair they had down. I scanned the room, the release of tension was palpable, these last twelve weeks had been filled with stress and anxiety and tonight it was all coming out. I supped on my pint and blew my cheeks out. *Thank the Lord that is over.*

****

The final report showed that South Coast Comprehensive was a good school, with well-behaved students, high-quality teaching and good outcomes. It recommended further training and development on the use of ICT, (no surprise there!), improvements to the way student books were marked and progress recorded and reported, and a focus on raising standards in English and Maths, (again, no surprise there.) My department was deemed to be good with some outstanding features such as the quality of the curriculum, including the depth of planning. *I'll take that!*

The next year or so saw changes to the teaching of English and Maths, the development of a whole school marking and recording strategy that standardized the way books were marked and how staff graded and recorded information, and of course investment in ICT (Information and computer technology). There were action plans, strategies and INSET training on a whole range of things that were highlighted in the report. It seemed to fire up the school to improve in all areas, not just those highlighted. So perhaps it wasn't that bad after all.

CHAPTER ELEVEN

The rise of the machines

The ICT suite was one room that had been converted to house thirty Amstrad PCWs. The computer age had entered South Coast Comprehensive School. Students had one lesson once a fortnight where they learned to type and use a word processor. The staff could also share the space but had to wait for the room to be free or after school. I was keen to get involved in the technological age, as until now the most exciting development I had seen was the whiteboard and dry wipe marker pens! Then I walked into the staffroom one Monday morning and saw, what I can only describe as something out of Star Trek, placed on a table behind the door, I was almost overwhelmed. It was a BBC computer. A beast of a machine with a large keyboard with what seemed like hundreds of buttons. The cream-coloured TV screen sat on top of the thick metal computer housing. Next to it was a box of floppy discs almost six inches across. Apparently, one disc could store up to twenty average-sized documents. Each floppy disc had a label with a staff name on it. I flicked through them, found mine, picked it out of the box and held it up. My own floppy disc. *This is amazing, but what am I going to do with it?* There was a note attached to the screen.

> Training on the use of the BBC computer will be given to all staff who wish to use it. Each day after school for the next week.

It was signed by Steve the ICT teacher. He used to teach Maths but now taught children how to type, use PCWs and computers. He was a bit of an expert. I quickly signed up for the training the same night. I wanted to be in at the start. The school had recently bought into SIMS the school software management system and had employed a SIMS manager, a fearsome woman called Janice. She appeared to control the school from her office next to the Head teacher's office. The whirr of a dot matrix printer could often be heard producing lists and official documents. The school was due to install computers in every office so that senior leaders Heads of House, deputies and department heads had access to SIMS. We were all due to have training at County Hall, where there was a room full of computers where staff from all over Sussex could train to use SIMS.

"So there you have it, everything you need to know to get you started on using the BBC" Steve handed out a stapled booklet that went through, step by step, what he had just shown five of us huddled around the BBC. "Any questions?"

"What happens if I fill up my disc?" said Sally Le Croix a little anxiously.

"We have plenty more, 50 pence each to staff. We charge the children more," said Steve with a big grin.

At that moment David Grant, the eccentric, wig-wearing, Art teacher swept in. "It is the beginning of the end!" he said dramatically. "In ten years none of us will be able to write using a pen."

"Shut up, David!" said Steve. "That's what they said about art when the camera was invented, but you're still in a job!" We all laughed.

"You wait and see," he cried, "It will kill the art of writing neatly." He disappeared off outside for a smoke.

****

I sat at the BBC computer and pressed the 'on button'. *Here we go, let's see if this is worth all the fuss,* I thought. Next to me was the stapled instruction sheet that Steve had handed out a few days earlier. I needed to write a Year Ten test about the features of a Christian Church. All the questions were written in rough on my notepad. This would be a chance to see if I could type and set out a document. There were about ten short answer questions plus a couple of questions that required longer answers. With a deep breath, I set off on what was to be the start of a huge change in my teaching career.

"How do I get it to stop typing across the page and go down a line?" I called to no one in particular. I picked up the instruction sheet to see if that would help. I scanned it and discovered something called a return button. I pressed it and the cursor dropped a line. "Got it!" I called, in case anyone was listening. It was just like a typewriter. I remembered trying to use my mum's typewriter when I was a child. There was a big chrome handle that you flicked and the roller on the machine turned the paper, slightly moving it upwards so that you could type on the line below. That was clumsy, this was instant. Wow!

"How do I do capital letters?" Once again, none one was listening. *Am I the only one interested in learning this new skill?* I shook my head in disgust.

After about forty minutes the warning bell sounded for the end of lunchtime and the noise of children flooding back into the building filled my ears. I picked out my floppy disk from the box on the side and inserted it into the slot. The machine whirred and clicked and then the word "Save?" appeared in a box on the blue screen. It was flashing. I hit the return button and the machine buzzed and clicked again until my work was transformed from type on a screen to magnetic data on the disk.

I looked at my work so far, still on the screen. Five questions complete. *Not bad. But it could do with underlining the headings and leaving space to write answers. How do I do that?* My brain was full, that would have to wait. I had Year Seven class to teach. I ejected the disk, returned it to the box of disks on the table and left feeling proud as punch.

Over the next week, I sat at the BBC every lunchtime for forty minutes, learning to type with two fingers; embedding in my brain the basic skills of word processing. The space bar, the return button, how to underline, and even how to write in bold became second nature. What was holding me back was the speed of my typing. It was dreadfully slow.

"Da Dah!" I raised my hands in triumph as I hit the print button and the dot matrix printer began to chatter like the "Vidi printer" on Grandstand on a Saturday afternoon. At last, my Year Ten test was complete. I grinned like the Cheshire Cat as the test appeared line by line. As the last line appeared, I carefully ripped it off after the paper had scrolled out to the next perforated section. Slowly, I removed the perforated sides and wandered over to the photocopier. Having lifted the lid, I placed my precious test on the glass plate. I tapped in 30 copies and hit the copy button. The photocopier read the document; the top moving as it scanned the paper, then, as if by magic, copies of my test began to spew out, pristine and clear. I was genuinely impressed. It took me nearly four hours to produce, but it was legible, neat and had spaces for answers. This was the way forward, no more hand-written sheets. *I wonder if it is possible to add some pictures. How would you do that?* I was quite excited at the prospect.

"What's Windows?" I whispered to Jackie Jones, my partner in the RE department. We were sitting in a staff training session in early September 1992. Steve, the ICT teacher was revealing how the school had invested in new computers for all offices and the two computer rooms. They were to be installed with Windows 3.1 and a document-writing programme called

Microsoft Word. All staff were to sign up for training on how to use both these pieces of software.

"I think it helps you navigate your computer and helps you do things." She shrugged her shoulders and pulled a quizzical face. Steve was explaining the benefits of "Windows" but he faced some fierce opposition from some of the older staff. David Grant in particular was vocal about the apocalyptic nature of computers and how this was the slippery slope to a world of uneducated people who were devoid of any fine art, English or Mathematic skills.

"We're turning into a nation of screen watchers instead of reading or appreciating the arts. This is a downward spiral, mark my words!" His voice was raised and his finger was pointing as if proclaiming something prophetic from God.

"We're all doomed!" I called out in the style of Fraser from Dad's Army. It broke the tension and people laughed but it earned me a stern look from the Head Teacher, Melanie Franks.

For the next hour, Steve talked us through the benefits of Windows 3.1 and how programmes like Microsoft Word and Publisher would transform our work. There was even an opportunity to include digital pictures into our documents via the use of a floppy disk containing stock images as well as some real photographs that were part of the programme. I tried taking notes but was blown away by what these new computer software programmes could do, so much better than the BBC computer.

"Right, in you go please, find your seats and get your books out as quickly as possible!" I was covering a Year Ten maths lesson. I was a bit frustrated as I had planned to use the time to practise my ICT skills and produce a worksheet for Year Nine on the Five Pillars of Islam. The classroom was on the second floor overlooking the playground. I hoped the teacher had left some notes about what they were to do; otherwise, the lesson became incredibly stressful. Maths was never a strong subject for me, so I needed clear guidance. Two things happened as I entered the classroom after all the children. Firstly, I noticed the new computer on the teacher's desk. *Excellent, at least I might get a chance to play around and practise creating my worksheet.* Secondly, I noticed a movement from outside the window on the left of the classroom. I took in the scene quickly. The central window was slightly ajar. Outside the window was a ledge about four feet wide, it was in reality, the flat, concrete roof of the porch to the door below that led to the playground. The movement was a human head, from Mustafa Ibrahim or Mussy as everyone called him. Mussy was hiding on the window ledge. Mussy and I had a love-hate relationship, he hated my subject but I loved his mischievous sense of humour and how he would always try to catch me out. He was at it again, hiding on the ledge and then, I expect, he wanted to surprise me. The darker side of my nature took over. Casually, as I entered the room, I strolled over to the window and closed it. "Brrrr, it's cold in here. Who left that window open?" I said with great drama. There were a few giggles behind me. Clearly, the class knew what was going on. I made my way to the desk at the front and was relieved to see the teacher's mark book with register and a sheet of paper taped to the desk with work for the class to do.

"Right, settle down please, I'll take the register then I will explain your work. Please make sure you have your maths book, textbook and pens etc. for today's lesson." I began to call the register with a firm and authoritative voice. The class quickly settled. As I continued down the list calling out names and marking them off in the teacher's planner, I was interrupted by a loud knocking. I knew exactly what it was. Mussy, banging on the window. He was still crouching down out of sight, trying to play a joke on me. I pretended I did not know who it was. "Please stop that, whoever you are, you are interrupting me." I got to Mussy's name on the register.

"Mussy?" I paused, knowing he could not answer. "Mussy? Has anyone seen Mussy?" There were giggles and fidgeting from around the room. Some were clearly enjoying it, thinking the joke was on me. A few of the gentler and kind students, I could see, were feeling uncomfortable. One of them got up and approached the desk just as the knocking repeated. Mussy was banging louder on the window from his crouched position. The girl who approached the desk was called Blessing. She was Afro-Caribbean, one of an increasing number of non-white students, that helped the school become genuinely multicultural. Blessing was a studious and kind girl who always wanted to help. "Blessing, don't say anything," called one lad from the back. She turned back to the lad and then to me. She didn't know what to do. I held up my hand to quieten the class and turned to Blessing. "I will put you out of your misery, Blessing, I know exactly what you are going to say." She looked at me with a puzzled look. She was about to speak when I held my finger to my mouth to shush the class. I smiled at her and whispered to her to sit back down.

"Listen you lot," I said with a grin. "I know exactly what's going on. I wasn't born yesterday. Mussy is out on the ledge, banging on the window. He thinks he is tricking me, but we are going to trick him."

"Yay!" "Yes," How did you know?" Several in the room called out at once. I shushed them again as Mussy banged on the window for the third time. I just saw his head pop below the window as I turned. With great drama and with a conspiratorial tone I hushed them and made them listen to me. I spoke quietly so that there was no chance of Mussy hearing.

"Mussy is not exactly a ninja, I saw him on the ledge as I came into the room. That's why I shut the window. Now let's all ignore him and get on with the lesson." I turned back to the whiteboard and began to write up the work they had to do for their maths lesson. There was a lot of excited chatter and laughter at the prospect of leaving Mussy on the ledge.

"Sir, it's spitting outside, the forecast on the TV last night said heavy rain," said one lad, one of Mussy's friends.

"It's a good job there is no one hiding on the ledge then, otherwise they'd get very wet," I said with a grin and a wink. Several of the class laughed. "Remember, ignore him. We don't know he is there, do we?"

For the next ten minutes, the class did well ignoring Mussy, who tried to grab their attention by popping up and pulling faces through the window. The rain came in and large drops of rain began to fall before all of a sudden there was a sharp downpour.

"Sir, what are you going to do?" The boy who was concerned that Blessing was going to grass Mussy up, was now concerned for his welfare. "What do you think I should do?" I wandered over to the window and looked out. Mussy was crouched down with his blazer covering his head to keep the rain off. "We don't know he's there, so what can we do?" I turned my back to the window and stood facing the room. The class were waiting for me to respond.

"Shall we let him in?" I asked.

"Let him stay out there, it's his fault he's wet," said one. "A taste of his own medicine," said another. A third also demanded that he remain outside as justice for trying to trick me. No one spoke up for Mussy, not even his mates, who were enjoying the spectacle and grateful it was not them. My compassionate side kicked in, also, if he fell off the porch roof, I'd probably get the sack.

"I'll be kind. I will let him back in but promise me you won't tell him I knew. Let him think he outwitted me." There were groans of disapproval but in the end a sense of agreement that it was right to let him in. With one last wink and grin, I turned back to the window and opened it.

"Oh my goodness!" I said in mock shock. "What on earth are you doing out there? You're soaking wet. Come on in. That was a silly thing to do. Why did you climb out there?" It was a pantomime performance from me. The class were laughing along. Mussy stood up on the ledge. At first, he looked crestfallen at being very wet, but as he climbed back into the room his face lit up. He had tricked me. The class were laughing and cheering, playing their part.

"Got ya, sir. I've been out there all along, it was me banging on the window." He stood dripping and beaming. "Well, I am shocked, Mussy." I turned to the class. "Did you know about this?" As a class, they responded, "No sir!" laughing as they did so.

"Come on Mussy, take that wet blazer off and sit down. You really got me that time. Mind you that was dangerous. Please don't do it again." My voice sounded stern as if I was cross but inside I was laughing. *Jack Turner one, Mussy nil.*

The rest of the lesson passed without incident, Mussy sat dripping at his desk, his mates chattering about his heroics, laying it on thick, not letting him know that he had been duped. The rest of the class got on with their maths, and I even managed to insert some clip art onto a document, using Microsoft Word, so the cover lesson wasn't a total waste of time.

"Mussy, a word please," I called him over as the class filed out at the end of the lesson.

"You knew, didn't you? You knew I was out there." Mussy said, a little disappointed. "Who grassed me up?" "No one did, I spotted you as I came in." I smiled at him.

"I suppose I've got a detention."

"Listen Mussy, you're a good kid, with a lot of potential. I like you, you make me laugh. However, you can't pull stunts like that. If you had fallen, you'd have broken a leg or worse and I'd have been out of a job." Mussy looked up, stunned. He hadn't realised that.

"Sorry, sir." He was genuine.

"I'm sorry too, I shouldn't have left you there. But it was funny."

He looked up and smiled. "You got me, fair and square. It was my own fault."

"I'll do a deal with you Mussy. I let you off and you start to respect my subject and have a go in lessons. But don't lose that adventurous side of you." He looked at me, thought about it and held out his hand. "Deal!"

****

The 1990s rolled on with speed and technology with it. I was still getting used to having an email address and people sending me messages that popped up on my computer in my office when in the staffroom one day I saw Martin Simpson, the Deputy Head. He was sitting at one of the staffroom computers with a couple of people standing around. One of whom was Steve, the ICT teacher, who was teaching him something. Martin looked up and called me over. "Jack, come and have a look at this, it is incredible!" I joined the huddle and listened as Steve continued.

"Ok, so, in the box on the screen, type a question, any question." Steve pointed to a box on the screen with a flashing cursor. Martin thought for a moment and then began to type his question. I read it to myself as he typed it into the box. *Who is the manager of Birmingham City FC?* Martin was an avid Blues fan. He would talk football at any opportunity. We often discussed our woes, both of us supporting teams in the lower divisions.

The computer thought for a few seconds and the page slowly

began to change. A new page appeared with a selection of writing, some in blue typeface. Steve explained that these were called links. Most of them mentioned Birmingham City.

"Now click the top link," said Steve enthusiastically. Martin moved the computer mouse down to the top link until the arrow was over the blue writing.

"Press the left-hand mouse button," continued Steve.

Martin obeyed the instruction and slowly a page filled the screen. As we waited for the new page to load, it became clear that it was filled with information about Birmingham City Football Club.

"Barry Fry!" said Steve triumphantly. The page had finished loading.

"Bloody Hell," said Martin, "that's brilliant" I echoed his opinion.

"What is this?" I was fascinated.

"This is called 'Ask Jeeves.' It is what is known as a search engine. You type in a question and it will give you the answer. Steve smiled smugly as he imparted this wisdom to us all gathered there.

"How does it know the answers?" I asked again.

"It doesn't, it searches for them on the World Wide Web." He smiled again, enthusiastically.

"What? What is the…" I struggled to remember.

"World Wide Web. It is a series of computer sites all over the world that this computer is talking to. It connects to them and finds answers." Steve was in his element.

"But how?" This time Sally asked the question. But it could have been me. Steve began to explain in detail how the World Wide Web worked.

"There aren't that many sites yet, but as this improves, the whole world will be connected and we can find out anything. The more sites people create; the more information we can access."

This time I asked the questions. "How do you make a site? How are they connected?" I tried to follow Steve's answer but was still too enthralled watching the screen change from page to page as Martin typed new questions for 'Ask Jeeves' to find answers to.

"So anyone with a computer can do this?" Sally asked again.

"Yes, the computer uses your phone line to connect to other machines. We won't need textbooks soon. Children can look things up for themselves." Steve was enjoying himself.

"We'll all be out of a job soon! Maybe David Grant was right!" I winked at Sally as I spoke.

****

"Sir?" said Johnny Miller, a tall, good-looking Year Ten boy whose only interest in life was football. "Do you think we'll beat Germany in the Semi-final?" I smiled at him. There was a twinkle in his eye. He brushed his mop of blonde hair back away from his face.

"I'm not sure what that has to do with your work. You are supposed to be writing up your research on the death penalty." My Year Ten class were working in one of the two computer suites. Their task was to produce a piece of work that represented different opinions on the death penalty, including a range of religious responses. This class was the fruit of three years' work in developing RE and PSHE as a whole school curriculum subject, including Short Course GCSE as well as a full course group. I had proved to Martin Simpson the need for a further full-time RE teacher and had won the battle. Penny Williams had joined the department as a newly qualified teacher after completing her PGCE placement with us. She was a big hit with the children, enthusiastic, bubbly and creative. This class had been researching using the textbooks in the main classroom and had homework to research further. Today was their opportunity to use Microsoft Word or Publisher to present their findings. I had hoped that this may make my life easier in reading the work of those whose handwriting often resembled the ramblings of a drunk spider. The boys in particular enjoyed any opportunity to sit at a computer and try things out. It was a tough job keeping them on task. Johnny Millar had done a good job of distracting me.

"Sir, please, will we win? What do you think? We've got the SAS up front!" Johnny was determined to get me to respond. I shook my head, smiled and spoke. "Okay, okay. After the mess we made of it in 1990 at the world cup against the Germans, I don't hold out much hope. If it goes to penalties we're stuffed."

"Oh, come on, Sir, we've got Shearer and Sheringham. We will easily win." I admired his optimism, but I had seen enough of England since 1970 when I first remember seeing them play, that we generally stuffed it up in the latter stages.

"Herr Schmidt seems to think Germany will cruise through!" I countered his hope with the comment. Uli Schmidt was a teacher from Germany who was on a year-long exchange. He was a tall and authoritative man with a shock of silver hair. The banter in the staff room had steadily risen as the tournament progressed and Uli and the PE department in particular spent a great deal of time poring over stats and reports and discussing the matches they had watched. I wasn't averse to joining in.

"Rubbish!" said Johnny, and several others muttered their assent. The boys were getting distracted from the death penalty. The irony of the word penalty was lost on them.

"He's bound to say that. He's been winding us up all week! He'll be sorry tomorrow morning when England are in the final and

Germany are licking their wounds!" I raised an eyebrow at his confidence. I wished I could share it.

"Back to work, boys, and the rest of you!" I looked at my watch. "You've got thirty minutes to finish your essay. Remember, you must present at least two different views, and include some reference to a clear religious view, either Christian or Muslim. Try to use a quotation from the Bible or the Qur'an. Your opinion must be explained and referenced against one of the other views you presented.

"Sir?" Johnny continued. "I haven't got a Bible quote to use. Can you help me?"

I sighed. "How about 'love your enemy.' Jesus said that. How could you use that to support or oppose one of the arguments?

"Does that mean I have to love the German football team?" Johnny was on a roll.

"Definitely!"

I wandered the room examining the work that was being produced. Occasionally I would catch the odd boy playing Solitaire on screen. The work varied enormously; there was a range of fonts and sizes on display, and those who had researched a lot used a much smaller font. I reflected on how easy this might be to interpret and mark. I thought of David Grant's voice of doom some years back and countered it in my head. *O brave new world that has such people in it! The Tempest,* I thought, but I wasn't sure. The world of education was certainly changing fast and we needed to be brave to embrace it, to overcome our fear of change. *Change, the biggest barrier to progress in schools.* A dismal but reasonable reflection I thought, picturing David Grant again.

CHAPTER TWELVE

Assemblies

Sometimes I daydream. I sat at my desk in the House Office at South Coast Comprehensive School. I am one of the five Heads of House and also the Head of the RE and PSHE Department. Mary Johnson is my formidable deputy. She is loved and hated equally by the students to whom she teaches maths and those in Columbus House. I was trying to plan an assembly but my mind was blank. So I was daydreaming. I recalled my school days in the 1970s in a south-west London, all-boys, secondary modern school. Assemblies were very different then; fortunately, they no longer function similarly.

I stood in a long line of boys, all from my form. I was about halfway down the line in the middle of the hall. There were one thousand boys crammed into the giant sports hall. I held in my hands a green school hymn book, we were handed one on the way into each assembly. The plastic cover that protected it was ripped and the spine of the book was damaged. Someone had picked at it, ripping most of it away. At the end of each row stood a scowling teacher, their beady eyes ensuring we did not misbehave. I was nervous, I could hear the Headmaster's voice telling boys off as he walked up and down each row, inspecting the uniform and tugging on hair if it was below the collar of your blazer.

"Chip" the Headmaster was getting closer. His real name was Fisher but everyone called him "Chip" but never to his face. He was a short but ferocious man who believed that the boys in his school were as good as any from any private school like Eton or Harrow, and he treated us in that way. He was incredibly strict, but if you

were good at anything he would encourage you and support you to be the best. Consequently, I played Rugby for the school (football wasn't allowed) and then joined the rowing squad. As a result of Chip's passion, I got to row at the School's Regatta at Henley and many other top rowing events for schools. He encouraged all boys to engage in sports, travel and academic excellence and the school ran many trips abroad as well as educational visits to all the big museums, galleries and theatres. I sweated slightly, nervously waiting for Chip to come past me. I discreetly checked my tie and prayed my hair wasn't too long. I snuck a glance at the boy next to me, Ben Roberts. He'd definitely get his hair tugged. The style was like David Cassidy's but longer in length. Chip would never allow that!

My mind wandered again to singing in assembly and the awful experiences we had murdering classic Christian hymns. *One thousand boys mumbling along to Onward Christian Soldiers, resenting every minute, hearts hardening toward any semblance of faith in the religion of Christianity. The teachers walked the lines singing loudly trying to make us sing with pride and gusto. In reality, we all tried to think of rude words to sing instead and not get caught.*

I was back in the present and I shook my head at the memories. *Thank God they're not like that today.* I was still no closer to writing a fifteen-minute assembly.

At that moment, Martin Simpson poked his head around my office door with a big grin on his face. "Jack, any chance you could do me a massive favour?"

"Yep, go for it. What can I do?" I was a little nervous as it often involved some kind of extra work.

"Have you prepared for House Assembly tomorrow? Can I step in and take over?" His eyes pleaded with me.

"What? You want to take my assembly." I stressed the word 'want'. "Normally you guys at the top try to wheedle out of it. What's going on?" I sensed he was up to something, but he was the Deputy Head. Who was I to argue?

"Of course, I'll put mine on hold. It can be saved for another time," I lied, smiling inside. *Sorry, Lord!* I prayed briefly.

"Brilliant, thanks, Jack. If you start off as usual with any notices and then hand over to me." Martin seemed very upbeat for someone who had just taken on an extra job. I sat back in my chair after he left and felt that somehow I'd been stitched up but I couldn't work out how. After a while, I gave up trying and got back to work.

****

I stood at the front of the hall, next to a large wooden lectern, trying to give the impression of authority and wisdom. Classes of children filed in quietly and sat in chairs that were neatly arranged in rows. The challenge of House assemblies is pitching it at the correct level. There were eleven-year-old children and young people of sixteen and every age in between. There were two hundred different opinions on music, film, sport, religion, morals and everything else. The art of a good assembly was finding something that entertained the Year Sevens and was not too deep for Year Nine pubescent students whose brains were swimming with hormones, and something cool enough to be appreciated by Year Eleven. Normally this involved something visual or comical for the younger ones, some music with a message that could be appreciated by the older ones and a simple yet striking message based on true life for the brain-addled mid-section.

As the final class filed in and sat in their assigned seats, and form teachers ticked their students off on their registers to mark them as present, I stepped forward and began to address the cohort of Columbus House.

"Good morning Columbus House," I spoke in a loud, confident

voice, the hall settled. A few of the Year Sevens were still in primary school mode and began to chant back, "Good Morning Mr..." but soon realised their error. There were a few giggles from their peers and some groans from the Year Elevens. I smiled and waited for the hall to quieten again.

"Welcome to our assembly on this fine morning. Mr Simpson is going to lead our assembly this morning but first some notices." As I began to read out a selection of notices about sports events, charity cake sales and reminders to return slips about trips, the door at the back of the hall opened and the Head, Melanie Franks, followed by the senior leadership team filed in. Choudhry, Lovejoy and Higgins. *Sounded like a firm of Solicitors* I thought. It momentarily threw me off my stride.

"...so please remember to walk on the left, remain silent and obey the signs that say 'No Entry' or 'Exam in progress.' Our Year Elevens need support from you all during their mock exams." I turned to Mr Simpson. "Over to you, Mr Simpson. Please welcome Mr Simpson to our assembly in the usual friendly Columbus way." I started to clap and the rest of the hall followed suit, enthusiastically. Martin Simpson was a popular member of staff.

I stood and watched the senior team. *Why are they here? What's going on?* The only time all the team were in the same assembly was on the last day of term when we crammed everyone in for a final assembly before sending them off for the holidays. Something was up.

Martin began to speak. I wasn't really paying attention as I was still perturbed by the arrival of the SLT. They just stood and watched. Choudhry was smirking as if he knew something that no one else did. Melanie Franks stood impassive, with no emotion. *I bet that's a skill you learn at Head Teacher training courses,* I thought childishly. The others occasionally muttered to each other.

Suddenly my attention was caught by the restlessness of a

couple of my staff. I stared at them. They looked bemused as if they couldn't follow what was being said by Martin. I tuned in to his assembly.

"... so that evening as I tucked into my brioche bun and Pinot Grigio..."

What is he talking about? Brioche bun and white wine?

"I reflected on the sweetness of the bun and the dryness of the wine and compared it to my life..." Martin continued.

Eh? I continued to listen, puzzled by the bizarre connections he was making. I scanned the hall. The Year Sevens sat in silence, the Year Eleven were beginning to fidget. To all intents and purposes, the Year Nines were asleep.

"I thought about how life is like mashed potato, sometimes too runny and sometimes lumpy..." Martin seemed to be rambling.

What the...? What on earth is he talking about? This is nonsense. What is he playing at? I shrugged my shoulders at the bemused staff who were worriedly looking at me for guidance.

"... and then of course there is the aardvark! What an incredible creature, look how it has evolved over millennia to adapt to its surroundings and be able to survive. We must remember to be like aardvarks, becoming adaptable. Accepting change..."

"Eating ants!" the teenage male voice came from somewhere at the back. Laughter erupted amongst the ranks at the back of the hall.

Teachers standing around that part of the hall sprang into action to quieten the students.

I laughed inside and tried not to smile. *Smart kid, I like him!* Martin Simpson stopped speaking. He too smiled. He waited to continue.

"No, not eating ants, but we can learn a lot from ants; their industry and teamwork for example leads to building tremendous communities all creating success for each other."

That's the first sensible thing you've said.

"Back to the main point…" said Martin.

Point? There's a point to all this? I realised I was pulling a bemused face and tried to rectify it quickly. I glanced at the SLT standing at the back. All now appeared to be enjoying what must be the worst assembly I have seen. (Except when Year Eight boys are involved in running assembly, and then it always ends up with a mock fight or one of them trying to perform a rap they have written.)

"So if we really want to understand the meaning of life, and of course, the answer is not 42…" He waited for his comic moment to have an impact. There was none, except from the staff of a certain age. *Clearly, no child in Columbus House has read Hitchhiker's Guide to the Galaxy.*

"…um", Martin was disappointed. "Of course, the answer is 'Pepperami,' that amazing spicy sausage in a foil pack. Life is just like a 'Pepperami.' Sometimes we struggle to open it up and it takes force. Life is like that too. Sometimes we struggle to find the happiness we search for and life is a struggle…"

I could see several of my staff beginning to laugh, trying to maintain a sense of decorum, but failing. Melanie Franks was grinning like a Cheshire Cat.

I put my hand on my forehead and began to shake my head. I could not believe what I was hearing. A few of the Year Sevens near me had noticed my reaction and were whispering. I couldn't blame them.

Martin was still rambling. His message was confusing and distracted.

"So, Columbus House, what we can all take away from this is the need to be like 'Blu Tak', strong, pliable and sticky. Sticking to what we believe, but pliable enough to see the views of others and strong enough to hold our life together. Thank you." He stepped back from the lectern. There was silence around the hall. No one knew what to do. Normally applause begins automatically, but today there was stunned silence. I quickly stepped up to replace him at the Lectern.

"Thank you, Mr Simpson, for that … er… interesting assembly. Very thought-provoking. Now please let's give Mr Simpson a big thank you from us all." I began the applause. Ripples of clapping began, people unsure of what they had just witnessed. Then suddenly one Year Eleven boy stood up. "Bravo! Well done Simpson, aardvarks rule!" This sparked off the whole of Year Eleven who rose to their feet cheering and clapping. There were whistles followed by more shouting. Soon the whole cohort was applauding and cheering. I let it roll for a moment and then raised my hands in the air and signalled for them to settle. They did, gradually.

Martin Simpson stood there, beaming and staring at the SLT. They turned and filed out.

That afternoon, it was my turn to poke my head around Martin's office door.

"What the heck was that all about this morning? Aardvarks? Pepperami? Pinot Grigio? That was awful! What were you playing at and why were Melanie and the others standing around at the back?" I was still a bit confused and it had been brooding in my mind all day. Several of my tutors had also asked the same questions as me.

"What? What do you mean?" Martin sat behind his desk, hiding behind his monitor. However, there was a grin on his face.

"Don't give me that, Martin, you know full well what I mean? What were you guys up to in assembly this morning? It was a joke. I'm surprised they behaved so well considering the mess you made of talking to them."

Martin was now laughing, at me and the whole situation. At my frustration and posturing as well as the story that lay behind it.

"Okay, okay... calm down. It was a joke. Well, more of a challenge really. In the SLT meeting yesterday we were discussing assemblies and themes. Melanie told us a story of a challenge that happened in her old school, how the leadership team challenged her to include six random words in an assembly and see if anyone noticed." I shook my head gently, understanding beginning to dawn on me.

"...so yesterday we agreed to do it again. I got the short straw, but they didn't tell me the words until this morning. I had no idea what I was going to say." Martin sat back in his chair grinning.

"Let me guess... Brioche, Pinot Grigio, mashed potato, aardvark, Pepperami and Blu Tak" I counted them off on my fingers as I spoke. Martin just grinned. "You bas***d", I mouthed. After all, he was still my boss. I was laughing now at the absurdity of the situation.

"I was making it up as I went along." Martin was laughing as he spoke.

"Yeah, I noticed. So did the staff and the Year Elevens. Not sure about the rest!" I sat down in one of the comfy chairs in his office. "I can't believe you had the nerve... I mean the meaning of life is Pepperami?" For the next twenty minutes, we chatted, laughed and replayed the events of the worst assembly ever.

****

End-of-term assemblies at South Coast Comprehensive School were a big tradition. They were also a feat of incredible logistics. One thousand students, squashed into the hall and gym. The latter was separated by folding doors that could be opened to create one huge space. On final assembly day, the doors were opened and chairs were put out for students in years Nine to Eleven. Years Seven and Eight sat on the floor. It was the only way to fit them all in. It took over an hour to get everyone in place. Student runners calling individual tutor groups to the hall, led by their tutor. They brought with them all their bags and coats. No one went back inside after they were dismissed. By the time the assembly began the poor Year Sevens had been sat on a parquet floor for sixty minutes surrounded by their coats and bags.

It had been a long and difficult term; Ofsted had been and gone, leaving the staff battle-scarred. The weather had been difficult meaning there had been many wet and cold days where students could not go outside. This in itself caused increased stress for everyone, including the children. To cap it all Christmas was five days away. For the past two weeks students had become overly excited, attempting to introduce Christmas into every lesson. Tinsel was in evidence, as were reindeer antler hair bands and even Santa beards. In the mix of this chaos, Year Eleven had sat mock GCSE exams. Staff were desperately trying to get everything marked before the holiday so that no work needed to be done in the two-week break. Children and staff had had enough. We all needed a holiday!

The final Year Eleven students filed in, and Christmas music played over the sound system. I had been placed in charge of the music and sound system as the ICT technician was absent with flu and I knew how to operate it. As the last strains of "I wish it could be Christmas every day" by Wizard faded out, Melanie Franks stepped up onto the stage at the front of the hall. She wore a red two-piece skirt and Jacket and had tied some tinsel in her hair. *Very Christmassy.* Behind her on the stage was the school orchestra ready to belt out some Christmas tunes. Along the front of the stage, facing the whole school was the choir. This mainly constituted of girls with the occasional boy to help with the baritone parts. The whole staff crammed themselves in around the edges, trying to keep a look out for miscreant children who were not engaging in the end-of-term celebrations. Melanie Franks stepped forward and welcomed everyone, as if they had a choice to be there.

"It has been a long and challenging term for all of us and I want to say thank you to you all for your excellent efforts, especially during our inspection, during the poor weather and for supporting our Year Eleven students…"

Melanie Franks continued for about five minutes thanking everyone. Several rounds of applause were given before the choir sang two pieces, Leonard Cohen's 'Hallelujah' and 'Baby It's cold outside.' There was quiet applause from the school but enthusiastic clapping from the staff. *Wasted on children,* I thought meanly. It's not really, the more you expose children to a wide range of music, drama and literature, the more they will appreciate it. It takes time. I recalled being the same.

I stood in the corner by the stage, controlling the sound, from a portable sound desk. There was some poetry, followed by a list of students who had achieved well-earned merit certificates. Sports results were read out. I beamed as it was announced that my Year Eight team had reached the semi-finals of both the South East Sussex and the Sussex Cup at U13 level. I coached them weekly and drove them all over Sussex in the school minibus. I felt like Alex Ferguson. As the assembly finally drew to a close, the band played a medley of Christmas songs culminating in Slade's "Merry Christmas Everyone." People sang along, arms waving. The atmosphere was a mixture of Christmas joy and relief that the ordeal of the final assembly was nearly over. It had been going on for nearly an hour.

There was fidgeting and students were eager to leave for their Christmas holiday. Some Year Sevens tried to stand. They were quickly and quietly told to remain. Melanie Franks spoke for a final time.

"Thank you all, have an amazing Christmas and return ready to learn. We will wait, and remain seated until the doors are opened to the playground and then you will be dismissed year by year. Remember you cannot go back into school. Tutors please be ready to open the doors and dismiss the school, but first, we will listen to our final piece of music." There were some groans and mumbles from across the school, gathered in the hall and gym.

As I had been put in charge of the music, I had selected what I thought was an appropriate piece. After all, it had been a difficult term. I hit the play button and the CD began to whirr.

Trumpets and drums began to sound in a march that at first caused confusion. The harsh beat of the drums was not at all Christmassy but almost sounded military. Then suddenly the familiarity of the theme from 'The Great Escape' began to emerge. The whistling effect of the orchestra playing the oh-so-familiar rhythm. Melanie looked at me with a little sternness; I shrugged and smiled at her. She relented, shook her head and began to grin. I looked around the hall, the staff were grinning, and the students looked confused. Some of the older ones understood and cheered and joined in with the tune. The Fire exits opened and students began to file out into the playground. It was a very grey and dark sky. Just as the students began to emerge from the hall, finally escaping from school for a much-earned and needed rest, large droplets of rain began to fall. Slowly at first and then, as if someone had burst a balloon full of water, the heavens opened and it poured down. Torrential rain. There were screams as students fled for cover under porches and the trees on the edge of the playground. Some tried to re-enter the school but were turned away by eager teachers wanting to get to the staff lunch and down a beer or two. The music played out to its conclusion and the hall was empty bar the staff. The floor was littered with bits of tinsel, empty envelopes that once contained cards, Christmas wrapping paper and sweet wrappers. It was hot and steamy.

The rain dissipated quickly and the sun broke through. *Perfect timing!* Damp children began to make their way home across the playground and out into the street. *What an end to a long and challenging term,* I thought. The site team were already busy with brooms and stacking chairs. I packed up the audio equipment and locked the box. *I need a beer!*

****

Assemblies are a key part in promoting the virtues and ethos of any school. The broadly Christian nature, that the Government require provides a big window of opportunity to share outstanding moral stories, historical characters, contemporary heroes and good old messages of right and wrong. In the secondary phase of education corporate singing and prayer have vanished, giving opportunity for the watering down of clear Christian teaching. Some say this is a good thing, others a bad thing. I am somewhere in the middle. I can't say that I am an advocate of prayer and singing in schools, but a more open and honest approach to sharing the Christian faith and its values seems reasonable given the nation's heritage and history. So when Ofsted came calling in the spring of 2005 the new Head Teacher, Paul Hawkins, a stocky, balding Scotsman who looked more like a bouncer than a teacher approached me to lead a Columbus House assembly.

"Jack," he said, his Glaswegian accent strong and intimidating. "I need you to lead the assembly when the inspectors are here. You have a talent for it. Wednesday morning. Is it prepared already?" The call from Ofsted had come yesterday. Two inspectors were coming on Wednesday and Thursday. I winked at him confidently and said, "Born ready!" He grinned back, "That's my boy. I knew you would do it." He patted me on the shoulder in a fatherly way. He was about fifteen years older than me. This was his first headship after serving in a North London school as a deputy for ten years.

I ran through the assembly in my head, as he walked away down the corridor. Fortunately for me, it was already planned. We had a termly theme. This term was British heroes. My Assembly was called 'Chocolate is good for you,' and was all about the Cadbury brothers and the vision of George Cadbury to build a village for his workers called Bournville. It was his Christian faith that inspired him to create a better life for his factory workers. As I ran through it in my head, I made sure I ticked all the boxes and more, to ensure that our inspector could see our ethos and virtues on display.

Students filed in quietly as Shanks and Bigfoot, "Sweet Like Chocolate" boomed out across the hall. The PowerPoint on the big screen showed a large bar of chocolate with the title "Chocolate is good for you."

Mary Johnson stepped forward and settled the house. The music stopped, and calm descended on the hall. Mary began to read out a few brief notices before she handed over to me. I sat on the stage looking relaxed. The inspector, a woman of about sixty who was apparently a former head teacher who not only was an inspector but also trained new head teachers walked in followed by Paul Hawkins. She sat in an empty seat at the end of a row. Mary Johnson finished her notices and handed over to me. I slipped off the stage and stepped forward.

"Morning all." There were a few muttered responses. "Well thank you for that, at least some of you are awake this morning. I must apologise, I was running late today and so have not had any breakfast." I pulled out a bar of Cadbury Fruit and Nut from behind the lectern. "I found this hidden in Ms Johnson's drawers." There was a smirk and a grin from Mary. Several of my tutors cracked a smile. The joke went over the heads of all the children. "Would you mind if I had some now?"

I cracked open the packet and broke off a couple of squares and put them in my mouth. I patrolled along the front of the hall eating my chocolate. I offered a bit to a Year Seven, who was unsure what to do. I winked at her and encouraged her to take a piece. She did. Others began to ask. I walked away. There was expectation building in the room.

"Mmm… lovely. Does anyone here like chocolate?" The year Sevens and eights in the front rows went crazy. Hands up and calling out "Me, Me, I do!"

I proceeded to do a short quiz on the benefits of chocolate and facts about it. I threw Cadbury Heroes to those who got answers right and I threw extra as well just to keep it interesting. As the assembly progressed I ran through the Bournville story and how the faith of the Cadbury brothers led them to create a unique village in the country for the factory workers, something not seen in Victorian times. Using images and stories I drew out the virtues of compassion and generosity and linked them to the Christian faith. At the close, I picked on some Year Elevens to recap, for a prize, of course, more Heroes. Fifteen minutes passed in a flash and the House filed out, many smiling and talking about chocolate.

Paul and the inspector approached me. I was introduced and shook her hand. I smiled my best smile and looked hopeful.

"Thank you, Jack, much appreciated. Good assembly." Paul was always one to thank you quickly, to make you feel encouraged.

"Yes, thank you, Mr Turner. I thoroughly enjoyed your assembly. You have a real talent for drawing in the students and not only entertaining them but giving a strong and powerful message. I was not aware of the story behind Bournville. Very interesting." She smiled and seemed genuinely interested. "It was clear that the students were listening and engaged. The school values came through. Well done." She paused and then came the 'but.' *Here comes the 'but'. I knew she'd find something.*

"But just one point to note. It would have been good to have some music as the students entered, it just sets the tone rather than silence."

If you'd been on time, you would have heard it. "Actually, I think you missed it, you were probably delayed by the Head." I gave him a knowing look. "Sweet like Chocolate, an appropriate theme I think."

"Ah!" She nodded. *Jack Turner one, Inspector nil.*

****

One of the things that is inevitable in every school is change. It is of course the only constant, as they say. When Paul Hawkins became the Head Teacher, the idea of a final assembly at the end of each term was swiftly replaced by House Assemblies (or Communities, as they were now known.) Each community had a final assembly for thirty minutes at Christmas and in the summer. It was still a logistical feat moving students in and out of the hall throughout the day. The poor orchestra and choir now had four assemblies to perform rather than just one. It was a long day for the music department.

As head of Columbus Community, I was responsible for planning my own assembly. The choir and orchestra would perform set pieces throughout the day, but in between, I had to plan something festive. Each Head of Community would borrow ideas from each other to reduce planning, but I really wanted to do something different.

"How about a visit from Santa?" said Penny Williams as we sat in our department meeting moderating Year-Eleven mock exams. "You could dress up as Santa, come in from the back, dish out a few sweets etc. to the kids and then ask different staff if they've been good or not."

"Interesting!" I put my red pen down and sat there for a

moment.

"You could even get old Lovejoy and a few of the other senior leaders to sit on your lap. It could become a bit of a sketch. The kids would love it." Penny was really going for it. "They'd do it if you asked them beforehand! Your tutors would definitely be up for it!"

"You could be right. It certainly makes a change from poems and a bit of sombre reflection." My mind was heading off in a planning direction. All hope of moderating was lost. The Year Elevens would have to wait.

Mary Johnson was leading the Columbus Christmas assembly. The Orchestra had played a Christmas medley (the same one they did every year!) and the Choir had sung a couple of great Christmassy songs. It was nearly time for Santa to make his entrance. I thought back to the last forty-eight hours and the conversations I had had convincing not only the hippy-like Francesca Lovejoy but also Paul Hawkins, the big burly Scottish Headteacher, to play stooge to my Santa. It took some doing but they reluctantly agreed. They were concerned about decorum and learning, whereas I was more interested in creating an experience they might actually remember and enjoy. My tutors, of course, were very keen and would ham it up nicely to entertain the community.

I heard my cue and burst through the rear doors. "Ho, Ho, Ho!" I boomed in my best Santa voice. I was wearing the traditional Santa outfit; red trousers and jacket, a big black belt, wellington boots, a big red hat and of course a fake beard! I strode around the back of the hall, greeting children in a Santa-like way. The cushion stuffed under my jacket kept slipping despite being tied in with string. I kept heaving it up.

"Ho, ho, ho! How are we all? Have we all been good?" I began to throw sweets out from a sack that I was carrying. Children jumped and lurched forwards to try and catch them.

"It's Turner!" said one year-eight lad, in a slightly disappointed way.

"No, no, no! I'm Santa. Mr Turner is off sick! Here my child, have a sweet!" I handed him a sweet and winked at him and moved on swiftly.

The atmosphere was one of fun and laughter. I could see Lovejoy and Hawkins standing on the far side, looking a little uncomfortable.

I stopped in front of one of my tutors, a young History teacher called Paul Rogers. He was young enough to have been at the school when I had first started teaching, and here he was now a member of my team.

"Mr Rogers, have you been a good boy this year?" There was a cheer from some of his tutor group, sitting nearby.

"I'm always good Santa!" He said coyly.

"What would you like for Christmas?" I was really beginning to get into the Santa role. I put my arm around his shoulder and waited for his reply.

"Well, if it's not too much trouble and you can fit it on your sleigh…" The children around were laughing and enjoying seeing teachers acting the fool. It made us human and therefore more approachable.

"… I would love a new drum kit!" Paul played in a local pub band. Many of the older year Eleven students knew this and had seen him perform at the weekends.

I moved on around the room, throwing sweets, causing mayhem, and interacting with students and staff, asking them what they wanted for Christmas. Eventually, I reached the front. I was slightly out of breath. I held up my hand to silence the children and gradually they began to settle.

"My goodness, too many mince pies, I'm not as fit as I thought!" I wobbled my fake belly and heaved it back into place.

"Go on Turner, take that beard off, we know it's you!" I recognised the voice of a cheeky year Ten lad, a future alpha male, but not yet there.

"Now, now, Tommy, we must all believe in Santa or we won't get any presents, will we, boys and girls?" I spread my hands out wide to encourage them to respond. They did in equal measure of agreement and derision. I could see my tutors laughing and enjoying the spectacle. Lovejoy and Hawkins both smiled a little nervously.

At the front of the stage where I now stood, just in front of the orchestra a big comfy chair had miraculously appeared. It was decorated with tinsel and had a sign attached to the top that said "Santa's special chair." I sat down in it and the assembled children began to settle down, expecting me to recount some poem or story. But I had other plans.

"Today, we have two very special visitors to our assembly," I said in my best Santa voice. I motioned to Lovejoy and Hawkins. A round of applause began.

"Welcome, welcome..." My beard was getting a bit soggy and it was difficult to speak. I kept having to spit bits of it out. It made the Year Seven laugh.

"Come now Ms Lovejoy, come and visit me here." Francesca Lovejoy stepped forward and climbed the steps to the stage. I patted my lap and indicated for her to sit down.

She looked at me nervously, worried about her status and authority. Cautiously she sat on the edge of my lap. A cheer went up from across the rows of Year Eleven, some whistles and clapping. I held up a hand to settle them down.

"Now, Ms Lovejoy, have you been a good girl this year?" More cheers erupted. I could see the staff grinning and enjoying the spectacle. I put my arm around her shoulder in a Santa-friendly way, eliciting more cheers.

"Well," she said. "I think so! I can't remember being naughty."

To my surprise, Francesca was embracing the moment. She began to relax and overact, to the delight of the assembled students. She reeled off a list of presents she would like, including diamonds and a new car. The children were delighted.

"Well, I have in my sack a very special present, just for you, because you've been so good!" There were 'oohs' and 'ahs' from across the hall. I pulled out a little wrapped box of chocolates and gave it to her. She hopped off my lap, and took a bow, the children, clapped and cheered.

"Well now, who's next? Ah yes, Mr Hawkins" I gestured to him and he came forward onto the stage. He stood next to me, looking down. It was hard to tell if he was in the mood or in a mood. I took a chance. I patted my lap and indicated he should sit down. There was a moment when I thought I had got it wrong and he wouldn't play. *I'm in trouble.* But then he plonked himself squarely on my lap and nearly winded me! A roar went up across the room, cheering and clapping. The whole of Columbus Community, staff included, joined in.

I adjusted myself to get comfier and waited until the hall had settled.

"My my, you have grown, haven't you? Too much cake and beer." I pulled a face behind his back as if he weighed a great deal. The children who saw it giggled with delight.

"Have you been a good boy?" My Santa voice was struggling and I was trying not to laugh.

Paul Hawkins then did the best thing I have ever seen any head do. In his most broad Glaswegian accent in an aggressive tone, he spoke.

"I'm always good, and if anyone says different, send 'em to me an I'll correct 'em. Ya know what I mean?" He held up a threatening fist. "I'll no have anyone say I'm ne good." For a moment many students in the hall couldn't decide if he was acting or serious.

"Would you like a present, Mr Hawkins?" I was struggling to keep it together.

"Aye, and nothing crappy!" The staff were lapping it up and the older students were enthralled by their Headteacher. I dug into my sack and pulled out a small bottle of whisky, a miniature.

Still using his best (or worst) Glaswegian accent, Hawkins thanked me. "Thank ya Santa, yer a good lad!" He stood up and raised the bottle of whisky to acknowledge the students who were now cheering and clapping. I stood up and came down off the stage. I began waving to the students, "Merry Christmas, Merry Christmas!" I threw the last remaining sweets from my bag and left the hall the way I came in. The orchestra struck up "Merry Christmas Everyone" by Slade.

I slumped against the wall outside in the corridor, I was exhausted. The door opened again and out walked Lovejoy and Hawkins. "Brilliant Jack, good idea, thanks for the pressies." Hawkins' accent had returned to the less severe version.

"Yes, thanks Jack, my favourite chocolate. How did you know?"

As quick as a flash I replied, "Santa knows everything."

****

Sometimes a school can break with tradition and in 1998 when England were in the World Cup in France, the first match was during school time. It had taken much persuasion from the sportier staff to allow the whole school to watch (if they chose to) England's opening match against Tunisia.

"I still can't believe the Head went for it!" I said as I filed into the hall, leading my RE class.

"It was only the Maths department who raised a major objection. They're getting to do Maths with those who don't want to watch. There's only a handful." Martin Simpson, the Deputy Head and ardent football fan, had pressed the Headteacher on the issue as soon as the schedule was announced.

"Mathematicians have no soul," I joked, "it serves them right." He grinned back at me, knowing that my deputy in Columbus House was a mathematician. Football fever had struck South Coast Comprehensive School, as it had the whole nation of England. Glen Hoddle's men had promised to bring it home! There was even an updated version of the Lightning Seeds Football Anthem. Flags adorned school classrooms as well as every car that passed by and many houses were draped in the St George's flag. There was a real sense of optimism that this time we wouldn't fall to penalties against the Germans as we had in '96.

The hall was packed with children and staff, the BBC was on the big screen and the teams were lining up. There was a buzz of excitement in the hall, cheering and singing. As the national anthem sounded and the sound of "God Save the Queen" began to play, almost everyone stood and it became absolutely quiet. No one had primed them. It was as if this moment in history was significant and they all wanted to be a part of it. I am not a keen royalist. I have time for the Queen but beyond that, I have little interest in them, but this moved me. As the camera finished scanning the players and the anthem ended, everyone sat down. The French announcer on the TV called for people to rise for the national anthem of Tunisia. One young boy, Samir, stood alone in the middle of the hall, whilst all around him stared. Samir was from Tunisia. With a hand on his heart, he stood proudly. There was silence. I could see several staff, both male and female, welling up at his courage. I was overwhelmed by it. What bravery, what courage! When the anthem finished, the whole school began to clap for him acknowledging his defiant-like act of nationalism. One boy against nine hundred or so.

"That was the best assembly ever sir! Come on England!" said one rather excited Year Seven boy as he filed out of the hall and made his way home. Sometimes, schools just need to ride on the wave of a national event rather than try to maintain the stance that an hour's Maths or English or any subject is more important for the development of rounded human beings than taking part in a whole school fun event. That day the children learned a lot about each other and about respect. Respect for traditions like the national anthem and respect for Samir and his homeland.

CHAPTER THIRTEEN

The Alex Ferguson Years

When Phil, the shell-suited head of PE, came to me and asked if I would take over the coaching of our year eight football team, how could I refuse? Not only was he a fellow Christian and a good mate, but here was my chance to show that I could coach as well as play. It was September 1993, I was in my early thirties and still playing football regularly, much to the despair of my wife Sandy who was left with the boys on Saturday afternoons. I was a goalkeeper. Jack "The Cat" Turner, they called me. I think that referred to my ability to sleep curled around the foot of the goalpost rather than to any real agility. I had played football since about the age of seven and more latterly represented my university and a host of local pub and club sides. I currently play for my local church team in the Sussex League.

"Of course I will, I'd love to!" I was genuinely excited to be asked. I loved football and here was my chance to show I knew something about the game.

"You can drive the bus, can't you? Your first match is already fixed, the first round of the U13 Sussex Cup versus St Saviours. They won the U12 competition last year." Phil patted me on the back and handed me a list of names. "These are the boys who played last year, you may want to hold a trial again and pick a fresh squad." Phil smiled at me, in a way that said, "I've just stitched you up, sucker!"

"They are a tricky bunch of lads, but with some decent players, you might be able to beat St Saviours." I got the feeling my managerial career might be short-lived.

"Sir, we'll never beat St Saviours! We lost six nil last year and that was with Jason King playing, but he's gone to private school. We'll never win without him!" Apparently, Jason King was their talisman, their top scorer. We were in a huddle on the edge of the pitch at a school in the Sussex Weald. I was trying to encourage them and instil in them some of the ideas I shared in the two training sessions I had managed to have.

"Johnny, stop worrying! You didn't win with Jason, last year, perhaps you will do better if you all believe you have the ability to play. I went around each member of the squad and highlighted a positive quality and skill they had. "Paul, you're a great keeper, you have the height, and agility and you scare attackers when you rush out toward them." I turned and pointed at another shorter, dark-haired boy, "Nick, you have got pace, tricky feet and a fierce shot. You're the next Jason King!" A couple of his mates nudged him and patted him on the head.

"Ali and Johnny, you boys scare me! You're taller and more muscular than any other year eight kids I know. Nothing will get past you…" They looked at each other. Johnny blushed. It matched his flaming red hair.

"Now get out there, remember your jobs, encourage each other, work hard and most of all enjoy it. Don't worry, it isn't the World Cup Final!" I sent them off for a final warm-up before kick-off. *You're such a liar, Jack! Enjoy it? I'm nervous as hell.*

The noise on the bus on the way back to school was ear-splitting. The boys were buzzing. After an edgy but goalless first half, my boys started to gain confidence. Ali and Johnny were indeed rocks at the back, very little got past them. Anything that did, Paul our giant, agile keeper mopped up with ease. St Saviours began to get panicky and sloppy, feeling the match was not going their way. Some careless passing allowed Nick to dribble his way around three defenders and pass it into the net beyond a static goalkeeper. The boys began to press and cause more errors and a second goal came when Nick controlled a cross from the left, turned the defender and rifled a shot in from the edge of the box. The match was secured when Ali and Johnny drew the taller defenders away at a corner allowing the diminutive Nick to leap like a salmon, unmarked, and head in a third goal.

"Sir, I can't believe it, we beat St Saviours. Nick was brilliant!" Jonny was so excited as were the remainder of the squad. They were loud, boisterous and unable to contain their joy at winning.

"Jason King? Who's he? We've got Nick Jenkins! Hat-trick hero." I joined in their excitement, to help them see that they could be successful without their supposed talisman. "When you guys worked together and for each other, you played great football. Do you remember how they fell apart when they started to panic and argue?"

"We stuffed them, they were crap!" Ali shouted loudly from the back of the bus. A big grin on his face.

"Language Ali, language!" I called back. Despite my joy at their win, I still needed to ensure they behaved appropriately. By the time we arrived back at school, the car park was nearly empty. The boys piled out of the bus, grabbing their bags and coats. "Remember, boys, teamwork makes the dream work!" Johnny turned and faced me. His shock of red hair was a mess and he had a massive grin across his freckled face. "Sir, that is so lame, don't ever say it again!"

As the autumn months rolled on into the winter and the new year, the confidence from their initial win continued to grow with each win. The team cruised through three more rounds of the Sussex Cup winning each by several goals. They also topped the town league and were thus in the quarterfinals of the South East Sussex Cup as well. We trained each week and I got to know the boys well, their strengths and weakness' as players and, more importantly as human beings. They lived and breathed football, so I could also use that desire to help them in the classroom. It was a rule that if they got a detention or missed homework, then they missed a match. This caused Adam consternation as he did not believe I would drop him for the quarter-final match. Adam was a great defensive midfielder. He was short and stocky and he never held back in his tackling. In the classroom, he was a rogue; cheeky to the point of being rude and often unwilling to work at his best in lessons he did not like.

"Sir, you can't! It's not fair. Please, please let me play." He was welling up. He had lied about a detention he received and had played in the previous round instead of going to the maths detention he had been set.

"Adam, you knew the rule. You knew what I would say, and you lied because you knew. You deceived the maths teacher and you lied to me. What should I do, ignore the rules just for you? That's not fair either. You can come along and be part of the squad, but you won't play." Adam lost control; his anger flared up. He turned to one of the nearby metal lockers and kicked it hard. It dented. "F**king shit, Turner, you're a f**king shit!" He stormed off. My stomach turned, not about being sworn at, that's par for the course, but because I felt awful for Adam. I knew how much he wanted to play. *If I give in to him now, I will have lost this team forever. I'll be a walkover.*

"Jack, can you not let him play, please? Just for this game? It's the quarter-final!" Phil held out his shell-suited arm and passed me a letter from Adam's mum. I read it and handed it back. I shrugged my shoulders. "So? He hates me, his mum thinks I'm useless. Phil, if you don't back me now then every time I make an unpopular decision with these lads then they will just ignore me, I might as well give up now." There was steel in my voice. I was not normally so assertive but would not be moved. "I'll call his mum, we've chatted before."

It was a crisp January afternoon; it was a lunchtime kick-off so the boys had eaten an early lunch before we got on the bus. The bus was quiet all the way to Crowborough as we travelled to the quarterfinal. The boys changed in silence and went slowly out onto the pitch to warm up. The sun was shining but it was cold. None of them smiled or joked as they usually did. Their mood was sombre. My team talk, good as it was in my view, was received as if I had passed the death sentence on them all. I sent them off to play in a match that they would lose unless I could do something to change their mood.

By halftime they were two–nil down, there was no communication, and they were not playing with any determination or desire. Adam stood next to our kit bag and bucket, his arms folded and a face of thunder stared at me. *This is your fault Adam, not mine,* but I couldn't say that to him. The boys reluctantly huddled around, I passed out oranges and water. They looked defeated. Adam sauntered up and stood behind me.

"Now look, I don't care whether you hate me or not, whether you think it's all my fault or not. It was my rule and my choice. Adam screwed up, he knows it, you know it. If I let him get away with it, then what? You all would try it on. I care just as much about your education and your academic success as I do about us winning a football match. In fact, more so." I stared them down and waited. "If you want to throw away this match to spite me, then go ahead, just carry on as you have been and you will lose heavily. But if you really care about your football and you want to win a trophy this year, then let it go. If you turn this around, then Adam is back for the semi-final. Are you going to let him down? Are you going to make him miss that opportunity? Now get the hell out there and play to win, stop sulking!" I stepped back and let Adam into the fold. "Now he's back, see! Adam, tell them to go and win and not to be so bloody stupid!" The swear word slipped out before I could stop it. Several of them began to giggle, and a couple smiled. Very quickly the mood changed and they began to chatter.

"Lads," Adam said, "Listen. Sir is right. It was my fault. I'm sorry I let you down and Sir I'm sorry I let you down." There was a twinkle in his eye, the thunder was gone. The mood swiftly changed. There were shouts of "Come on!" and "Let's go!" as they sprinted back onto the pitch. Adam looked up at me and smiled. I ruffled his hair. "Well done, good speech. Let's hope it works." It did work. They pulled the second half around and won three-two. Nick, the new talisman scored two and Johnny headed in the winner from a corner in the last five minutes.

The semi-final was a tight affair. We were playing at a school in Chichester. We were drawn away from home. The boys were overwhelmed by the facilities. The pitch was pristine, like a carpet, it was flat and well-maintained. The changing facilities were unlike any they had ever seen, spacious, clean and undamaged. They felt like they were playing at Wembley. It was just before the February half-term holiday. It was bitterly cold even though the sun was shining, and there was a blustery wind. The match was in the closing stages and we were winning two-one. The pitch had helped us, the even bounce and the slick passing allowed us to play a good passing game. It was pretty comfortable for the boys and they sensed a victory. With about three minutes to go their tall, lanky frontman broke through the midfield and sprinted into the eighteen-yard box. Paul our keeper stepped forward three paces and set himself, preparing for a shot. Ali cut across from the penalty spot, stuck out a leg to tackle him and was fractionally late. He took the player and the ball, in that order. I was running the line, and in an instant, my flag went up and I was flagging for a penalty. The ref saw me, blew his whistle and pointed to the spot. One of our parents who travelled with us for support as his son was in the team rushed over to me, swearing. "What the f**k did you do that for?" He continued to abuse me verbally berating me for my poor decision-making. "It was clearly a foul!" I replied, I could feel my heart rate increase, I was getting stressed. Some of the boys ran over to me and began to complain. I squared up to the dad, who was taller than me and clearly used to confrontation, "If you can't be civil in front of the boys, you need to leave the pitch side." I waited, my heart racing. Fortunately for me, he backed down. I couldn't allow myself to be drawn into a fracas.

After the final whistle, the boys reluctantly gathered around me. They were despondent and upset with me.

"Sir, why did you flag? We would have won if you didn't"

"You could have let it go, sir!" Their complaints continued for a full minute. I stayed and let them grumble.

"Finished?" My voice was stern, almost angry. I was cross, not with my decision, it was correct but cross with my team for doubting my integrity. "Listen!" I was sharp with them. "I'm no cheat, we win fairly or not at all. I don't want to get to a final by cheating. Do you?" I stared them out.

"But sir…" Johnny was still upset and wanted to argue.

"No Johnny, we do it the right way. That team have little left, they were flagging. That penalty was their first attack in the second half. You were all over them. Nick has goals in him, get the ball to him quickly. Make the runs through the lines Nick," I pointed at him for emphasis. Johnny, Ali, put the ball out wide to Adam or Sam and let's play diagonals over the top and let Nick run on. He has the beating of the defenders every time. They are tired." I stared hard at them. "Do you want to go to the final? Or are you ready to give up?" I almost felt like Churchill giving his rousing speech about fighting them on the beaches!

Within three minutes of extra time starting, we had scored

again. Nick had raced through beyond the back line and latched on to a diagonal ball from Adam. He rounded the keeper and slotted home into an empty net. Two more followed in quick succession before the break. In the second period of extra time, the pace eased. The opposition was spent; they knew they were beaten. A final thunderbolt from Adam made it six. We were in the final.

The PE teacher, from the Chichester school, shook my hand at the end as the boys trooped off. "Well done, your boys did well. A brave decision to flag for a penalty against your own side. You don't see it often. I wouldn't have flagged it." I smiled inside.

"It was a penalty. We have to play it as we see it, any other way sends the wrong message to the boys." I wanted to make my point.

"Still brave…" He turned and walked off to console his team. I saw the parent standing by the bus looking a little shameful. "Sorry, you were right. I shouldn't have lost it!" He held out his hand. I shook it.

It was a cold March night and the breeze was coming off the sea. Newhaven Town FC was hosting the Under 13 Sussex Cup final between South Coast Comprehensive and Oakwood School from Crawley. The floodlights were on and there was a slight mist. It was an eerie sight. I prowled the touchline, shouting instructions and encouraging the team. I was wearing a thick winter-type coat, light brown with a dark faux fur collar. My school suit was underneath. I felt like a proper football manager. The two teams were evenly matched and it was a tough match, ebbing and flowing, neither side really taking control. Paul had made a couple of excellent stops to keep us in it, but at the same time, we had hit the post and had a shot cleared off the line.

As the match drew towards its conclusion and extra time

loomed we gained a corner. Ali took it, an in-swinger, Johnny rose to head it but was jostled out of the way. He fell. There was a moment when everyone stopped thinking the ref would blow for a penalty. He didn't. The ball dropped to a lad called Chris, he was a left midfielder. He controlled it easily, pushed it to his right to make space and struck a low drive toward the goal. He was the only one who hadn't stopped, expecting a penalty. The ball swept past two defenders who just watched. The keeper made an effort to dive but was woefully short and the ball rolled swiftly into the bottom right corner of the net. The whistle went, and the ref pointed to the centre spot. Goal!

Within minutes the final whistle went; we had won! I trotted over to their manager shook his hand and then turned and sprinted onto the pitch! It was reminiscent of Bob Stokoe after Sunderland beat Leeds at Wembley in 1973. I made a beeline for Chris the goal scorer, picked him up and swung him around! The team were running to us, cheering and shouting.

"You did it, sir! You won the cup!" Chris was keen to give me the glory.

"No Chris, you guys did it." I turned to the boys huddled around, smiles all around. "I told you; 'teamwork makes the dream work!'" I was bundled. The boys grabbed me and jumped on me, cheering and shouting. I was on the floor surrounded by a host of excited and happy boys who had achieved what they thought was impossible.

It didn't stop there. That season we also won the South East Sussex Cup, beating our neighbouring school and fiercest rivals. We also won that same cup for the following three years, until that team left school. Undefeated in four years. We were semi-finalists twice more in the Sussex Cup, but never achieved the heady heights of a cup double again. As the team grew and matured (if that's what they did?), they became more challenging to manage, teenage hormones kicked in, and alpha male syndrome developed amongst them all. Driving them through Sussex on cold wintery evenings became more difficult as their boisterousness was mingled with testosterone and increasing size. Despite all of this we forged a relationship based on respect (most of the time) and a love of football.

****

P.S.: It's not just the kids!

A significant number of male staff at South Coast Comprehensive were very sporty and competitive, therefore it was no surprise that there was a staff football team in the winter and cricket in the summer. There were four other local schools and we played Friday night fixtures in the Autumn, Spring and Summer. In fact, unbeknown to the other schools, Phil, the shell-suited head of PE, had created a league table and posted our results with a match report each time we played another school. Monday morning, gathered around the noticeboard reading Phil's match report, hoping for a mention, helped develop a huge sense of camaraderie amongst the male staff. We would relive the matches in the staffroom at break times, laughing and joking, winding each other up over our good, bad or indifferent performances.

"Jack The Cat Turner strikes again! How on earth did you reach that shot in the top corner? I've not seen you leap that far before!" Martin Simpson slapped me on the back as we read the match report. Inwardly I glowed with pride. Even I thought it was a cracking save. I was impressed with myself.

"Natural talent, mate, some of us are blessed with it. And also with a large dose of humility." I poked him in the ribs and stepped back quickly before he retaliated. We had beaten our local rival school from across town and my save had kept the score at two –one, which turned out to be the final result.

"Ah, but to get into this team as a keeper you only need a

modicum of talent, there is not much competition." The banter went back and forth both of us trying to outdo the other. In fairness to Martin, he was a good midfielder, one of those who could see what was about to happen and be at the right place to intercept or place a pass. He was a PE teacher, so he ought to be half decent.

Each match was played with an equal balance of fun and competitiveness. No team wanted to lose, so fought hard, but there was always an element of camaraderie between the staff from different schools. In our industry, we were all on the same team.

At the end of each season, we even had a trophy night, a meal out, some speeches and some semi-serious and not-so-serious awards. I was the first to give an after-dinner speech. I had no idea what to do.   "A Life between the sticks" was my title. It wasn't a huge success and I took some grief. At the time, after dinner speaking wasn't a strong weapon in my armoury. Now if they had asked me to do an assembly with visual aids and a PowerPoint, or preach the Gospel in church then that would be different. I never realised the difference in skill and technique that were needed, or maybe it was a passion for the topic or a heckling audience. Whatever it was, my first efforts at after-dinner speaking are best forgotten.

Football was serious stuff, we even went on a football tour, sometime in the early 2000s. I was coerced into driving the minibus, full of past-their-prime teachers going on a weekend football tour. It was organised by one of our former colleagues, who still played with us. He had gone on to work for a sports company and had connections with Sport England and the England football set-up. We started with a home match versus the local university side on Friday evening after school. (Drawn 2-2) It was followed by a meal in the pub opposite the pitch and then we headed off in the bus to Harlow and the Sport England's training camp. We stayed on the campus and trained the following morning, followed by a match against some of the England Youth coaches. (Lost 3-1). That Saturday night in Harlow was spent at a curry house: 17 teachers, curry and beer. Apparently, some of the team stayed out very late. When Sunday morning arrived we were lined up to face a team of teenagers and early twenties, all potential or existing England youth players. We looked old and tired and bleary-eyed compared to the strapping young lads opposite us. Our captain was nowhere to be seen. His hangover was so intense he did not fully wake up until it was nearly all over. He sauntered over to the pitch side midway through the second half munching on a bacon roll. By that time, we were losing about eight- one. Surprisingly I played quite well in those three games. The scores would not reflect that, but I can say, I played on the Sport England training pitch and against England youth players.

The cricket was no less serious. The match sign-up sheet required you to sign up using your initials and surname, just like a pro-cricket team sheet.

"Jack, you can't sign up with just your name!" Phil was adamant. "Write it properly. Look at everyone else!" I stared at the sheet. My name "Jack" stood out as being different from the rest. All the others were initials and a Surname: M. S Simpson, P. T Perch, I. C Smith etc. I raised my eyebrows and shook my head. "Ok, ok!" I crossed it out and wrote it in correctly. J.E Turner.

"Remember, full whites, no shorts, we have to look the part." Phil was insistent. Cricket was not my game. I like to watch it and follow it on TV but I've never played, only in staff matches. I can slow bowl and field well, but my batting is a bit random. I have no idea what I am really doing. I was there to make up the numbers and have a good time. The best match of the season was always the staff versus pupils. There were sandwiches and drinks and it was a great time to get to know some of the older students in a less formal way. Invariably the staff always won. If it was close, then Phil would somehow manipulate the rules for scoring in favour of the staff.

"Jack you're on, you have two overs to bowl. We need a couple of wickets to swing it in our favour." Phil tossed me the ball. My bowling is slow, which sometimes tricks the less experienced and talented batter. It can also be a little wayward. This also throws the batter into confusion.

"Bowl it down the leg side and try and get him to swing at it. We can usually get a catch if they mis-hit it." Phil was giving me my final instructions. *Bowl it down the leg side? It'll be lucky to make it to the other end. I have no idea where this will go once it leaves my hand!* If only Phil realised I really had no idea what I was doing. I stepped up and bowled a long, looping bowl down the off side, the year eleven boy stepped forward and calmly drove it into mid-off where there was no fielder. It went for four.

"Leg side" whispered Phil. As he handed me the ball. I made a show of rubbing it on my trousers. Not sure why they do that, but it looked good.

"Yep, I'll try, my brain says leg side but my hand does something else. Give me football every time." Phil patted me on the back. I stepped up again, desperately trying to aim down the leg side. The ball left my hand with the same looping arc as before, but this time down the leg side.

"Wide!" called the white-coated umpire. He signalled with his hands. The ball was tossed back to me and I caught it one-handed. I turned back and almost prayed for a faster and straighter delivery. The sun was behind me and the young batsman's helmet was slightly large, it shielded his eyes not only from the sun but from the ground two yards in front of him. *If only I could bowl a straight one, a little faster, then maybe...* I let my thought tail away and stepped up to bowl. This time I put a bit more pace on the ball and released it slightly later. It went straight down the middle, bounced two yards in front of the batter, stayed straight and slipped between his bat and pad. It struck the centre stump knocking it clean out! A cheer went up, from my teammates.

"Yeeesss!" I screamed and punched the air. I took the plaudits as if I had done it on purpose. I was patted on the back and generally congratulated. I felt like Bob Willis getting his 8-43 against the Aussies in 1981. My second over also produced a wicket. I finally got a ball down the leg side, the batter swung at it, it took a nick and went straight to the leg slip, which happened to be Phil. He tossed the ball up in the air, ran over to me and said: "See, I told you! Get it down the leg side!" I grinned. *If only you knew!* My innings was not so glorious; I was out after six balls scoring just 7 runs. Enough said.

We won, as always. We ate the food, drank the drinks and made the students feel like they were adults. After they had gone home we sat together outside the clubhouse bar and relived our victory over a couple of pints. The sun shone down on us that Friday evening in July.

CHAPTER FOURTEEN

A season of development

Always expect the unexpected in teaching. That's one thing that became blindingly obvious when, out of the blue, the University of Brighton asked me to do some lecturing for their undergrad/post-grad courses. It was the summer term in the late 1990s when Paul Hawkins, the stocky Scottish Head Teacher walked into my classroom after school.

"Jack, I've had a request from Brighton University." I was puzzled. The school obviously had links with both Brighton and Sussex Universities because of PGCE (Post Graduate Certificate in Education) teacher training, The RE department trained two students a year, and we were building a reputation for being a top school for trainees.

"What do they want? We can't accommodate a third student; we don't have the timetable space." I did not want to overburden my team, they worked hard enough already.

"No, no," smiled Paul. "this is something totally different. Professor Rodney Holding wants you to teach part-time at Brighton." He handed me a letter. I scanned it: there in black and white was the offer to teach both undergraduates and PGCE students. Rod Holding ran the RE department at Brighton, including the post-graduate RE teacher training. He was a lovely bloke aged about sixty, with a big bushy beard and was quite deaf in one ear. He looked like a professor from the 1970s Open University TV programmes. I reread the pertinent passage of the letter again.

...Invited to teach undergraduates a course in Biblical Ethics and to teach Postgraduates principles of RE teaching in

the Secondary Sector. Both sessions are scheduled for teaching

on a Tuesday Pm at 2 pm and 4 pm on the Falmer campus.

The Re Department at South Coast Comprehensive School would

receive an annual honorarium of £400…

"What do you think?" Paul was smiling. "It would be an excellent opportunity for you. It would broaden your experience and look excellent on your C.V. If you want to do it, we will have to act fast to amend next year's timetable. We will need to cut your allocation by two hours. Penny is light on her timetable; she can take up the slack.

"Yes, of course, I'll do it. It sounds fantastic." Inside I was panicking. *Why me? Am I good enough? What if I can't do it? This is so different to anything I've done before.*

"It is a real feather in your cap, Jack. Well done. This shows that what you are doing here is being recognised. You are doing an excellent job. Well done. I will get straight on it and ask Martin to work on the timetable." He patted me on the back, turned and left. I was stunned.

"Well done!" Sandy leaned over and gave me a kiss. We were sitting on the patio in the evening sunshine. She held up her glass of wine and I clinked it with mine. "Cheers," she said. "To my academic, university teaching husband." Sandy was my rock. She supported, counselled, put up with and slept with me. What more did I need? Sandy worked at the local junior school where many of my students came from. We would swap stories each day, she would warn me of certain students arriving in year seven, and I would regale her with stories of how some of her former students were managing at South Coast Comprehensive. It always seemed to surprise some students that teachers knew each other or were married to each other. My mind wandered to a recent conversation with a little Year Seven lad.

"Sir? In my old school, I had a teacher called Miss Turner. I liked her better than the other lady we had, who always shouted." Stuart was a gentle and kind Year Seven boy who sometimes was a little slow on the uptake.

"Don't tell me, Stuart, let me guess! She is about this tall." I gestured with my hand approximating her height. "She has blonde wavy hair, blue eyes and a lovely smile." Stuart was stunned. "Yes, sir, but how do you know that?" Stuart was genuinely surprised.

"Dur!" said another lad called Ian. "Keep up Stuart, they both have the same name, they're brother and sister, dozy." He sat back smugly.

"Close, Ian, I am married to her." There was some laughter and some "Wahey's" from the class. "Really?" said Stuart.

"Yes, really!" I replied.

The drive to Brighton was always a frantic rush. I would dash from my lesson before lunch, jump into the car and head off to Brighton. It was a 30-minute drive and then I had to find a parking space in the small and crowded carpark. The day I walked into my first lecture with a group of undergraduates I was petrified. *I am going to be found out. They'll discover I am a fraud, just a secondary teacher and not proficient in higher education.* Similar thoughts buzzed through my brain. The tables in the small classroom were arranged in a square, so all could see each other. There was a whiteboard at one end and a window at the other. I sat at the desk with the whiteboard behind me. It was five minutes to two. No one else was there. For a moment I panicked thinking I was in the wrong place. I checked my class list and room number. Finding I was in the correct room, I relaxed slightly. Just then the door opened and in filed several people. All of them were eighteen or nineteen years old, mainly young women with two young men as well. After a couple more moments all the seats were filled and the numbers matched those on my list. I was set to go.

"Welcome to 'Biblical Ethics' course code RE126. If this is not what you were expecting, then now is a good time to leave." I paused. A couple of people smiled at my poor attempt at humour to break the ice. "I'm Jack Turner, a part-time lecturer here and a practising secondary teacher in RE at South Coast Comprehensive, along the coast. Please call me Jack. Now let's see who we have got here." I looked up and smiled, hoping I was conveying a sense that I knew what I was doing.

"I know this is cheesy, but as I call your name please tell me something about you. Just to break the ice." There were some smiles and a little muttering, but no one objected. It quickly became apparent that the students were equally nervous. My first session was really to assess where their understanding was in terms of biblical knowledge. I began to ask them to tell me their favourite Bible story explaining why it was so and what could be learned from it. It soon became apparent that even though these were students studying religion, faith and practice for a degree in Religious Studies their biblical knowledge was patchy, to say the least. I relaxed slightly, realising that these young people saw me as the expert with insight and knowledge they did not have about biblical ethics.

As the weeks progressed, my confidence to teach at a higher level grew. Their understanding of key theological concepts was greater than I expected, meaning progress was faster. We enjoyed delving into the Decalogue, elements of other Old Testament laws as well as the ethics of Jesus, Peter and Paul as seen in the New Testament. The discussions were lively so I could develop their appreciation of the differences between the Old and New Testaments relating to law and grace.

"I'm struggling, Jack," said one student called Claire. "Does Christianity promote faith in Jesus or obedience to the laws in the Bible, there seems to be a contradiction. On the one hand, you have the Ten Commandments and the Old Testament laws, some of which, by the way, are bizarre! On the other, you have Jesus promoting love for your enemy and declaring himself to be the way to heaven. Which is it?" She held up her hands in a gesture of confusion. There were nods of agreement around the room.   I looked around the gathered students, "Does anyone want to offer a response to Claire's question?" I was hoping at least some had grasped the basics of Christian theology and ethics. We were only a few weeks into the course, so it was early days.   Silence fell across the small classroom and the proverbial tumbleweed floated across the room in my mind's eye.

"OK, let me try and explain it again." I made myself comfy in the seat and began. "Paul, in the letter to the Romans, sets out this exact point to convince the Roman Jews that adherence to Jewish law was not needed for Gentile Christians." A hand wavered in the room, not sure if she should raise it. "Yes, Caz." I paused a second and then continued. "Gentile?" she nodded in an embarrassed way. "Never be embarrassed by not knowing anything. We all have different levels of knowledge and understanding." I smiled at her encouragingly. "A Gentile is basically a non-Jewish person. The Church in Rome was a mixture of Jews, Greeks or Gentiles." She nodded and made a note on her pad.

"As I was saying, Paul sets out the case for faith in Jesus over and above adherence to the Old Testament law…" I continued to explain for about ten minutes. Occasionally questions were asked and I answered them.

"So simply put, the Law only reveals human sin, it cannot rescue us from it. It points out and shows us that we cannot restore our relationship with God through our own good work. It makes us realise our need of salvation. Jesus, his death and resurrection provide the means for sin to be forgiven and a relationship with God to be restored. Paul then explains what life is intended to be like when you put faith in Jesus. The law of love, God's love not our version, is the basis of life, not adherence to a set of rules. The Christian life is a response to God's love, seen in Jesus, not an attempt to be good enough." I sat back and waited for the questions. One of the young men who was called Mark piped up. "So, am I correct in saying that Christians 'do good'" he made speech marks with his fingers in the air, "not in an attempt to get into heaven, but as a response to receiving their 'ticket' so to speak." Again he made speech marks when he said ticket. I smiled at his use of language to express his thoughts.

"If you mean, they try to respond in loving ways to people around them because God loved them first, and Jesus died for them, then yes!" I wanted him to begin to use more appropriate terminology.

"So why does the Church teach about being good to get to heaven, if it is all about faith?" Mark was really thinking now.

"Excellent!" I was genuinely pleased that Mark was thinking this through. "That stems from the Roman Catholic Church in the Middle Ages attempting to control behaviour by scaring people into thinking their eternal soul was in danger if they misbehaved. To an extent they were right, but also they missed the Biblical truth of grace and salvation through faith; that any sin is forgivable if you ask and put your faith in Jesus. This is where Martin Luther and the Protestant Reformation come in." A few more questions followed that revealed the depth of their understanding. It was quite encouraging. *Maybe I can do this after all.*

As the weeks progressed their understanding increased and their final essays were pretty good. I had a mark scheme given by Rod Holding and it was a joy to mark work from students who really wanted to impress.

The postgraduate students were different. They were battle-hardened, some were straight from their degree and others coming late into teaching, men and women in their thirties or forties. Their questioning was more focused, their understanding of education clearer, they were more intense and passionate. I knew that I had to pre-empt as many of their questions as possible. The purpose of the course was to teach them how to teach RE, what it was like to be an RE teacher and some practical tips on planning and preparing for teaching practice. In doing this, I discovered that I actually knew a great deal about educational practice, what worked and did not. I knew a lot about how children responded to things, and how to engage them in activities in which they were not initially interested. I discovered that I was actually a good storyteller using stories and concrete examples to convey ideas and themes. This was a skill that I hadn't realised I was using every day.

"Let me put it this way, tell them a good story, with a personal slant that supports an idea you are trying to embed and the chances are they will remember the story and then connect the teaching to it. Our brains are hard-wired for stories, it is the way we learn about the world, ourselves, morality and ethics. Without stories, our lives would be very dull." I was responding to a question from a student in his early thirties who was coming into education after a time in the retail industry. He couldn't see the need for stories. "Why not just give them the facts to learn?" he had argued. I continued my defence of storytelling. "Why do you think Maths' exam questions have a little story attached to them rather than just a sum to answer? It makes it more intriguing and interesting." He nodded acceptance, but I wasn't going to let an opportunity for a joke go begging. "For example," I continued. "If Maggie has three apples and Johnny has four, they both give one each to Gita, how long does it take to get to Manchester on the train if it leaves at 9.15 am" There were smatterings of laughter and the occasional groan. Even my protagonist raised a smile.

"There, you see that is much more interesting and fun."

The three years I spent teaching part-time at Brighton were professionally fulfilling as well as thoroughly enjoyable, if not exhausting on a Tuesday afternoon. Not only did it provide good opportunities to cherry-pick trainees but it also gave me a personal boost to my confidence as a professional. After three years l took an opportunity to join SACRE (The Standing Advisory Council for Religious Education) and become part of the working party writing the new Agreed Syllabus for RE in East Sussex. This in turn led me to become involved in county training, delivering CPD on topics like assessing, identifying and recording progress in RE. Alongside this, I marked GCSE RE exams, an invaluable experience in increasing the department's grades. Little did I know that all this was a preparation for the next phase in my career, one which I never thought I would take - the step into senior leadership.

****

In teaching, it is not possible to focus on just one role. As a middle leader, you are expected to juggle multiple roles which develop your practice, serving to improve the lives and success of students as well as enhance the reputation of the school. Time is therefore split, often unevenly, between classroom practice, pastoral care, developing initiatives and involvement in extracurricular activities. Often it meant working at weekends or in your holiday time.

The fourth Thursday in August is always stressful and full of anxiety in secondary schools. It is of course the day that GCSE results are released to students. It is a day of joy and a day of tears, a day of relief and a day of despair, a day of hope and a day of regret. Students milled around outside in the playground having received their results. Staff mingled with them, congratulating or consoling, encouraging and counselling to ensure that every student left smiling, or at least with a sense that all was not lost.

Jackie Jones, the efficient, non-paid deputy in the RE Department, Penny Williams our newest recruit and I sat in my classroom poring over the first-ever set of whole cohort RE GCSE (short course) results. I had persuaded the Head Teacher, with the help of Martin Simpson, the deputy, to expand RE provision and provide every child with the opportunity to do RE GCSE. At first a short course, but with the plan to develop it into a full-blown RE GCSE. That had been two years previously and now the first results were in. Had we succeeded in our mission to broaden the horizons of our students? Had we managed to help them think spiritually, creatively as well as academically? Of course we had!

"Bloody hell," said Penny with a sense of disbelief. "65% A-C in our first year!" She grinned. I was pretty pleased myself. We needed a strong set of results to justify the faith put in us by the Head and governors, who had not been fully convinced it was a good idea to invest an extra hour of curriculum time in RE. "Not only that but 23% grade A/A*!" It was Jackie's turn to look up and declare our greatness.

"I told you… we are the Mary Poppins dept. Practically perfect in every way!" I smiled at my own joke and thankfully the others did as well. "Well done both of you, excellent results. Look at the breakdown. All our classes performed on a par. No one did significantly better or worse and we all have our share of top grades." I was brimming with pride in a job well done. Not only had we achieved results only 2-3% below English, Maths and Science but we had done it in only one hour a week. Full-course subjects get five hours over a fortnight. This was to be the start of the growth of the RE empire at South Coast Comprehensive School.

When the turnout for the 2001 General Election was so low, Tony Blair's government pushed through compulsory citizenship lessons into the National Curriculum. The plans had been on the back burner since the late nineties as resistance to the idea was strong. In my view, the natural place for delivery was of course in RE. This was my chance to expand the department further. With a plan in my hand and a PowerPoint on my memory stick, I attended the leadership team meeting where I presented a rock-solid case for expansion for all students not only to do citizenship in KS3 RE but also to extend the KS4 classes to teach GCSE Citizenship. With each objection raised, I guided them back to the law, to the National Curriculum and to the benefits of experts teaching it rather than overworked and time-constrained tutors.

"Well done Jack, I think they will go for it." Martin was quietly shepherding me out of the meeting, my presentation complete. "I can't see how they can refuse. This is government-led." I was excited and determined to get the development off the ground. Martin smiled one of his infectious smiles that tended to charm everyone who experienced it. "We will look at it seriously. I know that Paul is keen, but it is whether we can persuade the governors and the finance manager." Paul Hawkins, the Head Teacher, looked and sounded like a bouncer from a Glasgow red-light district nightclub. "I am happy to present to the governors if needed. Let me know! We need this Martin; the school needs it." *Maybe I'm laying it on a bit thick, but hey if you don't ask you don't get.*

The following September, there was a new subject in Year Ten, Social Studies. Three hours per fortnight. It was taught by a mixture of the RE team and other interested volunteers who were keen on Citizenship. We planned a curriculum that would deliver, RE and Citizenship GCSE as well as PSHE. It was tough going and there was some resistance from the less motivated students.

"Sir, why are we doing this? My mum says it's a waste of time and we should be doing more English." Tommy was a thick-set lad with a shock of long black hair that hung over his eyes.

He was constantly moving it so he could see. Unfortunately, one teacher made the mistake of commenting on that fact and suggested he had a haircut. What followed was a series of complicated phone calls and meetings, including with the member of staff, his union rep, the parents and the lad all in one room with Paul Hawkins. An embarrassing apology had to be made and the parents left smugly, having undermined the school and the teacher and ultimately negatively impacted on their son's education. He now believed he could say or do anything and teachers wouldn't react for fear of his parents. I sighed inwardly and responded to Tommy. "If I gave you three more hours a week of English, would you work in those hours, would it ensure you got an A grade?" Knowing how Tommy hated reading and writing, I thought I was on to a winner. I waited. His eyes narrowed as he struggled for a response. In the end, he just 'humphed' loudly and sat back in his chair. I leapt for joy inwardly but outwardly said, "Tommy, we all need to broaden our horizons, find out new things, get our brains working and thinking differently. We all have plenty to learn." He wasn't buying it but it stopped him from arguing for a week or two.

****

"Look, there is a clear formula the exam board uses to mark questions. If we teach the kids to write in a certain style, and as long as the content is accurate, they will pick up maximum marks." I was sharing some insights I had received from an examiner's training conference. It was early summer and the exam season was almost beginning.

"We can't confuse them," said Penny, "it is too late to change it now."

"I agree, but we need to start now with the Year Tens. I know we will see a significant increase in results if we do this." I was determined to implement some new strategies to improve exam grades.

"How about we use the English dept. PEE paragraph approach," said Jackie enthusiastically. "Just need to ensure that they reference Jesus, the Church or the Bible in their answers."

"Jesus, Church, Bible... Jesus, Church, Bible..." Penny was chewing the three words over, trying to think of a way to get these ideas into a format that kids could remember.

"J, C, B," she said out loud to no one in particular. And then it happened, that moment of genius, that fortuitous connection that is made in your mind.

"J, C, B, the big yellow diggers!" I said to them both.

"Eh?" said Jackie. Penny looked puzzled.

"JCB is the name given to commercial digging machines. Those things that dig up roads, move rubble etc. on building sites. You build using a JCB. We can build essays and exam answers using JCB." An idea was formulating. "We teach the kids to build their exam answers using the English dept. PEE paragraph that they already know, but we introduce a big yellow digger a JCB... Jesus, Church, Bible!" They began to catch on.

"Yes," said Penny," we can have pictures of big yellow diggers on the walls, to prompt them which can be in their books as well."

"How about we give them a set list of basic quotes or teachings, say three from Jesus, three from Church teaching and three from other parts of the Bible? That is their stock, go to set of quotes," said Jackie enthusiastically as she began scribbling down some of the basic quotations that we used regularly. We were on a roll. By the end of the meeting, we had a fully formulated strategy for improving exam technique. It not only included posters of diggers but also clearly taught ways to answer exam questions. We would also teach them the mark scheme so that they understood why some answers were better than others. It clearly paid off. The following year saw a 7% increase in top grades with more achieving grade A/A*.

The Mary Poppins reputation of the RE Department increased over the next five years. (Well in our eyes anyway). The exam results crept up to hit the dizzy heights of the early 70%, still in less time than a full course GCSE and the students were receiving two short course certificates. The department was contributing significantly to the whole school's results and student progress; we were also taking the lead in some CPD on marking and feedback. We were on the up!

"What's this for?" said Penny eying up the custard doughnuts I had bought. We were in a department meeting. "Just a thank you, for all your efforts this term. I really need to say thank you to you two a lot more. Without you both, this department would be nothing. You deserve it." I got up from my place walked around the table and hugged them both.

" Ooo…er vicar, you're making me blush," said Penny. Jackie nearly choked on her doughnut.

I loved my department - they made my job a joy. Yes, it was hard, yes it was stressful, and at times you wanted to throttle a kid and sometimes the Head Teacher. In the end, you didn't. You realised that the kid was just struggling to communicate and probably dealing with a lot of crap at home and the Head Teacher was no different from you; wanting the best for the kids but not always being able to get it because of constraints of budgets, government edicts and difficult governors. At the end of the day, you made a difference to some kids and that is all that counted.

CHAPTER FIFTEEN

Terry, the head-butt, the threat and the stolen laptop

One of the great things about being a pastoral leader in a school is that you never know what is going to happen on any given day. As Head of Columbus House at South Coast Comprehensive School, I was responsible for the welfare and academic progress of two hundred students aged eleven to sixteen. Invariably one or more of them were sent to my office each day for some behavioural or academic issue for me to resolve or mediate.

Terry was one of those boys who found school a real challenge. Some less sympathetic teachers might have called him "feral", "disturbed" or "a pain in the bloody backside" but I just felt sorry for him. Yes, he could be troublesome and disobedient, but his life outside of school was dreadful. He would have fitted into the cast of "Oliver" perfectly, as one of Fagin's boys. He did not know how to respond appropriately to people because he had never been taught to by his parent, who struggled herself. I sighed and smiled as Terry was handed over to my care by the "on-call" teacher.

"Sit down Terry and tell me all about it" He plonked himself down in a chair and stretched his legs out. He didn't usually say much to me and this occasion was no different. He shrugged his shoulders. He had been removed from maths for attempting to climb out of the window. He saw school more like a prison camp and he was "Hilts, The Cooler King" from the Great Escape, always looking for a way out. He spent a lot of time in solitary, in my office, or outside the Head Teacher's office. When he had arrived from Junior school, his TA (teaching assistant) had spoken to me directly to pass on strategic information that would help me and the SEND dept. support him appropriately. I recalled the TA saying quite clearly. "Be careful when you are walking in the corridor with him. Walk behind him, not in front, or he will mysteriously disappear. He is very slippery."

He sat silently, head bowed for about fifteen minutes. I was unable to get him to speak. As I worked at my desk, Martin Simpson popped his head around the door. "Can I have a word?" He noticed Terry sitting there quietly and added "Outside." I got up and left the office, standing in the corridor a few feet away from my office door. Martin and I chatted about Terry. Apparently, the reason he had tried to escape the maths room was that he had stolen a girl's purse from her bag.

"Ok, let's go back and talk to him. Let me start, Martin. For what it is worth, he does trust me, slightly." He nodded and we returned to the office. We had been outside for a minute maximum. Terry was gone. The chair was empty!

"Shit!" said Martin, "He probably heard us chatting and legged it." He turned and looked up and down the corridor. "He can't have got far. Call me if you see him." He patted his walkie-talkie. I stepped into my office, retrieved my walkie-talkie and locked the office after me. For the next thirty minutes, we scoured the school, investigating all the usual hiding places, including the girl's toilets. He had been known to elude staff by hiding in there. There was no sign of him anywhere. We rendezvoused at my office and I unlocked the door. There sat Terry, in the chair, legs stretched out and a big grin on his face. On my desk was the purse.

"What the…? How did you get in here Terry? I locked the door!" I was more than surprised.

"Are you sure you locked it, Jack?"

I gave Martin a stern stare. "You just watched me unlock it!"

Terry sat there grinning like the proverbial Cheshire Cat. "Come on then, Terry, how did you do it?" I was impressed and troubled at the same time.

"Have you got a master key?" chirped Martin from behind me.

Without speaking, Terry stood up, crouched down and crawled under the student work desk next to the door of my office. He poked his head out and grinned. "I never left, Sir."

"Is that the purse you took, Terry?" Martin was becoming 'bad cop' to my 'good'.

He nodded and hung his head. "I knew I wouldn't get away with it, once you locked me in the room." He looked at me then turned to Martin. "I heard you tell Turner that I took it. Then I got locked in." My heart bled for him. He was definitely a rogue, but he was a lovable rogue.

Later that day Wayne was sitting in my office. Wayne was a Year Ten boy who would rather be out on the street, wheeling and dealing, than be in school. He came from a traveller family, and he and his sister would often disappear for a few weeks, especially in the summer. He had threatened to stab another student who had made fun of his sister.

"I don't care," he said angrily, "he deserves it. He shouldn't talk about my sister like that." It was no use reasoning with him at present; he would not take in that his behaviour was equally unreasonable.

"Threatening people is wrong Wayne. We don't tolerate it here at school." I spoke in a gentle and calm way. I learned long ago that getting angry with certain children just provokes a mirrored response. "I know people," said Wayne in a style that was meant to intimidate me. "If I ask them, they'll stab him for me. I could get you stabbed too." He stared at me, his eyes still burning with rage. He was definitely trying to scare me. *It's not working Wayne; you don't scare me. I know you too well. You're all talk.* What I actually said was: "That's very interesting, Wayne, but that won't solve all your problems, will it? Anyway, you will miss me if you have me killed!" I smiled. He softened a little, his body began to relax, the anger in his eyes began to fade. I left him to sit whilst I got back to work at my desk. After several minutes I went back to sit next to him.

"Have you ever said anything nasty to anyone, Wayne?" I was taking a risk by asking. He looked at me oddly. "Of course I have, I'm no wimp!" The anger flared up momentarily.

"Did you ever think how your words might make others feel?"

He shook his head, "Na!"

"So really, Wayne, you are no better than that boy who talked about your sister, are you?"

"S'pose not." I could see him thinking, the cogs turning. "What you sayin'?"

"I'm saying, do you deserve to be stabbed for the nasty things you said?" I spoke quietly but firmly not wanting to arouse the anger in him.

"Wayne, your mum believes in the Bible, doesn't she?" I knew she claimed to be a devout Catholic.

"Yeah, an' so do I." He looked a bit defensive.

"Well, in the Bible, Jesus says that we should treat people how we want to be treated. So, if you don't want to be stabbed, you shouldn't stab others."

"S'pose so. But you just can't let people get away with stuff." Wayne was still determined to be right.

"No, but you can choose a different way to respond. You always have a choice." I stood up and went back to my desk. "I will leave you to think about it."

I never did get stabbed, nor did the boy. Wayne served his detention peacefully and I like to think that what I said to him made a difference. He never threatened to stab anyone else, but it didn't prevent him from finding himself in further trouble.

****

Pedro had been asked to sit in my office for his own protection. He was a relatively new boy in Year Nine, having arrived from South America. His English was good but his understanding of British school culture was lacking. He had upset a Year Ten boy, Andrew, by asking his girlfriend out. She, in turn, had told Andrew who had instantly sought him out at break time and started a fight. They had been separated by duty staff, but Andrew had escaped custody and was on the prowl seeking further vengeance.

Pedro had a bruised eye and was nursing a cold pack on it as he sat in my office. I was chatting with him, trying to ascertain exactly what he had done and what had caused the fight. Pedro was bemused. In his eyes, he had done no wrong. Andrew, a blond, good-looking lad, was full of fury and needed to reassert his alpha male status amongst his peers, who had laughed at him when Pedro had the audacity to speak to his girlfriend.

Suddenly the door to my office burst open and Andrew attempted to enter. Both Pedro and I jumped up. Pedro darted behind my desk for cover and I stepped toward Andrew. As he tried to enter I barred his way, placing my arms on either side of the door frame.

"Get out of my way! I'm going to f**king kill him" The rage in his voice was fierce. The red mist had descended.

"I can't do that, Andrew, you know that." I stood my ground at the door. I could hear other staff approaching in the corridor.

"I said… get out of my way." He started to push past me, first by grabbing my arm to move it and then by trying to sneak beneath it. Each time I manoeuvred myself to stop him from entering the room. Pedro was crouching behind my desk.

Andrew continued to push against me, trying to gain access to Pedro. I raised my voice a little to speak firmly.

"Andrew, that's enough! Step back." As Martin and the Headteacher arrived, I grabbed hold of Andrew's shoulders to keep him from forcing his way into the room. At that moment he stepped forward and head-butted me. The pain sliced through my head. I stepped back. Fortunately for me, his aim was out, he had landed his forehead not on my nose, but on my forehead. I shook my head and refocused. The Head and Martin had hold of a screaming Andrew. He was swearing, cursing and wriggling in an attempt to break free. I stepped forward and spoke to him. "Andrew, stop now before you make it even worse." He looked at me and saw the big red mark on my forehead and realised he had made a huge mistake. He slumped and stopped and allowed himself to be led away.

We sat in my office, Pedro with a cold pack on his eye, me with one on my forehead. "Are you sure you are all right?" Mary Johnson Deputy Head of House enquired. She looked concerned for us both. She handed me a cup of sugared tea. I sipped it and it soothed me. Nectar, working its way to my senses and relieving the stress. My body was in a slight shock, but the colour in my cheeks had returned. "I'm fine, really. I am more concerned with Pedro and Andrew, that we get this resolved."

"Leave that to me, you should go home!" I gave her a stare. There was no way I was leaving early. I wasn't even that bad, although my head did hurt a little. I finished my tea, took some paracetamol and went back to work.

Pedro took a day off to let his bruise come out. He was quite proud, but he had learned a valuable lesson about British school life. I never saw Andrew again. He spent the remainder of his time in education at another school. I hope he learned a valuable lesson as well.

****

As always, my office was a haven or a prison for students. On a cold winter's day, Sharon turned up at my office. Sharon was a (wayward) teenager who also had a younger brother in Columbus House. I had many dealings with both Sharon and Jason. On the occasions I had to speak with their father, he often reminded me that either of them could break my neck in one blow. They were both black belts in some martial art that I had never heard of. They had a challenging life. Their mother had passed away when they were young and dad struggled with his mobility and walked with sticks. He had brought them up to be independent and rely on no one. However, this was backfiring as both Sharon and Jason refused any support and help at school and both really needed it.

"I've been sent here by the office as I am late!" Sharon spoke with a somewhat harsh tone.

She plonked herself down in a chair and took off her large sheepskin-style winter coat. "I don't know what lesson I've got. Can I have a timetable?"

"How are you, Sharon? Your dad ok?" She shrugged, not wanting to engage with me. I tapped in a few details on my PC and pulled up her timetable. I clicked print and sent it to the photocopier in the staffroom a few doors down the corridor.

"Hold tight, I'll be back in a tick with your timetable. Try not to lose it, eh?" I smiled, trying to engage her on a social level. She just sat there.

I was back within a minute and handed her the timetable. She took it in one hand, stood and walked out, carrying her big winter coat folded into a bundle. I settled down to work for the rest of the lesson.

At the end of the day, Mary came into the office and sat down at her desk. "Where's my laptop?" There was concern in her voice. "Have you moved it?"

"No, I've not been in here since I locked up after Sharon went to class. That was after break time. I was on lunch duty after that. It's been locked all day." It had become practice to lock offices after a spate of petty thefts.

"Well it has gone, it was definitely here first thing. I was working on it." Mary was getting agitated. "All my data is on there. Everything!"

"Are you certain you didn't take it to your room?" I couldn't imagine how it had gone missing.

"The only other person who has been in here is Sharon. She left with me and I locked up. I can't see how she could have…" I stopped in mid-sentence. "I was out of the room for a minute whilst I printed her timetable. Surely she couldn't have taken it. I would have noticed!"

We were huddled around the TV monitor in the ICT office watching a playback of the feed from outside my office.

"Look, there's Sharon leaving my office. There is no laptop." I was genuinely puzzled.

"Look at her coat," said Mary pointing at the screen. Look how she's holding it."

"Tim, can you track her on the other cameras?" Tim was our ICT guy, the resident expert on all things computer, both hardware and software. He flicked a switch and a new playback started from the same time period. Sharon was walking down a parallel corridor. She stopped, looked around to see if the corridor was empty, then she knelt down laid her coat on the ground, unwrapped it and there was the laptop. She opened her big school bag and slipped it inside, put her coat on and carried on walking. The next camera showed her leaving the site and heading right up the street towards her home.

"I'll give Dad a call. Mary, can you call Linda at the police liaison and get her to go up to the house. The quicker we get there the more chance of retrieval." I was saddened by Sharon's actions. I knew the family struggled, but I also knew Dad would be mortified to see the CCTV footage. *You're throwing it all away Sharon, for what? A laptop?* I picked up the phone and began to punch in the numbers.

"She didn't have a chance to mess it up or even get into it. Linda was in the area, so was quick to respond." There was relief in Mary's voice. Her laptop had become her life and contained all her work and data on all the children in Columbus House. I was pleased for Mary but I was sad for Sharon, Jason and their dad. A family struggling to survive loss, illness and low income. There are times when you wished you could do more, but the reality is there is not enough money in the system or the staffing to support such families. The chances were, Sharon and Jason would continue the cycle of low income and low education unless, by some educational miracle, they chose to engage.

CHAPTER SIXTEEN

CPD and the fart

Continuing professional development or CPD for short is one of those things that teachers love or hate. If you are running it, you generally think it is brilliant. If you are new to teaching you are often keen to get heavily involved in it. If, like me, you have taught long enough to be teaching children's children, then you can take it or leave it. Sometimes CPD can be the last thing you need at that moment in time but, by the time it is over, it was worth it. You did learn something that developed your classroom practice; maybe you bonded with a new staff member, got to know a TA a little more or just enjoyed the food. At other times CPD can be downright awful. School leaders have the habit of inviting former teachers into school, usually ones who have been out of circulation for a while and have a book to promote, to let the rest of us know what they have discovered through new research. For teachers who've been in the classroom for a while, they know that in the words of Solomon "There is nothing new under the sun." Much of the modern CPD is a rehash of older ideas with further research and a wider evidence base. Still, it is good to refresh your practice and be open to new ways of doing things. I clearly recall deciding not to become like the four grumpy older teachers I saw on my first day in education. I had to be careful not to fall into that trap.

I sat in the hall listening to the speaker espousing the benefits of meditation, controlled breathing, sleep and a whole host of other well-being techniques and activities. This was going to be a long day! My mind wandered, which in fact was one of his well-being techniques, so technically I was paying attention. Every time he introduced a new technique to improve student and teacher well-being, I thought *that's in the Bible, that's not new!* I began searching my brain for memorized scripture to support my theory. They began popping into my mind...

Be still and know that I am God. Come to me all who are weary and heavy laden... do not be anxious about anything... they flowed into my mind until I began to lose track. I made a mental note to do my own research.

I looked down at the agenda for the day as the speaker continued to explain why it was not good to drink alcohol in the evening. *Seriously, you're talking to teachers.* I then noticed the next session after the coffee break.

Session 2. Practical experience of relaxation techniques. A Workshop for all staff

The drama department will lead different groups in a variety of relaxation

techniques that can be used in your classroom for your pupils or your own

personal benefit. Please see the lists by the door to discover which group

you are in and your workshop location.

I sighed inwardly. *Oh God, please no. I'm going to have to pretend to be a tree or some other stupid idea.* I generally found relaxation techniques rather stressful and had never discovered their benefits. This was probably due to my cynical attitude and the desire not to look like a complete numpty, sitting cross-legged on the floor, humming like an overheated circuit board. I could feel myself tensing at the thought of the session. I genuinely hated all those activities that the Drama Dept. love to do. As a secretly shy person, I was not keen on putting myself on show or doing things with which I was not confident. *Why do they assume that everybody loves to do this kind of stuff? THEY DON'T!* The morning was becoming a total loss for me. *What a waste of time.* I sat back in my chair and allowed my mind to wander. *I like to relax by playing sports, watching a film, spending time in prayer and going to church. I know how to relax; I don't need 'experts' telling me.* The rest of the session was wasted on me; I had lost interest.

I sipped my coffee and wandered over to the board to discover which group I was in and where I was to be subjected to the humiliation of icebreakers and 'fun' drama games. My thoughts reflected the grumpy old teachers from 1984 on my first day. I chastised myself. *Come on, Jack let go! Don't worry about looking like a fool, everyone else will be doing the same and having the same anxiety. Just get on with it and have fun. It's better than teaching 9X3 today!*

I filtered into the hall where my session was to be held. Bruce Stockman, the head of Drama was leading the session. There were about twenty of us. Bruce was about forty years old, slightly camp, seriously loud and bold; almost a stereotypical drama teacher, if there is such a thing.

"Welcome lovelies, take your shoes off and chuck them in the corner by the door," he pointed vaguely in the direction from which we all had just entered. "Spread out around the hall, find your own space and stand absolutely still and quiet." We fussed about taking our shoes off and muttered and chattered whilst we found spaces. I could see several female staff bunching together, wanting to stand next to each other, seeking security from friendships and gender. The men, I noticed, didn't speak much at all. Many of them looked downcast and uneasy. I felt their discomfort. *At least it is not just me.* When we were all in position, Bruce continued,

"Let your arms dangle loosely, shake them as if you're shaking off water." He demonstrated it for us. I watched carefully. The women engaged energetically, the men less so and with an embarrassed expression.

"Now, slowly lower your head so you are stretching the back

of your neck. Nice and slow. Keep your breathing steady, in through the nose and out through the mouth." All of a sudden you could hear people breathing, exaggerating their breaths. "Now lift your head slowly and turn it to the left and the right. Try to look over your shoulder." I followed the instructions and to be honest it felt good. I hadn't anticipated that. I was surprised. The cynic in me was being squeezed out with every neck stretch. Bruce led us through several more stretches and exercises, including some voice exercises. After fifteen minutes, I was feeling relaxed and ready to face up to anything. For the first time, I thought, *this really does work!*

"Okay everyone, shake those arms again!" We all did; this time I noticed more energy from the men and even a few smiles. I was almost converted to relaxation techniques when it all fell apart.

"The next set of exercises requires us to sit on the floor, cross-legged. Ladies if you are wearing a skirt or dress, either face away from the gents or sit in a more dignified way." There were a few mutters and one or two near-the-knuckle comments from the PE staff present.

"Crikey, no one wants to see your pants Lizzy!" grinned Phil from his shell suit. Lizzy was head of Girls PE. She was about fifty years old, an old school PE teacher. "What makes you think I'm wearing any?" Her response caused laughter around the room. Phil feigned being sick. "Please, say you're joking!" Their banter was friendly and not malicious. They had been working together for years, their time was often spent in one-upmanship. The atmosphere was truly relaxed but Bruce was getting a little irritated as his workshop was being side-tracked. "Come on, sit down, let's not lose the mood." People began to sit. I looked around me to ensure I was not going to sit on anyone nor be accused of staring at someone's knickers. As I did so, quite unexpectedly my buttocks released an enormous fart. It was huge and noisy. There was no way it would go unnoticed and it didn't.

"What the f**k was that?" Sam White the head of Science' voice boomed across the hall. He was laughing hysterically. So much so that he leaned back from his sitting position and hit his head on the parquet floor. He laughed all the more! I was mortified. Amanda Wyatt, the new head of Art, called to me in her Irish brogue, "Jack, my love, was that you? My God that was a beauty!" She collapsed against a fellow member of staff giggling like a child. The room was in chaos, there were giggles and laughter from all quarters. All pretence of adulthood was gone. We were all full-blown kids giggling at a fart. In the end, I had no option but to join in. I could feel that my face was flushed with embarrassment, but I had to save face somehow. All my dignity was gone; how could I regain some modicum of it?

"Sorry everyone, Bruce," I held up my hand in a gesture of apology. "It seems your relaxation techniques went too far!" I grinned trying to make light of this most embarrassing moment.

"No follow through, I hope!" Sam piped up, still giggling. The flow of giggles erupted again. I was beginning to enjoy the moment; the initial embarrassment was fading. I found it very funny but I could see Bruce was getting a little agitated.

"Sorry Bruce, really sorry! I genuinely wasn't expecting that!" I held up my hand again in apology, grinning like a naughty school kid. He smiled recognising that I was not wholly responsible for destroying his workshop. The human body has a way of taking over sometimes.

The staffroom door opened and in walked Martin Simpson, the Deputy Head. He strode up behind me and blew a massive raspberry in my ear. I jumped, not expecting it. "Bloody hell Simpson, you scared the crap out of me!"

"You should be used to that! I hear you can destroy a whole workshop with one fart! That's impressive." I was about to vent a reply when he held up his hand. "Now, now, remember, Jesus is watching!" He motioned to the ceiling with his eyes and pointed upward with his finger. He was grinning, enjoying the opportunity to rib me. I narrowed my eyes and stared hard at him. At that moment Jackie walked in and ruffled my hair, "All right windy?"

"Don't you start!" I was enjoying the attention, but if only it could have been for something positive. It was just after lunch and staff were preparing for the afternoon sessions on the well-being INSET day. There were a variety of workshops on meditation, Pilates, yoga, watercolour painting, creative writing and a host of other pastimes and hobbies. In truth, the most relaxing thing I could have done that afternoon was to tidy out my cupboard or catch up on some marking. That would have reduced my stress more than doing stretches or attempting to paint a landscape. Penny, the third member of the RE department, sidled up to me and linked her arm through mine and rested her head on my shoulder. She was always overly demonstrative and I found it uncomfortable. She looked me in the eyes and spoke softly to me. "Jack, I've been to the toilet, so I should be all right for the yoga this afternoon." She pulled away from me and scampered across the room giggling. "You sod!" I was laughing. "I thought you were being kind and compassionate? I'll have you sharpening pencils all afternoon!" I called in a mock authoritarian manner.

"What's all the fuss?" It was Linda Higgins, the other deputy head, it was her final year in teaching. Her role had changed recently to focus on staff training, including links with the universities and trainee teachers. She had organised the CPD today and was issuing feedback forms to staff.

"Jack, you can have yours now, rather than me put it in your pigeonhole." She handed me a feedback form. "Give poor Bruce a good comment, he was upset this morning. Apparently, someone ruined his session." I rolled my eyes and held my hands up "Mea culpa. Is there anyone in school who hasn't heard about my fart?”

“It will be a long time before you live this one down!” Linda smiled as she spoke. I shook my head in mock disbelief.

Penny, who was looking out of the window onto the carpark called across the room. “Hey, Jack!” I turned to acknowledge her. “Look here, South East Today have just turned up with a camera crew, they’re all wearing gas masks!” Several people in the room began to laugh, especially my closest colleagues, Martin, Linda and Jackie. I screwed up my feedback sheet and threw it at Penny. “Shut up and make your farty boss a coffee!”

It did indeed take a long time for the memory to fade. But even then, when, some years later, whilst visiting a neighbouring school I met up with Amanda Wyatt who was now a Deputy Head, she promptly reminded me of the day I farted in a CPD session. I am so glad to have made such a lasting impression on colleagues.

CHAPTER SEVENTEEN

Vive La France

I t was a fateful day when the school trip brochure appeared in my pigeonhole in September 2005. I was now Head of Year Nine, and academic and pastoral care was now done by year group. I had taken them on as new Year Sevens and would see them through all five years. The house pastoral care system had been relegated to a means for organising sports. I flipped through the pages as I sat at my desk one lunchtime. One trip stood out. The advertisement hit the spot.

"Treat your students to a post-SATs holiday to Disneyland Paris!"

As I read the advert and the details, I had a soft and mushy moment where I thought, *wouldn't it be great to take my year group on this holiday.* And that was it, I was consumed for the next ten months planning the best post-SATs holiday for my year group. Within a week I had gained approval from the senior team and governors to take one hundred students in two coaches on a weekend trip to Paris in early July 2006. With a provisional booking made, I set about the task of organising the biggest trip of my school career so far. Who would have thought that taking one hundred teenagers to France would be so difficult? I spent almost every spare moment on the phone with the company, to parents, checking the basics, like did they have a passport, did they get travel sick? Were there any medical conditions I needed to be aware of? My file grew fatter and fatter as the months passed.

"Jack, do you realise that the Sunday we are in Paris is the night of the World Cup Final?" It was two months before we were due to leave early on the Friday morning of 7th July. John Perkins, a science teacher and one of my Year Nine tutors, had popped his head around the office door. I looked at him in disbelief. How could I have made such a big mistake?

"We won't go all the way; we'll lose on penalties to the Germans in the quarters!" I tried to make it sound convincing, but there were many lads going who would be devastated and might pull out of the trip if England got to the finals. That afternoon I called the hotel where we were due to stay and spoke to Henri in reception. I remembered him from my free reconnaissance trip at Easter. I took my youngest son Sam and we stayed in what was effectively a Travelodge on the outskirts of Paris. We had a free day at Disney. Henri assured me that there was a television available to use and that it could be booked by my group. I booked it and gave a sigh of relief. *If we actually do get to the final, at least we can watch it.* We were actually due to go and see Wild Bill Hickok's Wild West Show, but I was sure that some of the boys would prefer to watch the football. I'd cross that bridge when I came to it.

It was a long first night after we arrived at the hotel. The kids were so excited that it was nearly 2 am before it was all quiet and I managed to crawl into bed. The staff and I had spent four hours patrolling the two floors of rooms that we had booked for us. At breakfast, the bleary-eyed staff were met by bright and excited teenagers, eager to get going. It was going to be a long weekend.

"Sir, what time are we leaving for Parc Asterix?" said Tommy, a slightly stocky lad with black curly hair. He was still chewing on his toast and a little piece flew out and nearly landed in my cereal. He didn't notice. I smiled politely at him. "9.30 on the dot. You need to be at the coaches by twenty past. Tommy, can you go round and remind everyone?" He nodded eagerly and pottered off to all the tables in the dining room. I had already done a morning briefing explaining the routine for the day. It couldn't hurt to have it repeated. The staff with me were excellent, taking control of most things, leaving me to liaise with the tour company, hotel and parks. I was so blessed to have such a great team with me. The day in Parc Asterix went without a hitch and they were overawed with the massive wooden rollercoaster Tonnerre De Zeus.

"Sir, it's awesome, there is a massive wooden rollercoaster. Come and have a look." Shelly was one of those girls who was popular, kind, hard-working and pretty. A rare breed. I was sitting quietly having a coffee and a pain au chocolat in one of the many cafés in the park. I was on duty. The kids knew where to find a member of staff at all times. We were on a rota an hour at a time to cover the eight hours in the park. I pulled a face, not wanting to leave the sanctuary of the café. Just then Kate, one of my colleagues, strolled up to relieve me. *Bad timing Kate!* I gulped down my coffee, picked up my pain au chocolat and headed off with a group of my students, led by Shelly, to observe the wonder that was Tonnerre De Zeus.

"Sir, what's happening tonight again?" Tommy was nothing if not consistent. He had forgotten the itinerary and he had a mouth full of chocolate. We were sitting on the coach on the way back to the hotel after a full-on day at Parc Asterix. I had not lost a student, there had been no injuries and as far as I could tell no one had fallen out with anyone else (So far!) For me, that was a winning day.

"Tommy, have you got a sieve for a brain? I told you in the briefing, you've all had an itinerary, and we had a big meeting about it all with your parents before we came. Surely you must remember something?" He was one of those loveable kids who were just a bit disorganised and needed constant reminders of everything. "And how much chocolate have you eaten today?" He shrugged. "Dunno? Three, maybe four bars."

"If you puke in the coach, I'll be cross." He grinned at me with chocolaty teeth. "We are going to have some dinner at the hotel, then we are off to central Paris for a boat trip on the River Seine and we will see the Eiffel Tower."

"Cool!" He turned and meandered back to his seat finishing his chocolate bar.

It was the evening and we were sailing down the Seine in the dwindling sunshine on a pleasure cruiser. The sights and sounds of Paris passing us by. It was warm and all the students were seated on benches on the top deck. As I strolled around ensuring they were not disturbing other passengers, I noticed several of the students waving at passers-by who were enjoying a walk on the riverbank. They waved back, it appeared to be an idyllic scene; children innocently waving. All of a sudden there was shrieking and laughter. Students pointing towards the riverbank. I turned to see what the fuss was all about.

"Look, sir!" said Sophie, a tall dark haired girl. She pointed to the riverbank. A man had dropped his trousers and was mooning. It was followed by two more young men on the bank. All three, pointing their bums toward the boat. The laughter was hysterical from the boat.

"Calm down! It's only a bottom!" I tried to play down the incident.

"Three bums actually!" Sophie replied, struggling to contain her laughter. As I continued to try and distract them from what was in essence a humorous moment I heard a shout.

"Leon, no, don't do it!" It was Kate, one of the other staff members. She was walking swiftly towards Leon. But it was too late. Leon had stood up turned his backside to the river bank and dropped his trousers and pants. He returned the moon. There were shrieks of delight and the word spread quickly so that kids ran from all around the top deck to see the sight of Leon mooning at French citizens.

Kate tried to stand between him and the railing of the boat to hide him from the riverbank. "For God's sake pull your pants up!" she shouted. All around her the kids were in fits of laughter. Cameras were out taking photos.

"What were you thinking Leon?" I scolded him as he buckled up his belt. He sat back down on the bench. Crowds of kids gathered around like footballers pressing the referee after a foul. I shooed them away and gradually other staff arrived to manage the students. I sat down next to Leon.

"What on earth did you do that for?" I was supposed to be cross with him, but I could see the funny side. It took a lot of composure to hold my nerve and be stern with him. "You promised me you would behave on this trip. You've let me and the school down!"

Leon had only just made it onto the trip. He was a loveable rogue, but his behaviour log at school counted against him. He had a history of disobedience and truancy, along with a short fuse. I had spoken clearly with him and his parents about expectations of behaviour before I accepted him on the trip. I was taking a risk. "Trust me Sir, I'll behave," he had told me with puppy eyes that could melt your heart. It was no wonder so many of the girls in the year fancied him. Up until now, Leon had been good to his word.

"Sir?" His face looked genuinely shocked that I was cross. "I couldn't let them get away with that. It was a matter of national pride! They threw down a challenge! What was I supposed to do? Ignore it?"

"Well yes, actually. That would have been a better option." *National pride? A challenge?* Inside my head, I was laughing. I could imagine what went through his mind.

"Anyway sir, look at the fun we've had. No one will forget this boat trip!" Leon just grinned triumphantly and took the adulation from his peers for the rest of the trip. I needed to sanction him for his misconduct, but he was right. It was a highlight and a memory made that none of his friends would forget. In the end, his sanction was more of a punishment for me than for him. He spent an hour in my company the next day in Disneyland Park.

As it turned out, England lost to Portugal on penalties in the quarter-finals, so the pressure was off and we could enjoy the Wild Bill Hickok show without worry. By the time we returned to our hotel the world cup final between France and Italy was going into extra time. I had planned a final night party for the students. The small conference room at the hotel was set up with chairs and a few tables and there was music. I supplied copious amounts of cola and lemonade plus sandwiches and cake. The eight staff took turns supervising whilst the rest sat around a small television in reception watching the football. Let me just set the scene a little more. We were staying in Paris on the night of the World Cup Final in which France was playing. The nation of France was on tenterhooks as extra time turned sour when Zidane head-butted Materazzi and was sent off. The nation's hero turned villain and ultimately cost them the title. Italy went on to win on penalties. The mood in Paris changed from celebration to mourning and frustration.

The party was petering out and many of the kids had gone to bed, exhausted after three long days. I was clearing up the detritus whilst other staff were supervising bedtime. Outside, the celebration fireworks for winning the World Cup were now the fireworks of discontent. Henri the receptionist appeared at the door.

"Monsieur Turner, there is a phone call for you at reception."

His accent was classic. I was puzzled.

"Mr Turner, it is Mrs Glover, calling from England, Tommy's mother. Is everything all right?" Her voice was filled with fear and panic. "Tommy has just phoned me to say that the hotel is under attack! Bombs are going off all around." For a second I thought it was a wind-up by one of the other staff with me. Just then a loud firework exploded outside the hotel. There was a small gathering of youths letting off bangers and shouting. There were car horns beeping in the distance and more fireworks. I understood.

"It's okay Mrs Glover, we are not under attack. Tommy has got the wrong end of the stick. It is just the local youth letting off fireworks. France just lost the World Cup Final. They were expected to win. There was to be a city-wide celebration. We are definitely not under attack!" I was trying not to laugh. For a moment there was silence on the phone.

"Oh my God! I am so sorry; I feel like such a fool. Tommy told me not to phone. Please don't tell him I called. He'll be so embarrassed." I could feel her embarrassment but understood her concern.

"It's fine, I won't say a word to him. I promise." I was dying to laugh but had to hold it together. I was faithful and kept the promise until the day the Year Group left South Coast Comprehensive. It made a great and embarrassing story as part of my final assembly for them.

It was early morning before the fireworks and beeping horns finally subsided, Paris had finally come to terms with their team's loss. I got to bed at about 3 am only to be up at 7 am for the long journey home.

I sat in a café in the *City Europe* shopping complex along with several other staff, enjoying a coffee and cake. We were exhausted. It had been a long four days and it was nearly over.

I DON'T CARE WHO STARTED IT

Just the ferry and one more coach ride and we were home again. The only downside was that it was straight back to work at eight tomorrow morning.

"Sir, sir!" the voice rang out. "Mr Turner come quickly!" I looked up and saw two girls running toward us. I stood up from the table and went towards them. They looked scared.

"What's happened?" I assumed that there had been an accident of sorts or a fight between students.

"It's Sophie," said the girl, whose name was Claire. She was out of breath. "We've been looking for you!"

"What is it? What's wrong?" I could see the panic in her eyes. Sophie was her friend.

"Sophie's been arrested and taken away!" There were tears in her eyes, she was panicking.

"Kate!" I turned and motioned to her. "Look after Claire." I turned to the other girl who seemed more composed. Her name was Hannah.

"Hannah, do you know where Sophie is?" She nodded "Yes, we went with her. The policeman told us to find you."

"Lead the way." I smiled reassuringly. "It will be fine, I am sure." *Sophie, what have you done?*

The gendarme was tall, dark-haired and sported a thick moustache. His uniform was pristine and I could not help but notice the large automatic pistol strapped to his belt. Sophie sat crying in a chair behind a desk in a stark interview room. We were inside the local Gendarmerie at *City Europe.* I held out my hand to greet the officer but he just stared at me. In his best English, he spoke. "Ziz is not a simple matter. Ziz girl is one of your students, yes?" "Yes, she is, her name is Sophie," I spoke firmly in response to his stern manner. He was not going to intimidate me. "Why have you arrested her? What is it you think she has done?" I stood next to her, hand on her shoulder in a protective manner. She looked up at me, her make-up streaked with tears. I was cross, both at her and at the gendarme.

"Pleaz, zit down. She is a thief. She stole from ze Carrefour supermarket." I took the seat next to Sophie. She looked at me briefly then lowered her head in shame. She had done it. *You stupid, girl.*

"Sophie was…er spotted… by our store detective and it was on CCTV. She tried to leave ze store before she had paid." His voice was gravelly and stern. His eyes were cold. He spoke as if she had committed some terrorist atrocity. I was expecting to hear that she had taken cash from the till or tried to take some item of clothing or even a TV. So when I asked, "What did she steal?" I was dumbfounded when the gendarme produced an item from his jacket pocket. It looked like a pair of scissors but with a strangely shaped pad where the blades should be. I turned to Sophie, then looked the gendarme in the eyes. "What on earth is it?" He pushed it across the table for me to take a closer look. I picked it up and saw a tag. "Recourbe-cils" with a price of €3.20. I was none the wiser. I made a face that indicated I was confused. The gendarme picked the item up and held it towards his eye. "Zey curl ze eyelash."

For a second I was dumbstruck. Then I got really cross. I turned to Sophie and spoke harshly to her. "What were you thinking, Sophie? What possessed you to do such a stupid thing? Had you run out of money? Couldn't you borrow some?" I took a deep breath before I said something I would later regret. I turned my attention to Inspector Clouseau sitting opposite us. "Was all this really worth it? Bringing her in here? Look at her she's a kid. It's €3.20 for heaven's sake! Just take it off her and kick her out. Why make all this fuss?" I was tired, cross and just needed to get home.

"You want to prosecute her, for this?" I waved a hand toward the curlers on the desk. "Seriously."

"Monsieur, it is ze policy of *City Europe*. Sophie 'az committed a crime." He pulled out a form and wanted to take down details.

"No, this is nonsense. We are on the ferry in ninety minutes. We will be gone. Sophie is never coming back here." I pulled my wallet out of my pocket and dropped a €5 on the table. I stood up. "Come on Sophie, we're going." I grabbed her hand as she got up and began walking toward the exit. "Monsieur!" His voice was sharp and stern. I turned to see him standing, hand on his gun. In his other hand, he held out the eyelash curlers. "Zey are yours now!" I rolled my eyes at the ridiculous situation, took them and left.

"Sir, I am so sorry, please sir!" she pleaded. I was almost dragging Sophie down the concourse back to the café. "Don't speak to me Sophie, you are in so much trouble!" I plonked her down in a chair next to Kate and the other staff. "Sit there and don't move!" I had a face like thunder and a voice to match. Kate looked up at me in concern. "Jack, what's happened?" I walked away a few paces and as I did so the whole scene replayed in my head and I began to see the ludicrous nature of it. My heart rate began to drop and the adrenaline ebbed away. I felt in my pocket and pulled out the eyelash curlers. I shook my head. *Bloody stupid thing to do. He had a gun!* I began to laugh.

Sophie spent the rest of the journey sitting next to me, crying and sniffing. Her friends rallied around her trying to give her comfort but for those outside her circle of friends there was a mix of disappointment and "there but for the grace of God..." She was excluded for a day for bringing the school into disrepute and banned from further school trips. The eyelash curlers? Well, they found a new home in Sandy's make-up bag!

The coaches were queuing to board the ferry, nothing was moving yet. Most of the kids were sleepy, the rest hyper on chocolate and cola. My mobile rang, it was Kate, the leading staff member on the other bus. "Jack, we have an issue here. A possible medical emergency."

"I'm on my way!" I felt sick in my stomach. We had got this far without any medical issues. Picking up my bag containing the folder with all the pupil details and medical forms, just in case, I hopped off the coach and ran to the next one down.

"It's Hayley! She seems to be going into a diabetic episode. She is semi-responsive and talking gibberish." Hayley was the only diabetic on the trip. She was a smart girl, who generally managed her condition without fuss. I went down to her seat on the bus. The other staff had evacuated the bus to give her space. They were doing a great job managing the students who had a habit of making everything into a drama. One girl was crying, being comforted by three others, who looked anxiously on.

"Do we know if she has eaten correctly today? Has she checked her sugar levels?" My heart was racing and my stress increasing.

"Last time I checked in with her at lunchtime she was ok, she had just tested." I could see the concern on Kate's face. She was responsible for Hayley's welfare being the official medic on the trip. I looked at her and spoke gently. "Hayley, it's Mr Turner. Have you had your meals today?" I could see her pupils were dilating and she was not responding. She smiled weakly before closing her eyes.

"Call the paramedics! Kate get her insulin pen and give her a shot." Kate rummaged in Hayley's bag and pulled out the insulin pen. John, another staff member rushed off to speak to a gendarme, who quickly called the paramedics. Kate primed the pen and thrust it into Hayley's thigh, holding it in until the full dose was released.

"She's got her packed lunch, here, unopened, and her drink is only half gone." Kate was now searching her bag to see if

Hayley had been on top of her food intake today.

By the time the ambulance arrived and two delightful French paramedics examined Hayley, she was awake and chatting. She munched on a biscuit and looked sheepish.

"I'm happy to stay behind with her," said Kate. The paramedics wanted to take her to the local hospital for a check-up. However, the ferry was due to leave in 30 minutes.

"That's great, and thank you, but I have just spoken to Hayley's mum. She says that once the insulin kicks in Hayley usually recovers very quickly. She should be okay to travel. She says thank you for spotting it and being so quick to act."

The paramedics stood patiently waiting. Hayley was on a gurney by the ambulance. All the kids on the coach stared out of the window. I went to tell the paramedics the outcome of my conversation with mum. They seemed happy but still gave Hayley one more check before signing her over to me.

"I'm not sure I can walk yet; I still feel wobbly." The colour had returned to her cheeks and her eyes were normal.

"No problem! If you will permit me, I will carry you on to the coach." I looked at her and smiled.

"Go for it, sir!" I scooped her up and she clung to me, arms around my neck. There was a massive cheer from the coaches and Hayley waved to them all.

As the bus pulled up outside the school in the early evening sunshine, I was relieved. *Thank goodness that's over. Remind me never to suggest something so stupid again!* In truth, we had a great time. I enjoyed it and so had all the kids. New memories were made, new friendships forged and potentially the initial development of decent human beings. Well that's what I was telling myself. It was all worth it.

CHAPTER EIGHTEEN

Martin

Martin Simpson had been at South Coast Comprehensive longer than I had. He had started as a PE teacher and done most jobs including Head of Department and House Head. He was a good Deputy Head and lived for the school. We had become great colleagues and good friends. We shared the same outlook on education, which included ensuring that all children were given opportunities to shine in whatever sphere they could. We spent time discussing religion and faith; he had rejected the faith of his family and considered himself a Humanist. He would bombard me with facts and figures about evolution and the cosmos and I would respond with scripture and explanations of Genesis that gave him pause for thought. We would debate the merits and faults of our respective football teams, Leicester City and Fulham, both having torrid times until the early 2000s when they began to enjoy some success.

Martin was my go-to man for support with anything to do with the curriculum. He was a supporter of RE and PSHE, having taught both. He supported and backed me when I introduced the whole cohort RE/Citizenship at GCSE. Together we took on whole school activities such as "Enterprise Weeks" where students devised a business plan in four days and presented it to real bank managers. We played together in the staff football and cricket teams, and our kids went to the same junior school. When he died suddenly, it rocked the school and changed the direction of my career.

****

It was a cold, crisp Sunday evening and I had just returned from an evening service at church when the phone rang. Sandy answered it.

"Jack, it's for you. It's Paul." She held out the phone for me to take. "Paul who?" I queried.

"Your boss, Paul!" I pulled a face of bemusement and took the phone from her.

"Hi," I wasn't sure what to call him, he never called people at home.

"Jack, I have some sad news. It's Martin Simpson, he died this morning." He paused to let the news sink in.

"What? How? An accident?" My head was spinning; I had only spoken to him on Friday after school. We were making plans for a meeting next week.

"He was playing football for the Accies." The Accies were the Brighton University staff team, The Academics, they played in a local Sunday League. "He just collapsed on the pitch."

"I don't understand, he was so fit and healthy. What about Shelly?" They called her straight after they called the ambulance. By the time she got to the pitch, he was gone." Paul's voice was wavering. He and Martin were close. A tear welled up in my eye as I thought of Martin. Memories flooded into my head. All the things we had done together.

"I am so sorry, Jack, I know you two were good friends."

"You also, Paul. What are you going to do tomorrow? Anything I can do to help, please let me know. Use me, I want to help." We ended the conversation; I put the phone down and hugged Sandy. I was lost for words, my brain felt scrambled. *How could he be gone? He was fit, sporty and only about five years older than me.* A tear leaked from my eye and dripped onto Sandy's jumper.

The next few days passed in a blur. The initial staff meeting on

Monday was the most difficult I have ever experienced. There were tears and several staff went home, unable to manage their own grief as well as that of the students. It was followed by a series of assemblies led by Paul, who conveyed the news to all the students. The school had a muted atmosphere all day, and students looked shocked and dazed by the news. Staff were on hand to support those who were visibly distressed and County Hall provided grief counsellors who were available all week.

His death left a huge hole in the life of the school. His personality, presence and skill were sorely missed. The school was closed on the day of his funeral, which was attended by over two hundred people, including former staff, students and of course family and friends. It even made the local paper, such was his influence locally.

"I keep wanting to go and talk to him. I need to ask him for help." I sat at my desk in the office I used to share with Mary. She was now a Year Head in her own right. She sat in a comfy chair opposite. Her mug of tea steamed. "I know what you mean. He always had a solution. Always a smile and a way of dealing with you that made you feel supported and valued." We were reminiscing about Martin, as many staff were doing on regular occasions. It seemed to help the healing process. "Yep, despite being a massive pain in the neck, on so many occasions, he was a great friend and Deputy Head." Mary grinned at my description of Martin. She nodded, understanding that our relationship had been one of banter, insult and deep respect.

"Have you seen the advert for his job? It's up on the board and goes out in the TES* this week." Mary's comment made Martin's death seem final. He wasn't coming back. It had been over a month since his death and funeral and the school was coming to terms with the tragedy and was ready to move on.

"Yeah, I saw, they are taking the opportunity to do a bit of a reshuffle and develop the structure. Apparently, we are going to have 'Directors of Learning' as well as an extra Deputy. How are they paying for all that?" I was secretly curious about this new role as I was becoming slightly weary of dealing with student behaviour, progress and the seemingly endless stream of parents wanting to grumble about 'poor Johnny's unfair detention', or the unreasonable decision to exclude little Suzy for repeatedly slapping a Year Seven around the head. *Maybe this is an opportunity for me to make a change. A new direction. After all, I've been doing this role as Head of Year for fifteen years. Time for a change.*

"The big news is, that both Linda Higgins and Sam Lovejoy are retiring and Choudri is off to be a Deputy Head in Wandsworth. That's a big chunk of the leadership team. Paul has money to play with and wants to change the feel of the team." Mary always seemed to know what was going on before anyone else.

"How do you know all this? Where do you get your information from?" I was constantly amazed by her knowledge of what was going on at the senior level in school. "How do you do it?" She smiled innocently. "It helps to be best friends with the Head's PA." I laughed. We continued our post-school wind-down, before the rigours of department meetings.

*TES =Times Educational Supplement

Martin would always remain one of my favourite work colleagues. His wit, his passion for the children and his desire to see the best for them was second to none. He had been a massive help to me over so many years and I vowed to take what I learned from him, forward in my career. I was forty-six years old, I still had time to make a difference.

"I think you should do it," said Sandy, flicking through the paperwork relating to the job of 'Director of Learning for the

Human World'. "It sounds like a grand title, and it is on the leadership pay scale."

"It's basically a faculty head for Humanities. With an extra leadership role attached. I'd be overseeing the development of the curriculum in History, Geography and RE, monitoring progress and being responsible for the implementation of school strategies in the 'Directorate.'" I was quite excited but at the same time guilty.

"I feel bad about it. If Martin were still alive, this job probably wouldn't exist. I wouldn't even be considering a change." Sandy snuggled up next to me on the sofa and rested her head on my shoulder. "If Martin were here, he'd be helping you write your application. You must go for it. You have worked hard; you've been a success in every role. Why not have a go at this? I am pretty sure you can do it." She kissed me on the cheek. Just then my eldest son Joe walked into the room. He dumped his bag on the floor and, noticing the school logo, picked up the papers from the coffee table. He was home for the weekend from Uni.

"New job. Eh? Look at that salary! Does that mean you will give me an allowance?" He smirked.

"I haven't even applied for it yet! Slow down. And no, it doesn't, I'm already paying for your accommodation, fat chance of getting pocket money." I stood up and gave him a big hug.

That evening I began the process of drafting an application for the role of 'Director of Learning for the Human World.' It was a decision that would alter the course of my career and bring much joy and no less frustration.

****

"Congratulations, Jack!" Paul Hawkins, the Head teacher, stood up moved around the table, and stuck out his hand to shake mine. I had just accepted the role of 'Director of Learning for the Human World,' after a day of rigorous interviews. I had been one of five interviewees, all of whom I thought were better than me. What swung it my way was the student interview. A panel of six students interviewed each candidate and fed back to the Head teacher. They asked me to tell a joke.

"Mr Turner," said the Year Eleven Head student, "please could you tell us a joke." I was a little taken aback, I had not expected that. Fortunately, I am blessed with a "dad-like" sense of humour, so jokes often flow freely. "Of course." I pulled an old Tommy Cooper joke out of the bag. "There were two fish in a tank, one said to the other; 'You drive and I'll man the gun.'" There was a moment when I thought it had missed the mark, but then they all groaned. The rest of the interview was a breeze after that, they knew I could be trusted.

"So, Jack, the plan is to have you up and running in your new role after Easter, this gives you plenty of time to settle in before September. You'll be busy, Penny is already moving on and I hear Jackie is applying to work at County Hall for the Careers Service." I nodded. I knew about Penny; she was off to teach sixth-form RE at the local college. Jackie had asked me to be a referee but I had not heard any further news. I could have a whole new RE Dept. in September.

As it turned out there were changes all over the school and by the time September arrived, the Human World Directorate was over sixty per cent new staff, and the senior team, of which I was now a part, was almost all new faces. Not only that, but the new Humanities block was ready and I would be taking over new rooms and a new office.

As the summer holiday arrived and Sandy and I went off on a special 25th Wedding anniversary holiday, I felt quite nervous about September, it felt like I was starting at a whole new school. *I hope I haven't jumped out of the frying pan into the fire.* I had a nagging thought that I had bitten off more than I could chew.

PART THREE
The leadership years
2009-2021

CHAPTER NINETEEN

The times, they are a-changin'

(Bob Dylan)

I walked into room 211, one of the new specialist Humanities rooms. I was nervous. I had sat through two different senior meetings and a staff meeting, where the Head had gone through the results and set out the vision (again). The tension in my body had risen as the morning progressed. It was INSET day in September 2009 and I was the new Assistant Head Teacher, Director for the Human World (a fancy way of saying Humanities). I had an agenda to get through that had been set at my 'Directors meeting' earlier but I needed to set the tone. Most of my staff were new, I had just started the role, so it was up to me to dictate how I was to lead this team. *Deep breath Jack, you can do this.*

"Morning all, I hope the morning has gone well so far." I settled myself into the empty seat next to the desktop PC. The projector was on, displaying the school logo and a picture of the front of the school. *Very corporate.* "Please help yourself to brownies, I persuaded Sandy to make some last night. A welcome gift for you." Sandy's brownies were always crisp on the top and gooey in the middle with chunks of choc chip to bite on. Everyone always loved them.

"Oh my God, they're great," came the muffled voice of Cassie the new Head of RE. This was swiftly followed by mutters of assent from everyone around the table. "Exquisite!" "So gooey," "I love them, what's the recipe?" I smiled a chocolatey smile, *round one to me.* From then on Sandy's brownies were the stuff of legend, baked each term as a treat, to encourage, embolden and comfort the Humanities staff.

"Let's get on," I said in a semi-formal way. The room settled down quickly into a rhythm of eating, drinking and listening. It was comfortable, the way I liked it.

"Before we start on the main agenda, I just want to say welcome to our new staff and welcome back to the rest. It is great to see you all here. Let's go round and do some introductions. Tell us your name, role and three words that sum up your summer. I'll go first." I paused for dramatic effect. "Jack Turner, Director for Human World: anniversary, holiday, Africa." There were a few oohs and aahs. I looked at the person on my left.

"Cassie Brandon, Head of RE and PSHE: comics, cats and Star Wars. I know that's four but you can't separate star from wars." People laughed and smiled. *Perfect.* Cassie was assertive and strong-willed. She was a Buddhist, practised kickboxing (which I could never quite understand) and was a great teacher. Already she had plans to develop and expand the department.

"Karen Cooper, NQT in the RE Dept; travel, Prosecco, boyfriend." Karen had trained at the school the previous year, she was already a top-class practitioner. Karen was enthusiastic, bouncy, a stylish dresser and pretty, as noted by all the boys in the top two years.

"James Thompson, Head of Geography: cycling, camping, festivals." Again there were oohs about the festivals and questions related to them.

"Keep going!" I encouraged.

"Amy Watson, Lead Teacher and Head of History: Brighton FC, walking holiday and pubs." Amy had been at the school many years, we had shared several adventures, and we also shared similar educational values. Amy was often outspoken about the direction in which the school was going.

The introductions continued at a pace. Clem Vine and Sue James introduced themselves as part of the History department; Linda Mason and Carole Jones to the Geography department. As the meeting progressed, I realised that this was a high-performing team with clear and resolute core educational values. On the one hand, we would gel well as we shared a similar outlook, but, on the other, I foresaw the potential for conflict with the senior team over management issues and whole school decisions. These independent and critical thinkers would not take poor leadership lying down. I had my work cut out to convince them I was up to the task of guiding them through the current educational landscape and keeping their values intact.

****

"This seems very restrictive Jack, I can't see why we need to teach in this formulaic way." Clem, the unofficial second in command of the History Department was becoming irritated. We had been bouncing the idea of a set lesson format around the Humanities meeting for about thirty minutes. "It is designed to show clear progression in a lesson and provide an opportunity for Assessment for Learning (AFL). It is what Ofsted are recommending, or so I have been told." I was a little sceptical that it had actually been an Ofsted directive, but it had been sold to me as that by the core leadership team of the school.

"I get that, Jack, but I just think there are other ways of doing this without restricting our planning to a basic three-part lesson." Clem was on a roll. "What if I need to show a documentary or film? I can't do that if I have to have a starter, middle and plenary. You can still do AFL without those three parts, just stop the film and ask pertinent questions." There were nods from the Geography Department.

Cassie stepped in. "I think it works well, most of our lessons could be adapted over time to fit the model."

"Not every lesson needs to fit the model, but we have to move in this direction. When observations or inspections happen, the expectation is that you follow this model." I was trying to steer a middle course. The new model of lesson planning made sense up to a point. It did encourage variety, AFL and made room for progression and stopped lessons from being monotone, passive and teacher-led. However, for the more creative teacher, they could be restrictive, not allowing for innovation, surprise or going deep into a topic. AFL and three-part lessons were top of the educational agenda and it was my job to implement them across my team. Not surprisingly they had strong opinions. *I wish I was leading the Maths Department; they just seem to do as they're told!*

"This is good practice Clem, it will encourage a more balanced style of lesson and ensure a greater level of participation from students." Amy spoke with her Lead Teacher hat on rather than as a colleague in the History Department. "The research suggests that this style of lesson and greater use of AFL techniques will produce faster and more sustained progress."

"Oh okay, but I'm not going to re-plan every lesson in this style." She was both frustrated and resigned to the outcome at the same time. She sank back in her chair and folded her arms.

"Clem," I said encouragingly, "no one is expecting you to. You know as well as anyone that nothing remains constant in education. This is the current trend, we should run with it, see how it goes and evaluate it. If it turns out it makes no difference, well then… we can review it." I was making that last part up, I didn't have the authority to say that, but it seemed to make sense. Clem was great, a fine teacher with a strong heart for student welfare and a passion for History. However, she found change a challenge, especially when the benefit was not obvious. It wasn't that she was opposed to change, it was just that change for change's sake was not a good enough reason for her, so she fought it.

I slumped myself down in a chair in the staffroom and stretched out. It was the end of the first week back and I was already shattered. Clem sat down alongside me. "Sorry for being a pain in the arse in the meeting on INSET day," she said with genuine feeling.

"It's no problem, I would rather you spoke your mind and we talked about everything, however difficult, than you just kept quiet and became resentful about stuff."

She smiled. "Thanks, that's what I like about you. You listen and even if we can't change your mind, at least you listen and understand. It's a strength. I get the feeling some of the others on the senior team are not so willing to listen. I hear there was a row in the English meeting and they all got told to 'Do as they're told!'"

I raised an eyebrow, I had not heard that. "Well, that's something to be thankful for! Coffee?" I stood up and walked over to the kitchen area. "Who keeps stealing all the blooming teaspoons? It's only September and they're all gone!" I began scrabbling around in the drawers searching for an elusive spoon.

"Tell me about your plans for the department, Cassie." Cassie and I were in my office having a line management meeting, having been through the usual progress and data elements, highlighting underachievers, recent outcomes, plans to rectify and any staff issues, we were now on to the interesting part of the meeting.

"Well," she said with a conspiratorial tone, "Karen and I have been exploring how we can develop the department. We believe that with all three of us, and one part-timer, we could deliver not only whole cohort GCSE full course but also improve our PSHE delivery. We would need five hours over the ten-day timetable..." I raised an eyebrow, a bit like Roger Moore does when he is playing James Bond.

She regaled me with facts and figures for thirty minutes, setting out how it could be achieved through a mixture of changing hours in KS3 and improving KS4 provision so we could deliver top-class RE/PSHE across all five years leading to a GCSE qualification for everyone. "Oh, and by the way, we want to call it Philosophy and Ethics."

I was curious. "Why?"

"It removes the instant stigma that RE has and changes the emphasis from religious teaching to critical thinking. We still deliver the SACRE curriculum but the emphasis is on developing a more critical approach rather than just 'learning about' and 'learning from.'" She was quoting the SACRE attainment targets. She wanted the children to have a better experience than just 'learning about'. This was all about thinking independently and learning to debate, argue and empathise.

"Put a detailed plan together and let's present it. With luck, we could be up and running for next September. I love it!"

Cassie beamed at me, looked over her glasses and spoke; "I want us to be the best in Sussex for both RE and PSHE, I know your background and what you have done here, so I need you with me."

"Cassie, I am with you all the way. Your role is to convince the senior team; I have to balance your interests against those of the wider school vision. But to be honest the more 'Philosophy and Ethics' the better in my book."

I felt like I was settling into my new role well, my reduced teaching load gave me more time for other leadership duties such as running line management meetings, attending other strategy meetings, detention duties and of course the obligatory break time duties and ON CALL. For the uninitiated,

ON CALL is the emergency service of the school. For every hour of the day, a member of the leadership team or pastoral team is ready to respond to any emergency that might crop up. This usually involved patrolling the corridors and popping into classrooms to unofficially monitor classroom practice and student behaviour. However, most of the time you dealt with kids who were feeling ill or being disruptive.

Mosmil or 'Mos' was ethnically from Bangladesh, although he had been born in London but his family had moved south to the coast. They ran an excellent restaurant in town. I walked into the classroom where Mos was studying Ethics with Karen Cooper, my walkie-talkie in hand.

"Ah! Mr Turner, thank you. Mos is feeling ill and not really engaging with the lesson." She indicated where Mos was sitting. His head was down on the table resting in his hands, his elbows spread wide. "He says he feels sick, but strangely he often feels sick in my lessons." Karen smirked and a few of the kids around smiled. Mos was not a keen learner. He was capable but was not interested in anything but making money. However, he had yet to recognise that a good education would increase his chances of wealth in the future.

"Yes, I see, I have heard that Mos also feels sick in English, Maths and Science too. Very strange. Perhaps he is allergic to school?" There were more smirks from the class who knew Mos to be one of those who tried to fool teachers on a regular basis.

"Come on Mos, sit up, let's take a look at you." I knelt down by his desk. Mos raised his head from the table. He looked a little green as if he were about to faint. "Have you eaten or drunk today?" He nodded weakly. *Are you playing me for a fool or are you really ill?* I thought it wise not to risk it. He could sit outside my office with a glass of water. "Can you give him some work, Miss Cooper, please? She scurried around for a worksheet as I collected his book and equipment. Slowly Mos got up and we left the room. I was expecting him to perk up immediately after leaving, his plan to evade work having succeeded but he didn't. By the time we got to the stairs, he was leaning on the wall.

"Sir, I really don't feel too good."

"What is it Mos, where does it hurt?" I was beginning to wonder if he was actually ill.

"I think I am going to be sick." With that he leaned over the top of the stairs opened his mouth and a deluge of vomit erupted from it. It kept coming like a volcano in full lava mode. It flowed down the stairs like a river of yellow, chunky, viscous and smelly liquid. I had to work hard not to join him. I retched a couple of times, keeping my mouth closed for fear of adding to the mess. I had never seen one person produce such an amount of vomit in one go.

"Mos, don't move!" He was about to go downstairs towards the medical room. He would have slipped and caused even more chaos. He retched again and a further explosion of chunky yellow liquid erupted from him. The stench was almost overpowering. I turned away and took a deep breath. I flicked the switch on my walkie-talkie to channel one and called for the site team. "Andy, are you there? Andy, we have an emergency in the Humanities corridor south stairs, a student has vomited a bucket load of sick!" There was a quick crackle of static and Andy replied: "On my way, just need to get the trolley." The school had an emergency trolley loaded with equipment for just such emergencies. *Poor Andy, wait 'till he sees this lot, it'll take ages to clean. Rather him than me!*

"Right, Mos. Any more to come out or are you okay to get to the Medical room? I need to stay and stop anyone using the stairs. I will let them know you are coming; the nurse will meet you. Go the other way along and down and round past the hall." He nodded weakly. I called the medical room and advised the nurse of his imminent arrival. I watched him traipse along the corridor. I could hear the sounds of classes packing away and glanced at my watch. "Seriously?" I bemoaned the end of the lesson. Slipping back into Karen's classroom I asked her to guard the top of the stairs and send people back down the corridor.

"At least he really was ill and not trying to skive the lesson, poor lad."

"Wait until you see the mess, then you can say poor Mr Turner, I had to witness it!" Karen laughed. I picked my way down the stairs trying not to step in Mos's churned-up stomach contents and stood at the bottom of the stairs just as the bell went. The next five minutes were hell. The next three sentences were on repeat.

"No, you can't go up there!"

But sir, my class is just there, please…"

"No you can't go up there, please go around. The stairs are closed."

It was the start of the summer term and I sat in a progress meeting. I hated these meetings with a passion, they seemed such a waste of time and in my opinion, there was a smarter way of sharing this information. The premise was this; the names of identified underachievers from the most recent data capture were on screen for all to see. The subjects in which they were not making progress were highlighted. A traffic light system was used to identify them. The reds being the most significant underachievers. The spreadsheet on the screen was filled with names and blocks of red or amber with a smattering of green below subject headings. Each director had to give an account of why a student was underachieving and what was in place to support them. Now don't misunderstand me. The principle was sound; it was just the methodology of the meeting that I found to be poor. The meetings often lasted for at least two hours after school and Directors went through their identified students explaining in detail what was being done for them. There were various stages of intervention which were assigned to these students and time was spent deciding to move students up or down the various stages. What bugged me the most was that Humanities was generally fourth or fifth in line by which time no one cared anymore, they just wanted to go home. I would sit and listen to endless stories of students and anecdotes about them, not really caring what Maths or English were doing to support a particular student. I knew what my departments needed to do, so why did I need to know what everyone else was doing? It would frustrate me; I could have been doing something more useful. It was about 5.50 pm on a beautifully sunny Spring afternoon when at last it was my turn to share my data and reveal our department strategies. I was in mid-flow:

"… so with Francesca, she is struggling with her essays, this is what is causing her low marks in assessments. We have put in place…"

"Ah, yes Francesca, there is an issue here, she is in trouble with me because of her uniform…" Andrew Potter, the Senior Assistant Head Teacher butted in. "She has consistently been wearing the wrong shoes…" His voice was his usual booming tone that dominated a room. I was furious with him. I had sat there in silence for nearly two hours listening to him and others wittering on and now he had the audacity to interrupt me in my only opportunity to contribute. Without too much thought I spoke loudly and firmly to counteract his voice.

"I'm sorry Andrew, I hadn't realised that I had finished speaking! I wasn't aware that your concern over shoes was more important than her success in her GCSEs." There was grit and frustration in my tone. Andrew stopped, his eyes wide in surprise. The rest of the room was a little stunned. They were not used to seeing me be quite so frustrated. They were also not used to seeing Andrew Potter stopped in mid-flow. I could see one or two smiling.

"Apologies, Jack. Carry on." Andrew looked angry but his voice was quieter.

As we left the meeting, Andrew called to me. "Jack, have you a moment?" I shrugged and made my way around the room to where he sat. Andrew was the son of a 'Windrush' couple. He had been raised in South London and spoke with a clear London accent. I liked him a lot. He was the pastoral lead at the school and had responsibility for the Year Heads as well as managing the lead teachers. He was an outstanding science teacher and the kids had a marmite relationship with him. If your uniform was even slightly out he would spot it from at least a hundred yards away and he had a habit of stopping in the corridor and following a student with his eyes wide if he saw uniform irregularities. It would make the kids laugh if you were not the one being stared at. Then he would call your name loudly and ask you to give an account of why you were not in uniform. He would often run everywhere, usually because he was late for a lesson. He had a passion for chocolate bars, which he used as fuel for the day, but he was as fit and slim as he burned so much energy. He was a bit like Tigger from Winnie the Pooh.

"Jack, I want to apologise, I was out of order. It was your turn. I shouldn't have interrupted."

"No problem, I shouldn't have embarrassed you that way either. So we're both in the wrong." We smiled and accepted the mutual apologies. "I just get so frustrated in those meetings they're such a waste of time." Andrew gave me a wide-eyed stare of disbelief.

"What do you mean?"

"I think there are better ways of sharing this information. To be honest, I don't care what the Science Department do to raise achievement, and if you are honest do you really care what I am doing? Do you study my data and ask how my underachievers are doing?"

He shook his head. "I take your point, so how should we do this?"

"The whole point of these meetings is to support students, that's why we're here. I don't think this is helpful at all." We sat and chatted it through and as we did Sally Le Croix came and sat with us. I had known Sally since I began teaching. She had left South Coast Comprehensive some years ago to be a head of Modern Languages at a school in Brighton. She returned in September as Deputy Head, having done a variety of leadership roles across Sussex. I was thrilled, Sally and I had always been good friends and colleagues.

She listened attentively and finally said, "I think we need to look at this more seriously. I think there is mileage in what you said. I could see your frustration and to be honest, two hours or so of this kind of meeting is too much. Let's bring it up at the senior team meeting." *Thank you, thank you, thank you.*

I sat in the back of Eve Reynold's classroom; I was observing her as part of our internal monitoring and appraisal process. Eve was a Technology teacher; I knew little about the subject specifics but was really there to see if her general practice had improved. She had been at the school for several years and recently had been struggling in lessons. There had been several behaviour issues, poor results and student progress was limited. There had been interventions by the department and lead teachers and she was now on a support plan to improve her practice. This was a voluntary observation and she had asked me to come and watch her teach a Year Nine class in their final planning lesson before embarking on a 'wooden box project'. I liked Eve; she was a kind, gentle person, but teaching was not really her strength. She was really an artist and designer who had not found a career in the creative industry so came into teaching. It always puzzled me how some teachers made it through training when they clearly were not cut out for it. The lesson so far had been slow to start and there was confusion about where the student's books were located. Many of the kids in the class were unsettled and did not have the right equipment. Eve was struggling to get them sorted. I leaned across to a quiet girl who was waiting patiently for the lesson to begin.

"Is it always like this at the start?" I asked innocently. Children were always brutally honest about their lessons, if you asked the right kid you would gain an accurate picture of the teacher.

"Yeah, mostly," she whispered. I smiled at her and asked her if she knew what they were supposed to be learning. She explained it quite well, but I knew from experience that this girl was a bright button and always knew what was going on. The lesson progressed and Eve began to explain how to complete the design of their boxes, what to include on their diagram labels, explaining how to draw the joints they would use. I wandered around the class, watching the students and listening to Eve. Her questioning was generally closed and only elicited monosyllabic answers. It did not give the opportunity for students to show learning or progress. She often ignored the boys and picked on girls whom she knew would give correct responses. Several boys became disaffected and their work rate quickly dropped off. Eve ignored them wanting to avoid a conflict. She was not doing herself any favours. I was here to help her and support her but she was ignoring basic teaching skills and practice.

"Tell me about your work," I asked one lad whom I knew to have a specific learning need. "How has Miss Reynolds explained it to you? Has she spoken to you and shown you what to do?" I flicked through his planning book to see if there was evidence of feedback. "Dunno," he said and shrugged. "Tell me what you have to do to make your box." I looked up and saw Eve looking in my direction, she smiled nervously. The lad proceeded to explain the basic ideas as he understood them, but he clearly had no understanding of why he was doing the work.

After an hour, I knew that the conversation with Eve was going to be difficult. I was optimistic that, because she had asked for me to observe her, she would take the constructive criticism in the way it was offered. This was the part of the job I really hated. It was not in my nature to deliberately upset people. I knew Eve was going to be upset.

"Listen, Eve, you have two formal observations to go as part of your support plan. You have to show a degree of improvement." Eve was sniffing and wiping her nose. The conversation had been a challenge but she had recognised her issues and that some basic practices could be improved. "Let's meet weekly and see how you are getting on. I can support you with the planning that you are doing with Paul your Lead teacher. You can turn this around Eve, this is partly about organisation and timing, if we get those right then we can work on the other skills. Deal?"

"Deal." She smiled. "Thanks, Jack, I know I can do better, I owe it to the kids." I sighed as she left my office. It was 5 pm on a May afternoon the sun was out and it was warm. I could hear the sounds of the last of the kids leaving school after sports clubs and I still had Year Ten lessons to plan before tomorrow as well as a proposal to finalise how we do feedback to students in a more consistent fashion across the school. *That'll teach me to open my mouth in the Directors meeting.* To be fair, it needs sorting and I was keen to take it on.

CHAPTER TWENTY

Frustration and Firefighting –
Not cut out for the top?

The new Head Teacher of South Coast Academy (Part of the Sussex Learning Trust) had been appointed to take the school from County Council control to Academy status. He was a tall, slim, man of West African descent with the intriguing name of Dexter McCormack. He had been an English teacher and served as a deputy in a school in Birmingham for over a decade. It was September 2014 and I sat in his office with Cassie. We were having our exam results review meeting. I had already sat through the History and Geography meetings (both had done well, with results in the 70%s and slightly above forecast), and I was sitting comfortably as Director of Humanities because the Philosophy and Ethics results were also excellent. Cassie had achieved the highest set of results the department had ever had, with 85% of students achieving A*-C and 30% getting A/A*.

"Congratulations Cassie, well done to you and your department. The switch to whole cohort Philosophy and Ethics has certainly paid off. I know my predecessor was a little nervous about it, but you have clearly proved him wrong. You have won over the hearts and minds of not only many on the staff but also the student body. Feedback from student surveys suggests a high degree of satisfaction with the subject across all ages." He had a calm and soothing voice, which could be deceptive if he had an ulterior motive. I looked across at Cassie. She was beaming. The department, including me, had worked hard to improve the results each year. This was our third cohort through and each time the results were better.

"Thank you, we do try to ensure that everyone can not only attain good grades but achieve excellent progress," Cassie spoke enthusiastically.

I interjected, "Yes, our progress data is also in line with predictions and just about the right side of the line." The meeting continued in a positive vein for a further twenty minutes with Cassie and I explaining further developments planned in the Philosophy and Ethics Department and Dexter asking pertinent questions to ensure we were in line with the school vision and improvement plan. It was also due to be an Ofsted year so we had to show we were 'Ofsted ready'.

"Jack, before you go, have you got a moment? I have something to tell you." Dexter's calm and quiet voice was strangely unsettling. He was about to chuck a grenade into my life. I sat back down in the chair and watched as Cassie closed the door behind her.

"Jack, I have been impressed with the work you have done with Eve Reynolds in Technology. Her trajectory is upward and recent observations are much improved. I know you missed out on the CPD and data roles that were on offer last year. You interviewed well, it was a shame there was not a role for you." I nodded sagely as if understanding his disappointment. In reality, I was glad I missed out on both those promotions to the 'top table' of school leadership. I had observed the stress and worry lines on the other staff who were the lucky ones to receive invites to the top table, I wasn't convinced it was worth it. *What do you want me to do? Will I have a choice? Here it comes!*

"I've thought about this long and hard and I am making you Director of Technology as well as Humanities. Tom can't lead Science, Technology and manage 'Curriculum and Timetable.'" He paused, waiting for me to respond. I didn't. I was thinking hard! *Technology? What do I know about that? What's the catch?*

Dexter continued, "Their results are poor, the teaching quality is below par and you have proven with Humanities that you can lead a successful team. The challenge is now: Can you improve a failing team?"

"Do I have a choice?"

"No."

"In which case I accept. I will need a reduction in teaching hours, I won't be able to manage another team without more time to meet and lead them." If I was going to be stitched up, then at least I was going to try and get some concessions.

"Not this year, maybe next." Dexter was noncommittal.

"Then don't expect miracles."

"I'm not, just improvements. It starts today, I have already told Tom you are taking over Technology from him." I stared momentarily at Dexter. This was a done deal even before he spoke to me.

"I bet he was overjoyed at the news." Dexter smiled at the tone of my voice. He knew how difficult the Technology Department were. Tom would be thrilled to be shot of them. I got up to leave and Dexter spoke again.

"Just one more thing…" I stopped and turned to face him. "I also want you to take over responsibility for the whole school strategy on homework."

"What?" I was stunned. "I thought Andrew ran that? What is going on?"

"Andrew has exams and admissions. His role as the Pastoral Lead is also huge, he cannot manage this as well." Dexter smiled. My heart sank. I felt I had just been given the England manager's job. No one really wants it, and when you are doing it all you get is grief, even when it's going well. Make one error and you are tainted forever.

"Can I think it over?" I was desperate not to take it on but I was caught between a rock and a hard place.

"You will need an outstanding reason not to do it, Jack. I expect you to accept. You will be part of the Core Leadership Team as of tomorrow." With that, the meeting was over. I walked out into the corridor, my head was spinning and I had the definite feeling I had just been shafted.

"What are those?" The voice was loud and it reverberated down the corridor. Andrew Potter the Senior Assistant Head stood wide-eyed staring at a pair of trainers on the feet of a year eight boy. He stood one hand on his hip, he leant forward, the other arm stretched out, hand pointing at the trainers as if they were a manifestation of Satan himself. The crowds in the corridor parted like the Red Sea and left the poor boy and Andrew in a stand-off.

"What are those?" His finger trembled as it pointed at the trainers.

"Trainers, sir!" It was bravado for the watching crowd. He was scared, as most students were when Potter caught them out of uniform. "Come with me, right now... hurry up." Potter released from his pose scurried off towards his office, the poor Year Eight boy trailing in his wake. There was relief among the watching masses that their imperfect uniform had gone unnoticed.

The incident released me from my sense of bemusement about my new job role. The crowds began to move and I was forced to move along with them. "Walk on the left, please! Coats off and please be aware of what your bag is doing, there are small children who are bag height!"

****

"At the end of the day, Jack, it's a promotion. You should be proud and pleased that Dexter has seen what you can do."

Sandy kissed me on the forehead and snuggled up next to me on the sofa.

"I know, but it's not like I asked for it, it was thrust on me. There is no more time to do it, I'm still teaching 65% of the time and now he wants me to improve the Technology Department and revamp the whole school strategy on homework. I just feel I'm being taken for a ride, that's all." I was feeling sorry for myself, mainly because the rest of the Core Team who had similar responsibilities had 15% extra time in which to do the role, plus more money.

"Just give it a go Jack, I'm sure you can do it. Just stay at work an extra hour, it's not like we live a long way from the school." We literally lived around the corner, it was a five-minute walk. Sandy was always understanding and willing to support me. She also was now in a full-time role as a Year Head in a large junior school, it was not as if she would be at home waiting for me. "Do it for a couple of years and if you don't like it, step away. There is no shame in that."

"You're right. I just feel a bit railroaded into senior leadership and I am not sure I am suited for all the cut and thrust of it. I am more interested in the students and helping them to succeed." I had begun to see a disconnect between what the school and/or government wanted and what the children actually needed. It was bringing me into conflict more and more with my colleagues higher up the school ladder. I picked up my wine glass and offered a toast with Sandy. "To Jack Turner, Technology Supremo and Homework wizard. Here's hoping!" We clinked glasses but I had a deep sense of foreboding.

By the end of that academic year, I had spent more time on Technology and homework than I had ensuring that Humanities remained on an upward trend. The Technology team were great people: kind, friendly and very keen to do well. I got to know them not only as colleagues but as friends as well. The biggest issue I faced was a stubbornness in their practice, the belief that their systems were perfect and that what they were doing was good enough; it was just the quality of the children that caused their poor results. It was as if they did not want to hear that maybe their practice was not the best. Let's face it, nobody wants to hear that. I tried to be gentle and supportive, tweaking things slowly to improve outcomes and trying to get the team to realise that there were better ways of planning, teaching, recording, assessing and marking that would improve outcomes across their subjects. Although progress in the August 2015 GCSE results was showing improvements, the actual grades were well below par.

"Jim, you keep telling me that everything is fine with the way you are teaching and that nothing needs to change, but the results don't bear that out. We can't take this to Dexter without a serious plan for improvement." We sat in his workshop amongst the sawdust. The smell of fresh-cut wood was appealing and the August sun streamed through the windows. Jim was the Head of Technology, a tall man of similar age to me, a good craftsman who got the children to make incredible things, but his teaching style, team management, record keeping and administration were letting him down. He was trying to defend his position.

"Jack, you know the calibre of kids we get, they dump anyone who can't cope with writing in my classes. How am I expected to get them higher grades if they won't or can't write? All they want to do is make stuff. The GCSE is only 20% practical. I've told the leadership this countless times. They don't listen. I get the blame for their failure to provide proper courses for those who are not academic." Jim was adamant the results were not his fault.

"It's clear the strategies for support we put in place didn't work..." I was cut off by Jim.

"Of course they bloody didn't, these kids were never going to turn up to extra lessons or after-school clubs, that's their nature! Anyway bloody Maths and English always took them. Did they pass English and Maths? No, they didn't, yet I'm the one getting it in the neck!" The truth was, that Jim's teaching was not up to standard, he was complacent and did not challenge poor teaching in his own team. As a result, they had all let things slide. The problem was, Jim was a friend and I found it incredibly hard to tell him this. Everyone could see it, yet it was down to me to sort it out. *This is why I am not cut out for the top. I don't like upsetting people.*

"Jim, have you thought any more about dropping the GCSE and going to BTech? That way it is a lot more practical, more coursework and a higher chance of improved student progress."

"What, and lose the kudos of GCSE? They will dump even more of the less desirable students on me."

"Listen Jim, I'm not sure Dexter will want to run GCSE again after these results, he will want a change." In fact, I know he did. He had told me so earlier in the summer after Jim had lost several pieces of coursework and students had to redo it after school. It had been a difficult time.

"He has it in for me, I know. He wants me out." Jim was getting very agitated.

"No, he wants what is best for the students and we have to deliver that. Now let's present him with a plan he can't resist and a determination to become the most improved subject next year." I was desperately trying to be positive, but we both knew the meeting in September was going to be very difficult.

****

As I sat in the hall leading homework detention duty after school on a Thursday in May, I recalled a leadership meeting back in September. My proposal for the introduction of a whole school homework app called "My homework" was met with little enthusiasm. It would have revolutionised the setting and recording of all homework and even informed parents who could check what had been set for their children.

"It looks amazing Jack, but we would like you to develop it through the school website which we are updating at present. Work with Danny on this, he is in overall charge of the ICT strategy at the school." Danny was on the senior team, he was a good man and skilled at his job.

My heart sank, I was disappointed. "Can I ask why you made this decision?" Dexter smiled at me and the rest of the senior team sat in silence. I scanned their faces. They clearly had known this was coming. Why didn't I?

"Well, for one it is expensive, £5000 is a lot to invest in something that is unproven. Also, we were already committed to a major website update that would include homework provision and the possibility of our own app." As always Dexter smiled as he spoke, his voice always gentle and soothing.

"I wish I had been informed of this when you asked me to take this role on. I wouldn't have wasted hours of research time. I could have been working with Danny on it for the last six months. You could have told me there were limitations and pointed me in the right direction." The tone of my voice betrayed my frustration. "Also, it is not unproven. Every other school in the town has invested in it and it has revolutionised the level of homework completion and satisfaction from parents. It's a winner." I was determined to let Dexter know I thought he was wrong.

"I appreciate your efforts Jack, and what we believe is that the homework extensions of the website, when they are completed, will do a similar job and will save us money."

"Sir, can we go now? It is 4.30." A little lad piped up. I looked up at the dozen students who had shown up for detention. There should have been twenty, so now I had another thirty minutes of admin to do setting them school detention, informing parents, logging it on the SIMS system. I stood up and wandered around the hall looking at the work they were supposed to be doing. Some staff had failed to provide the missed homework, so the children were still behind in their studies, others had completed what had been set, but it bore little resemblance to any quality work of which they were capable. I was beginning to wonder if the detention was worth the effort.

"Okay pack up your work and place it in the box at the front, any scrap paper put in the recycling bin and off you go." I smiled at them all as they were dismissed.

"Bye sir, I expect I'll see you next week," said the same lad.

"No, just do your homework!" I responded cheerily.

"Na!" He grinned cheekily as he left the hall. I shook my head in despair. At that moment Danny walked in looking pleased with himself.

"Jack, have you got ten minutes? The website upgrade is complete; we can begin to launch it with staff ready for September."

"But Danny, this system requires every subject to have planned every homework in advance, with dates attached and have it all in place for September." We sat in his office huddled around his PC.

"Yes, the idea is we populate every subject area with homework for the year, with links to PDFs or websites etc. Once it is up and running, all staff need to do is to tell the kids which number homework it is and when it is due. For example, you could say to your Year Tens, 'This week it is homework 5 on topic 4 due in on so and so date.' It's simple."

"But can parents access this? Are they instantly informed when homework is set?" This was looking like a lot of work for the staff to do before September.

"They can access it via the website but they don't get informed when it is set or if it is completed." Danny could see where I was leading with my questions.

"So this is more work for staff, not as good for parents, and requires the student to tell their parents they have homework. How much did this upgrade cost?" Danny went quiet for a moment. I waited. "There may be an app in a year or so that will do a lot more than just homework, this is just the start." I nodded sagely.

"So we get the staff to do a load of work on this for one or two years, just to dump it for an app similar to the one I proposed last September." Silence.

"Well, thanks for this. I will have to sell it to the staff. We can't expect them to populate a whole year's worth of homework by September. Let's try six weeks at a time eh?" I tried unsuccessfully to hide my frustration.

"Jack, I know it's not what you wanted, but this will work in the long run." Danny was sympathetic, he had experienced something similar with smart boards and TVs.

"Yeah okay. Let's just plan this and get going. I am too tired to argue it." I sighed.

As I juggled the stresses of the Technology Department and the endless concerns that being the homework guru gave me, the Humanities Faculty had its own issues to face. One of my team had been suspended for a breach of safeguarding and was under investigation, there were rumours and counter rumours and I had been appointed this person's contact at school. I was bound to secrecy until all investigation was over. The daily questions from the rest of the team wanting to know information and how much longer cover work was to be set. caused me daily headaches.

"I am really sorry, Cass, I can't say anything. We just have to ride it out." The staff member in question was a new member of the Philosophy and Ethics team. The team had expanded again several years back and now had three full-time members plus myself and another part-timer. Sue Jennings was new in the department in September. She was bubbly and creative but also a little emotionally stunted. This often led to her being rather abrupt and causing offence to others. She was a marmite character. The issue was that Cass and Karen in the department didn't like marmite. To me, Sue was okay. A little annoying and overconfident but she was genuinely keen to learn the trade. Sue had made a serious error of judgement and had failed to pass on a safeguarding concern quickly enough. As soon as she had told me I explained to her the need to pass it on to the Deputy Head. I was as surprised as anyone when she disappeared and I found myself being interviewed about how long I had known about the issue. Sue was off for three weeks whilst the case was investigated. She ended up with a warning and a note on her record. But for those three weeks, I took the brunt of it.

"I'm really sorry Jack, I placed you in a difficult position." Sue was nearly in tears.

"It's not a problem, I am glad you are back. Just tell everyone you had a virus or something."

"I am not sure if I can stay after July, I am applying for a job in Lewes. I need a fresh start." Part of me was relieved when she said that, a feeling that I felt guilty about, which added to my stress. *Aaargh!*

"Harry, what are you doing outside my office?" I stood over

him as he sat on a blue plastic chair in the corridor.

He looked up and smiled at me, "I'm not allowed in History."

"What, again? What is it this time?" I looked down at him with puzzlement in my eyes. Harry struggled with his history teacher. I was never sure whether it was all his fault, his teacher's fault or a lack of compromise. Probably the latter.

"I came into class with a drink in my hand and Miss just shouted and told me to get out!" Harry followed me into the office carrying the chair and then left it by the door, blocking the entrance and plonked himself in a comfier seat. I picked up the chair and stacked it in the corner.

"So, let me get this straight. Miss James shouted at the top of her voice telling you to get out because you had a drink in your hand." I tried to make it sound like a ridiculous thing to have done. To test his nerve.

"Yes, exactly!" Harry was no angel, he was in and out of scrapes regularly, but essentially a good kid.

"What was the drink?" I asked innocently. I knew the answer. Harry only ever drank Cola. His bag was usually filled with cans and biscuits.

"Cola." He grinned.

"You know full well that fizzy drinks are banned, and you know that your parents have been told not to let you bring them in. Did miss offer to take it from you? Did she ask you to stop drinking it?" I was hoping he would say 'yes', but I knew the answer would be 'no'. Sue James was a good teacher but she was very black-and-white, there was no compromise on anything. It was her way or nothing. She had a tendency to overreact rather than try a soft approach first. "Come on, Harry, let's go and speak to her and see if we can get you back into the lesson."

We stood outside Sue's classroom, Harry looking sheepish.

"I'm sorry but he can't come back until he promises never to drink fizzy drinks in my room again. He needs to apologize for breaking school rules." Sue's feathers were ruffled and she was wanting to stand her ground. She was holding the door to her classroom and occasionally looking in to check her class were behaving. "I can't have Harry flouting the rules in such a blatant manner."

"I understand Miss James, but we do need a resolution quickly, Harry doesn't want to miss any more History, do you, Harry?" *For goodness sake agree with me!*

Harry nodded and smiled. "I understand you shouted at him before giving him a chance to give you his drink?" *I hope she falls for it; I need to get on with other work.*

"Well, I ur …um… possibly. … It's not the first time, so I was expecting an argument." Sue was flustered. I nodded and smiled politely. "Harry, what do you say to miss?"

"Sorry, miss." His head bowed.

"No more fizzy drinks or I will be contacting home again!" I made my voice sound stern and fatherly at the same time.

"Miss James, are you ok with that?" She nodded and opened the door for Harry to enter.

"Sorry," she whispered to me as she shut the door. I blew a big sigh and turned to leave, just then my radio crackled into life.

"On call and any senior staff, we have smokers in the north boy's toilets and two girls trying to jump the fence by the bike sheds." The static made it difficult to hear. But I got the gist.

"On my way."

CHAPTER TWENTY-ONE

Condoms Across the Curriculum

"Sir, why have you got a box of dildos on your desk?" It was the same every year. Henry thought he was being funny, but it was not original. All the boys laughed and some of the girls too. Others in the room quietly smiled, thinking Mr Turner would be embarrassed. They were out of luck.

"Actually, Henry, they are demonstrators, as you well know. Now I know that many of you have been looking forward to this lesson ever since we began this particular Sex Ed unit, but this is one of the most important lessons you will ever have." It was summer term and this was a Year Nine class. This particular PSHE topic was a Sex Ed one with a focus on healthy relationships, safe sex, and STIs. It was one of my favourite topics as well. Not only did it give me a chance to speak about the sacredness of sex from a Christian perspective, but it was also a chance to watch the bravado of many boys and girls melt away in the face of putting a condom on a large plastic or rubber demonstrator.

The lesson was progressing well; the class were well-behaved because they understood that immaturity would mean no condoms. We had re-capped the concept of consent and mutual agreement, religious attitudes versus secular ones and respect for all.

"Look," said Henry pointing and laughing, "there are blue willies!" I smiled; this happened every lesson. "Yes Henry, they're Smurf willies!" There was a chorus of laughter.

"Now remember, what are they?" Several hands shot up, including Henry's. "Henry, if you say dildo, I'll send you out." Henry lowered his hand and sulked.

"Anna, please enlighten us, I know I can trust you to be sensible." Anna smiled and spoke with confidence. "They're demonstrators, sir, not dildos. Anyway, they're not like my mum's." There were suddenly hoots of laughter and jeering mainly from the boys. I raised my voice a touch,

"Anna, too much information." I was trying not to smirk. Fatimah, my lovely Iraqi teaching assistant, blushed but I could tell she was giggling. "Now everyone, what is one of our key rules of PSHE…" I started the answer for them to give them a clue, "What is said in the room…"

There was a chorus of responses, "Stays in the room!"

"Excellent, that means we don't go around the whole of Year Nine telling everyone what Anna's mum has got." I was careful not to use the word dildo again as it would just reignite the disruption.

"Anna, for your fantastic answer can you please hand out a demonstrator to everyone in the class? Henry, you can distribute the condoms. No stealing any, I know exactly how many there are!" Anna stood up and picked up the box from my desk, Henry followed suit. There was a buzz of excitement and anticipation from most of the room. Some, however, were a little nervous. "Listen, everyone, remember, if you feel uncomfortable doing this, then please just observe. Allow Anna and Henry to give you the equipment but you don't have to take part." I could see relief flood over one girl's face, a shy girl, quiet, hardworking and easily anxious.

"Who wants a black one?" Anna held up a large black plastic penis and waved it around. "Hurry up, Anna, don't give them choice or we'll be here all day."

As the demonstrators and condoms were distributed, I flicked the PowerPoint onto the next slide. On the screen, several bullet points described the steps needed to successfully open, use and dispose of a condom. "Okay, everyone, looking this way, condoms and demonstrators on the desk, no touching them until we know what to do." I looked around, ensuring that all were following my instructions. Once I was satisfied I had reached optimum obedience I continued.

"Look at the slide. Simon, can you please read the first instruction." Simon looked up and read the bullet point confidently. "First find the expiry date and the CE mark or British kite mark." I pointed out to the class where they could find it and why it was important.

"You mean condoms go out of date?" Sarah called out.

"Yes, they do, and remember, hand up if you want to contribute. Does anyone know what happens to the latex after the expiry date?" I looked around hopefully.

"Do they split sir?" said one lad. "Well done, Tommy. They are more prone to splitting because the latex begins to perish. Why is that a problem?"

"You don't want it splitting when you're fu.. bonking!" Henry was beaming.

"Thank you, Henry. Remember, let's use more classroom-friendly terms, 'having sex', not bonking or any other term, eh?" I gave him a gentle stare to remind him of how close he was to being disruptive.

The lesson continued at a pace; the class learned how to open the pack, remove the condom, squeeze the tip to release the air and roll it down the demonstrator.

"Sir, mine's stuck, it won't move!" Tommy was trying to push his condom down the demonstrator but it was stuck firm.

"Everyone stop!" I waited until the noise died. "What has Tommy forgotten to check?"

"He's got it inside out! He didn't check his Mexican hat!" Sarah called out.

"Well done, Sarah. You must check that the condom looks like a Mexican sombrero, a pointy top with a thick rim. Then you know it's the right way round." I walked over to Tommy's seat and helped him reorganise his condom. "Get it right this time, Tommy. You don't want any future partner ending up pregnant do you?" Tommy shook his head, the thought of a girlfriend frightened him. He was too consumed by his Xbox, it was all he ever spoke about.

"Sir, genuine question, what if you're gay? Why do you need a condom?" Henry was sitting next to Tommy and had successfully sheathed his demonstrator.

"Brilliant question, Henry, can anyone help answer Henry's question? Why do gay men need to use condoms?" A raft of hands shot in the air.

"Gemma, can you tell us?"

"STIs! Gay men can still catch STIs, and so can lesbians." Gemma smiled proudly as she spoke. She had recently come out as gay and was keen to support LGBTQ people. She wore rainbow badges on her blazer and was part of the school's diversity club.

"Excellent, Gemma, full marks!" I looked around the room and could see most of the class had completed the first part of the condom challenge. On almost every desk there was a demonstrator sheathed correctly.

"Ugh. Ur..."

"What's the matter, Shannon?" She waved her hands about as if trying to flick off a bug.

"It's just so sticky, sir. It's horrible."

"That is the spermicide and lubricant that are essential for the condom to be effective. It is necessary. Hang on and when we have all got those condoms off, we can clean our hands and our demonstrators." I showed them a big box of wet wipes.

By the time the lesson was nearly over, the class had successfully removed the condom, tied it in a knot and been told never to throw them down the toilet but to wrap them up and place them in the bin. With the room nearly tidy and everything wiped and clean, Shannon came up to me and asked a question.

"Sir, do you have to have sex?"

"What do you mean, Shannon?" I felt she needed some reassurance that not being interested yet in sex was totally acceptable.

"I'm just not interested in all this stuff. Why are we learning about it now if the law says we can't do it until we're sixteen anyway?" I was right, she was anxious. "Shannon, can I share your concern with the class, I expect there are others who feel the same." She nodded and went to sit down.

"Okay, finally, let's think about why we have done this lesson." I stood at the front, we had ten minutes to go, just enough time to get them reflecting.

"So we don't get pregnant!" "So we don't get STIs!" the answers kept coming. I raised my hands to indicate silence and waited. The room settled.

"I am really thinking about this from a different angle. You lot are only 14, so why are we teaching you this when the law says you cannot consent to sex until sixteen? Some of you here are getting interested in sex right now." There were a few "waheys" from some of the more testosterone-filled boys. "But many of you are not interested in sex. It is not on your radar or the horizon just yet. And that is good." I paused a moment, just to think about where I was taking this. "There will be a time for most of you when you will find a partner, fall in love, maybe get married, and want to have sex to show your love and commitment. It is good to know how to do that safely and consensually. It is better to be prepared than unprepared. No one here is promoting sex as something you have to do, but it is a big part of human existence and life. To learn about it in a safe and secure environment where you can ask questions and get good answers is very important." I began to wander the room as I got into my final few sentences.

"Everyone has a different perspective on sex and sexuality. What we want to do here at South Coast School is to ensure that you understand the different perspectives and know how to make positive and healthy choices as you grow into adults. Never rush into sex just because you think everyone is doing it. They're not. Take your time and don't let anyone pressure you." A few more questions followed and the class completed the quiz in their books, just to check if they had fully understood the lesson.

****

"I've invited the local PSHE adviser from East Sussex to come and do a mini inspection. I believe we offer some of the best PSHE in the county. I want us to be recognised as outstanding." Cass was sharing in our department meeting. She was now the strategic lead for PSHE and Karen Cooper had taken over as head of the department. The new third member of the team, Becca, was also present. Becca was what was called an NQT, but now they had a new name, which I could never remember. She was well-liked by us all and already a skilled practitioner. *She won't stay too long before she is a Head of Department.* It was the Spring of 2017.

"The last Ofsted specifically mentioned PSHE as being a highlight and commented on the good practice." I was keen to point that out and remind Cass that as a team we were already pretty good.

"I know, but Dexter is still nervous about our 'Love Life' day, so I thought if an inspector sees it and commends it, it should reassure him that a day spent celebrating and recapping five years of quality sex education is a worthwhile thing." Love Life Day was exactly as Cass described. A whole day where Year Eleven were off Timetable, just before their exams, to celebrate and recall their five years of Sex Education. There were workshops on pregnancy and birth, understanding our body parts, and the links between alcohol and sex. We ran a condom Olympics, where facts and myths about condoms were explored, as well as 'Doctors and Patients' where students pretended to be doctors and diagnosed and offered suggested treatments for a range of STIs. It was a fun-packed day where many of the other staff got to see and appreciate the role of PSHE and PSHE teachers in the school.

"I like your thinking Cass, so is she coming on Love Life Day?" She nodded in agreement and then explained how the mini-inspection would work.

I handed out four condoms, each one blown up like a balloon ready to burst, to the four unsuspecting volunteers from the Year Eleven students. The rest of the year group was watching and chatting excitedly. The mood in the hall was celebratory. We were in the middle of the condom Olympics. We had already discovered that over 5 litres of water could be poured into a condom and that it was possible to fit three unopened tins of beans into a single condom, each fact demonstrating that a condom splitting is unlikely unless poorly used or out of date. There had been much cheering and laughing as the events took place. Even the more negative students were engaging in this type of learning. Cass explained that the challenge was to rub different types of oil or lubrication onto the condom. The point being, oil-based lube would perish the latex and pop the condom. The kids began. One kid holding the condom another rubbing sun tan or baby lotion onto it.

'Boom' one of the condoms exploded. There was a shriek from the girl who was massaging the oil on the stretched surface of the condom. Several other shrieks followed as the first row of students in the hall were covered in lube! Howls of laughter filled the room. Sadly for me, I was standing too close and found I had a face full of lube! However, it made many laugh. As I wiped lube off my face, the poor girl who had experienced the full blast of it looked like she had been rescued from a bottle of washing-up liquid. She was giggling and laughing as she wiped her face with tissues handed to her by Cass.

Cass spoke into the microphone at the front of the stage. "Settle down. Thank you, contestants, clean yourselves up and sit back down. Can anyone explain why that condom exploded?" She scanned the hall. Many hands went up and several people called out.

"Oil-based lube will quickly perish the latex!"

"Excellent," said Cass enthusiastically, "Therefore...?" she held out her hands and shrugged to indicate a 'so what?' pose. More shouts from the floor.

"Only use water-based, proper sex lube, not sun cream or other stuff." The kids knew their stuff.

The Local Authority advisor sat at the back, grinning, and jotted down a few notes. If I did not know she was a PSHE advisor, I probably would have guessed. She had purple hair, large leafy earrings that dangled and swung every time she moved, and a very colourful and flouncy dress, with a chiffon scarf. She was about my age, in her mid-fifties. I looked in her direction. *You couldn't get a more stereotypical image of a PSHE guru than that.*

The final session of the day was a whole-year group quiz in the hall. Every IPad the school possessed had been handed out and the kids were in small teams. Cass had devised an online quiz to finally test their understanding. There were prizes at stake and the kids were excited. Two hundred and

270

forty sixteen-year-olds were keen to take part in a quiz that led to cash vouchers, chocolates and stickers. (Year Eleven love a good sticker!) Becca in the sound booth was rapidly blocking rude names that appeared on the team name list. Whilst rude, they were extremely clever and quite funny. Eventually, the students caught on and the team names morphed into ones that were just about passable by school standards. Questions from everything to naming body parts, where to get help if you have an STI, and how to treat them, as well as a video observation round, proved to be a huge success. The winning teams received not only rapturous applause from their peers but their vouchers, chocolates and, of course, stickers.

"I'm knackered!" said Cass as we slumped down in the staff room having cleared the hall of the detritus of the day.

"Yeah, but it was brilliant, as always!" Karen lay flat out across several seats, trying to muster up the energy to make a cup of tea! "I need a glass of wine!"

"Me too," said Becca.

"Come on, let's go down the pub and celebrate. After all, it is Friday. We made it through another week, another 'Love Life Day' and almost another term. We deserve it!"

I looked at the three amazing women in the Ethics and Philosophy Department. *I love these women; this is what proper education is all about. Giving it all, all day for the kids to have a better opportunity for success.*

"Sir, you're old, what do you think about creation and God making the world?" It was a year Ten GCSE lesson, one of my favourite topics that explored the very nature of God and creation.

"What are you saying, Poppy, that I was there at creation, so I should know the answers?" I smirked as I spoke. I knew what she meant but it was an opportunity to build positive relationships by using humour.

"No, no sir, I just meant…"

"Just meant what?" There were a few giggles and smiles around the room from those enjoying Poppy squirm.

"I… I..I just meant you have been teaching a long time, you know the answers."

"So you are calling me old?" I knew Poppy well, she went to the same Church as I did, and I knew her parents. This was banter. I was teasing her because I knew how she would react and she didn't let me down.

"Well if you put it like that then, yes, you must be at least 65!" She was almost laughing as she spoke.

"Well, thank you, Poppy, I was about to forgive you, but maybe I won't." The class were revelling in the banter and loved the fact that I could be teased and not take offence. She had one more riposte. "I thought you were a Christian; you're supposed to forgive."

"Touché!… now let's get on. A great question, by the way. Why don't we open it up and see what others think first, then I will outline a broadly Christian perspective." The class settled back into work mode and began to share personal views on God, creation and evolution. It created a healthy debate, with views from across the spectrum.

I drew a big circle on the board, "If this circle represents the total knowledge in the universe, how much of that knowledge do humans actually know? Half? A quarter? More or less?"

A few brave students suggested amounts but we eventually settled on a very, very thin slice of a pie chart to represent human knowledge.

"So, you atheists out there who are convinced that there is no God and that creation could not take place are basing that view on this tiny portion of knowledge?" I pointed to the thin slice of pie. "Is it not logical to assume that a God could exist, given the tiny portion of knowledge and understanding that we possess? Atheists at best should be agnostic." I wandered the room as I spoke.

"But sir, surely you could argue the opposite based on the same principle?" Ted was a bright lad, who would argue most things with me as a matter of course. The perfect Ethics student.

"Well done, Ted, yes, you could. The argument can work both ways. So what makes the difference? Why do some fall on the side of belief and some on the side of atheism?" I looked around the room hoping that someone would pick up on my train of thought. I continued. "Why am I a believer and Ted is not?"

"Upbringing?" said one girl. "Brainwashing?" said another, half-jokingly.

"Aah, but who has been brainwashed, Ted or me?" There was a moment's silence as the class realised that their preconceptions of religious upbringing leading to being 'brainwashed' could also apply to an atheistic upbringing.

"What happened to Paul on the road to Damascus?" We had recently covered this in a lesson on religious experience. A few hands shot up.

"Yes, Katy." I smiled hopefully.

"Experience, some kind of contact with God?" She was unsure if her answer was correct.

"Perfect, Katy, well done." She swelled up with pride. "If I said that God had spoken to me somehow or answered my prayers, or appeared to me, you might call me mad, delusional, mistaken or even a liar, but you cannot deny my experience. My experience remains true for me. No argument can destroy it."

"But surely it's all psychological and not real." Ted was keen to respond and develop the debate. I moved the mouse on my desktop and clicked the play button on the MP3 file. Indiana Jones clicked into life. He was about to find the fabled Holy Grail and had followed the clues in his father's book all the way, but now he had to step off a cliff. He had to believe he would not fall and could cross the massive ravine without dying. He stepped off the edge. He appeared to be floating. There was an 'invisible bridge' that could only be seen once you were on it. I stopped the clip.

"So, what has this got to do with our debate?" I waited, giving them some thinking time.

"Ted, any ideas? Katy?...anyone?" Poppy put her hand up.

"It is about faith, he had to have faith. He knew it didn't seem logical to step off, but he had to have faith. The book told him he needed to take a leap of faith. That's the same with belief in God." *I knew she wouldn't let me down.*

"Fantastic Poppy, well done. Yes, belief in God is not an intellectual acceptance of a set of rules or beliefs, it requires faith. It requires a person to accept those truths and act on them. It is only after that step, that the truth of God becomes a reality. Without a step of faith, no one will believe in God. When St Paul had a religious experience and encountered God it changed him completely. Was he a liar? Was he delusional? Or did he experience something and then put his complete faith in it?" There were a few nods of assent but some were confused.

"Ok, everyone up on their feet. If you don't get this, find someone who does. Team up. Those who understand it, explain it to them. You have five minutes." I wandered the room, ensuring that they paired up and correcting any mistakes in translation. *This is what it is all about, getting young people to think, reflect and understand. I love it.* I smiled to myself. This was the best part of my job.

To be honest, leadership takes its toll on your classroom

practice. Time for planning, marking and being creative becomes secondary to meetings, strategy, monitoring others, and exploring data. Only a small portion of my time was now spent in the practice of teaching, I was much more of a manager and leader. When I thought about this, it often saddened me to think that so many excellent teachers moved up to leadership and the children missed out on their expertise. Not that I thought of myself as an excellent teacher.

CHAPTER TWENTY-TWO
A cloud and a thunderbolt

November 2018 brought with it a storm cloud to my career. For the first time, I found myself unable to manage, not only some of the more difficult students but also my leadership role. I began to feel weighed down and burdened by it as if I was not performing it with the same level of enthusiasm and commitment that I needed and wanted. I found that I became less patient with the children and it required more effort to maintain a level acceptable as a school leader. This was not what I had expected. I felt confused and frustrated. I wanted to be the best I could be, but at the same time felt that my job was a waste of time.

As I walked up the path towards the school gate it felt like a cloud was descending over my head, a cloud of depression. I had never suffered from depression but it felt that way. I was no longer looking forward to work. It hit me like a thunderbolt. I stopped in my tracks. *I'm not enjoying my job anymore; I don't care as much as I used to.* I sighed, took a deep breath and gave myself a stern talking to and walked on. *Pull yourself together, Jack. Everyone feels like this at some point. You're nothing special. Just get on with it and you'll be fine.* I began to recall what had brought about this change in my disposition.

Dexter sat at the head of the table; Clem Vine, now Head of History, sat next to me. He cleared his throat and spoke. "Thank you for coming. You know the process, we are here to explore the History Department results, and find a path forward to improved outcomes." The History Department results were on a two-year slump. From my perspective as Head of Faculty, it was a combination of the quality of students and a reluctance by the department to embrace some of the changes to practice that the leadership were demanding. The history teachers were all good or outstanding in every observation for the last three or four years, but little had changed in terms of how they planned and taught and progress was erratic. It was as if they were in a bubble and could not or would not let the bubble burst. Clem was on the defensive.

"To be fair, 30% of our students don't have a reading age sufficient enough to read and interpret the questions. How are they expected to be successful? I did warn you about this last year, I presented the data to you. Five of those who significantly underperformed had long-term absence issues. How were they supposed to achieve if they were never in class?" Clem continued her defence, stating reasons and supporting them with data. I was always impressed by her arguments, they seemed to make sense even if I disagreed. Dexter waited until Clem had finished, turned to me and asked if I had anything to add. I paused and thought carefully. Clem was right in what she said, but at the same time, there was no denying that the History Department was going through a rough time.

"Yes, I do agree with Clem's assessment of the results. Some of the decisions made by leadership about adding to the cohort new student arrivals to the school who have no History background have negatively impacted the results. At the same time, I feel more could have been done to support struggling or disengaged students." I felt Clem bristle. She believed her role was to offer support, not to chase after those who repeatedly chose to ignore it. It was the seesaw principle. Work with those who could easily tip the balance; the others will either fall off or slide closer to the tipping point. Clem went on the attack.

"That's not true. After school support was offered, I emailed parents regularly, and I explained what work had been missed and where to find it on the school website. What else am I reasonably supposed to do? If they don't want to engage I can't force them." She was riled and I felt for her. A part of me agreed with all she said and another believed that she was fighting a losing battle. The rest of me felt numb, not interested. *Give it a rest, Dexter, Clem is working hard. Clem, wake up and realise you will never win this argument. This is such a waste of time.* It was the last thought that really shook me. I didn't care enough that some of those who underperformed in History were being failed. I felt tired of the process of picking through the bones trying to find someone or something to blame for underachievement. *Sometimes it just happens. Life is bigger than GCSE results.*

I sat in my office staring at the screen of my PC and wondering what had happened to learning for learning sake. Progress 8 and Attainment 8 data filled the screen. It was mind-numbingly boring, and I hated data. Yes, it had its place in supporting progress, but it was restricting the curriculum, teaching styles and educational enjoyment for both student and teacher. All the focus was on improving the data and, in my opinion, it had sucked the life out of teaching. Everything was assessment focussed, soft and hard assessments, testing every few weeks, and exam practice each lesson. There was no time for reflection, debate, or learning something new just for the joy of it. Everything from Year Seven upward was all about passing GCSE. I began to hate it. *I didn't come into teaching to sit poring over numbers on a spreadsheet, this won't help students become rounded, compassionate and useful members of society.* I began to curse Michael Gove and his Baccalaureate. I was sitting with my head in my hands when the Deputy Head Sally Le Croix knocked on the door.

"Everything all right, Jack? You look fed up."

"It's bloody Michael Gove and his Progress 8 nonsense." My tone gave away the fact she was correct about my mood. She leaned her head to one side and smiled sympathetically. "Mind if I sit down?"

"Go ahead, how can I help you?" I pointed to a comfy chair and she sat down.

"If I am honest, Dexter asked me to speak to you. He has noticed that you have become a bit negative in meetings. You often disagree with the decisions being made and question everything. Is everything okay with you? You are a good leader, Jack, well respected, but recently you…" I interrupted her.

"I know, I am sorry, I just can't agree with the current state of the whole system and I struggle with the fact that no one else seems to see the issues." With that, I began to pour out my disillusionment with a host of things, some national, some internal and some personal.

"Why does nobody see that making every child do History or Geography or ancient, bloody Hebrew, is just a waste of time. It's a false way to improve the quality of education. Not everyone is academically minded, some need to be doing useful, practical skills." My rant continued with occasional interruptions from Sally. She was a good friend and a good deputy head; she listened and allowed me to offload.

"Have you noticed that I am no longer asked to do anything upfront? Everyone else gets to, but not me. No important assemblies, no parent meetings, no taking the lead on new initiatives. Why is that, Sally? Does Dexter not rate me? Am I not doing a good enough job?" Sally sat uncomfortably in her seat. "Have you spotted the new homework app that Danny has bought as part of his ICT role? I asked for something similar several years back but was told we were going via the website. Remember? Now he introduces this app and all is jolly and good. It's like I don't exist on that leadership team, I am not valued and not really part of it. I am definitely a second-class citizen here." I hadn't planned to say any of that. It had just come out. Perhaps I had reached the tipping point?

"Well, I wasn't expecting that!" Sally sat back in her chair and breathed out a big sigh. "I don't know what to say except I am sorry. I am sorry you feel that way. There is certainly no deliberate plan to ostracise you. You are valued and respected. You have been here a long time, you have experience."

"Yes, but from where I am sitting, I am not heard, I don't have a voice. I am ignored." Sally shook her head. "No Jack, that's not true." We sat in silence for a moment, neither of us knowing what to say next.

"Anyway Sally, enough of my woes, why did you pop in, not just to see how I was? I am sure there was something else."

"Actually Jack, there is, but perhaps now is not the time." Sally smiled and began to get up from her seat.

"No, no, Sally spit it out. We've come this far. You can't leave me wondering." She sighed and looked burdened. "This is just going to reinforce your feelings, Jack, but it certainly was not intended that way. Dexter wants me to take control of Technology. You've done it for several years and the results have not improved quickly enough. He has some plans for the area and wants me to head up the changes." My stomach tightened and my stress levels rose. "Also, Danny has asked to take on homework as it is now linked to the app." I sat back in my chair and couldn't decide whether to laugh or cry.

"Well, that's bloody brilliant. Thanks, Sally!" I was cross at the messenger; I knew I shouldn't be.

"Jack…" Sally leant forward to touch my arm in reassurance. I pulled it away.

"No! All the work I've put into Technology and Homework. All the work the staff have put into the website fiasco that Dexter promised would work and now I'm thrown on the rubbish heap, and he sends you to do it, one of my oldest friends and colleagues!" I shook my head in disbelief. *Unbelievable!*

I sat in my office reflecting after Sally had left. She felt bad but it was her job and I shouldn't have taken it out on her. I needed to apologise. I texted Sandy to tell her what had happened and how cross I was. She responded quickly.

Why so cross? You hated those jobs from the start. Perhaps it is for the best.

You are a good classroom teacher, your team like you. Talk later. XXX

Sandy had left teaching a year ago and now worked at our church, it had changed her whole outlook on life. She didn't miss teaching and had found another path. Perhaps I should do the same? I sat quietly for a moment and then began to pray. I felt a real sense of peace flood through me. I needed to begin to let go. *The truth is I am quite happy that I've lost those roles, I don't really have the passion for them. They were a distraction and something I never wanted. Move on.*

"If you don't like leadership at that level, Jack, don't do it! Step back." Sandy and I were sitting up in bed drinking tea. It was our usual time to reflect on life before we slept.

"Yeah, but if I step down from the core team back to just being Head of Faculty, we lose about £4000 a year."

"I don't care about the money, if you're not happy, then change! You are a great teacher; you don't need the money or the stress. Step back. I'll support you whatever you choose." She leaned over and kissed me. *What would I do without you, Sandy?*

The little cloud descended on me every morning as I approached the school and lifted as I left. The feelings of stress and anxiety increased as the year went on despite being relieved of extra leadership duties. I followed Sandy's advice and stepped off the top tier of leadership at Christmas. It was a relief and gave me back some of the joy I had previously experienced. However, the overarching feeling that this was all a waste of my time not only remained but steadily grew. I worked hard each day, forcing myself to deliver high-quality lessons, be the Head of Faculty my team needed, and support the leadership as best I could but deep down there was a real sense of pointlessness. *Why am I doing this?* Everything at school seemed petty and unimportant in the grand scheme of life.

On the surface, I did my job well, everything was now fine with leadership. I contributed, did as asked and led my team, but inside the fire was out. It was time to leave. *Time to leave? But what else is there to do? I know nothing but teaching. I have no other skills. I don't know what else to do.* These thoughts permeated my mind for the next few months until Sandy said something that felt like it changed my life.

"Jack, if you are still unhappy at work, look for something else, or go part-time. You're 57 in the Summer, and lots of people nearing retirement go part-time. I'm pretty sure we can afford it. Talk to the pension guy again. See what he says."

This is scary. Part-time work? Retirement? Can I? Should I? These thoughts almost consumed me and began to have a positive impact on my life at school. The cloud began to lift, I could see daylight, a light at the end of the tunnel and it wasn't an oncoming train!

****

The crackle of static on the walkie-talkie caught my attention. I was wandering the field in the summer sun at lunchtime. It seemed to be a peaceful day, the children were calm and it was warm on my face as I patrolled the large field.

"A large number of Year 11 are storming onto the field, looking for the Year Tens. Apparently, there is an issue. It looks like a fight is brewing. All senior staff to the field, please."

I turned to see a posse of about thirty Year Eleven boys charging onto the field toward some Year Tens who were playing football. I was close by so stepped toward to intervene. I could see others running to support; Sally, Danny, and several of the pastoral team. I was in position first, facing the hoard of thirty. I held up my hands, palms outward in a 'stop' gesture.

"Stop, please. Year Eleven, calm down." The shouting from the mob was intense, several younger students ran for safety, others ran towards the posse to see what was happening, the atmosphere was quickly growing hostile.

"Out of the way sir! You can't stop us!" The boy was correct, I couldn't, but it was my job to intervene to stop a fight. I repeated my call for calm and cried out "Stop." Just then Jakob, a burly lad, who had been at the school a long time and knew me well, cried out. "Get out of my way!"

"No, stop!" He barged into me with some force, his momentum sent me flying and I landed on my back. The walkie-talkie fell from my hand. I was winded and banged my head on the hard sun-baked ground. It felt like slow motion as it does in the movies. I rolled over and began to sit up. "Stay still, Jack, don't move." It was Sally. She was kneeling beside me. I could hear the rumpus going on beyond me and the staff shouting to control the students. A crowd of onlookers had gathered around most of whom were shocked to see a teacher on the ground injured. *Ouch! How am I going to live this down?* I sat up and took a few deep breaths.

"I'm okay, he just winded me and I banged my head." Sally helped me up and handed me back my walkie-talkie."

"Are you all right, sir? I saw what happened, that boy pushed you over." She pointed to Jakob who had momentarily stopped and then continued his pursuit in the hope of getting lost in the crowd. Others agreed with the concerned Year Seven girl.

"I'm fine, he just caught me off guard." *If they believe that, they'll believe anything.*

"Caroline, can you write down what you saw, please and hand it into my office as soon as possible." Sally was on the case. "Yes, miss." She turned and ran to get her bag. By now a large crowd was following Sally and me off the field wanting to see what was going to happen next. Other lunchtime staff arrived to disperse them and by the time we got back to my office it was quiet.

"I'm fine, Sally, everything's fine." The adrenalin was fading away and I was feeling a bit shaky. I sipped on a cup of hot sweet tea, it helped. *Why does tea help?* By the end of lunchtime, I had been visited by several of my team, concerned for my welfare and then Dexter arrived.

"Jack, how are you feeling? Did he hurt you? We have Jakob in Danny's office; he is writing a statement but he accepts he pushed you over."

"At least that's something. He usually denies wrongdoing and argues the hind legs off a donkey." Dexter smiled at my attempt to behave in a normal way after such an incident. To be honest, I didn't think it was so bad. It was mob mentality, not malicious, but maybe the bang on the head had addled my brain.

"Take the day off tomorrow and we will see you on Monday" Dexter stood up and put his hand on my shoulder. "You're a good man Jack, valued and important to the school. Make sure you are fully recovered before you return." With that comment, he left the office.

"You're not going to work. He told you to take the day off!" Sandy was indignant.

"I'm fine! Really. Anyway, I have a light day today, and I don't want to be chasing my tail and planning things over the weekend. I hate working at weekends."

"Why don't you go part-time, three days a week, then you

would never need to work at the weekend again!" Sandy had suggested this several months back. *Really? Could I?*

"What? Are you serious? No, I couldn't I'd feel too guilty."

"About what? Being knocked over by a thug of a boy, being treated like you don't matter? Why feel guilty?" *She's got a point.*

"Let's talk about it properly tonight. It's too late for next year, the timetable is almost built and the staffing is pretty much settled barring any late resignations next week." It was close to the May holiday when the final deadline for leaving in the summer was permitted.

"Jakob will be permanently excluded; however, he will come into school to sit his exams. He will do them all in my office, under my supervision. He has written you a letter of apology." Dexter handed me a piece of A4 file paper.

> Dear Mr Turner,
>
> I am so sorry about knocking you over. I do not normally do such things.
>
> I was part of the crowd of angry boys chasing someone. I don't even know who.
>
> I hope that you are okay and that you were not hurt. Please forgive me.
>
> I deserve to be excluded for what I did, but could you find it in your heart to
>
> Let me go to Prom. I have already bought my suit.
>
> Jakob.

I read it twice then folded it up and put it in my pocket. "Thank you for your support, Dexter, it is much appreciated."

"There is no need, we cannot allow that kind of behaviour, however unintentional it may or may not have been. We have to act firmly. I will leave it up to you to decide if you think he should go to Prom."

"No way!" "That's outrageous!" "F**k off, that's nuts!" The responses from my team were clear. They did not want to see Jakob at Prom.

"Jack, you can't seriously let him go to Prom, after what he did to you?" Cass was incensed.

"I know. My head says 'no way' but look at the letter." I showed her the handwritten note.

"He seems genuinely remorseful, Cass." I was torn.

"He's a devious bas***d, that's what he is. He is manipulative, sexist, intimidating and arrogant." Cass had spent two years teaching him Philosophy and Ethics. "He constantly undermines my authority, and is intimidating to anyone who dares to have an opinion other than his." Cass was furious at the thought that Jakob might be given a 'get out of jail free' card by me.

"But he needs to know that it is okay between us. I bear no grudge. From my point of view, he is forgiven."

"But he also needs his comeuppance! He has to realise that there are consequences to his actions. You can't let him off." She wagged a finger at me.

"But..."

"If you go all Christian on me, I'll scream!" Suddenly we both stopped, then burst out laughing at the absurdity of her comment.

"I can't help it, Cass, it's who I am!" I discovered years ago that my faith was no longer something I did, it had become who I was. She smiled and then hugged me. "Do what you have to, Jack. I'm not sure I could be so forgiving."

Andrew Potter stood in front of me in the corridor. It was after school; a few stragglers were heading home. Andrew stared at them intently, checking their uniform was correct, his eyes wide and intimidating. He had a chocolate bar in one hand and had just taken a bite.

"So, Jack, what do you want to do about Jakob? Can he come to Prom?" Andrew was organising it. It was his baby!

"What's your view? I don't want to go overboard on punishment. He has been excluded, missed out on all the revision sessions and extra classes. I am not sure that banning him from Prom will benefit anyone."

Andrew took another bite of his chocolate. He had a habit of laughing out loud at almost everything; he laughed.

"Well, I see your point, but it is your call. There are mixed views about it." He was clearly wanting to me to take responsibility for the decision. I didn't want to.

"To be honest, Andrew, I don't care. I'm not going to Prom, I never do, it's not my thing! I'm not bothered what you decide. I will leave it to you." I shrugged, turned away and left him munching on his chocolate.

****

"The pension guy says it will have no significant impact on your pension, a few quid. So you might as well go for it. We can afford the cut in pay, we just save less each month. I am more concerned for you, Jack, than the money. I have not liked seeing you so down and fed up. If this makes you happier, then I'm all for it!" Sandy leaned in and kissed me.

"Thanks, I just feel so guilty. It is my job to look after everyone. I've always worked full-time." I really was feeling troubled. The thought of going three days a week filled me with excitement but at the same time, it went against everything I had known was right. I was the hunter-gatherer in the family, Sandy had taken the part-time roles. Was it now time to swap?

Oh Lord, I really need some help, here!

CHAPTER TWENTY-THREE

COVID: a life-changing experience

As I walked up the path to work there was a spring in my step. The previous day I received confirmation that my request to go part-time had been approved and I would be working Monday to Wednesday from September 2020. A job share with Angela Ritzini, another member of the ever-expanding Philosophy and Ethics Department, had been negotiated. Angie was an experienced teacher who had moved to the area and the school snapped her up. She only wanted part-time so a job share with her was ideal.

It was mid-March 2020, the sun was out and we were heading towards the Easter holiday. The thought of part-time was making the light at the end of the tunnel move closer, I was feeling content. *I can do two years part-time and then walk away. I can do that, it's easy.*

"Sir," said Ojo, a Year Ten lad with tight cornrow hair that fascinated his peers, and with enough charm to mask his poor punctuality. He always had something to say. "Do you think they'll close the school? The Coronavirus is spreading. I've heard rumours that Boris is going to close schools." We were in registration time on a Tuesday morning. I covered this tutor group every Tuesday.

"No, I don't think so. School is too important. It's all a bit over the top. It won't spread all over the country. We'll be fine." I was pretty confident that this was a storm in a teacup….hmm.

"I'm not taking chances!" He pulled his bandana from his

pocket and turned it into a mask covering his mouth and nose. I laughed. *This is absurd, it's all out of proportion; it's just a virus a few people have got.*

The following day the world changed. Years Seven to Nine were told not to come back to school until further notice. Only the GCSE years were left in school, and by the end of the week, Boris Johnson had shut down the nation. COVID-19 was a pandemic. All schools were closed, shops apart from supermarkets shut, and all industries except essential ones needed to supply food and energy were to close. They called it 'lockdown'! Initially, it was for two weeks as a circuit breaker to stop the virus from spreading but it went on for months.

I read the email again, just to be sure.

> To all teaching staff

> The training on 'Microsoft Teams' that we have all done will be intensified so

> that all teaching staff will be able to continue work. Please watch the training

> videos and familiarise yourself with Teams. Work will need to be set for all

> classes to access. Please ensure that departments have created online tasks

> that can be completed independently by students. Further training will be

> given to staff on how to deliver live lessons once the students are familiar with

> Teams and we have identified who needs access to laptops or tablets.

South Coast Academy had been training all its staff on Teams for about a year as part of its Technology Policy. Online work was being used as homework, and activities that could be marked easily and automatically were used regularly. Most staff were familiar with it. The intensification meant learning how to meet together online through technology and how to deliver 'live' lessons.

I sat in my office, it was eerily quiet for 9 am. There was a handful of staff in the building. I sipped my coffee as I began to monitor the online work that had been set by the Humanities Team. *This is crazy, I can't believe we're doing this.* I sat reflecting on how the whole of the teaching world in the UK had suddenly changed. The implications were massive. My computer began to make a noise like a telephone, I clicked the accept button and Sally appeared on screen. She was in her office on the other side of the school.

"Hi Jack, we need to talk about exam data. The word from Government so far is that we have to rank Year Eleven on where they are now, not what they might get." Sally proceeded to explain that Heads of Departments needed to collect data to show what grade every child was currently at and then rank them in subdivided sections within a grade boundary. My head was spinning after the Teams call, but I went straight into another meeting with Cass, Clem and James my three department heads. Their faces appeared on screen. All of them were at home, sitting on sofas or around a kitchen table. It seemed bizarre to think of working in this way. By the end of the day, I was quite tired and had a headache. The combination of facing a screen all day, the stress of trying to collate data and get used to a whole new way of working was causing my brain to overheat.

"Jack, what are you doing in the building? You should be at home. Take your laptop and work from there, please. We're trying to lock down as much of the school as we can. All the corridors have been sanitized and the classrooms thoroughly cleaned. We don't want to have to keep on doing it." Sally called from the far end of the Humanities corridor; she had spotted me returning from the toilet.

"Do I have to? It is so much easier to work in school." I pleaded with her. My laptop was slow and only had one screen, whereas my office PC was fast with two monitors.

"Go and don't come back until you are told to!" She wagged a finger at me, instructing me to go, grinning as she did so.

"Bully!" I retorted with an equal grin. "If you insist!"

The next few months were the weirdest I've ever experienced. I worked at my desk in our office at home, Sandy set up a desk in our bedroom and my youngest son worked in his bedroom. Amazingly our Wi-Fi coped! Initially, my days were structured as follows. I worked online from 8 am until 1 pm, taking a coffee break at eleven. I set online tasks for classes, marked work that had been returned and attended numerous Teams meetings about GCSE grades, and how to deliver online 'live' lessons. For the remainder of my time, I liaised with my Humanities team, encouraging them, monitoring their work and updating resources ready for when we eventually got back to teaching. The afternoons were my own. They were spent in the sunshine in my garden or taking the compulsory walk that Boris permitted us to do. I watched the daily COVID updates on the BBC and in the evenings Sandy and I gorged ourselves on Netflix box sets. Trips to the supermarket became early morning adventures, attempting to beat the long queues, to ensure we had enough toilet rolls, eggs and bread.

"This is the life, eh? Work in the morning and relax all afternoon in the garden." I was sitting on a garden chair looking at my newly erected shed. COVID had given me the time to build a base and get a shed delivered, painted and constructed. I had the tidiest shed in town.

"It certainly gives you a taste of the quiet life, retirement and easy living." Sandy sipped her tea and picked up the paperback she was reading. *She's not wrong. I could get used to this quite easily.* I settled back to enjoy the warm early summer sun stroke my face.

As the Summer arrived and COVID restrictions slowly began to lift, staff at South Coast Academy were expected to be in school for the final six weeks. There were, of course, no children except those whose parents worked in the NHS or were vulnerable in some way. The team of TAs and associate staff who had looked after them all this time looked exhausted. I sat at my desk, staring at my monitor, the Teams meeting had been going on for over an hour. Andrew Potter had been explaining how the school was going to be organised into bubbles for any potential return to school in September.

"It means, of course, that some staff will need to move offices, at least temporarily whilst the bubbles are in place. We need Year Heads to be located in the heart of their bubble and not in a different one. We can't have pupils mixing bubbles." I could see what was coming. My office was at the heart of what was to be the Year Eight Bubble. I was going to be asked to move. Dexter took over from Andrew. "Classes will be in zones or bubbles and students will remain in those bubbles, except for ICT and drama. This means that no member of staff will have a permanent classroom base. We all become nomadic and move to where the children are." Even over the ether, I could hear the groans. Questions began popping up in the chat, electronic hands were raised. Staff keen for clarification. I double-checked that my microphone was off and said in a loud voice, "This is going to be a nightmare, a shambles." I shook my head in despair. The cloud that had followed me for over a year, that had lifted during lockdown, suddenly came over the horizon and settled on my head. I felt an overwhelming sense of doom.

"Jack, we asked you here to this meeting to discuss your role as Faculty Head for Humanities." It was July, two weeks to go before the summer break. The classroom was light and airy and the sun was shining through the window. Dexter sat at one table, I sat at another and Sally at a third. We were the regulation two metres apart.

"I have been wondering how this would work. It would be good if Cass or James stepped up to help on the days that I am not in school. Thursday and Friday. I haven't mentioned it yet, but it seems like a good opportunity for career development for them." I was quite upbeat about the prospect. It seemed to me to be an obvious and simple solution.

"We have an alternative plan," said Dexter calmly. "We would like you to take on the leadership role of 'Recovery Curriculum.' As you will be part-time we feel that you will not be able to fully fulfil your responsibilities as Head of Faculty." Dexter paused to give me time to think. I looked at Sally. She was clearly uncomfortable about being in the room. She had been my friend since we met in 1984. She did not like what was happening to me any more than I did. *That is the price you pay for leadership. Difficult conversations with friends.*

"How do you feel about that, Jack?" Dexter smiled and leaned his head to the side.

"To be honest, I am a bit nonplussed. I was not expecting anything like this. I thought I was here to discuss how I can continue as Head of Faculty. This is a bolt from the blue." My heart was racing, adrenaline was pumping, I was angry.

"I thought you knew." Dexter looked at Sally. Sally looked back.

"It seems there has been a lack of communication, Jack. I am sorry about that. We thought you knew." Dexter was genuinely surprised, as was Sally. Somewhere down the line, the wires got crossed and I got burned.

I regained a bit of composure and tried to collect my thoughts. *I've been dumped out of my office and put in an old staff toilet on the far side of the school, now I've lost my role, the one thing that is keeping me going.* In the office shake-up, due to COVID, I had lost my nice new office to one of the Heads of Year as it was central to the bubble the year would be in. My new office was across the school, away from the Humanities classrooms. It was formerly a staff toilet, but the toilet had been removed and the cubicle was now a cupboard, the outer cloakroom was a makeshift storeroom for cleaning equipment. It had been tidied up and decorated for me, with a new desk, but it had pipes all over the ceiling and down the walls. I felt like Harry, that boy wizard, who lived under the stairs.

"I have no idea what recovery curriculum means. It sounds like some sort of made-up job. What if I say no?" I was trying to stay calm and professional, but I felt, once again, that I was being stitched up.

"It certainly is not a made-up job; many schools are going down this route post-COVID restrictions. It is about ensuring students can recover; emotionally, psychologically and academically once they return in September. There has already been a lot of research done about it. We would like to be at the forefront of practice in this area. Will you do it, Jack?" Dexter was enthusiastic as he spoke and handed me a sheaf of papers.

"Just some headlines and thoughts from some of the research to get you going." I took the papers and glanced down at them. *I hate reading research, absolutely hate it! This is my worst nightmare, trawling through research.*

"Do I have a choice?" I looked at both Dexter and Sally. She did not make eye contact; she knew I was angry with her.

"Not really, Jack. Look we're having an INSET day on the last day of term to prepare for September when the children are back. I'd like you to present a session on the recovery curriculum. Get the staff thinking about it. You'll be in the hall with the TAs and support staff and it will be beamed around the school on Teams."

"It looks like a done deal, then. I have no choice but to agree. Who will be taking over the Humanities? I will need to liaise with them about the handover." I tried to make it sound positive, but it was hard. I had been kicked in the head!

"Norman Black. He knows of course and is waiting for you to make contact. You can tell your team immediately. Give them time to adjust." My heart sank! *Norman Black! That's not going to go down well.* Norman was a nice bloke, he was a senior assistant head, Ofsted inspector, responsible for a myriad of organisational things behind the scenes, and to cap it all he was a mathematician. In the eyes of the Humanities team, he came across as if he were on the autistic spectrum, everything was by the book, black and white, right or wrong. Not an ideal humanitarian. *What does he know about Humanities?*

Dexter stood up and left the room, leaving Sally and me alone.

"Jack, I am so sorry. I thought you knew. He was supposed to have warned you weeks ago."

"I can't believe it. Do you see why I feel under threat and undervalued? It's all right for you. You made a success at leadership, but I struggled. I couldn't separate the leadership role from being a friend to my colleagues. You can't do both. I always had a foot in both camps."

"Jack, that's a strength. The rest of the leadership team admires you for that. You can be a thorn in their side, that's true, but for all the right reasons. You care. You care about the children and you care about your staff. Your team love you. Not every leader can say that." Sally stood up and came over to me, careful to observe COVID protocols. "Come on, I'll make you a cuppa."

"It's all right for you, you're retiring in two weeks. I'm still stuck here!" I was jealous, Sally was getting out at the right time.

****

September 2020 saw the school partitioned off into five zones, separate playgrounds and eating areas. Different entrances and exits for year groups, sanitiser dispensers on the walls every ten metres around the school and a host of other new features to ensure children remained separate, COVID free and safe. New routines were soon established, such as staff LFT testing twice a week, and students being issued with box after box of LFT tests, many of which were discarded or destroyed and never used.

"Please go around, you can't cut through. It is not your zone." I stood barring the way to the Humanities corridor.

"But I need to get to the maths rooms." The student pointed down the corridor. Maths rooms were adjacent to the Humanities at the far end of the corridor.

"You know full well you cannot go down there. Walk round. The way you were shown at the start of term." The student 'humphed' and turned away. This was a daily occurrence at every change of lesson and every break. Somehow, COVID restrictions that applied to the nation didn't seem to apply to teenagers. The concept of doing something for the common good was still alien to them, despite three months of 'lockdown'.

"It's all nonsense of course," said Amy Watson. She stood two metres away holding a cup of tea. It was break time and we were on duty.

"What, COVID?" I looked up in surprise. I knew Amy wasn't a COVID denier.

"No, all this bubble stuff. It's pointless. Everyone knows they all leave school via different exits but they all meet up outside the school, kiss, cuddle, fight, and mess about. It makes what we do here totally redundant!"

I grinned and nodded in agreement, "Makes life fun though, eh? Trying to have a philosophical debate in a science lab with Year Ten or doing science in an RE room? You can't do group work, share resources, pens or books."

"Yep, also you miss fifteen minutes of every lesson whilst they line up in their playgrounds waiting to be led to their room." We continued to bemoan the COVID school systems in place and longed to be back in our own classrooms once again, instead of running across the school to get to a room or to pick up a class waiting in the playground. The bell sounded and we went outside to find our respective classes that were supposed to be lining up quietly.

As the year progressed, the behaviour of the children grew steadily worse. Their confinement to a particular set of rooms, mixing with only a limited set of people, contributed to higher anxiety and more outbursts of disruption. In some classes, tensions rose, and the ability to move children between rooms to give them space had been removed, they were trapped. As I developed my new role as 'Recovery Curriculum Coordinator' I presented a plan to staff that involved giving time to talk about COVID experiences, offering support to anxious students, and setting out plans to re-engage students with reading, writing and learning. It was a good plan, well received by all, but, in reality, all teachers wanted to do was to catch up on missing work with the children. Time-to-talk activities went out of the window very quickly, once the results of a school-wide survey that I did suggested that the vast majority of children were happy, not affected by COVID and keen to get on with work. I was battling the tide of missed curriculum time. Teachers didn't want to waste time on 'recovery'. There were exams to do.

Whilst Dexter and the leadership team made all the right

noises about supporting me, it was clear their focus was on exam results and catching up on missed lessons. I got that, I understood it.

"Jack, just do what you can in the three days a week you have." That was Dexter's approach, which to me said I was down the pecking order. Maybe I was, maybe I was just getting a bit old and cynical.

When the schools were closed again in November 2020, I felt like all my work, however, minimally it had been received, was wasted. It would all need to start again. I sat in my office, the pipes gurgling above me as someone upstairs flushed a toilet. The school was quiet and I was about to start an online lesson. Staff were in school unless they were vulnerable in some way, it was a peaceful place to be. The children began to log on to the lesson and I started teaching. The slide presentation worked well, I responded to questions in the chat space and occasionally took questions from the disconnected voice of a student. Sometimes I wondered if anyone was listening to me. *They could have all logged on and then cleared off to watch Netflix.*

The days and weeks passed quickly, I fell into an easy routine of online lessons and marking. It was straightforward, but it was dull. I attended meetings about exams and ranking students again, using exam papers to provide evidence for Year Eleven to be properly assessed. It was all routine, and I became bored. My recovery role had been shelved since no children were in school. I would resurrect it once they came back. If they did.

In contrast, my days off were filled with interest. Thursdays I spent with Sandy, who also had a day off work, and Fridays I volunteered at church helping out the ministry team. On those days I felt alive, fresh, and inspired. I looked forward to them each week. The contrast was so stark that on a cold January Thursday morning in 2021, as Sandy and I went for a walk in the park, she said:

"Jack, just do it. Retire from teaching. You've done enough

time. Nearly 37 years. That's long enough." We were chatting about how we were both feeling about work, COVID and life and Sandy, knowing me as she did, could see clearly how disillusioned I was with school.

"You love it on your days off, you are so much happier. You wear your heart on your sleeve, you know."

I smiled thoughtfully and was about to argue, but she placed her finger over my mouth to silence me. She then kissed me.

"I know what you are going to say. 'I feel guilty, I have to provide for you, blah, blah blah!" I smiled at her poor impression of me. "But you know what, you deserve it. You have looked after me and the boys, and you've worked hard. You have been the best teacher you could have been. Look at all those people you keep meeting in town, that you once taught. They all remember you fondly. You're a good teacher. Now it's your time. Go for it!"

I stopped in the park turned to face her and held her hands. "Thank you, I still feel uncomfortable about it. It goes against the grain. Thank you for supporting me and enabling me to become the teacher I am. But you are right it is time to let go." I kissed her, she squeezed my hands and we continued our walk.

It took me a few weeks to pluck up the courage to write the email to Dexter but when I hit the send button, a sense of relief flooded through me. The light at the end of the tunnel was clear, I could see beyond the tunnel, and it looked amazing.

"I can't believe it, Jack, you're going? What are we going to do? Who will look after us?" Cass was the first to be told of my decision.

"Norman's doing a good job, isn't he?" I knew that Cass struggled with Norman, he was too task focused and lacked the vision that Cass and Karen had for the Philosophy and Ethics Department. She scoffed and I grinned. She stepped toward me and hugged me, defying the two-metre protocol.

"Careful," I joked, "you might catch something!"

"I don't care, we're all going to miss you. You have been our leader for a long time, you have cared and looked out for us." Her comments encouraged me and reminded me that, despite what I thought were failings in my career, I had been a successful leader, one who had developed an area for the curriculum and improved it.

When the children returned to school in March 2021, it confirmed to me that I had made the correct choice. The cloud returned to my mind at the start of the week and lifted as I left school on Wednesday evenings. The hustle and bustle of school life, COVID restrictions and zones or bubbles were something I would be glad to leave behind. COVID had finally killed my passion for education. The last twelve weeks of my school career passed quickly and I worked hard to ensure that the legacy that I would leave would be positive. The work on recovery was picked up again and I handed it on as a package of activities and principles to support children. Whether it would ever be used I did not know. Every book was marked, every lesson delivered as best as I could, and all my files and planning were organised for someone else to use.

The sun was hot; the whole staff were gathered out in the playground around tables. Food was being eaten and speeches were underway. Staff sat in sunglasses, hats and tee shirts. It was the last day of term. My final moments in South Coast Comprehensive. I was feeling quite emotional. I had cleared out my office of personal items and taken them home the night before. I wanted to walk out, head held high without looking like I had been dismissed.

As I stood to make my farewell speech, I was strangely nervous, I slipped my notes from my pocket and stood behind the microphone. I spoke of funny incidents, Katy and her fluffy handcuffs, the disappearing snow, and my pride as a football coach. I finished by reading a letter I received from a student called Sylvie. She had been a tearaway, a troubled teenager, angry and aggressive. I had been her year head for five years.

"Dear Sir

I hope you remember me. I just want to say thank you for all you did for me during my time at school. I know that I was very naughty and that you tried so hard to help me. I now realise that the compassion, care and support you showed came from your faith. Shortly after I left, I too became a Christian and turned my life around. I have recently obtained a first-class honours degree in Environmental Science from Greenwich University. I thought you might like to know that what you did was not wasted.

Love from Sylvie x

There was a tear in my eye as I read it. I took a deep breath and finished my speech.

"So any of you youngsters thinking about quitting, don't. You are making a difference. I made a difference to Sylvie, and probably to many more. It is this letter that I received several years ago that made me realise that despite all the difficulties, knockbacks and struggles we might encounter, we are making difference in the lives of children. We are giving them opportunities. I can confidently step away from teaching, knowing that my efforts have not been in vain." I paused and then took the biggest risk I've taken as a Christian teacher.

"I would like to finish by praying for you all. I know not many of you are believers, but please bear with me." I began to pray for the staff, just a short prayer of thanksgiving for them, for protection over them and a blessing on them. When I said "Amen" I was expecting silence but there was a resounding echo of "Amen" and then a round of applause that went on for what seemed ages. I made my way back to my seat, people patted me on the back, shook my hand and congratulated me.

"Well done Jack, great speech."

"Thank you for praying, never seen that done before."

"I'm going to miss you, Jack, Keep in touch! Let's play golf sometime!"

I smiled, waved and chatted as I sat back down and waited for the next speech. Dexter was leaving too.

I stood alone in the hall, slipped off my trainers and stood in my white sports socks. The sun shone through the windows revealing the motes in the dustlight. I began to run across the hall and then slid across, raising my arms for balance. I laughed as I almost lost balance and tumbled onto the floor. I turned and skidded back to my shoes. *I've always wanted to do that.*

The cloud didn't lift that day as I walked up the path from school. It had not been there for at least a fortnight. I felt joy and peace. I had done a good job, I had touched people's lives, I had made a difference.

ABOUT THE AUTHOR

Jez Taylor

Jez Taylor trained at Roehampton to be an RE teacher in the Secondary phase of education. He has worked in three different state schools across Sussex during his thirty-seven-year career. During this time, he was a Head of Department, Head of House/Year, Head of a faculty and an Assistant Head Teacher with a wide variety of responsibilities. Not only has he taught RE but also English, History, Geography, PSHE, Careers, Citizenship, ICT and PE. He now  lives happily in retirement by the Sussex coast

BOOKS BY THIS AUTHOR

On This Rock (Peter The Rock Book 1)

2000 yrs. ago the nation of Israel was under the oppressive rule of the Romans. A young boy, Simon, grew up hearing the stories of freedom; stories of how God would send his Messiah to free Israel from all her enemies. He knew the prophecies; he dreamed the dreams of freedom. As a young married man, he lived to provide for his family; his dreams of freedom shattered by the power of Rome. That is until he meets a wandering Rabbi called Yeshua. His life gets turned upside down. Could this man be God's chosen Messiah? Simon finds himself on a journey of discovery which takes him from being a small-time fisherman to becoming the leader of a band of twelve revolutionaries who are set to change the world.

BOOKS BY THIS AUTHOR

I Will Build My Church (Peter The Rock Book 2)

Jesus has ascended to heaven and the fledgling Church is led by Peter, who discovers that with God's power, he is able to see God's kingdom grow. Encountering many obstacles such as persecution, and dissension from within his community, he sees the Church flourish from being a small sect to a major influence in the Roman world. Essentially a family man, Peter has to make difficult choices to ensure he fulfils his duty to Jesus and his family. "I will build my Church" is book two in the series "Peter The Rock." book one is entitled: "On this rock."

Printed in Great Britain
by Amazon

36387768R00175